WAYFARER: AV494

SECOND EDITION

MATTHEW S COX

DIVISION ZERO PRESS

Wayfarer: AV494
A Novel
© 2016-2021 Matthew S. Cox

CONTENTS

INTRODUCTION

Welcome to the second edition of Wayfarer AV494. It's been a while since this book came out. Almost as soon as I first published it, I found myself second guessing one particular aspect of the story. Alas, there is no way for me to even hint at the explanation or reasons for what differs with this edition and the original (first two, though the second edition was only a change in publisher) without massive plot spoilers.

After much arguing with myself and endlessly pestering a few people (you know who you are, thank you) for opinions, I decided to make major edits to the story.

Suffice to say, this version is truer to my instinct for writing stories and less a slave to obeying genre conventions.

PERSEUS

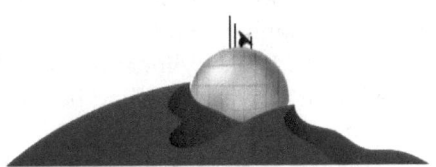

Unease permeated a vast expanse of endless blackness, as silent as the void of space. Kerys reached out into the emptiness… or at least tried to send an impulse down the nerves in her arm. She floated in the infinite silent nothingness, weightless, devoid of all sensation, unable to explain why her dream of jogging down the streets of her old neighborhood had stopped. Unable to tell if she could or could not move, dread built, the deepening fear pressing into her chest, constricting her lungs. The harder she tried to breathe, the stronger her awareness that she couldn't became.

Panic swirled into the need to scream—but her body refused to obey.

A faint *beep* broke the silence, derailing the spiraling sense of suffocation swallowing her mind. Her brain tried to seize on the direction the sound came from, desperate to construct any meaningful representation of environment. Alas, reality slipped through her fingers, ephemeral and nonexistent.

Beep.

Kerys stared at the void, trying to comprehend what happened to her.

Again and again, the weak electronic chirp taunted her, an ever-moving raven, black as midnight in a darkened room. She clung to the electronic disturbance, the only sensory information available to her. Each time it pulsed, she counted. Its tempo increased; the source drawing closer with each chime until it seemed to be emanating from inside her skull.

Beep. Beep. Beep.

2 | WAYFARER: AV494

The noise became intolerable. She tried to scream again, to grab her head, but couldn't move.

When her count reached fifty-eight, an explosion of tingling needlepoints swam over her body, every vein and capillary of her circulatory system on fire. She gasped; the rush of her breath deafening, echoing within a confined space. Minutes passed before a sense of having a physical form manifested within her consciousness. She lay in a body as leaden as stone.

I'm in stasis.

Her eyes snapped open.

Dim light suffused the space around her, lending an otherworldly azure glow to her plain white tank top and briefs. Each breath she released misted on the cover of a transparent cylinder, mere inches from her face. Loud beeping continued from above and behind her head.

I can't move... Something's wrong.

A human-shaped shadow drifted across the folds of a drab grey privacy curtain beyond the foot of her chamber. She focused her gaze on a blurry smear on the material. After a moment of staring, it resolved into words printed upon the plastic:

Avasar Biotech

The slogan 'worlds better' in much smaller text underlined the block lettering.

Kerys forced air into her chest, her nostrils tingling at the chill of the post-cryonic mist hanging in her chamber. Seconds became minutes. The first sign the chemical paralytic began to wear off came in the form of shivering. She struggled to raise her arms and breathe warmth into her hands.

The beeping stopped the instant she moved.

In the distance, a deep, resonant yawn echoed off the walls, a bellow appropriate for the end of a years-long sleep. Her pod shuddered with a heavy, mechanical *thud*. Kerys grabbed the cushions and yelped in surprise as the hatch opened, emitting a subdued hiss of pneumatics. A rush of chilly air invaded the coffin-sized chamber.

She sat up, brushing frost from her thighs and arms before swinging her legs over the side of the chair-bed. Dizziness convinced her not to try standing, so she slumped, head down and shivering, waiting for the fogginess of deep-freeze to fade.

"Hello," said a man outside the curtain while tapping his knuckles on the doorjamb. "Miss Loring? I'm Chris, with medical. Is it all right if I check a few things?"

"Yeah. Come on in." She reached up and massaged her left shoulder.

The curtain gave an audible *shhht* as her visitor pulled it aside. An athletic man, bald, with dark skin and a broad smile stepped in and pulled the curtain closed behind him. He wore a white jumpsuit bearing the six-armed Shiva logo of Avasar Biotech on the left breast pocket. Chris held up a thin silver tablet the size of a clipboard. Light from its screen tinted the front of his uniform faintly green.

"How do you feel?"

"Like a piece of steak some idiot put in the freezer unwrapped." She let her arm fall limp in her lap. "How are you so... *animated*?"

Chris chuckled. "Medical team thawed out two days ago so we'd be at a hundred percent for waking up the rest."

"That had to be boring." She forced a smile and stared at her blurry toes. "When are they going to turn the heat on? It's colder out here than it was in the pod."

A grid of blue laser light crawled up and down her chest, projected from a tiny black dot on the back of the silver tablet. Whatever appeared on the screen made Chris smile. "Well, looks like everything is normal... mostly."

"Mostly?" She raised an eyebrow.

"I think the pre-stasis agent hit you a little harder than normal." He tapped the screen twice. "Hmm. The dosage looks right for your recorded weight."

She kept her eyes down, thinking of the doctor back on Earth chiding her for not eating enough. "Is that bad?"

"How groggy do you feel? Are you experiencing any dizziness or feelings of vertigo?" He moved to stand in front of her and used a small light on the underside of his e-pad to examine her eyes.

Kerys sat straight, stretched, and exhaled. "It's not that bad. Like I overslept. Little dizziness, little blurred vision, but it's going away."

"Good. I wouldn't worry about it then." Chris held the e-pad to his chest. "Best to get up and about and move. Scan didn't pick up any ice crystals in your blood, so if you want to warm up with a shower, go right ahead."

She ground the heel of her hand into her eye socket. "There's not enough coffee on Earth to fix this."

"Welcome to the middle of nowhere." He started to leave, but paused at the curtain. "If you experience anything unusual—muscle soreness, numbness, inexplicable sharp pains—make sure you let one of us know."

"Yeah. I'll do that." Kerys bent forward and raked both hands at her scalp while staring down a tunnel of light brown hair at the dull steel floor between her feet. "Thanks."

"S'all good." Chris pulled the curtain closed and walked off, his shoes squeaking a few times before he stopped. "Hey, Mr. Trem, mind if I check on a few things?"

A man muttered in response. Another scrape of metal curtain rings sliding followed.

Kerys waited another minute or so for the fog to fade from her head, then forced herself to stand, weathering a momentary bout of pins and needles in her legs. She ambled over and opened the single locker on the left wall of her chamber, which held a dark blue jumpsuit and a pair of black boots. Her company ID already dangled from a plastic clip at the right breast pocket. Intending to take a shower right away, she gathered the stuff from the locker in a bundle and bumped the door shut with her knee.

Voices filled in the quiet outside in the hall, a few men and at least one woman. Everyone sounded as groggy as she felt. Gaze down, she shuffled out of her chamber and headed right, past another ten curtains on both sides. Two bathrooms, one marked 'women' and one marked 'men' branched off from the T at the end.

She headed for the women's area, entering a cloud of steam hanging in front of a row of lockers along the wall on the right. To the left, beyond a small steel bench, an older woman with streaks of grey in black hair stood under one of five showerheads, basking in the warmth. Kerys stuck her jumpsuit and boots in a random locker, then peeled off the underwear she'd been stuck in for…

Kerys stared at the tank top in her hand. *How long was I out? Two? Three years?* Regret for taking this job and excitement at what she might discover crashed head-to-head, leaving her feeling numb. She dropped the underwear on the bench and padded over to the showerhead farthest on the left, leaving one empty space between her and the other woman. A touchscreen offered several presets for water temp. She poked a blue square marked 105 degrees, and let out a moan of relief as water fell on her from above.

"Oh, hi there," said the woman. "You look happy to be awake."

"Hey." Kerys stood motionless, letting the water cascade over her. "Sorry. I know you introduced yourself before, but it's taking all my concentration to remember how to walk right now."

The woman chuckled. "That's okay, dear. I'm drawing a blank on your name too. I don't remember anyone else, really. Paula Driscoll, with Don's team."

A wave of embarrassment rose and fell. *Crap. She's my boss.* "Umm. Sorry… I'm Kerys Loring."

"Oh, yes. We'll be working together." Paula smiled, turning so the spray got her back. "And I'm sure this is more of me than you ever wanted to see. Don't mind my red face. I've never done one of these expeditions before. This is probably ordinary routine for you."

"I'm not seeing much of anything at the moment but the backs of my eyelids," said Kerys.

Hot water molded around her skull and ran down her body, chasing numbness from her toes. No one had bothered turning on the lights in the shower room, not that she cared.

"If I remember correctly," said Paula, "you were with the crew that made the find on Copernicus?"

Most of her grogginess evaporated. She grinned with a sense of pride. "Yeah. I'm actually the one who found the first—and still largest—validated relic."

Paula gave an annoyed sigh. "Shameful how they treated you. Suppose that's why you're here now?"

Kerys glanced to the right and caught herself staring at a sprawl of stretch marks on the woman's stomach. "Umm. Yeah. Thanks." She looked away, her enthusiasm dampened. "173 hours of work, and I barely got a footnote on the research paper. Doctor Furroughs got six million, and Doctor Teplitsky two-point-five. I guess it could be worse. That experience *did* get me this job."

Two fleshy *claps* came from Paula's hand meeting her belly. "Got two. Son and a daughter. No shame here, kiddo."

"Wow… You left your kids behind to come out here?"

The other shower cut off with an electric chirp. "Well, that's enough water for this old bird. Yes and no. Addison's almost twenty-five… or at least she was when I left. Alan turned twenty the day I accepted the job offer. They can survive without me for a couple years. I'd just be in their way."

Kerys couldn't think of anything to say so simply basked in the warm water. The sound of the spray and the rustling of Paula drying off and getting dressed soothed her. Eventually, her boss walked out, muttering about finding a break room. Relieved at the solitude, Kerys stretched a bit, letting the shower loosen her muscles. Other than Jaden, her younger brother, she hadn't left anyone behind on Earth she cared about. She'd left behind her ex as well, but he could stay gone.

Maybe a few thousand light years will give him a hint.

She jabbed her finger on the console to kill the water, dried herself off, and got dressed in her company-issued jumpsuit as well as the clean socks and underwear she'd stuffed into her boots before cryo.

After walking back past sixteen pairs of curtains, she reached an opening in the wall at the far end of the corridor where a ladder ran the length of a vertical shaft. A sign pointing up indicated 'flight deck,' 'staterooms,' and 'observation deck.' 'Shuttle bay,' and 'engineering' sat by a down-pointing arrow.

To her right, a closed door reduced several voices to indistinct murmurs. Kerys headed that way, eager to remind herself who else had been thrilled/foolish/reckless/careless/desperate enough to sign up for this job.

Five people sat around a cafeteria-style steel table at the center of a small lounge. A counter on the left held a Hydra machine as well as two racks full of the octagonal plastic trays containing dehydrated meals. The others picked at Salisbury steak, something pretending to be chicken, and an entrée she assumed to be meatloaf. Though all of it *looked* like a science project gone awry, the smell in the air proved intoxicating.

Don Bouchard, PhD, the head of the archaeology team, leaned over a tray with three light-brown lumps atop what appeared to be mashed potatoes. He scratched at his head, making his wild white-grey hair dance. "I've studied quite a few alien substances in my day, but I'm at a loss to explain what this is supposed to be."

"Fried chicken strips, I think," said a confident-sounding man.

Kerys glanced over at the source of the voice and caught herself staring at a fair-skinned soldier in a green camouflage jumpsuit. His sharp jawline and perfectly proportioned face made her wonder whatever possessed him to join the military. *He should be in movies…* The instant the glow in his blond hair from the overhead lights made her brain conjure up an angelic fantasy, he made eye contact… and she looked away.

"This food's like my ex-girlfriend," said a skinny guy with brown hair in a blue jumpsuit identical to hers. "Tastes a lot better if you close your eyes."

"Must you?" muttered Paula, sounding disgusted.

"Hmph." Don frowned.

A younger man in a military uniform next to Mr. Angel laughed until gravy dribbled from his nose.

Not wanting to become a target, Kerys faked a smile at the crass remark and helped herself to the next available meal in the rack. Hard nuggets rattled around in the plastic as she slid it into the Hydra. When she hit the 'go' button, the machine whirred to life, working to rapidly rehydrate and heat the contents.

Don sliced one of the nuggets in half. "I suspect you may be correct in your theory this is, or is at least attempting to be, chicken."

"Don't matter what it is—it's all we got," said the younger soldier. "Eventually, Hydra meals all wind up tasting the same: hot mush."

Mr. Angel chuckled. "Don't mind the FNG. This is his second hop, so he thinks he's a veteran."

The younger soldier picked at his eye with a middle finger.

A *ping* came from the Hydra. Kerys collected the steaming tray, pinching it between two fingers on each side, and rushed to drop it on the table before it scalded her fingers. Everyone paused to look at her as she stepped over the bench and sat. She managed a weak smile while picking at the clear plastic film covering her meal tray.

"You ever been this far out before, Foster?" asked Mr. Angel.

Kerys leaned forward to take a knife and fork from a small mesh bucket in the center of the table filled with utensils, staying stretched long enough to read the name over Mr. Angel's breast pocket: CPL Guillen, R.

He seemed to catch her staring and suppressed a smile.

"Naw." Foster shook his head. "Pretty sure this is a new record for me."

Corporal Guillen winked. "AV494 ain't far compared to some colonies. My first tour came with six years in the freezer, one way."

Kerys coughed on a mouthful of green beans.

"Oh, this planet isn't *too* far." Don plucked an e-pad off the table by his meal and held it up. A few finger taps opened an image of the Milky Way. "We're about here..." He pointed to a spot. "On the Perseus arm. Just a short hop from Earth, which is on the Orion Spur"—he slid his finger about a half-inch upward and to the right—"here."

"That don't look too far," said Foster.

"It's a matter of scale." Don closed the map and set the e-pad down. "It doesn't appear very long, but you'd be surprised."

"That's what she said." The skinny man winked.

"Must you, Marco?" asked Paula.

He grinned, shaking his head. "Oh, come on. We're inside a giant beer can out in the middle of space." Marco held up his little finger. "One rock the size of my pinky nail could kill us all if it hits the ship wrong. Lighten up a little."

Kerys swallowed hard.

"A little *esprit de corps* is not an unwise idea." Don examined a lump of chicken on his fork. "However, I would appreciate it if you'd tone down the sexual references."

The room hung in awkward silence for a few minutes. Kerys nibbled at her entrée, which might've been an attempt at pot roast.

"Hey, new girl," said Marco. "Somethin' wrong? You don't look too hungry."

She shrugged one shoulder. "Oh, you know... hurtling through space inside a beer can. Nervous... and excited about what's waiting for us down there."

Marco bobbed his head in an exaggerated nod. "Yeah. Say, anyone know why exactly we're here? I mean, aside from the giant paycheck?"

"The compensation for this job isn't unusual for the type of work," said Paula. "As far as I know, some of Avasar's people stumbled on something they think shows evidence of non-human civilization."

"There's been a facility here for quite some time already." Don chewed a nugget, made an appraising face, and eventually seemed to decide he liked the flavor.

Kerys pushed food around her tray, staring at the whorls of steam wafting past her fork. "It's not like it's unheard of. We've found alien construction and artifacts before."

Don held up a finger until he swallowed. "Indeed. In the eighty-two years since the commercialization of translight travel, there've been over forty-six finds at various colony and research outposts. We're well beyond wondering *if* aliens exist, and have moved on to trying to understand what they are... or were."

"Were?" asked Corporal Guillen. "That kinda sounds like you think they're all dead."

Don offered a whimsical shrug. "Based on what I've seen... dusty relics and half-buried sites, there's been no evidence of activity within the last seven centuries. For all we know, any aliens proximal to Earth, or with the technology to get there, have died out already."

"Maybe they got close enough to get a look at us, and said 'fuck that." Foster glanced around. "We're a pretty screwed up species."

"The galaxy is over a hundred thousand light years across." Paula tapped her fork on an empty tray in thought. "Billions of stars and planets. It's a mathematical certainty that there's some other life out there we just haven't run into yet."

"So, what's got everyone so worked up over this place?" asked Marco. "The plants?"

"Precisely!" Don thrust his hand up for emphasis, accidentally tossing a glop of mashed potato from his fork to the table. "Thus far, on every planet where we've discovered signs of intelligent construction, there's been no active biological life. This is the first time I've ever heard of there being life on the same world at the time humans find it."

"Most of the other sites appear to have either experienced extinction-level events or been tiny, almost like remote outposts," said Kerys. Hundreds of still images flashed by in her memory. "I can think of three: Demeter-11, IX144, and Ptolemy Major, where the site teams did find fossilized evidence suggesting water *had* been present in the past, but none remained."

Paula looked impressed. "I worked with the Demeter team when I was your age, doing analysis from a lab safe on Earth. It's true. We found geological evidence of prior water, but something tore away that planet's atmosphere eons before human boots ever touched its surface."

"Sorry… you are?" asked Marco.

"Kerys." She stabbed more green beans and nibbled.

"Marco Trem." He offered a hand. "Since you're wearing blue, I guess you're on my team. Xenoarchaeology?"

"Yeah." She shook hands.

"MIT?" asked Marco.

"Berkeley." Kerys stirred the contents of her tray's 'meat' section around. "This'll be my fourth site."

"Nice. Second for me."

"You've met Doctor Bouchard during the preflight interview process," said Paula. "He's our project lead."

Kerys looked at the white-haired man for a few seconds before her gaze slipped over to Corporal Guillen.

Paula grinned. "As you know, the military subsidizes most interstellar travel. Ships this size always come with a security detachment."

"Rick Guillen." The corporal offered his hand. "Private Foster here and I are rotating in, assigned to Wayfarer Outpost for six months. Maybe we'll catch the same ship back home."

Marco laughed. "Six months… if only we get done that fast. Be nice."

"You can call me Ed." Private Foster smiled at Kerys.

"Good Lord, is that boy even eighteen yet?" asked Paula. "My son looks older than you."

Don chuckled.

"Twenty, ma'am." Private Foster saluted.

She couldn't remember how long the job contract stipulated, having been too excited for this chance to retain such a trivial detail. "Umm, I'm not really sure how long we'll be here."

"That all depends on what we find." Don dropped his fork on the empty tray. "However, the shortest amount of time we'll be on site is six months."

Marco rubbed his chin. "You know what's weird to think about? If we *are* out of here in six months, the ship that'll take us home is already on its way here."

Corporal Guillen looked down at the table, as if staring deep into the metal at some other reality. After a moment, he spoke without looking up. "Two years, nine months, twelve days, and three hours. I'm legally thirty-nine, but biologically twenty-six since I've pulled so much cryo time."

"Wow, that's—" Kerys froze at the sudden, loud groaning of metal emanating from everywhere—along with heavy bangs.

The corporal disregarded the noise, twirling a fork around in his fingers. Everyone else looked like a pack of startled raccoons caught raiding the pantry.

"Please tell me that's normal." Marco stared at the ceiling. "That's gotta be normal, right? The ship's supposed to sound like it's being bent in half?"

"Heh." Corporal Guillen flipped the fork up and caught it. "It's from the ship decelerating out of translight. I'm no astrophysicist, but something about moving at that speed does funny things with matter. The hull stretches out a little."

Kerys dropped her fork in her still half-full tray, appetite gone. "That's... umm... interesting."

"Our primary objective here"—Don cleared his throat—"is to evaluate and assess suspected signs of nonhuman civilization the Avasar Biotech people found. According to the information I've been given, the site is only a short distance from Wayfarer Outpost. A complete accident they decided to set up there."

Paula examined her e-pad. Light from its screen painted a shadow of her on the wall behind her. "They chose the location for its proximity to the largest... I suppose 'forest' would be the best term. Aerial photography shows a rocky ridgeline passing northeast to southwest at the bottom of a downgrade, a little farther than a half mile from the outpost. Here, I've got the photos up."

She handed her e-pad around. Kerys took it from Marco and spent a few minutes staring at a jagged line of dark grey mountains surrounded by a black field interspersed with shiny flecks.

"What's the composition of that soil?" asked Kerys.

"Mostly silica," said Don, "as well as traces of other crystals, and an element or two we've never seen before. I'm told it can have sharp edges. Disturbing it raises clouds of micro-fine particles that would be like breathing razor blades."

Kerys shivered.

"I wouldn't worry about that." Corporal Guillen traced a circle around his head. "The atmosphere's not compatible with humans. If you go outside without a suit, you'll have much bigger problems than accidentally inhaling sharp dust."

The smell of food from her tray shifted from uninteresting to nauseating. She nudged it away.

"Wayfarer Outpost was set up four years and two months ago," said Don. "There's no need to experience anxiety. The facility is a series of individual pods connected by modular tubes. Each building is capable of lasting quite a while if isolated from the rest."

Paula gestured at her e-pad. "I didn't see any reports of weather patterns indicative of concern. The planet has water and rain."

Kerys stared at the glittering black sand, smiling at the prospect of new scenery. A far cry from Earth, not at all safe, but a welcome change for a while. Despite the danger of the alien landscape, she couldn't help but find it beautiful.

"Hey, you done with that?" Foster reached across the table toward her, flicking his fingers closed against his palm a few times.

She handed him the e-pad.

"Gonna finish your... whatever that is?" Marco gestured at her half-eaten tray.

"I'm full. Go right ahead." She pushed it toward him.

"Much obliged." He winked and dug in. "Oh, hey—pot roast. I didn't know they made Hydra pot roast."

"They don't. That's the steak," said Foster.

Kerys's gut churned. "How long until we arrive?"

Corporal Guillen checked his armband. "Four hours nineteen minutes. Everyone's got an assigned stateroom on Deck B. There's also a small fitness center at the aft end of the hallway there. Med crew's made a mess of the lounge, but they've got some vids there if you need to kill boredom."

It didn't seem real that she'd been asleep and motionless for almost three years. They'd said she wouldn't even dream, but she had a few... though for all she knew, those dreams occupied fleeting moments between the onset of the anesthetic and the initiation of the freeze. Getting her body moving again seemed like a good idea, though considering she'd just eaten, nothing too strenuous.

"Right." Kerys stood. "Guess I'll walk around a little, maybe check out the fitness center."

Don got up and offered a hand. "Glad to have you with us, Miss Loring. I'm sure your experience will prove valuable planetside."

"Thanks, doctor." She shivered with anticipation, much the way she figured the first humans to set foot on a planet outside the solar system did so many years ago. "I can't wait."

Kerys crossed from the café to the ladder and climbed up one level to Deck B. A few of the plain metal doors had strips of white tape with names written on them in black marker. She stopped at the third on the right, upon which someone had written 'Loring, K.' Curiosity got the better of her and she pulled the sliding door aside to peer in at a modest stateroom with a foam pad bunk, grey blanket, and a tiny desk.

A thin-screen terminal bore bright amber lettering: ‹New Messages: 14›

"What?" Kerys blinked, clinging to the wall while staring at the display. Once surprise wore off, she eased into the room and slid the door closed behind her.

After taking a seat at the desk, she poked the screen, which presented her with a green fingerprint login box. She pressed her thumb to the monitor, waiting for a thin blue line to sweep past. A second later, the black background changed to a generic flowery meadow with bright blue sky and fluffy clouds. Kerys tapped the icon flashing with the shape of an envelope, opening a black window containing fourteen individual tiles.

Each small box had her little brother Jaden's face in it, mostly smiling. On the far left, he looked much like she remembered, about ten. In the most recent message on the other end, he appeared noticeably older.

Tears gathered at the corners of her eyes. *He's gotta be thirteen now.* Jaden had been a surprise... Her mother had him only five months before Kerys moved out to go to college. *I'm shocked Mom kept him.* She'd seen him on and off for holidays and the like, until he discovered she'd gone into space—at which point he wanted to know all about everything. The last site had been a mere seven-month cryo trip, so she hadn't missed *too* much.

"Three years..."

She tapped the first message.

"Hey, Ker! I know you're like sleeping now while the ship is flying, but they said I can send you these vid mails, and you'd get them when you woke up. I got an A on the project you helped with. Mr. Davis didn't believe me at first, thought I made it up. He was gonna fail me, but Mom went off on him. He wound up calling the people you used to work for and they verified it. Now I'm like a celebrity."

Kerys draped herself back in the seat, listening to her little brother talk on and on about how excited he was that she got another chance to 'research alien ruins and stuff.' One message into the next, he filled her in on life back home. He got a new game system for his eleventh birthday and spent twenty minutes talking about how one of the games made him think of her roaming around an alien planet. In the fifth video, a bright green plastic lattice encased his left arm. He'd broken it playing lacrosse and had to wear the 'stupid thing' for two days until the nanosurgery finished.

Watching him get older before her eyes summoned a lump in her throat. She grasped the front of her neck on the twelfth video when he let slip that he wished she could be there for Christmas. His somberness didn't last long, and soon he resumed barraging her with questions about her expedition.

Though he projected excitement, the sense that he missed her grew stronger with each successive message. She left the last second of the final video on freeze-frame. Not since the rep from Avasar made contact had she once hesitated at their offer. The chance to visit another planet and find alien civilization had been too strong a call to resist. Only now, staring into her brother's slate-blue eyes, did she feel a pang of doubt that she'd made a mistake.

The boy hadn't paid much attention to her until he'd turned nine. Before that, he'd been a bit of a brat, snapping that she couldn't tell him what to do because he already had a mother and didn't need two. For reasons she still didn't quite understand, Kerys had gone from unwanted 'second parent' to adored 'big sis' overnight. Six years was a lot of time to lose from her brother's life. Even if she turned around right away, he'd be sixteen before she got back to Earth. In a paradoxical way, she'd 'be there' during what remained of his childhood more from far away, even if the video messages took a month to make the trip.

Once, she tried to wrap her brain around how they could manage to send transmissions through space folds, but pages of technical documents made her head explode. She only remembered something about the folds being tiny. They hadn't developed the technology enough to squeeze starships into them, which could've cut the travel time on this trip to four weeks instead of three years. Of course, a data transmission from AV494 orbit to Earth via the SFT took a month, that didn't mean a ship would too. Her brain swam with jargon about exponential power curves.

"Ugh." She rubbed her nose, stared at Jaden for another few minutes, and hit a key to record a message.

"Hey, kiddo. We just woke up about forty minutes ago. It's hard to believe I've been asleep for so long and missed so much." She concentrated on not choking up. "I'm sorry for disappearing on you, but you know how important this could be. I'm higher up the food chain this time, so if we find something, I won't get left out." She waved at the wall behind her. "This is my luxurious stateroom, a little bigger than your closet. I won't be in it long. A couple hours from now, a shuttle's going to take us to the planet's surface, and then this ship will turn around and head right back to Earth.

"No one's really sure what's down there, at least as far as alien stuff goes. People have been on this planet for a while already, studying the plants. There's water here, so I'm *really* excited we might find something no one has ever documented before. It's going to be a lot of hard work, but I'm so anxious to get started, I'm shaking."

She held up her hands, allowing the camera to record her fluttering fingers.

"This is the chance of a lifetime. If someone at Avasar decided to put this outpost a little farther north or south, they never would've found the excavation site. Ugh. The few hours I'm stuck in this ship waiting are going to feel like forever. At least since I'm awake now, I'll be able to send you messages back. I'll try to send one off every couple days."

Kerys bounced in the seat, commenting about random things she could remember from her brother's messages. Eventually, the file size limit flashed a warning.

"Okay, bud. I've only got twenty seconds left. Wish me luck!"

The video window shrank to a small square, flashing in time with the word ‹sending› beneath it. Eighteen seconds later, it flashed 'transmission successful,' and returned to the main messaging window.

"Ugh." Kerys moved from the chair to the bed and stretched out.

Anxiety, anticipation, guilt, and fear got into a battle royal in her gut.

Despite that, she grinned at the drab ceiling overhead. In a little over two hours, a shuttle would take her team down to Wayfarer Outpost, and hopefully, a career-making discovery.

"I can do this." She closed her eyes. "I have to do this. We're going to make history."

2

REENTRY

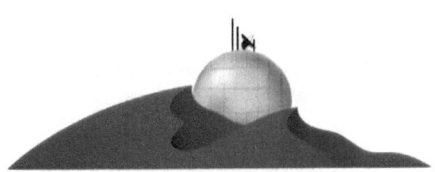

Hours of staring at her stateroom ceiling dragged on forever.

Fifty minutes prior to launch, Marco poked his head in to let Kerys know Don asked everyone to help load the team's gear. For whatever reason, all the archaeology equipment had to make the flight in the starship's cargo hold instead of being pre-loaded in the shuttle. She'd gotten up with little protest, as having something to do—even physical labor—would make the time vanish in a blur of activity. After she lugged her two duffel bags packed with company-issued jumpsuits and other clothes to the shuttle, she helped the rest of the team carry the rigid cases containing the research equipment.

From random conversation while moving heavy objects, she learned the *Avasar 4* had a length of 184 meters, and its designers thought the cargo area needed to be as far away from the shuttle compartment in the nose as possible. She also learned that 184 meters feels like five hundred when walking backwards while holding up one end of a two-hundred-pound trunk. Fortunately, the shuttle's rear door opened downward into a ramp with direct access to its cargo hold. Two immense ion thruster pods jutted out on either side of the opening, each bearing one folded wing.

"I can go first if you want," said Marco, "just swivel the box around."

"S'okay." Kerys grunted, straining to look back over her shoulder as she edged toward the ramp. "Besides, you just wanna give me the heavy end going uphill."

He chuckled.

Grunting, she heaved up on the handles, lugging the ponderous burden into the shuttle's hold. Six steps in, Marco stopped without warning. She yelped and almost fell over trying not to drop it.

"Hey! Careful! Why'd you stop?"

He nodded toward an open space beneath a rack. "Let's drop it here and push it. If you back in there, you won't be able to get out."

"Oh." She exhaled. "Yeah, good idea."

They set the case down and took a momentary breather. Once she caught her breath, she moved to his side and they shoved the coffin-sized box in against the wall. Don strolled up the ramp, holding an e-pad and counting boxes.

Marco took a knee to secure a strap over the case. "At least the outpost's built already. My last hop, we spent the first week living in inflatables while we put the damn pods together."

Evidently satisfied at their placement of the equipment, Don smiled at them before exiting the cargo hold via a bulkhead door at the center of the inner wall.

"Ugh." She shivered. "I don't think I could've handled 'tents' again. Bad enough only having an inch of steel between me and death on this ship."

"Ship's hull's only a quarter-inch-thick." Marco winked. "Shuttle's got thicker sides."

"Thanks for that." She frowned.

He cinched the black nylon strap and stood. "Beats me why they worry about weight. Not like this thing has to float."

"They're worried about mass, not weight... inertia." Kerys wiped her hands on her jumpsuit and spent a few seconds staring at indentations the handle left on her fingers. *This is it. Another few minutes, and I'll be one of fewer than a hundred people to set foot on this planet.* Excitement whirled in her gut.

"So, you ready?" He pressed his fist to her shoulder and gave a light shove.

"Yeah." She grinned. "You?"

Marco leaned back, stretching. "Been waiting three years for this."

She rolled her eyes, shook her head, and chuckled as she headed for the same door Don went out. The space on the other side reminded her of a tiny commercial passenger vessel, twenty seats arranged in two rows of pairs. Don and Paula—engaged in a discussion planning the excavation—occupied the first two on the right side.

Vibration seeped into her boots as the cargo ramp door closed, sealing against the hull with a *clank*.

Guillen had taken the last aisle seat on the left row, its back against the wall separating the seating area from the cargo hold. Foster stood in the aisle, looking around as if unsure where to put himself. Kerys exchanged a pleasant smile as she scooted past him, and eased herself into the first seat in the left row, across the aisle from Don. Marco slipped into the seat behind her, leaning out to eavesdrop on the two bosses.

A short passageway continued forward to the flight deck, where a figure wearing a fancy helmet sat sipping coffee while occasionally poking a button on the console overhead. She rubbed her hands back and forth on her thighs out of nervousness rather than cold. A dull grey panel marked the wall to her left, where a window ought to be.

Damn. Would've liked a view. She frowned at the blank wall before looking to her right. "Doctor Bouchard? Any chance of a better view?"

"… at least two days from landing. It's regrettable, but policy." Don turned to look at her so fast his white hair fluffed up. "Of course. We'll be able to walk up front once we've breached the atmosphere."

"Attention everyone," said a man's voice from overhead speakers. "This is your pilot speaking. I'm afraid I have some bad news. The in-flight movie has been cancelled."

Marco feigned a groan of annoyance.

"We'll be departing the *Avasar 4* in about one minute. Just waiting on the final system checks. Flight time to Wayfarer Outpost is estimating at fifty-two minutes, but that may change based on wind conditions. If anyone forgot anything on the ship, speak up now. I'm about to depressurize the bay outside."

Foster hurried into a seat midway down the right aisle and strapped in. Kerys craned her neck to steal a glance at Guillen—who appeared to be sleeping. Any temptation she might have had to fantasize about the too-beautiful man evaporated to bafflement at how he could *sleep* at a moment like this. She faced forward and secured her belt. Nervousness built, and she found herself absentmindedly tapping her fingers together.

The room surrendered to silence for a short while before a loud hissing noise outside made her jump.

"All right everyone—at this point, opening any doors is a really bad idea," said the pilot. After a pause, he chuckled. "Need to ask everyone to stay seated and buckled in for at least the first ten minutes."

She clasped her hands together at her chin, trying not to shake from eagerness. Everything she'd ever dreamed of since graduation waited for her down on the planet's surface.

A soft rumbling from behind built into a mild roar that rattled the ship. A second later the shuttle dropped straight down; her body lurched up against the harness. She closed her eyes, grunting with a shift in weight that pinned her against the back of her seat.

Marco yelled, but she couldn't tell if he cheered or cried out in fear.

Four breaths later, the acceleration faded, leaving her floating, kept in her seat only by the safety harness. Her stomach did a backflip at the zero-g.

Paula said something the engines drowned out.

"Just breathe," said Don in a raised voice.

"Why is it so loud?" shouted Marco. "Isn't this space? Shouldn't it be like… silent?"

"If you think this is loud," said Corporal Guillen, "wait 'til you're on the way off-planet."

"Huh?" yelled Marco.

"We're not even using the main engines, the ones that break gravity." Guillen thrust his hand into the air, mimicking a space ship, before letting it fall into his lap. "Basically, right now, we're just falling like a rock with wings."

"Great," said Marco.

"Atmospheric entry in twenty-seven seconds," said the pilot over the PA system.

Marco leaned forward, yelling around the seatback into Kerys's ear. "Not re-entry?"

She shrugged. "I guess since we haven't come from this planet it can't be re-entry, right?"

"Oh." He nodded. "Yeah, that's a good point."

"Ten seconds," said the pilot.

Nine… eight… seven…

When her mental countdown hit two, the shuttle slammed into a wall of turbulence that made her feel like being in a car rolling down a hill after jumping a guardrail. She screamed, though couldn't even hear herself over the continuous thunder of the atmosphere battering the hull. All the noise and the shaking gave her nightmares of the shuttle breaking apart. After her lungs emptied, she kept trying to scream, forgetting how to breathe in.

Eventually, the shuddering ebbed, as did the deafening roar. She gasped for air. Once her head stopped spinning, she looked around at the others, feeling a little less embarrassed over screaming since Paula had apparently fainted. Don gave Paula a light shake, which woke her up in a flurry of flailing and screaming.

"Intense," said Foster. "Holy crap, that was awesome."

Corporal Guillen shrugged. "Air here is thinner than my last post. That drop kinda felt like Earth."

Kerys tuned out the soldiers' subsequent discussion about how 'rough' Guillen's last drop had been and enjoyed a moment of not being thrown around in her seat. Before long, floating ceased, and she eased down into the cushion.

"Well, gravity's back," said Don.

"Looks like the skies are friendly," said the pilot. "Plenty of room up here if anyone wants an aerial view."

Kerys unbuckled her harness and sprang to her feet, the first one down the short connecting corridor to the flight deck. A man in a black jumpsuit reclined on a padded chair surrounded by a console full of screens and buttons. One small joystick protruded from the right armrest of the chair, though he didn't touch it.

She shot a brief glance at a monitor screen in front of him, showing a graphical representation of a flight path, plus various data streams. Not bothering to attempt reading it, she turned her gaze to the wide cockpit window, admiring luminous puffs of vapor washing over the ship. As far as she could see, the dark indigo sky glowed with azure clouds. The local star sat beyond view, but imparted a glowing golden line across a curved horizon of glimmering onyx.

The others, except for Corporal Guillen, shuffled in behind her and formed a horseshoe around the pilot's chair. Marco pressed into Kerys from the right, squeezing her hip against the wall.

"So beautiful," whispered Paula.

"Sorry," Marco mumbled. "Little tight in here."

"It's all right." Kerys paid him no mind, mesmerized by the exterior.

"Amazing." Don whistled in awe. "Only a handful of people have ever seen this."

Kerys quivered with excitement. "It's almost scary to think of how many planets exist out here... and humanity could never hope to see even a significant fraction of them."

The crew fell silent for a few minutes. Gradually, the blackness of space faded to a dark blue, and the curvature of the ground flattened out. The shuttle dropped under cloud level, and a great expanse of glittering black dirt spread out below. Silvery rocks dotted the surface here and there, gleaming like chunks of pure silicon in the sunlight.

Those rocks have to be the size of houses to see them from this high up.

Metallic grey mountains to the left caught the glare of the local sun as well, but she tried to stare at them anyway despite having to squint. A few minutes later, Marco tapped her arm and pointed at an ocean far off to the right, a rich blue-green hue with teal-capped waves.

"Water..." whispered Kerys, leaning forward.

"It might look like water, but it could be liquid ammonia." The pilot tapped the console, causing the primary display to switch to a diagram of the shuttle. He seemed satisfied and switched back to the flight path.

Everyone swayed to the right as the shuttle banked, holding a gradual turn for a few seconds before leveling off.

"It *is* water, at least close enough to support some form of plant life here." Don smiled. "However, I wouldn't want to drink it."

"Hey," said Marco. "You didn't touch the stick and the ship just turned… are you even doing anything?"

The pilot swiveled his chair around to face the crew. "Yep. I'm fulfilling regulations. These things are so automated now, the only reason I'm still even here is due to bureaucracy." He paused, as if realizing something, then smiled wider. "Oh, I do have to push a start button."

"Bureaucracy?" asked Kerys. "Aren't you a pilot?"

"Well, yes…" He tapped a winged emblem on his breast pocket over the name '1LT Serrano, A.' "On contract to Avasar Biotech. If I'm not here, the company loses about three-point-eight billion in assistance. Military regulations require a live pilot. Avasar hates paying me."

"Well, I feel a lot better having a human in the loop." Paula smiled at Lieutenant Serrano. "I don't feel comfortable trusting my life to computers."

"Yeah," said Marco. "One lazy idiot in a cube somewhere forgets a comma and we crash."

Lieutenant Serrano grinned. "This software's thirty years old. They wrote it back in like 2093 or something. Bugs are fixed." He swung around to face forward again. "Sometimes I do take the stick for old times' sake."

"Look there." Paula pointed ahead and left.

A swath of color spread over the glittery black ground straight ahead, like a massive patch of lichen growing on a rock. Ribbons of violet, periwinkle blue, white, and shades in between spanned an area likely hundreds of miles across. Several of the crew whispered in awe at the beauty of it.

"What is that?" Private Foster pointed at the colorful anomaly.

"That's the forest," said Don. "It's located in something of a valley exposed to wind coming off the ocean. This is the largest collection of plant life on this planet. There are other localized pockets, but they are much smaller."

"Looks like moss on LSD," said Marco.

Don laughed.

"The trees here resemble broccoli… only about a hundred feet tall." Paula held on to the pilot's chair to steady herself as the shuttle adjusted course to the right a few degrees.

Kerys peered around at the landscape. Mountains, miles and miles of sparkling black sand, a giant greenish ocean, and a thick run of 'trees.' *This is like a weird dream.* As beautiful as it all was, everything about this place felt deadly. She swallowed, but refused to let fear chip away at her hope. She'd spend most of her time on this planet in a cavern picking at ruins, or sitting inside an office studying images. The toxicity of the environment wouldn't matter.

She let out a slow breath, thought back to yoga class, and tried to center herself, pushing anxiety out into the floor. The shuttle descended to about five hundred feet and cruised over black desert for another twenty minutes before another, much smaller, line of mountains rose into view on the right. The mirror-like surface caught the sunlight with a flash that caused the canopy to auto-darken.

"There we are." Don pointed ahead. "The reason we're here is under that ridge."

A blinking yellow triangle appeared on the windscreen, superimposed on a speck of white.

"We're in transponder range of Wayfarer." Lieutenant Serrano tapped a button on a touchscreen to the left of the primary display before poking the triangle. "Wayfarer ground control, this is *Avasar-4* shuttle. We're three minutes out and looking good. Requesting clearance to land."

"Copy, shuttle." A woman's voice emanated from speakers overhead. "Pad's clear. Come on down."

Kerys stared wide-eyed at the distant forest as it grew from a patch of 'moss' to a collection of ominous stalks that towered over the nearby landscape. Beneath the rainbow of broccoli-like florets forming the canopy, the trunks of each 'tree' all had the same dull periwinkle blue color. Dark spaces between them stirred a deep and primal unease, as if a monster from a childhood storybook waited for her in the shrouded gloom.

A collection of white structures drew closer upon the inky dunes. Eight pods of varying size clustered around a central dome several stories taller, everything connected by silver and white tubes. Kerys grinned, thinking it resembled a bunch of take-out food containers someone plugged together with bendy straws—or perhaps an insanely expensive hamster habitat.

Red lights blinked in a steady rhythm from a group of antennas at the dome's top. To the west, a huge, rectangular structure emitted plumes of white vapor. North of it, a pair of smaller rectangles sat almost close enough to be touching, glowing with many small windows around the outside. Judging by their spacing as well as the density of tiny windows, she assumed them to hold crew quarters. A tall cube-shaped building stood to the east of the central dome, with a pair of oblong structures at the southeast corner. Despite having been in operation for years, the buildings of Wayfarer Outpost gleamed white, as if taken out of their packaging only hours ago.

Good sign. The atmosphere isn't overly harsh on the outpost.

A huge hexagonal pad sat a short distance northeast of the outpost, the shuttle's likely destination. Moving dark spots on the metal grating became evident as people in e-suits once the shuttle got closer—a group waiting for them.

"Gotta ask everyone to go grab a seat again," said Lieutenant Serrano. "If someone gets hurt during landing, it's on me."

The crew shuffled back to the seating area. Kerys buckled in, but excitement kept her leg bouncing.

Deceleration made her lean forward. Engine noise changed pitch, growing higher and louder for a few seconds. The shuttle came to a stop in midair, rotated to the left, and descended. Tangible relief swept over the crew at the creak of the landing pads absorbing the ship's weight.

Lieutenant Serrano walked in, without his helmet. "There's e-suits for everyone in the cargo hold in lockers along the starboard side. The door's not going to be opened until everyone's had their suits checked by either myself, Corporal Guillen, or Private Foster."

Murmurs of agreement spread over the crew. Kerys followed them to the cargo hold and stopped at the first available locker. She grasped the handle, but hesitated at the sight of 'Trem, Marco' written on tape.

He tapped her on the shoulder and pointed at hers, two doors to the left.

"Thanks."

She sidestepped and opened her locker, revealing a dark suit with oversized metal boots and reinforced matte-black panels on the forearms, elbows, knees, and chest. A blue metallic collar ringed the neck, matching the underside of the helmet. It had some similarities to the suit she'd worn on her last job, though its backpack unit looked about half the size. She pulled it out to check it over, trying to decide if they'd given her a newer model or gone cheap. The fasteners and clips appeared to be more or less in the same place. A hatch at the lower right corner of the backpack pod bore the label 'CBP.'

Curiosity got the better of her. She fussed at it until the panel opened, sliding back on small, hinged arms to expose a grey plastic disc about four inches across. Cyan-hued light glowed from the seam around it.

"First time?" asked Corporal Guillen, at her side.

Kerys startled. "Umm. Not really. Just haven't seen this model of suit before." She shifted her eyes to the left. Warmth spread over her face at his proximity, at his chest hovering inches from her arm. He'd already donned his suit, except for the helmet, and gained a few inches of height.

"The design isn't *that* new. These are operations suits, for delicate work. You probably used the Galileos on your last site?"

"Yeah." She grasped a folding handle set into the disc, twisted it, and pulled out a cylinder nine inches long filled with a gelatinous blue mass. The empty cylinder walls emitted strong white light. "Never saw one of these before though."

"That's the next-gen re-breather filter. Based on synthetic bacteria or something."

"Cyanobacteria," said Don from across the room. "That little canister is the next best thing to having an entire forest of trees in your backpack."

Corporal Guillen gestured at it. "The Galileos had about a seventy-two-hour limit before the filter pack needed a recharge, but they weighed fifty-four pounds. These Nomad suits are good for about thirty before you need to swap out the pod. Course, ya ask me, I wouldn't feel too safe past twenty."

"Right…" She put the canister back, closed the hatch, and pulled the suit open. He motioned to help, but she slipped into it without hesitation. "I *have* worn e-suits before, you know."

He smiled. "These are a lot lighter and more comfortable. Helmet's got a wider field of view, and the gloves are thinner, so you can do whatever it is you scientist types do. Only real problem with them is they put the fasteners in an awkward place. Hard to work them yourself."

She stooped to hit buttons on the boots, which caused them to split open on powered struts. "Us scientist types?" A grin spread over her face, and she found herself not minding him hovering so close. "I suppose you'll have to show me how to put this thing on."

He chuckled, indicating the boots with a nod. "Looks like you got the hang of it."

Kerys stared at his perfect face for a second or two before she caught herself doing it, and averted her eyes while stepping into the suit. As soon as her weight pressed down, the metal boots closed around her normal boots with a soft *hiss*. She stuck her arms in the sleeves, then reached up and guided the rigid helmet ring down over her head.

"Four primary fasteners hold the chest plates closed. One at each shoulder, one on either side right above the belt line." Corporal Guillen sealed up the back of her suit and gave her a pat on the shoulder. "Not bad."

Not bad yourself. She resisted the urge to wink and sighed in her mind. *I'm not here to find a date. There's alien relics to dig up.*

"Suit's got the usual feature set. Micro spotlights on the shoulders, integrated communications suite in the helmet. It'll auto-join the comm net, but you won't be able to talk until you identify. When you first boot up, you'll be listening, but no one will know you're there until you log in."

She nodded and grabbed the helmet. "How long 'til we go EVO?"

"As soon as everyone's suited. Might as well seal up."

"Right." She gathered her hair into a bun and held it in place while lowering the helmet on. It met the ring with an audible click, and tiny motors locked it in place. A HUD appeared on the visor, showing the filter pod life on the lower right as 99% [29.56 H]. A small bar on the left contained a row of names:

Doc B
SSG Gensch
CPL Mitchell
ElectricWeasel
Paula
PFC Morrow
SGT Coleman
Marco T
[Login]

"What's taking them so long?" asked a young woman in tandem with a yellow dot appearing by the name Mitchell.

The dot went out, and another came on by 'SSG Gensch.' A thick, scratchy voice conjuring the image of an older man flooded her helmet. "Give 'em a moment. They're prettyin' up for us."

"Come on, people," said PFC Morrow. "I wanna get off this goddamned rock."

Marco laughed, lighting up his dot. "Oh, we're gettin' nice and ready for you boys. Takin' me forever to decide what to wear."

The others must be outside. Kerys stared at the bottom line and blinked both eyes in a slow, deliberate manner. The word 'Login' disappeared.

"Kerys," said Kerys.

The system spelled her name 'Kerris.' She sighed and blinked at her name again. "Modify spelling. K-e-r-y-s." A second blink confirmed it.

"Plus one," said Doctor Bouchard.

"Hi," said Kerys.

Paula waved as her voice came over the comm. "Hello."

Corporal Guillen patted and tugged at her suit in several places before giving her left shoulder a squeeze and flashing a thumbs up. "You're good to go."

She smiled to herself, watching him walk over to Marco for a suit check. Even in the form-obscuring e-suit, he cut a striking figure. That he hadn't hit on her or even commented on her looks made him feel strange and appealing already. *That's going to take getting used to.* She grumbled to herself. *Forget him. He's back on Earth.*

After the soldiers put their helmets on and checked each other's suits, Lieutenant Serrano (who hadn't put on an e-suit) jogged out of the cargo hold, sealing the door behind him. Corporal Guillen approached a panel by the rear door and rested his hand on the wall.

"Heads up, people. About to reclaim the air in there. If anyone gets flashing red or orange stuff on their HUD, speak up fast. A solid red indicator is normal."

Murmurs of agreement came from the archaeology team. Kerys nodded.

"Come on, come on," said a female voice. The dot by SGT Coleman lit up. "Nine damn months is over."

"What are you gonna name him?" asked SSG Gensch.

"Genscher," said Coleman.

"Ouch." The gruff older man chuckled, his gritty voice grinding in her helmet. "You'd do that to your kid?"

PFC Morrow laughed. "Your dad did it to *you*."

"Depressurizing," said Guillen.

A red dot blinked on at the top center of Kerys's field of view, indicating the suit detected no breathable air outside. She looked down at her gloved hands, flexed the fingers, and rotated them around to test flexibility. *Yeah, this won't be too bad. The Galileo suit was like trying to work in mittens.*

Corporal Guillen pounded a button, and the rear wall opened outward, extending into a ramp. Two men and two women in camo-green e-suits approached. One pair held rifles across their chests; the others each lugged a pair of overpacked duffel bags. The soldiers with the bags rushed up the ramp and dropped their bags on the floor before clasping arms in greeting with Corporal Guillen and Private Foster.

Doctor Bouchard led the way down the ramp, followed by Paula. Marco traipsed along behind them. Kerys kept a hand on a hydraulic strut for balance as she made her way out of the shuttle onto the landing pad. When she reached the end of the metal gridding, her boots hit the sparkly ground with a *crunch*, sinking a good inch as if she'd stepped in loose sand. Flakes and chips of varying size appeared dark or gleamed like mirrors depending on how they lay. She crouched and scooped a handful, wiggling her fingers to let the glinting crystals rain back to the surface.

It's like black diamond snow.

"Careful, uhh, Kerys," said a woman.

She glanced left, catching the last second of a yellow dot lit up by Corporal Mitchell's name. "Sorry?"

"The regolith here consists of flakes and crystals. Some of them are sharp enough to damage an e-suit. You're walking on a pile of knives. Boots are steel, so no big…"

"Crap. That's right. Sorry, not thinking. It's so mesmerizing to look at." She stood straight and waved her hand about to get rid of any traces.

"Everyone does that." Corporal Mitchell walked over. A halo of pale azure light inside the helmet illuminated a young, dark brown face with large, smiling eyes. "It's so pretty here, y'almost never think it's deadly."

Wow. She's practically still a kid.

"Yeah." Kerys held eye contact with the shorter woman for a second, offered a polite nod, and twisted to peer to her right. The ridge, her entire reason for being here, seemed more distant than she'd expected, on the far end of a long downhill slope. From where she stood, she could almost make out the glow of artificial lights at the bottom.

"All right, everyone," said Don. "We need to get our stuff off the shuttle before it can leave. There'll be plenty of time for sightseeing over the next... however many months we're here."

Kerys groaned, pivoted, and trudged back across the landing pad to the ramp. The departing soldiers helped unload as well, much to her surprise—though it made sense given they wanted to leave as soon as possible. It took about ten minutes to transfer the team's gear to a cargo skiff. Marco grabbed the skiff's handle and started pushing it toward the central dome.

Sergeant Gensch stepped in the way, pointing at a two-story square building south of the landing pad. "You'll be taking most of that gear into the excavation site as far as I understand. All this shit can sit in the garage for now. Personal belongings, obviously, go with everyone inside."

Kerys hurried over to the skiff and grabbed her two bags, as did Paula, Don, and Marco. She shot a sideways look at Corporal Guillen, who hadn't added his duffel to the pile. He bowed his helmet and kicked at the ground, as if trying not to laugh.

While Marco and Sergeant Gensch took the gear south to the vehicle garage, Corporal Mitchell led everyone else southeast, crossing about two hundred meters' worth of black sand to the central dome. Up close, the heart of Wayfarer Outpost loomed huge and foreboding, a five-story half-egg with narrow, armored windows like a militarized office building. Wisps of vapor whipped around the antenna array at the top, hinting at a stronger wind than the breeze gliding over the ground.

Mitchell led them to an open airlock at the northernmost point. Once everyone stepped inside, the outer door closed with a barely audible metallic scrape. Kerys gazed around at the immaculate white walls, the word 'Wayfarer' in large, black letters on the left, and Avasar Biotechnology on the right beside a life-sized Shiva silhouette logo.

The red dot vanished about twelve seconds later, and soon, the inner door split down the center and retracted into the walls, exposing a decent-sized room with more lockers, charging stations, and a group of people in jumpsuits. A Chinese woman in her early forties stood at the center of the group in an olive drab jumpsuit, arms folded, but smiling. Kerys gave the group a quick look as she went to drop her bags, and froze at the sight of a man in a forest green jumpsuit with thick black hair, a rich tan, and giant shit-eating grin.

Will Braxton.

Her ex-boyfriend.

The instant she processed who she looked at, her blood practically froze in her veins. If not for the airlock behind her being sealed shut, she might've tried to run for the departing shuttle. Instead, she backed up two steps until her e-suit's backpack module bumped the giant door.

What the fuck is he *doing here?*

She looked away and down before he could get a good look at her face, hoping the visor concealed her. In the bulky e-suit, she couldn't exactly stuff her hands in her armpits to stop them from shaking, so she made fists instead. Don, Paula, and Marco shuffled in, dropped their bags, and pulled their helmets off. Corporal Guillen and Private Foster formed up to the left of the archaeology team. Kerys wanted to stand behind them so *he* couldn't see her. She started to feel conspicuous as the only one left wearing a helmet, so she slouched over and pulled it off, letting her hair fall around her face.

Paula gave her an odd look and crept over. "Are you okay, hon?"

No. The room spun. *He's supposed to be on Earth. What the hell!* "Umm. Yeah, just a little dizzy."

The woman in the olive drab jumpsuit cleared her throat. "Hello everyone. I am Captain Emily Chen of the USIC. Although, this installation is not officially under the auspices of the US Interstellar Corps, since Avasar hasn't bothered to send any senior management, I am in charge." She paused for a few seconds to look the new arrivals over. "This will be your home for at least the next six months, if not longer. I say that because the next scheduled ship will not arrive for six months. In the event your task here runs longer than that, you'll be here for another six months. We are fully self-sufficient, and this facility can keep going for decades without supplies from Earth."

Six months. Kerys peered between two strands of hair at Will. *Six months stuck in a giant beer can with him.* The desire to scream in rage and cry canceled each other out and left her aiming a vacant stare at the floor. At a concerned glance from Paula, Kerys straightened her posture, but refused to look at him.

"I realize your team's mission is not the usual sort of thing Avasar Biotech deals with, but you'll be sharing some work areas and lab space with the bio teams." Captain Chen gestured at Will and an Indian woman, also in a green jumpsuit. "This is Doctor Annapurna Bhatia, our chief biologist, and Will Braxton, manager of our botanical science team."

"Hello," said Annapurna. "It's a pleasure to meet you."

"'Sup." Will offered a salute with two fingers.

Kerys clenched her fists. *Cocky bastard. You haven't changed at all.*

Paula leaned closer and whispered, "Something's up."

"No, I'm fine," whispered Kerys.

"Fine doesn't tremble." Paula put a hand on her arm.

Kerys sighed. "I'm not..." She looked down at herself. "Okay, maybe I am. I'm just excited about this job."

"I hope you're better at archaeology than you are at fibbing." Paula gave her a light squeeze. "I raised a daughter about your age."

A door on the east wall opened, admitting Marco and a muscular older man with thick white-grey hair in a brush cut and a matching mustache who didn't look terribly impressed with the new arrivals, though despite his gruff presence, something about him made him seem trustworthy. Both men carried their helmets, likely having entered via an airlock at the garage.

Marco trotted over to the rest of the team while the other man approached the three soldiers.

"You've obviously met"—Captain Chen glanced at her e-pad, reading—"Corporal Rick Guillen and Private Ed Foster already. The two of them along with Corporal Gina Mitchell here and Staff Sergeant Paul Gensch are part of the USIC presence on AV494. They're here to protect you all."

"Paul?" asked Gina. "Sarge actually has a first name?"

Sergeant Gensch's eyebrow crept up as he gave her a look somewhere between playful camaraderie and angry drill instructor.

"Protect us from what?" asked Don. "Have you encountered anything out there?"

Captain Chen smiled. "Mostly from each other, but in the event we encounter unidentified hostiles or foreign threats, they're here to make sure everyone goes home alive. And no, doctor, we haven't found anything alive here other than plants."

Kerys peered around Paula at Will. Argument after screaming argument replayed in her head. Every time he'd made her feel like a possession rather than a whole person came back in one flood of anguished grief. She'd wasted four years on him, counting the eleven months it took battling self-doubt to work up the courage to leave. *I didn't do anything wrong. He's an ass.* After hesitating too long, she'd finally left him after it became clear he would never change. Will got what Will wanted. No one else mattered—not even her, not even his parents. Sure, he could be charming, he looked amazing, and he had more confidence than anyone ought to, but she knew him too well to fall for that smile ever again.

A few times, she'd felt certain he'd hit her. He'd never gone that far, but watching him punch the wall or kick the dishwasher had frightened her every bit as much. She believed he tried as hard as he could to hold back since they hadn't gotten married... a spider pretending to be nice until its prey is stuck firmly in the web. He always apologized for scaring her afterward, but it never seemed genuine. She didn't trust he wouldn't do worse if he ever got angry enough.

A rumble in the ground from the shuttle lifting off hit her like a slamming door.

Stuck.

On this planet.

In this outpost.

With Will.

Inside an oasis of human-habitable space, a few thousand square feet surrounded by an entire planet of quick, painful death.

Continued conversation among the crew dragged down into an unintelligible murmur, as if everyone stood on the far side of the room. *He won't try anything here. He knows there's no damn chance.* She risked a peek again. Will hadn't appeared to recognize her. She started to breathe a sigh of relief until Captain Chen's next words pierced her veil of disorientation like a knife.

"This is Lars Deering, and Ellen Vickers. They're from our maintenance group, specialists with heavy equipment, and will be assisting your team with any heavy lifting or excavation you need done in there."

Kerys looked up at two people waving and nodding in greeting. The man seemed in his mid-twenties and had short blond hair, close-set blue eyes, and a wide chest. Next to him stood a six-foot-plus woman with a muscular physique, a military-style buzz cut of black hair, and a deep tan. Combat boots and camo-green fatigue pants fit her intimidating presence, though her black tank top with a Hello Kitty face on it did not. Kerys blinked at the dichotomy and almost smiled. If not for Will's presence, she'd likely have laughed.

"Doctor Bouchard, why don't you introduce your team?"

"Certainly, captain. All three are specialists in xenoarchaeology, which as you might imagine, is a pretty small world." Don chuckled. "This is Paula Driscoll, my right hand. She's our expert in pictographic languages and cryptography."

"Hello," said Paula.

"We brought Marco Trem on board at the last minute with a little help from the university's finance board." Don patted him on the back. "He's had some hands-on experience at a prior site, and well, it's not easy to come by people who've done this before... which leaves—"

"Kerys," said Will, sounding shocked and annoyed. "What are you doing here?"

He took a few steps closer, eyebrows furrowed. She suppressed the urge to flinch, knowing the look. Will hated when things happened he hadn't planned on, especially when those things got in the way of his wants. A memory of him red-faced with anger at a flat tire that delayed a trip to buy a new entertainment center came out of nowhere. A mere half-hour to deal with the tire, and he'd melted down.

He has no power over me. She squeezed her fists as hard as the e-suit gloves allowed and stared him in the eye. "I'm here to study the alien ruins your people found."

"Kerys's last team did remarkable work, but she, unfortunately, got left off the accolades." Don shook his head.

Will waved as if trying to send an improperly cooked steak back to the kitchen. "No... You can't. She can't stay here. It won't work."

"Is there a problem, Mr. Braxton?" Captain Chen raised an eyebrow.

"Uhh." Will stared at her, his expression strange and unreadable.

He looks hurt, almost worried. Kerys squinted. *No. I'm not falling for it. I'm not too damn brittle and delicate to be this far from Earth.*

"They got her on the cheap," said Marco with a wink. "Million-dollar experience, but no paperwork to back it up."

Don sighed. "It's not so much that as she wouldn't have been available for us. Her misfortune, alas, became our luck."

"Mr. Braxton?" Captain Chen raised her other eyebrow. "Is there something I should be aware of?"

"No, captain." Will set his fists on his hips and grumbled at the floor. "No problem. Forget it."

What's he scheming?

Fear gave way to anger. She leaned forward, aggressive, daring him to be his usual self.

Captain Chen glanced at Kerys. "I'll trust there will be no issues?"

Grr. She's looking at me like I'm *the problem.* She relaxed her hands. His reentering her life like a flaming meteor had been the absolute *last* thing she ever expected to find here... but she would not let him ruin it. "None from me." she said, steel in her voice.

The steel in her voice caused Will to hesitate for a second before putting on the plastic smile she so loathed. "Nah, just a shock is all."

"If you need to talk," whispered Paula. "I'm here."

Kerys glared at Will's back as he followed the others out of the room.

He hesitated at the door long enough to shoot her an irritated look before disappearing into the hallway.

Captain Chen clapped to break the tense silence. "Once you're all out of your e-suits, Corporal Mitchell will show you to your living quarters. I want you all to know that my door is always open." She smiled. "Welcome to Wayfarer."

3

ROUTINE

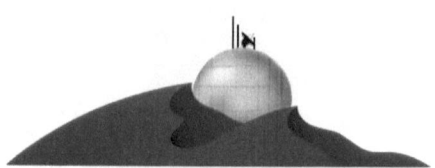

K erys sat on the edge of her bed, unsure if she should feel comforted or alarmed by its design.

The mattress occupying a hollow in the wall reminded her of a coffin. An automated hatch capable of sealing up in the event of atmospheric loss only worsened the claustrophobia. If the emergency system ever activated due to loss of atmosphere inside the dome, she'd be trapped like a fish in a tank, alive, but completely dependent on someone else showing up to find her.

Relax. This place is more solid than the Copernicus outpost... She shivered at the memory of what had basically been a heavy-duty plastic tent. Wayfarer's pods had four-inch-thick walls with reinforced windows.

"Heh. If anything breaches the hull, we'll all be way past the point where a trapdoor bed can help."

Distance from Will finally allowed her nerves to settle enough for her to once again think about the potential discoveries she might make. The odds of *him* ending up here seemed impossible until she thought about how few people worked in the field of xenobiology. Unless she changed careers, her future would likely continue to include working around him. *That* thought on top of watching the messages from her little brother again made her feel like she'd made a mistake coming out here. Being stuck on AV494 at least spared her from having to make a decision right away—though she considered leaving on the next shuttle regardless of what they found. To avoid ever seeing Will again, she'd change fields as soon as she could. Terrestrial archaeology would be the easiest choice but didn't exactly bring in the big bucks.

She'd packed her clothes away over two hours ago, but hadn't felt much motivation to move since Don gave her the bad news: Captain Chen ordered a hold on any of the new arrivals leaving the outpost for at least two days, pending medical evaluations. Sitting around inside, a half mile from making history, would be worse than three years in a cryo pod. At least for that, she'd been unconscious. Watching Will and the botany team head out to their research site in the forest hadn't helped.

Thinking of him got her nervously kneading her hands again. Aside from her time on ice, she'd been free of him for almost a year. She loved not having to validate herself, not having to worry if a lack of reply or a dish put down too hard meant he'd become angry with her. How long would he let her think she'd gotten away from him before he made a play to get her back? He'd probably just act like they never broke up and try to make everyone think she was crazy or unstable for saying they had.

He can try all he wants. I know what he's really like. I know all those fake faces he'll make.

She swiped her e-pad from the top of her desk, which folded down out of the wall below a hexagonal window the size of a dinner plate. It offered a meager view of the distant 'trees' shifting in wind strong enough to spin whorls of black dust off the ground into tiny tornados.

"Two days… This is going to suck."

The e-pad screen flickered to life at her touch, displaying the map of the Wayfarer outpost she'd opened out of boredom. Two rectangular pods at the northwest held all the living quarters. Her room occupied the more distant one from the dome. Only three rooms separated her from the northern end. A corridor ran south from the exit of her pod straight to the hydroponics facility—the massive western structure she'd noticed on the flight in. The outpost's power facility stood beyond the 'greenhouse' at the southwest corner, theoretically far enough away for the rest of the buildings to survive if it had a meltdown. To the southeast, two lab pods clustered together about a hundred meters from the start of the downhill grade leading to the excavation site. The vehicle garage, a square pod almost as big as the dome, but only one story high, sat to the east.

Everything connected to the dome by a series of semi-flexible tubes. The central structure had a map unto itself. Its five stories held the command area, communications controls, infirmary, fitness center, offices, cafeteria, backup power reactor, additional lab space, and Captain Chen's office at the top. Had Avasar sent a proper manager or VP to run the place, it would have been their office.

Kerys tossed the e-pad back to the desk with a sigh. She *could* go walking around to familiarize herself with the place, but the disappointment of being stuck inside doing nothing for two days sapped her energy.

After staring at the floor for some time, the idea of getting her medical check over with grew appealing enough to urge her into motion. Better to go wandering when Will had left to work in the forest so she wouldn't cross his path. As much as she told herself she'd stand up to him, she feared collapsing under pressure. For as long as she could get away with it, she'd act as if she hadn't encountered the one person capable of sucking the joy out of a journey to a breathtaking planet with actual living alien plants. Smiling to herself, she put on her 'inside shoes,' which reminded her of armored black sneakers, and left her room.

Strong overhead lights glared at her from super-white walls. Frigid air laced with a fragrance similar to hospital antiseptic blew in a noticeable breeze down the corridor. She shivered and tugged the zipper on her jumpsuit up a few inches. Silence made her feel like the only girl in the dorms who didn't want to go home for a holiday. That feeling, she knew well. Of course, everyone else would be at work now, except for the overnight people and the rest of her team. She hadn't a clue where any of them had gone.

Kerys headed to the right and wandered past twenty or so plain white doors on either side until she reached the ladder to the ground floor recessed in a shaft. She climbed down past several signs urging her to be careful—since Avasar cared about its employees and didn't want any injuries.

A heavier door at the south end of the pod opened to a short section of modular tunnel that connected south to the hydroponics pod with a left turn at the halfway mark. The sight of a large red handle labeled 'Do not pull – modular disconnect – Danger! Loss of atmosphere' out in the open stalled the breath in her throat.

No key? No code? Nothing? Just... sitting there? She shied away from it as if it would come to life and attack her.

Once the shock wore off, she crept into the tube and hooked a left to head toward the primary dome. About fifty meters later, she passed an opening leading to the other residence pod and continued past it another sixty meters to the dome. A six-inch-thick door had been locked open where the tube bolted to the hull. Aside from having only a little plastic between her and a fatal atmosphere, the place almost felt like a corporate office.

She emerged in an open atrium with a few benches and chairs. Like most of Wayfarer, hospital-white walls surrounded her. Traces of food aromas from the cafeteria muted the antiseptic odor clinging to everything. In the northeast, a corridor labeled 'garage' sat next to the cafeteria entrance. Another hallway led south from the atrium, with signs reading 'operations,' 'stairs,' 'labs,' and 'power.' Her e-pad map put the infirmary on the third floor, so she turned to her right down the hallway toward operations. Near what she estimated to be the center of the dome, she found a stairwell going up as well as down.

This place has a basement? Wow... Avasar went all out. Suppose they're intent on staying here a long time.

A few people she passed offered pleasant smiles as she made her way up six switchback flights to the third story. After a while of navigating corridors and peeking into office cubicles, she reached a hallway where the upper half of the walls were windows peering into conference rooms and cube farms. Two hallways later, she spotted an area with people seated at multi-workstation desks, reminiscent of a military command and control room. Kerys gazed at the operations center, watching them for a few minutes before her curiosity faded. She continued to the next corner. A short distance to the left, an archway led to an immaculate white corridor.

Much smaller than she expected, the infirmary consisted of two rooms: an unlit one with empty recovery beds, and a well-lit space where a dark-skinned man sat behind a desk with his feet up. Judging from the sounds of lasers and explosions on his terminal, he played a video game.

Kerys crept up to the open doorway. Her first attempt to knock on the metal doorjamb didn't make enough noise for him to notice, so she cleared her throat.

The man shifted his eyes to her without moving his body. A second later, the game paused and he bounced out of his chair with a broad smile. "Hello! Come in, come in." He gestured at a chair by his desk. "Please..."

Kerys approached, gazing past his desk at a pair of bulky surgical tables that looked like a cross between the dentist chair from hell and a tiny spacecraft. Both sat below egg-shaped swells on the ceiling brimming with slender robotic arms, lenses, and squiggly wires.

"I'm Doctor Sekhar, but please, call me Ravi if it's more comfortable for you." He smiled again, offering a hand.

Kerys accepted the handshake and sat. "Kerys Loring. They said I had to come in for a routine check."

"Ahh, yes. You're with the archaeology team that just arrived. They sent your files over." He scooted his chair in, tapping his finger on the terminal. "Pardon the game—I love being bored. It means no one is hurt."

She let off a nervous laugh. "I suppose that is a good thing."

The greenish tint on his white jumpsuit faded as the contents of the screen shifted. "Well then. Have you experienced anything unusual since being brought out of cryonic suspension? Muscle weakness? Cramps, tingles, soreness, headache, vertigo, numbness?" He leaned away from the monitor to smile at her.

Kerys shook her head. "No. Just a little restlessness. I want to get out there and see what they found that made them want to ship us all out here."

Doctor Sekhar nodded. "I can understand that. I haven't heard specifics, but Commander Chen has refused to let anyone near the site since they saw the carving."

"Carving?" Kerys perked up. "What kind of carving?"

"Oh." He offered an apologetic smile. "I'm not sure. I heard someone mention a survey team stumbled across what appeared to be a hallway cut into the rock, and something about markings on the wall they assumed to be writing."

Dammit! She sat on her hands, trembling with anticipation. "I can't wait to get out there and see for myself."

"It sounds exciting." He grinned at her before leaning close to the monitor again. "Well, let's see… They sent over your medical records. Everything looks good. No allergies, chronic conditions, anything of that nature?"

"Nothing I know of." She fidgeted.

"All right. I see you've spent time on an outpost before… Copernicus? So, you're already accustomed to tight quarters, not being able to go outside without a suit, the claustrophobia."

"This place is about ten times bigger than Cope was. Much less stressful."

He cringed. "Sorry to hear that. Most who come here show some signs of cabin fever within a month. There's a relaxation spa on the second floor, east part. Holographic beach, forest, and so on if you feel the need for 'fresh air.'"

"Wow. They really held nothing back here. This place even has a basement? They excavated under the dome?"

"They dug out a reservoir and ran an underground passage to the grow facility for more direct access to water." He waved his hand about. "Moisture collectors extract water from the atmosphere, purify it, and it's stored down there." He put on a mock stern face while pointing at her. "No swimming, since that's our drinking water."

"Right…"

"Might as well get the technical bits out of the way then." He stood and gestured at a flat white box on the ground against the wall. "Please come around the desk and stand on that."

She complied. As soon as she stepped up on the device, a blue dot appeared on the wall about even with the top of her head.

"Hmm. Your weight seems a little low. Have you been eating properly?"

"I've been frozen solid for three years and I'm all kinds of anxious." She picked at her jumpsuit pocket. "*Good* anxious I mean. What's sitting out in that cave could be one of the most significant finds in the history of humanity. I'm excited, and kinda nervous."

He tilted his head. "Is there something else? You look troubled."

Kerys sighed. *Crap. I have a sign on my forehead, don't I?* "I, uhh... yeah."

Doctor Sekhar gestured at the nearer surgical table. "Please relax there."

She eyed it, twitching.

"Only a routine scan." He clasped the e-pad to his chest and grinned. "Nothing will draw blood."

"Right." She hopped down off the scale and climbed up onto the medical station, reclining on black cushions much softer than they looked. Staring up at the shiny white egg and all its robotic protrusions stirred an uneasy feeling in the pit of her stomach, which worsened when a bright white seam lit up down the center. "So... what are you doing?"

The egg split apart about an inch, exposing three glowing green dots, projectors that covered her in a grid of laser lines.

"Body scan. Checking for injuries to bones, muscles, and vital organs... anything out of the ordinary. Please relax. This will only take a few minutes and requires no physical contact."

"Okay." She closed her eyes and tried to clear her thoughts.

Doctor Sekhar remained quiet for a little while as the machine thrummed and whirred. "You were about to mention something else contributing to your nervousness?"

Busted. "Just about the most cosmically bad luck imaginable. My ex is here."

"Your ex?"

Warmth tingled over her body, though she blamed the scanner. "I suppose it's not really that surprising. Both of us work in rare fields, and Avasar has deep pockets. Will's certainly driven enough to be near the top. I bet there's not even a hundred xeno-botanists on Earth, and I chose a field that gets made fun of. It pisses me off how stupid so many people are. There's literally more planets than we have numbers to be able to count, and they're convinced non-human life is a myth."

"And his presence here shocked you?"

She let the comforting tone of the doctor's voice settle her mind. "We met in school... Berkeley. Our majors had a lot of overlapping classes. Wound up getting an apartment together senior year. I suppose we had some good times, but after a while, it got harder and harder to ignore how much of an asshole he is."

The doctor pursed his lips and nodded, reading something on his e-pad. "I'm here to listen if you need an ear. Everything said in here is confidential. I hope he wasn't abusive."

"Not physically. At first, it was comforting to have a man in my life who had the confidence to make decisions and didn't need validation from anyone. I guess it started slow, a small disagreement about where to eat. I really wanted to go to this sushi place, but he had his mind set on Italian, and that was that. From there, I started to notice how everything was Will's way or no way at all. I felt like just another fancy expensive toy in his collection. For almost a year, I argued with myself, coming up with excuses like he's stressed out, or he's not going to stay like that, but he never changed."

"You can get up. The scan's done."

Kerys scratched at the side of her neck. "We dated for about two months before I decided to go to bed with him. Once I finally said yes that first time, I'd never told him no again when he wanted sex. The night I finally decided to leave him, I'd been let go from my first real job... I mean it wasn't anything grandiose, some part time grunt work at the California Science Center, tending to their space rocks. They decided to downsize the staff, and being new, I was one of the first to get the ax. Anyway, I took it hard. He didn't care I'd been crying on and off all day. His team made some kind of breakthrough and he came home all revved up and wanted to go out for dinner. Of course, to him, I was jealous of his success and trying to ruin his day. When we got back to the apartment, he wanted, umm... dessert."

Doctor Sekhar sighed.

"I wasn't in the mood. He flipped out. Kicked the nightstand, shouted, threw stuff. He didn't hit me though."

"He may as well have. Outbursts like that have almost the same effect."

She slid off the table to her feet and shrugged. "That was the first time I really felt afraid of him. I knew it would only get worse, so I told him I couldn't go on like that. He grabbed my arm when I tried to leave, started apologizing, but it felt *so* fake. Scripted like."

"It took a good deal of inner strength to get yourself out of that situation. Many suffer for years."

"Thanks." She rubbed her arms. "I'm afraid he's going to try something. He chased me for months. Phone calls, flowers, showing up unannounced. I almost trusted him again, but he always made me feel... I dunno, unclean. Like he was trying to sell me a bad used car. I thought he gave up when he just stopped cold, but now that I think about it… he'd probably taken the position here."

"I can't really discuss other personnel records, but he has been here a while considering the age of the facility." Doctor Sekhar offered a reassuring smile. "We strive to have a safe environment for everyone. If you feel threatened at any time, please let me know—or feel free to visit Captain Chen."

The worry needling at her gut ever since she saw Will here twisted deeper. He would definitely do something sooner or later, and already she could picture him shouting about her attempting to sabotage his career with bullshit. If she complained about him now, before he even did anything, it would only make her look bad. She forced a weak smile. "Thanks. I'm okay. He saw me already and kept his distance. I'm sure he understands we're done."

I can avoid him. He's out in the forest and I'm in a cave. I'll just keep to myself and stay out of his way. She nibbled on her lower lip, chiding herself for backing down before a conflict even started, but he'd been here for years. The crew of this place knew him, probably trusted him—he had that effect. She doubted anyone would believe her. Even the doctor, all smiles and warmth, might be jotting down comments about her being 'too sensitive' or 'not suited for deep space work.'

"So… umm… how'd the scan go?"

He looked up from the e-pad, smiling. "You're perfectly healthy. I've just submitted your medical clearance. Once the rest of your team has been here, you should be able to get started rooting around the caverns."

She grinned. Not even Will could ruin this for her. Kerys took a few breaths to calm down. True, whatever they found inside the cave had been convincing enough for Avasar Biotech to hire a xenoarchaeology team and fly them out here, but it didn't prove they'd stumbled across a career-making bonanza. Getting *too* excited wouldn't help.

The doctor made small talk for a little while, preferring human company to being alone in the infirmary with his video game. Eventually, a growl from her stomach gave her an excuse to get going, and the odd sensation of being hungry directed her to the cafeteria at the eastern side of the dome's ground floor. The entrance stood on the right side of the atrium, where the hall to the residence pods connected at the west, and a northern tube led off to the garage.

About two hours past lunchtime, she walked into a room containing rows and rows of shiny steel benches in the middle—and no other people. Smaller round tables lined the curving window at the outer wall. Rather than workers, a row of machines staffed a counter along the left next to stacks of plastic trays. The cafeteria gave people the option of grabbing a large selection of Hydra meals or waiting on line for 'fresher' food from a much smaller menu depending on what had been cooked.

An auto-attendant portioned out a plate of something masquerading as lasagna, which she carried to one of the window tables offering a view of the landscape between the lab pods on the right and the garage on the left.

Willowy bands of luminous cyan drifted across a stormy sky of blue-violet, flashing with the occasional streak of amethyst lightning reflecting on the silicon-grey mountains. Kerys stared at the shimmery rocks, hoping the future they contained for her would be good… or at least not bad. Daydreams of speaking at universities, meeting celebrities, maybe even the president, flickered across her brain.

The more she stared at the ridge, the more she smiled.

Will can go to hell. I'm glad I took this chance.

4

DAY ONE

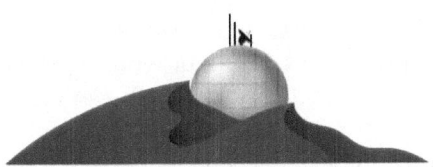

Anticipation complicated the task of opening the clasps on the shoulders of her e-suit.

Kerys grumbled under her breath when she caught herself pulling on the wrong side of the mechanism. The rest of the archaeology team, plus Corporal Mitchell and Private Foster, suited up with her in the ready room adjacent to the garage pod airlock. The din of idle conversation blended into the clatter of locker doors and e-suit parts, becoming a mess of meaningless sound.

She paused to collect herself, barely able to stop bouncing on her toes from excess energy. History could be less than an hour away. She opened her e-suit, stepped into it, and shrugged the front up to her shoulders before sitting on a plain steel bench with her arms draped over her knees, waiting.

Corporal Mitchell walked up behind her and helped snug her armor into position. Molded panels of rigid armor pressed into Kerys's chest. She adjusted it up a quarter-inch to fit better, before grasping the metal ring around her neck to keep it from digging into her throat. Mitchell secured the four fasteners around the armor, one at each shoulder and one on either side at the beltline. Each one closed with a faint squeak and click. After, the younger woman took a seat next to her and offered her back, smiling over her shoulder.

"Thanks, corporal." Kerys shifted sideways and got started returning the favor.

"No problem... and it's okay if you call me Gina." She peered back over her shoulder, her eyes radiating nervousness. "You're not enlisted, so it's not like required for you to use ranks or anything."

Guess I get to be big sister again. Is this kid even twenty yet? She smiled. "Is this your first off-world post?"

"Yeah." Gina looked down at her lap. "It's cool though. Ain't like I got no one missin' me back home. The Corps is my family."

"Sorry." Kerys braced one hand on Gina's shoulder and pushed the last clip closed. "There. All set."

"Don't be sorry. I came up in a shitty foster situation. Got my ass outta there when I turned sixteen. No one gonna save me but me, right? Street surfed a month or two 'fore I saw a recruitment ad. Didn't even lie about my age. Told 'em I was on my own"—she winked—"ain't as young as I look. Been three years now, but never got sent off-planet 'til this."

Kerys offered a sympathetic look. "I still can't get used to the whole freezing thing. So, you're nineteen but legally twenty-two. If not for the pod, I'd be over thirty. I'll take it. Cling to my twenties as long as I can."

Gina laughed, flashing a genuine smile for a few seconds before looking away and down as if embarrassed.

Ellen and Lars geared up in their e-suits on the other side of the room, then climbed into exoskeletons that made them close to ten feet tall. Ellen's exo had numerous Hello Kitty stickers on it, plus an airbrushed one in the center of the chest plate. Both flexed their arms and walked back and forth, as if testing to make sure everything worked. The repetitive clonking of metal boots on the floor rattled the room.

"Is everyone about ready then?" asked Don from near the airlock.

"S'pose that's our cue." Gina stood and grasped her helmet in both hands. She exhaled, forced a smile, and put it on.

"Yeah." Kerys packed her hair up and lowered her helmet over her head. Seconds after it made contact with the metal ring around her neck, tiny motors locked it in place, and a faint hiss whispered in her ears. A list of names appeared along the left side of her visor, with Don and Private Foster in a sub-window outlined in green. She stared at the login prompt in the sub-group, joining the private channel for her team. Within a second, 'CPL Mitchell' popped in below her name. "Gina, check me?"

Corporal Mitchell tugged and poked at Kerys's suit for a moment before giving her a pat on the helmet and a thumbs up. She moved on to check Marco while Private Foster helped Paula. Kerys focused on breathing at a normal rate for a little while before walking over to where Don waited for everyone. The HUD lit his pale cheeks yellowish green behind the visor.

"You look as excited as I am," said Don.

Kerys grinned. "I can't wait to see what's in there. Three days we've been stuck sitting on our asses."

He chuckled. "Like any other corporation, Avasar is worried about liability. They wanted to make sure everything checked out."

Marco approached and gave her a back pat. "Hey, new girl. You ready?"

"More than." Kerys rubbed her hands together.

Paula, Foster, and Mitchell walked over with Ellen and Lars clomping up behind them.

Don nodded to them before pivoting to face everyone. "All right. Today is our first entry to the cavern. I'd like to focus on mapping out the structure of the place in situ before we start digging or burrowing into walls. We've been allotted the use of a Warthog, which will make things a little easier on us."

"A what?" asked Marco.

"A Warthog. A small truck to carry us and our gear to the cave. It is, after all, 972 meters away from the outpost. I'm sure you don't want to spend all day going back and forth on foot carrying our supplies."

"Well, AV494 does have .94 Earth gravity, so it would be a *little* easier," said Paula.

Marco held up his right hand as if swearing an oath. "I'll take the vehicle."

Don chuckled. "I thought you might. So again, today, please focus on mapping and scanning. We'll be setting up the 3D modeler in the primary chamber. I trust you've all spent the past few days looking at the information I sent out?"

Paula and Marco nodded.

Kerys beamed. Don had shared some video he'd received from the Avasar people, showing a short tunnel to a large, rectangular chamber with a longer hallway heading to the left at the midway point that linked to a smaller chamber. The westernmost wall of the secondary room showed signs of collapse, though rather than a structural issue, it had a foreboding appearance, as though something the size of a bear had tunneled in.

"Everyone's suit's reading green," said Private Foster, a yellow dot glowing next to his name on her HUD in time with his voice.

"All right then. Let's not waste any more time." Don pressed a button that opened the inner door to the airlock.

Everyone hurried in. He hit another button, and the door closed behind them. As soon as it finished closing, he fiddled at a touchscreen mounted on the wall. Loud hissing filled the space, fading to silence within seconds. A red dot appeared at the top of her field of view indicating a toxic—or absent—atmosphere outside the suit. With a heavy *clunk* in the floor, the outer door parted down the middle and slid away to either side. Kerys followed the others out into a huge, square chamber.

On her left, five small quad ATVs stood next to shelves laden with tools, replacement parts, and batteries. The center of the room held a pair of giant six-wheeled rovers with enclosed cabins and sloped front ends. Massive pale grey tires came up to her helmet, a clue they'd been designed for extreme terrain. The open area in front of them looked large enough to hold another pair of the giant trucks. The archaeology team's gear had been stored on shelves along the right wall, near a trio of vehicles that resembled tiny flatbed trucks. A cube-shaped cabin large enough for two people sat atop the front wheels in front of a ten by four-foot platform.

Those must be the Warthogs.

Its wheels only came up to her knee, but the trip to the excavation site didn't require navigating huge rocks or uneven terrain, only a half-mile of razor-sharp beach sand. Marco's hand on her shoulder distracted her from thinking about how she could die any of ten different ways between the door and the cave.

"Hey. Give us a hand, huh?" Marco nodded toward the shelves.

Kerys followed him around the Warthogs, where Don went over the cases, tapping ones he identified as necessary for day one setup.

"It's okay, Doc," said Ellen. "We got this."

Ellen and Lars tossed the hundred-plus-pound boxes around like styrofoam coolers. Marco shrugged, smiling at not having to do manual labor. It took under a minute for the pair to transfer the equipment, and once they'd finished, they headed off on foot to the excavation site. Private Foster climbed in to drive the flatbed, with Don and Paula squeezed together with him up front. Marco started to climb up on the back end, but Gina waved him down.

"We got the quads." She pointed at the left wall. "Can't let you ride on back. Safety reasons."

"Oh, sweet." Marco hurried across the garage and hopped on the nearest quad. "Used to have somethin' like this back home."

Kerys mounted the next four-wheeler and examined the handlebars. The controls seemed straightforward: an off-on button, two squeeze brakes, and the right handgrip twisted to accelerate. A tiny screen between the handlebars showed a compass heading as well as battery charge at ninety-two percent, estimating four hours and nineteen minutes of driving.

"Need a hand?" asked Gina, sidling up next to her. "Controls are pretty simple."

"I think I can figure it out." Kerys flicked the button to 'on.' "Looks kinda obvious. I mean, it's a quad, not rocket science."

Marco laughed. "Driving a quad is *more* difficult than rocket science. That shit's all automated. The quads have more than one button."

The Warthog pulled away at a jogging pace, steering off in a gentle rightward arc after it passed the large door on the east face.

"Yeah, they're pretty basic. Just be easy on the throttle. That stuff out there is like the fake snow they use for movies. You twist that thing too hard, the quad'll burrow itself into the ground instead of going forward."

She flicked her thumb at the rubberized grip. "Right. Got it."

When Gina threw her leg over the next quad in line, Kerys walked hers backward away from the wall, then shifted the handlebars to point at the exit. The slightest twist at the right-side grip rocked the quad like one of the exo suits had kicked her from behind.

"Eep!" she yelled.

"Heh," said Gina, chuckling. "Tellin' you, these things wanna move."

Kerys leaned forward and let only the weight of her hand turn the grip. The quad lurched into motion, and within seconds, she bounced over waves in the black dunes. Her thighs grew sore from her legs' death grip on the machine, but she ignored the discomfort, too worried about being thrown or flipping.

Ahead of her, a little more than a half-mile of hill separated Wayfarer Outpost from the ridge. The two exoskeletons trudged side by side in a bounding walk, kicking up small puffs of ebon dust whenever their huge feet touched down. The rocky hillside gleamed with a dull grey sheen like an enormous nugget of raw silicon. Faint azure mist shrouded the peaks, twisting in a high-altitude wind.

Nervous from the incline, Kerys kept her fingers clamped tight for fear of taking a spill over the handlebars. Her quad gained on the Warthog with ease, blowing by it as if stationary. Hurtling down the hill, she zoomed past Ellen and Lars, who waved. Before she could look back at them, she hit a groove in the regolith and caught a few feet of air.

Shit... shit... shit... The quad came down hard, but she kept it upright, skidding sideways for a few seconds before regaining control.

"Easy there, Loring," said Don. "I know you're eager to get started, but there's no need to rush."

"She's from Cali. Thinks it's a jetski," said Marco, to chuckles.

"Uhh, this thing is a bit touchy." She let off the accelerator, allowing the machine to coast.

Gina pulled up alongside her, an obvious grin shining past the multicolored light saturating her face from the visor HUD. "Once you get used to the handling, it's easy. These things have gyroscopes, so it's *really* hard to roll them. Relax, don't drive like a jackass, and you'll be fine. I know it feels like you're going to tumble, but it won't. It'll throw you before it rolls."

"Right." Kerys looked back over her shoulder at the boxy Warthog plowing down the hill at the speed of a brisk walk. "Easier said…"

"Slow and easy," said Gina.

Marco laughed. "I've heard that before."

Don sighed over the comm.

Kerys stared up at the ridge, mesmerized by the metallic sheen of mountains rising higher and higher. As far as she could see to the right, the glimmering black 'sand' continued to the horizon. The hill blocked any view of the outpost behind her, causing a deepening feeling of being alone and isolated on a far-off world. She gave a wistful sigh and gingerly sped up, following the navigation line on the tiny screen between the handlebars. Soon, aluminum struts holding up banks of spotlights came into view up ahead, their beams apparent as cones of swirling mist illuminating a rectangular opening.

Interest distracted her from worry and took the place of confidence. She accelerated, shifting her weight back and forth in an automatic reflex to the moving terrain. When she didn't think about driving the quad, it seemed rather easy to control. Minutes later, she stopped by the entrance, gazing open-mouthed at construction that could only have been the product of a conscious mind. Kerys flicked the 'off' switch and dismounted, drawn to the stone as if by a magical lure.

Gina and Marco pulled up on either side of her quad.

"This is… amazing." Arm outstretched, Kerys walked over and touched the edge of the corridor. Perfectly smooth lines defined a doorway she estimated at twelve feet tall and five feet wide. The interior walls resembled dull mirrors, reflecting blurry swaths of color. "This is definitely not a natural formation."

Marco trotted over. "Whoa. This is serious. Never saw anything this obvious before. Mostly broken fragments and such. I suppose aliens exist after all. 'Course, what if we're like humanity that rose from the ashes after a way more advanced society blew itself up. Maybe humans made this ten thousand years ago."

"Were that the case," said Kerys, "we would've found some evidence suggesting humanity had regressed."

"What about the pyramids, or that Mayan calendar stuff? We *still* don't know how they did that. Think an older, collapsed human civilization is more likely than aliens coming to help?"

"I'm afraid I have to agree with Kerys here," said Don over the comm channel. "Had an older human civilization annihilated itself and set us back to the Stone Age, there would've been far more evident clues of its existence."

The Warthog pulled around in a turn, stopped, then backed up to the opening.

Don hopped out when it came to a stop and approached the tunnel. "All right. I know you're all eager to get inside, so let's take a look around before we lug everything in."

Kerys entered before he finished speaking, tracing her fingers across the wall to her left. The corridor grew dark after about ten paces. "Lights on."

LED bar lights on her shoulders activated, sending two rectangular beams into the murk ahead. White specks swirled in the glow, which illuminated a carved door a short distance away. Two stone slabs, the same semi-shiny grey as the mountains, hung open wide enough to admit a person. Damage at the center where the doors met made her cringe.

"I wish they waited for us before breaking down the doors." Kerys pushed at the slabs, opening them a little wider. Despite their size and likely weight, the massive stone doors glided without much effort.

"I've been studying images of those doors for hours," said Paula. "I'm sure the patterning is decorative. It doesn't seem like any form of language I can discern. I doubt they ruined anything significant in terms of understanding the purpose of this place."

"We're here," said Ellen. "Doc, you want us to start bringing your stuff in?"

Don turned to point his shoulder lights back at the opening. "Oh, I feel bad asking you to do all the work. My team can help."

"Nah, man." Lars laughed. "You guys are the smart ones. They pay us to pick stuff up and put it down."

"Or break rocks," said Ellen. "Don't worry about it. Just tell me where you want the stuff. It's not like it's heavy. The exo-suits do all the work."

Kerys stepped past the doors into a vast rectangular chamber. The walls had more of a natural cave look than the corridor, though the perfectly flat ceiling dispelled any notion this place had formed without the activity of living beings. Another passage near the midpoint of the room on the left appeared to lead to a secondary room. She approached the wall, brushing at it with her fingers. Silt fell away from her touch, and after a few seconds of pawing, she found hard, smooth stone a few inches deep.

"There's a substantial buildup of sediment around the walls," said Kerys.

Marco advanced to the right while Paula headed for the end opposite the entrance.

Don walked to the chamber's center. "Well, I suppose this would be a good place for our gear if you two are still willing to carry it in."

"Be right there," said Ellen.

Kerys kept brushing at the wall, knocking silt away. Before long, grooves and ferrules became apparent at about head level, suggesting a band of decorative engraving that went around the entire room. "Found something. More carvings."

"Something intelligent definitely made this place," said Paula.

"What do you think it is? A tomb?" Marco swatted his hands together to clear them of dust.

"That could be, though given the lack of any other detectable structures on the planet's surface, I'm more inclined to think it might have been some kind of outpost. Maybe these beings were explorers like us, not *from* here."

Heavy thudding emanated from the entrance passage.

Kerys glanced up as Ellen walked in carrying the giant case she'd helped Marco move to the shuttle. Lars entered behind her, lugging two smaller ones, each only about four feet long. They set the gear down with care and headed back outside.

"We should clear the walls before running the modeler," said Kerys.

"Indeed." Don opened one of the smaller cases. "Everyone grab a brush and let's get going."

Kerys retrieved a wide, soft brush, then returned to the spot she'd started. The others spread out to different parts of the room and set to the task of knocking the sediment away from the stone. She hummed to herself as she worked, grinning ear-to-ear. *This is real. This is actual evidence of non-human life. It's gotta be better than what we found on Copernicus.*

After bringing in the rest of the cases, Ellen and Lars occupied themselves by collecting the silt from the floor and taking it outside. All the while, they chatted with Don about his plans to excavate deeper into the mountainside based on sensor readings from the air. Blurs and distortions in the scans suggested at least nine total chambers existed here, with the innermost space easily six times the size of this one.

Gina and Private Foster helped with the silt clearing after Don assured them brushing the walls wouldn't damage anything.

For a while, Kerys managed to forget Will had ever existed. Chatter crisscrossed the comm as people discussed everything from Marco missing a real steak dinner to Ellen talking about her sister's four sons. Paula and Don discussed the pattern on the walls, both agreeing it syntactically meaningless, and intended for decoration.

"Hey, you think the aliens have corporations?" asked Lars.

Don laughed. "For their sake, I hope not."

"We don't know enough about them." Paula paused to study the wall. "We're not even sure what they look like."

"Or look*ed* like," said Marco. "They could be extinct."

"True." Kerys swept her brush down in broad strokes, knocking inches-deep caked-on silt to the ground. The pattern of ferrules continued, squared off lines forming spirals in an endless repetition. "I think I've seen something like this before. We found some engravings on Copernicus, and I also remember the same sort of thing in the archives back at Cal. We started calling them Atlanteans on Cope."

"What like the mythological continent?" asked Marco before chuckling. "You're saying aliens were on Earth now?"

She shrugged. "There's not enough evidence to support that, but some of the designs have striking similarities to what the Cornell group discovered."

"Oh, I heard about that." Paula twisted away from the wall to nod at her. "Some kind of ruins along the floor of the Mediterranean Sea."

Marco shook his head. "They didn't find any UFO parts down there."

"There are some thematic similarities in the patterns. I'm not saying aliens were at Atlantis, or that Atlantis even existed. It's just what my old team started calling the aliens because we wanted a quick name for them." Kerys stepped right, standing on tiptoe to extend her broom as high as possible.

"Hey, one thing that's been bugging me," said Marco. "What's Avasar bankrolling us for anyway? Not that I'm gonna turn down the paycheck, but why's a biopharma company interested in this stuff?"

"Tax breaks," said Ellen. "Donating to the sciences or some shit like that. Lets them get more money out of the military. Whatever it cost them to bring you guys out here, they get like six times that back. Lars here is the one who found the site."

"Aye." Lars nodded. "Captain Chen wanted us to check this ridge, see if we can get to the peaks to scout out a new location for some kind of long-range terrain scanner."

"*You're* the one who broke the door in?" asked Kerys.

Lars faced her, smiled, and shrugged his massive suit's arms. "I knocked."

"Avasar came to AV494 after a USIC deep space probe detected biological activity here. The life turned out to be plant matter, so the military contracted with Avasar Biotech. They've been here a couple years now studying the plants for possible medical or scientific applications." Gina tapped her brush against her boot to clear silt. "How did all this dust build up in a sealed chamber?"

"Perhaps it sat open for some time before being sealed," said Don. "Of course, that would imply some other sentient life discovered this place first and decided to close it off."

Paula pointed at the north wall. "We're only seeing the tip of the proverbial iceberg here. This site extends over a mile into the rock. There could've been an explosive event from deeper in that kicked up all this dust."

"They find anything good yet?" asked Marco.

"Well, they've managed to purify water." Gina laughed. "I heard them talking about it in the cafeteria last month. Without purification, the water here would kill us to drink, but the native plants use it. We can remove the toxic elements, but about a third of the plants they've found can't survive on 'human water.'"

"Interesting," said Don. "Makes me wonder if they'll be able to find any useful medical applications for them."

"That's over my pay grade." Gina shook her head.

Paula let off a startled gasp. "There's a door here!"

Everyone swarmed to her as she knocked silt from the wall around the center of the eastern wall, revealing a doorway in line with the passage to the outside. A featureless slab of silicon grey blocked it, set in a seam so perfect a sheet of paper wouldn't fit into it. The team spent a while examining the area, but could find no mechanism or means of opening the apparent door.

"That's gotta weigh thousands of pounds," said Marco. "Why would they use something so heavy for a door?"

Kerys traced her fingers down the glass-smooth surface. "Maybe it's a vault?"

"As exciting as this is," said Don, "we've got at least six months to study this site. There's no need to rush or do anything carelessly. Why don't we finish clearing the walls? Maybe there's something useful still hidden."

"Oh, like a security desk, something to uhh, 'buzz us in'?" Marco laughed.

The team got back to work, finishing off the remainder of the wall clearing in about twenty minutes. Their efforts exposed a band of carved pattern two feet tall around the entire room, but no sign of anything that might operate the door.

Don headed for the largest case, opening the lid to reveal a six-foot metal pole studded with boxy equipment. "This room's more or less clear. I'll get started on setting up the 3D scanner."

Everyone else migrated to the opening in the middle of the north wall, a short hallway leading to the secondary room, which also had a coating of silt, but not quite as thick. It had a square profile roughly half the size of the first room. A partial cave-in at the northwest corner looked like a mole the size of a compact car had gotten lost and crashed into the wall from the outside. Slabs of stone lay upon a mound of jet-black dirt that sparkled in the glare of shoulder-mounted spotlights. The video and still images made the collapse look worse than reality. Up close, it didn't seem anywhere near a threat to structural integrity.

While Marco examined the debris, Kerys headed straight to the north wall. Paula set to brushing nearest the hallway they'd entered from.

The last room had a door in line with the entrance. I wonder if the Atlanteans keep their patterns.

She got to brushing again, and within a few strokes, her efforts exposed a bit of flat metal embedded in the wall. "Ooh! Found something!" She attacked the area with fervor, soon unearthing a metal panel eight feet tall and three feet wide. Three rows of one-inch squares carved into the surface at her head level each contained a different symbol.

"That looks like writing." She peered back over her shoulder. "Paula? Come take a look at this."

The older woman hurried over, as did Marco.

"You're right, but… I don't think it's a phrase." Paula held up an e-pad and captured still photos of the object. "It almost looks like—"

"A keyboard," said Kerys. "I've seen symbols like this before on Copernicus." Images of pottery and slabs of stone laying half buried in craters came back to her. The surface of that planet reminded her a lot of Earth's moon, only with snowstorms. "That squiggle like a one-winged falcon was always at the top left."

"Hmm." Paula kept taking pictures. "Only one or two of these look familiar, but I've studied every known sample of alien language we've ever come across."

"Evidently not," muttered Marco. When she glared at him, he grinned. "Perhaps her Atlanteans are a different species?"

Paula sighed. "Must you call them Atlanteans? It makes them sound like mythology. Stories didn't"—she gestured emphatically at the wall —"build this."

"Sorry for mentioning it." Kerys slipped her e-pad from her belt and searched the file system for her old notes. "We needed a word. It was faster than constantly saying 'the aliens who may or may not have built this stuff.'"

"She's got a point." Marco chuckled. "Oh, the wall appears to be okay. The part that broke isn't load-bearing."

Paula glanced at the damage. "If it's not holding weight, what made it buckle?"

"Umm." Marco scratched at his helmet. "I'd have to dig inside to confirm, but it kinda looks like something exploded behind the wall. Could've been a pocket of trapped gas or a device."

"Defense mechanism?" asked Gina.

Marco flapped his arms. "Haven't had a chance to crawl in there and look yet."

Aha! Kerys tapped a folder containing pictures of the artifacts her team had uncovered on Copernicus. She held the e-pad with one hand, thumbing from image to image while absentmindedly brushing silt from the wall.

"What's that?" asked Paula, leaning closer.

"Stuff from the Copernicus site."

Again, Paula gasped. "How do you have that? I've been requesting to see those files for over a year, but Doctor Furroughs keeps refusing to share."

Kerys flashed a saccharin smile. "Well, I was *on* that team. I took these pics myself. And"—she wobbled her head side to side—"maybe I was obligated to delete them afterward, but they screwed me out of any credit or recognition. So… maybe it slipped my mind to clear the data."

"You know they could come after you for that," said Paula

"I doubt it. The only way I could have this is if I was there too, and they don't want to risk the fallout in case I make a big deal about being brushed aside. One of the major findings from that site was my work. This one mechanism, a machine that took up a room a little bigger than this one… I'm the one who figured out they used it to draw geothermal energy up from the ground for heat." She scowled. "When Doctor Furroughs couldn't disprove my theories, he decided to 'test think' about them being right, and then he realized it checked out, so they became *his* discovery. I mean, they couldn't have the kid only three years out of college figuring out something like that before the doctors."

Paula clapped her on the shoulder. "Sorry."

Blue laser light flickered in the corridor. Seconds later, Don, Ellen, and Lars hurried in, 'hurried' being a matter of relative for the large exo suits. The heavy tromping knocked dust off the ceiling and sent two large hunks of rock in the partial cave-in sliding to the floor.

"Careful!" shouted Paula.

Marco chuckled. "Hey, instead of all this brushing, maybe we could just have those two jump up and down."

"Nothing of the sort," said Don. "Too much risk of damage. I'll need to ask everyone to stay in here for at least fifteen minutes while the outer room is being scanned."

Kerys sat with her back to the wall, staring at the e-pad. *This has got to be some kind of keyboard.* Her fingers danced over the tiny eight-by-eight-inch screen, zooming and rotating pictures of the Copernicus ruins. The 'heat generator' room had similar markings, maybe one of the chambers in this place would hold a geothermal plant as well? The sixth image had what she searched for: a view of the side of a large, metal tank engraved with six symbols.

A one-winged hawk, a dot with a ring around it, a squiggle that resembled a cursive 'z,' a glyph composed of a square U with two vertical bars descending from the bottom, a mark with three lines spiraling clockwise together, and a complicated sigil that somewhat resembled a Japanese Kanji.

She found the same string of characters in another photo, etched into a slab of rock that had once been a wall. Minutes later, the string reappeared on the surface of a pottery vase. *I guess it isn't like a department name–'facilities' or some such.* She chuckled. *Why would they put that on vases? What if it's their god or something?* She blinked. *Maybe they do have corporations. Did I just learn 'ACME' in alien?*

"Hey check this out," said Marco. He pointed at a dark grey squiggle on the floor. "Looks like there could have been moisture in here at some point. This is dried mud that looks like the same silt that's on the walls."

"Interesting," said Don. "But what did that dribble from?"

Marco looked up. "Water vapor rises? Maybe it fell from the ceiling?"

Once the laser light show in the main chamber stopped, Don ambled off to check on the scanner. Paula followed, as did Lars, Ellen, and Private Foster. Gina hovered close by, leaning against the wall with one boot up.

When Kerys glanced up at her, she smiled. It didn't seem necessary to have armed soldiers around on a planet deserted for millennia. The chances of some other company sending a crew to steal their work, or some indigenous threat presenting itself seemed equally remote. Still, the woman exuded friendliness. Her earlier comment about running away from a bad home at sixteen to join the USIC made Kerys wonder if the girl suffered from simple loneliness.

"What'cha doin?" asked Gina the next time Kerys looked over at her.

"Those marks on the wall. I've seen something like them before. I'm trying to make sense of them. I keep finding the same series of characters." Kerys twisted to peer up at the slab, and though they did not form the sequence, all six of those symbols existed in the array.

Marco approached the metal panel and folded his arms. "Don's probably going to want to deep-scan that big door and find a way to open it. Looks like the main entrance. You know, now that I think about it, that space out there reminds me of a lobby."

"I think this is the way to open it." Kerys stood, gesturing at the fifteen buttons arranged in three rows of five. "It's like an access code panel. But... how long has it been dead? Might not work at all."

She traced her finger around the small square holding the one-winged hawk symbol at the center of the bottom row. "This is the first letter."

"Looks like a bowling pin with a splinter stickin' out of it," said Gina.

Kerys grinned. "I think it looks like a hawk."

"Yeah, I suppose if you've taken enough LSD." Marco chuckled.

She smirked. "Hmm." On a whim, she pressed the small square like a button.

The symbol glowed soft blue.

"Whoa," whispered Marco, taking a step back.

Gina pushed off the wall and got a ready grip on her rifle. "What did you do?"

Kerys shivered with delight. "It still works." The top-right button had a dot with a ring around it. She pushed it, and it lit up. All the way left in the middle row had the 'cursive z.' She pushed that one, and it glowed.

"Wait, stop." Marco grabbed her forearm. "We don't know what this is going to do."

"I've seen this... word written all over the place on the Atlantean artifacts we found on Copernicus. It's got to be either their name—like 'human' is to us—or maybe a deity they worship, or a company. They plaster it over everything like a label."

He let go but looked worried. "What if it's a self-destruct?"

"Uhh," said Gina, "if it is, it would be kinda stupid to put the password to nuke-it-all on everything, right?"

Kerys pushed the second button from the left on the top row, the mark that resembled a chalice. It too, glowed blue. "Yeah. If this was supposed to be secret, they wouldn't write it everywhere." She tapped the spiral mark button, second from the right in the middle row. It lit up as soon as she touched it.

"At least it's pretty." Marco yanked his e-pad off his belt and held it up. "I should probably be recording this."

"Good idea." She faced him. "This is Kerys Loring with the Avasar Biotech expedition on AV494. We've discovered alien ruins near the Wayfarer Outpost. While exploring them, we encountered what appears to be a control pad on the wall with a... form of keyboard. These glyphs are identical to others I observed on a previous site. I believe the same non-human species responsible for that site created this one. A pattern of these symbols recurred frequently on their artifacts, so I am attempting to enter that same sequence here to see if it might open the door. I'm joined by Marco Trem, and Corporal Gina Mitchell of the USIC."

"Why are you saying our names?" asked Gina.

Marco peered around the side of the e-pad. "In case we all die when she hits that last button."

"Umm." Gina stared at her.

Kerys shook her head. "This isn't going to kill anyone." She pressed her finger into the last button, the not-quite-Kanji. Rather than the button lighting up, the rest of them went dark.

"Huh, well… that was anticlimactic," said Marco.

She scowled at her e-pad. "Damn. I thought that would do som—"

The seam around the entire panel glowed blue. Kerys took a step back. The wall emitted a loud *click* and the tall metal plate opened inward, revealing a narrow corridor. Wisps of dust and silt whorled in the air flooded with azure light from deep inside.

"It's not a panel… it's a door." Kerys switched her e-pad to record video, and crept in, holding the device high.

"Wait." Gina put a hand on her shoulder. "Let me go first in case there's something in there."

"Yo, Doc," said Marco. "Kerys found a door. Got it open."

"What? Where?" yelled Don, alarm in his voice.

As Marco explained the buttons, Kerys advanced down a narrow tunnel despite Gina's tugging hand. The walls appeared to consist of individual silvery-grey bricks each about a foot tall by two feet long. Kerys pivoted the e-pad to the side.

"New section of the AV494 site shows evidence of intelligent construction, unlike the outer chambers, which appear to be carved from solid rock. This could be a false wall to conceal hidden spaces or mechanisms. Either that, or the mountain isn't solid."

"Maybe the mountains are artificial?" asked Marco. "Camouflage?"

Gina scooted in close behind her, as if trying to see over her shoulder.

Kerys walked deeper into the passage, taking slow, cautious steps until she emerged in another square chamber. Though much smaller than the outer room, this one had a vaulted pyramid ceiling three stories tall. At the center of the space, a shiny, dark object larger than their e-suit helmets hovered a few inches above a stone pedestal with no apparent means of support. It had an organic quality to its design, composed of tubes, vesicles, and membrane-like shrouds over connective tissue. The bizarre internal organ didn't look like anything found in human anatomy. It gleamed white wherever her shoulder-mounted lights hit it, suggesting it had either been petrified or been carved from stone decoratively. If anyone asked Kerys to guess what they looked at, she'd have said a heart. Thin portions of membrane and some of the tubes had a dark maroon hue, but the majority of its structure—including the sac-like parts—were black.

She raised her e-pad, tapped the screen to start a cataloging app, and held steady as thin green lines appeared around the artifact. It calculated its height at eighteen inches, fourteen inches wide, fourteen inches deep at the widest portions. Mass, density, and material composition came back as unknown.

Rapid footsteps scuffed to a halt near the door she'd opened.

"Kerys? Marco? Where are you?" Don's urgent voice came over comms, framed in a mild static crackle.

"Inside," whispered Kerys. She walked around the pedestal, recording video to capture the strange object from every angle.

Don squeezed into the chamber, Paula right behind him. Marco and Gina moved aside to let them pass, then gathered around the floating thing as well.

"This room seems like a shrine." Don stared upward.

"Or a missile silo." Gina peered up. "Why make something this tall if it's gonna be empty?"

"Could have religious connotations." Paula leaned close to the artifact. "How is it floating?"

"Magnets?" asked Kerys.

"Could it be biological?" Marco tilted his head. "Those membranes and tubes look like circulatory passages. Whoa. If this is a heart, those Atlanteans would have to be huge."

Paula grumbled. "Please stop calling them that."

Kerys stuck her hand in the space between the object and the pedestal.

"Gah!" Yelped Don. "Be careful! Don't touch anything until we know what we're dealing with."

"She technically didn't touch anything." Gina quirked an eyebrow.

"Well, it's definitely floating. I don't think it's a heart. If it was, whatever creature it came from wouldn't have been able to fit in here."

"That thing's pretty badass looking." Gina relaxed her rifle.

"Not reading any magnetic fields," muttered Marco.

Kerys stopped on the far side of the pedestal. She peered over the object at Don, Paula, and the hallway leading out of the hidden room. She opened her mouth to speak, but the air caught in her throat when she noticed two pairs of divots on the side facing her, each holding a rounded black oval. "It's... wow. Those look like eyes. I think this is a head."

"What?" Don rushed around to stand beside her. "I... can't even tell where the mouth would be, but those do look like eyes."

"Pareidolia," said Paula. "The human mind is programmed to recognize faces. You could be reading human features into something that isn't even close. These aliens could have had ten limbs, or none at all. Maybe they were serpents or floating gas-filled balloons. We don't even know if they *had* eyes. They might sense electromagnetism or heat. For all we know, this could be imaginary to them, the same way humans made statues of Medusa."

"Possible." Don leaned closer, putting his helmet nose to... something with the floating object. "Those depressions, the symmetry there, do seem like eyes. Given the *feeling* of this room, this could be a statue of an individual they revered."

"Maybe it's like a cult of personality thing? Their boss?" asked Marco.

"Or a tomb," said Kerys. "This could be a memorial for whoever's buried here."

"We'll need to get the DPMRI units in here and see what's inside the walls." Don raised his arm as if to look at a watch, but dropped it with a chuckle. "Darn suits. Oh, there it is. It's almost time for lunch."

Kerys reached out and touched a finger to the front of the 'head.' She tapped it twice. "Feels like stone."

The faint light between the head and the base flickered and went out. The head dropped a few inches, striking the pedestal with a heavy *thud*. Before anyone could do more than shout in surprise, it careened over to the side and crashed to the floor, landing on Marco's left foot.

He hit the ground, howling a stream of obscenities over the comm.

"Shit!" yelled Kerys. She dropped to one knee and grabbed the top of the alien object in both hands, straining to pull it off Marco's leg.

Gina swung her rifle on a strap over her shoulder and squatted next to her, also grabbing the 'head' to help. Between the two of them, they shifted it enough for Don and Paula to grasp the screaming Marco by the arms and drag him clear.

"Damn that hurts." Marco hissed and gasped for a few seconds. "I felt a crack. Think my shin broke."

Kerys cringed with guilt. "I'm sorry... I had no idea it would do that."

"Don't worry about it." Marco grunted as Gina and Don helped him upright to balance on his right leg. "Worst part is I'll be stuck inside for a couple days now."

"Heh. Give Doc something to do besides play video games." Gina pulled Marco's arm across her shoulder to support him. "I got ya."

Kerys stared at the artifact as Gina helped Marco off down the tunnel.

Don squatted over the head, testing the weight by tugging at it.

"Doctor Bouchard?" asked Captain Chen over the comm. "I'm being told your team made a discovery in there? And had an injury?"

"Yes. We found some kind of statue, I think. It was levitating via unknown means above a pedestal. Something caused the energy field to deactivate, and the relic fell on Mr. Trem's foot. I believe the man has a broken leg. He's on his way back."

"What sort of object did you locate?"

"I cannot say for sure. It seems to be a stone representation of either a heart, a head, or some as-yet-unknown internal organ or perhaps fictional creature. It behaves like stone but is not composed of any material humanity has previously encountered." Don looked up at Paula and Kerys, his expression pained.

"Bring it back with you for study. There is a quarantine access area attached to Lab Pod 1. All unknown items must undergo a thorough scan before being allowed in. Miss Vickers and Mr. Deering already know the drill."

"Marco just got hurt and she's worried about the head?" whispered Kerys.

Paula shrugged. "He's already injured and leaving this here won't help or hurt him. We're going to have to catalog it, anyway."

She stared down at the object. An unsettling sense of malice radiated from it, as though it glared at her for daring to disturb it. "Uhh." *If I say this thing feels awake, they're going to think I've cracked. Hell, I'm going to say I'm cracked. Stone heads don't have vibes.* "Is that wise?"

"That's why they have the quarantine." Don groaned as he stood from his squat. "I'll send Foster in here to help carry it. Bit too much for these old bones, and those exo suits won't fit down this hallway."

She tried to peel her gaze away from the alien head, but couldn't... inexplicably fearful of what it might do if she broke eye contact. "Right..." She swallowed the saliva gathering under her tongue. *I'm being superstitious.* A few quick breaths let her enthusiasm return. Nowhere before had humanity ever found the slightest clue what these 'Atlanteans,' or whatever they called themselves, looked like. She'd found what could be the first record of their appearance, at least from the neck up. That alone made the trip worth it.

Kerys patted the strange head. "Let's get it back then."

5

MESS

W ayfarer's quarantine module consisted of a tiny pod adjacent to the east-facing wall of Lab 1, connected by a short section of semi-flexible corridor. The specimen hatch made it look like an enormous toy oven. Inside, an array of sensors, filters, and scanning equipment would detect substances potentially dangerous to humans. Before Captain Chen would allow anything found outside into the atmosphere of the outpost, it had to pass a gauntlet of tests and yea/nay votes from the senior science staff.

Kerys sat on her quad about a hundred meters north of it, watching Ellen trudge back up the hill from the excavation site carrying the head, Lars at her side. Marco had ridden back in the Warthog, with Paula learning how to drive a quad for the return trip. Her first attempt had shot the four-wheeler out from under her, dumping her on her back. She didn't feel quite so foolish at her uncoordinated scramble down the hill earlier that day; at least she'd stayed on the vehicle. Everyone else had already gone inside via the garage.

The view to the south offered nothing but endless black sand, glinting here and there like thousands of miles of tiny black diamonds. No sign of plant life or any other mountains broke the monotony of the endless dunes. It seemed silly to think, but she pictured Earth as being somewhere far away on the other side of the desert. The isolation would've been almost welcome if not for Will being here.

Damn him. Why did he have to be such an ass? Why did he have to be here, of all places?

Ellen reached the quarantine pod and opened the specimen port. She set the head inside, shut the flap, and started the long walk to the garage.

I'm being an idiot standing here watching. What's she going to do? Steal the thing and run back to Earth to get all the credit? Chuckling to herself, she twisted the handlebars around and drove the quad the last two or three hundred meters to the garage opening. Getting used to the handling came easier than she'd expected. She guided the four-wheeler into the open space among the other quads with relative ease. After connecting the charging cable, she headed to the airlock... and waited.

Ten minutes later, Ellen and Lars tromped in the garage door.

"Thanks for waiting," said Ellen.

"No problem." Kerys smiled. "I figured working the console would be a pain in those exos."

Lars held up his hand, making the metal fingers open and close. "Not so much designed for precision."

Kerys edged left, leaning against the wall by the airlock control as the two people in bulky exo suits stepped past her. She hit the button to seal the outside door. A few seconds after it closed, the center button marked 'repressurize airlock' changed from red to green. Touching it filled the chamber with hissing, and soon the red 'no atmosphere' warning dot vanished from her HUD. Another tap at the touchscreen opened the inner doors.

Gina, already out of her e-suit, appeared to be hanging out in the changing area. Upon seeing Kerys, she stood from the locker bench and walked over. "Hey. Getting out of those suits alone is a pain in the ass unless you're a gymnast."

"Heh. Closest I got to gymnastics was some jiu-jitsu classes when I was in college." Kerys shuffled over to her locker and hit the helmet release. The seal broke with a *hiss* and a puff of pressurized air. Not until she'd taken a few breaths of inside atmosphere did it occur to her how much like rubber the suit's re-filtered air tasted.

"Creep issues?" Gina opened the clasps on Kerys's back, freeing her from the e-suit.

Hah. Just a little. "Yeah, major creep issues, but he's not why. I spent so much time studying or sleeping. Needed some activity, and I didn't have the time to get involved with any organized sports. I did yoga too, but kept falling asleep in the middle of the classes."

"Oh." Gina looked down.

Kerys stowed the helmet in the locker before letting the suit drop around her legs. "Sorry. I forgot."

"Naw, it's all good." Gina raised her head, flashing a weak smile. "I shouldn't assume you had an easy ride. You probably busted your ass to afford that fancy college."

"Nah. My mom paid for it." Kerys stepped out of the e-suit boots and hit the button to close them. "I think I'd rather have had to work my ass off. Didn't get along with her at all. I didn't really have a mother; I had a boss."

"Harsh." Gina winced. "'Least you had one. Sure she loved you in some way or 'nother."

Kerys stuffed the suit into the locker, closed the door a little harder than she intended, and shrugged. "If she did, she didn't show it much."

"Sorry." Gina bit her lip. "So... hungry?"

She exhaled. "Hey, it's not your fault. Suppose I might as well eat something."

They walked down the single 'hamster tube' connecting the garage pod to the central dome, accompanied by the repetitive *thunk* of boots and the clatter of tiny stones pelting the outside. Small portal windows passing on her right offered a view of the empty landing pad to the north where the shuttle had set down a few days before. Black dust skittered over the giant steel hexagon, lofted into spinning whorls before disappearing once more into the ground.

It's only been a few days... feels like I've been here for years.

She looked away and walked faster, as if her getting to the cafeteria four seconds sooner would somehow hasten the quarantine process. "We should check on Marco first."

"They're not going to keep him in the infirmary too long. He'll probably be out before we finish eating." Gina reached forward and hit the button to open the door where the tube connected to the dome. "Cutting edge medical tech and all that."

"Right." Kerys let out a slow breath.

"Hey don't blame yourself. You couldn't have known just touching it would make it drop."

Kerys followed an orange stripe on the wall marked 'cafeteria'. "I shouldn't have touched anything until we'd scanned it first. I pulled an amateur move 'cause I got too excited."

"Don't dwell on it. Holdin' on to guilt for somethin' like that'll drive you nuts."

"I suppose."

A din of voices flooded the cafeteria, spilling out into the atrium. Kerys followed Gina through the door, pausing to gaze in dismay at the large crowd packing the place, filling in rows of shiny silver tables. Don's wispy white hair caught her eye. A few seats appeared to be open near him, so she headed for the row of automats. The first bore the label 'General Tso.'

Oh, hell no. I don't even want to think about their version of Chinese food. She opted for the grilled chicken, and waited the forty seconds for the machine to warm and dispense it.

Once Gina got her food, they headed back toward Don, but Corporal Guillen had taken one of the only two adjacent spots. Kerys climbed over the bench and settled in between him and a thirty-something man in a green jumpsuit with light brown hair so neat it looked like he wasted an hour every morning in front of the mirror. He chatted with Don about the excavation site, a British accent evident in his voice.

Gina paused behind her, emitting a resigned sigh before slipping in on Corporal Guillen's right.

The grilled chicken didn't taste bad, but Kerys couldn't find much interest in it. Between wanting to go back out to the site, excitement about the discovery, and guilt over Marco's injury, her brain didn't have the extra space to accommodate the conversations flying around her. She pushed rice around with her fork while staring at the slab of chicken flecked in tiny green bits over 'grill marks' that looked too perfect to be real. Again and again in her mind, she thought about the head falling, and wondered if she could've stopped it or shoved Marco away rather than standing there like an idiot.

"Buck up, lass," said the man to her left. "Though, I completely understand. The food here's seven shades of awful."

"Says the Brit." Corporal Guillen raised a steel cup in toast and took a gulp of water.

"Kerys, this is Chris Mardling... he's with the botanical group."

Still staring at her food, she nodded. "Yeah, I got that from the green suit."

"Chemist actually." Chris offered a hand. "Pleasure to meet you. You're the one from Copernicus, right?"

"Yeah." She accepted his handshake but scrunched her eyebrows at him. "How do you know that?"

"Oh, Braxton's been running his mouth for months about them finding someone who'd worked on that project. As if you being here was his idea."

Kerys dropped her fork as her stomach did a backflip. *Son of a bitch. Is he why they contacted me?*

"Aye, the chicken's a right bit of awful, innit?"

Corporal Guillen chuckled. "You're from the UK, Chris. You're not permitted to complain about shitty food."

"Oh, is that so?" He put on a playful scowl. "Our food is just fine, thank you very much."

"I've been there," said Guillen. "You've got a strange definition of 'fine.'"

Kerys shrank in on herself as the men got into a playful argument back and forth in front of her about the intricacies of British cuisine.

"I don't know what manner of buffalo turns food orange, but it's an abject disaster," said Chris.

"What's up with that 'blood pudding' anyway? *That's* an abomination." Corporal Guillen impaled a golf ball sized orange nugget on his fork and ate it. "And this isn't buffalo chicken, it's Chinese."

Maybe I should've gotten the General Tso's... that actually doesn't smell too bad.

"Now wait just a minute…" Chris pointed at him.

"Your problem is that if food has flavor, you can't handle it. Everything over there is boiled to mush."

Chris laughed. "You're thinking of Irish food, mate." He peered at Kerys. "So, yeah, we're glad to have you."

Will seemed annoyed when he saw me. He couldn't be involved. "Braxton didn't know it was me on the way?"

"Don't think so." Chris chased a scattering of rice grains around his mostly empty tray. "Just knew Avasar hired someone with experience from that project. None of us thought they'd put that kind of budget to it."

She let off a sarcastic chuckle. "They didn't need to."

"Oh. That's too bad." Chris pursed his lips. "Wonder if that's what's got him out of sorts."

Kerys glanced at him. "What do you mean?"

"Right after your team landed, he came storming into the lab looking like Chen just told him he had to go home. Somewhere between shocked and angry."

She prodded at the chicken slab. "How many things did he break?"

"Just a cabinet door." Chris chuckled. "I guess you know him?"

"Unfortunately."

A grating whirr came from the vents for a few seconds, chugged to a stop, then sputtered up to a soft buzzing.

"Hey, Scotty, what's going on down there in engineering?" yelled a man.

"Oi, bastard," shouted a muscular red-haired man with a heavy accent. The big guy in the grey jumpsuit leaned up out of his chair to whip a steel cup at another man a few seats down. "You lot think 'et funny eh? Git stuffed."

Kerys covered her mouth to stifle a laugh.

Corporal Guillen leaned close to her and whispered, "That's MacLeod. He's the head of the maintenance team. Has a bit of a tendency to throw small metal objects at anyone who makes a 'Scotty' remark."

Grinding came from the vents for a few seconds before a muted *clunk*, then the abnormal sounds faded once more to the silent processing of air.

MacLeod stared up at the vent in the ceiling and cocked his jaw to the side.

"I'm going to go check on Marco." Kerys shifted her weight in preparation to stand, but Don put a hand on hers before she could get her rear end off the bench.

"At least finish the chicken. You need to keep up your strength out there, hostile environment and all that. Can't have you collapsing on us."

Paula gave her 'the look.' "And finish your veggies too, dear."

Kerys sighed. "Fine..."

After forcing down the entirety of the chicken, the green beans, and about two thirds of the rice, she got up and carried the tray to the nearest trash container. With one hand on her stomach to brace the uncomfortable sense of fullness inside her, she headed out of the cafeteria and hooked left to follow the hallway to the stairs.

About halfway down the corridor, Will came out of a doorway at a brisk stride, his attention glued to an e-pad with a glare making his displeasure at whatever he read obvious. He flicked his gaze to her for a second in reaction to a person in his way. She moved to let him pass, but upon recognizing her, he stopped and sighed.

"What are *you* doing here?"

Kerys folded her arms. "I could ask you the same thing."

"I work here."

She smirked. "So do I."

Will looked away to the left, scratching behind his right ear. "This is a bad idea. You're not going to handle it well out here... too far away from Earth. I'm pretty close to Captain Chen. We'll arrange for you to head back. Should be able to get you on one of the automated supply drops in a month."

"What?" She let her arms fall loose and glared at him. "Are you for real? Three years it took me to get out here and you think I'm too fragile for it? Ugh!" Kerys fumed. "You haven't changed at all, have you? Still think I'm helpless. You never let me make any decisions before, and— news flash, hotshot—we're not together anymore. Your opinions don't control me."

Her heart raced. She got light-headed, but forced herself not to show it. *Shit. I never snapped at him like this before.*

Will stared at her, no discernible emotion on his face. Her gaze locked on his hand, half expecting him to punch the wall. Maybe even her. *No, he couldn't be that reckless, could he?* Her throat tightened and a nigh imperceptible tremble started in her hands.

He broke eye contact again, sighing as he studied the floor. "Look, Kerys... All I'm saying is that I know how you and Jaden are. It's not fair to him for you to be so far out here. He needs emotional support. How could you leave him with your robot mother?"

The bundle of spiked nerves in her gut detonated to rage. "Leave him out of this! I'm already here, in case you hadn't noticed. It'd take another three years for me to go home. Even if I left right now, he'd be sixteen before I got back. I've already—" She covered her mouth with a hand, wiping at her cheek and nose. When she continued, her voice hovered a hair's breadth from a whisper. "I've already missed most of his childhood. Hell, I barely saw him at all for the first ten years."

"He's not yours, is he?" Will cocked an eyebrow. "You're what, eighteen when he was born? Is he really your brother, or did your mom agree to take him in?"

"Stop, Will. Just, stop. No. He's not mine. You're doing it again, jabbing your finger at my emotions to distract me. Why don't you want me here? Do you expect me to believe you're genuinely worried about little helpless me out in the cruel alien world? What, a girl can't handle science?"

He raised both hands. "That's got nothing to do with it, hon. As usual, you're jumping to conclusions and getting emotional over nothing."

Mouth open, she stared at him, too angry to shout. *You arrogant son of a bitch.*

"I just think this assignment is too dangerous for you. When you left, I... guess I stopped caring about everything. Took this job because it didn't matter if something happened to me anymore."

She looked away from the vulnerability in his eyes, not trusting it. *He's trying to make me feel bad for leaving him. Like it was my fault he is such a prick.* "I can handle this. It isn't my first outpost job. Copernicus only had glorified tents. This place is like a fortress compared."

He bit his lip. A second later, his expression of worry slithered into pride. "Nice work getting that door open."

"It's not going to work."

"You know, I just had an idea. I haven't felt the same since you left. Maybe you had a point."

"Oh, maybe." She frowned.

Will grinned.

His unibrow hasn't gotten any smaller. Dammit, how can he make it look sexy? She averted her gaze. *No. It's a trick. He's going to just do the same crap all over again once I get comfortable.*

"I think fate has a sense of humor. Maybe we were destined to—"

"No. We're destined to work in the same remote outpost for a while in close proximity. I know you, Will. Even if you managed to act human for the first couple of months, it's not going to last." She started past him for the stairway.

He grabbed her arm, pulling her close, head tilted. "You haven't let me finish yet. Walking off in the middle of a conversation is rude."

Kerys tried to back away from him, but he didn't let go. *We're not in the middle of a conversation—it's over.* The words stalled halfway from brain to mouth. She looked at his fingers pressing into her bicep. Everything and everyone she knew waited thousands of light years away. Her friends, her little brother, her entire support system. Any communication would take two months, one for her message to reach them, and another for the reply.

Alone.

Nothing wanted to work anymore. Her brain stopped processing. Her body stopped moving.

He's not letting go. Is he going to hit me? "I…" Old patterns of just doing whatever Will wanted so he didn't flip out reawakened. She stared down at the floor.

"Is there a problem here?" asked Corporal Guillen.

Kerys gulped and snapped her head up. Heat swam over her cheeks as though he'd walked in on her showering. She wasn't that person anymore, that weak-willed, shrinking college girl.

Will flashed his easy, charming—and entirely superficial—smile at him. "We were just catching up on old times."

"Yeah." She jerked her arm out of Will's grip. "He was just reminding me why I left him."

"Oh." Will glanced between them before giving her a wounded look. "That didn't take long."

Corporal Guillen hardened his glare.

"Asshole," muttered Kerys. "I'm not 'cheating' on you. For one thing, we broke up. It's not cheating when there's nothing to cheat on. Two, I'm not *with* him. I'm not *with* anyone. I'm here to study an ancient alien civilization, nothing more."

Will's teeth showed, perfect and sparkling, as his lips stretched into a broad smile. "Good to know."

Corporal Guillen turned in place, watching him walk off. "You okay?"

Despite her growing fear that Will wouldn't give up, she kept an outward calm. "Thanks. I should be okay."

"I understand if there's some history between you, but if at any time you don't feel safe, please tell someone. That's what we're here for."

Kerys nodded. "I will."

As soon as Corporal Guillen continued down the hall, she grasped her arm where Will's hand had been, cradling a tender spot she hoped wouldn't turn into a bruise.

6

THE FOREST FOR THE TREES

K erys reached the infirmary hall right as Marco ambled out of the treatment room, his foot and lower leg in a cast made of spider-web-pattern polymer. He wobbled on a metal cane, struggling to adapt to using it. At the sight of her, he stopped trying to walk, and smiled.

"Hey. It's not as bad as I thought. I should be cleared for EVO in about five days."

She blinked. "That's it? Five days?"

"Yeah, Avasar's got the latest meds. Some of it isn't even available outside the outpost yet. Doc said they've synthesized artificial stem cells from one type of fungus they found here, and it'll only take them a couple days to 'glue my bones back together.' Still can't put too much weight on it right now."

"I'm sorry." She bit her lip. "It was reckless of me to touch that thing and—"

"Forgiven. Hey, that's some exciting stuff, huh?" Marco winked. "Don't leave my name off the accolades and I'll take a busted foot. Deal?"

Kerys let out an angry laugh. "Yeah. No way would I ever do that to anyone. Need a hand getting somewhere?"

"I got it... but if you wanna take the walk in case I wind up on my ass." He hobbled forward. "So you think that's really a head?"

She crept along at his side. "Those indentations do resemble eyes, but Paula could have a point about how we see faces on things. I think it is, but I'm going to play it safe and refuse comment for now."

He tried to laugh, but wound up wincing. "Ouch."

At the stairs, he hesitated, unsure which foot to start with. Eventually, he tried leading with his cast-encased foot and nearly spilled forward. Kerys managed to grab on and keep him from tumbling headfirst. Marco fell straight down into a sitting position while the cane bounced down the first set of stairs to the landing.

A growl of suppressed pain leaked past his teeth.

Kerys clung to him to keep him from sliding after the cane. After a minute or two of gasping and wincing, he reached up, took hold of the railing, and pulled himself upright. "Uhh, maybe stairs are a bit much for my fledgling cane-wielding skills."

"Yeah. Put your arm around my shoulders and lean on me."

He did. Kerys helped him down to the landing, where Marco picked up his cane before they continued to the ground floor. After they stepped off the stairs, she held on a few seconds more until he got his balance. "Ugh. This is my fault. I'm so sorry."

"Bah." He tottered toward the cafeteria. "Doc said it would stop hurting in two days. All you did was give me some time to get paid for lying around doing nothing while we all become famous. I should be thanking you."

"You can still help out going over images and—"

Will hurried down the corridor in her direction. Instinctively, she felt the need to press herself into the wall to get away, but wound up standing like a statue.

"What?" asked Marco. He glanced from her deer-in-the-headlights eyes to Will. "What's up?"

Chris Mardling sprinted out of the cafeteria and intercepted Will about ten steps away. "Hey, Brax..."

Will closed his eyes the way he always did when he tried to swallow anger. By the time Chris caught up, he smiled. "Hey, Mard. What's up?"

"You've been summoned. Crew's assembling in the garage. We're supposed to head out in twelve minutes for a survey of cluster forty-two, or did you forget all about our sample gathering?"

"Right." Will shot a pleading look at Kerys. "I'll be there in a minute."

Chris shook his head. "Don't have a minute, pal. The shuttle's packed and we need your hands unloading it."

Shuttle? She blinked.

"I'll be *right* there." Will brushed past him and stepped over to Marco and Kerys.

"I'm not leaving, Will. I don't know how you got a shuttle here so fast, but you're not ruining my life twice."

He looked disappointed and worried, almost to the point of being believable. "No, this shuttle's been here. We use it for flying heavy equipment around. Wouldn't be able to use it to go home unless there's a starship waiting in orbit."

"Yeah." Marco laughed. "Without a translight drive, you'd be flying for thousands of years."

Will leaned closer, eyes widening. "Look, Kerys—"

"Come on, man!" yelled Chris. "Being the manager doesn't mean you get out of carrying boxes."

He sighed, staring at the ceiling. "We'll talk later."

She scowled at his back as he hurried to join Chris, and the two disappeared down the hallway leading to the garage pod.

No, we won't.

"What's up with that guy?" Marco raised an eyebrow.

"I broke up with him a couple years ago, but he hasn't gotten the memo."

"Oh. One of *those* jackasses." Marco switched his grip on the cane, holding it like a sword while grinning. "Say the word and I'll give him an attitude adjustment."

Kerys laughed. "It's all right. He's just a pushy, arrogant idiot." *He looked hurt. I'm not the one being unreasonable, am I?* Her smile faded. Could it have been her fault from day one? Had she been giving off signals that she wanted him to take control, to make all the decisions, to be the protector? What if he'd only done what he thought she wanted? She closed her eyes, her mind running back over hundreds of times he'd made her feel uncomfortable or frightened.

"Kerys?"

"I'm fine. I'm fine." She nodded, more to herself than him. *No. This is exactly what he wants to do. Make me feel like the bad guy. It's manipulation, nothing more.* "Just wound up about that relic."

Marco leaned on his cane. "If you mean fine in the sense of 'that woman is fine,' then I'll agree with you, but you don't look 'fine' like I think you meant it."

She chuckled, head bowed. "I'm a mess. A controlled mess, though. I met him in school. We dated a couple years, moved in together. Thought we'd wind up married, but he's really an asshat. Total control freak... and a manchild. Can't handle not getting what he wants. He never cared what I wanted. Everything had to be his way or not at all. I tried to tell myself he'd grow out of it or he'd change after the wedding, but I don't think I ever really believed it. I don't know what he's really capable of, but it's scary."

"Mmm. Well, I don't think your boy there's done." Marco held up the cane again. "The attitude adjuster is available if you need it."

"I hope it won't get to that point." She rested a hand on his arm. "No need for you to get dragged into his mess. All I need to do is stay focused on the job and pretend Will isn't even here."

She walked with Marco to the cafeteria and helped him get a tray of food. The smell of it made her gut clench on the way to a table. He sat, and she set the food tray down in front of him.

"You don't look so good." He lifted a forkful of whitish-brown matter to his mouth.

"Is that supposed to be fish?"

He shrugged while chewing. "Dunno, don't care. It tastes different from the blob on my tray last night, so that's a plus."

She put a hand over her mouth and nose.

"I can get myself back to my room. Last thing I need is you hurling all over me. A two-hundred-pound stone alien skull is plenty."

"Sorry." Kerys hung her head.

"Teasing. Relax. I already told Don it's no big deal. He doesn't think you were careless." Marco gave her hand a squeeze. "Go on, get some air or something."

"Damn. I never even thought about that. They must think I'm such a rookie."

His eyebrows rose in disbelief. "This from the woman who figured out a millennia old password and got a door open before their 'alien language expert.'"

"Hah. I have no idea what it means. I just saw that word… or maybe sentence before. I don't know if those are letters or whole words in pictograph."

"Right place, right time." He winked and ate another forkful of fish.

Kerys backed off. "That smell is getting to me."

He flicked his hand at the exit and smiled. "G'won. Get some air."

———

THE COMBINATION OF MARCO'S INJURY AND THE DISCOVERY OF THE HEAD caused either Don or Captain Chen to decide to keep the archaeology team inside for the rest of the day. Frustrated at not being able to get back to the ruins, Kerys spent an hour or so wandering the dome. The ground level had three airlocks, one at the north, one at the southeast between the garage and labs, and one at the southwest between the hydroponics pod and the supplemental power unit (aka reactor). The cafeteria, machine shop, air processing, battery room, and storage space took up most of that floor along with separate quarters for the military personnel, as opposed to their being in the residence pods to the northwest of the dome.

Kerys roamed around office cubicles on the second floor, where most of the botanical team worked when not out in the woods. Aside from the infirmary, the third level housed the fitness center, a lounge, and that virtual reality room where holographic projectors could create the illusion of being on Earth.

She spent a while on the third floor watching the command center, complete with a clear glass panel bearing a blue-line map of the area. On the fourth floor, she wandered past many closed doors, a couple offices, and some unused lab space. Since the outpost had dedicated external labs, no one used the small one built into the dome. Kerys didn't bother going up to the fifth and final level, as the sign by the stairwell indicated it held only 'Captain Chen's Quarters' and an 'Observatory.'

Three corridors led away from the west side of the dome: one at the northwest corner went back to the residence pods, one at the middle led to the hydroponic facility, and the southwestern link connected to a tube that ran all the way out to the pod housing the fusion reactor from which Wayfarer Outpost got most of its power.

Assuming the reactor to be off-limits, and not having any great desire to get closer to anything involving nuclear radiation, she let curiosity pull her to the hydroponics pod. A short tube linked it directly to the dome, the doors at both ends locked open. Green lights flickered on status panels, suggesting the system had the capability to react to pressure loss and seal itself if need be.

She stepped out of the tunnel into a room where a number of people in yellow jumpsuits inspected and packed vegetables into plastic trays. Some sliced up huge slabs of meat that resembled chicken breast, despite being almost four feet long. Aside from pleasant smiles of greeting, the workers didn't pay her much notice.

A white double door separated the room from a massive chamber beyond that appeared to take up the bulk of the pod's rectangular shape. Rows upon rows of liquid-filled tanks formed a veritable maze inside. Most had pale green fluid in which floated various vegetables at different stages of growth. The tanks farther from the door contained darker liquid with unrecognizable blobs.

Kerys leaned up to the window to get a better look, and stifled a squeal of shock when they opened, bathing her in hot, humid air laden with the stink of fertilizer. She backpedaled, gagging and coughing.

Two men working in the room behind her chuckled.

"What's blue mean?" asked one.

"Huh?" She faced him.

He gestured at her. "Your jumpsuit. Can't remember ever seeing a blue one before."

"Oh. Archaeology… actually xenoarchaeology."

"Neat." He nodded at the door. "You can go in if you want, just don't touch anything."

"Thanks. I'm just trying to familiarize myself with the layout of the place."

The workers nodded.

"Welcome to the ass end of nowhere," said the other guy.

Kerys stepped into the grow room. An overwhelming pungency of chemicals in the air watered her eyes and left the flavor of potting soil on her tongue. Intense lamps on the ceiling made it feel like a mid-summer day in a tropical rainforest. She coughed and took a few tentative steps forward, trying to get a better look at what floated in the more distant tanks. The ones near her forced her to stand on tiptoe to peer over them. Each had a small metal stairway to an attached catwalk, allowing worker access to the pools within.

Common vegetables hung from white plastic rods across the tops of the tanks, keeping the plants positioned in the liquid as if it were soil, with leaves and such above, and roots immersed. The heat got her dizzy by the time she reached the halfway point, and she stopped, leaning on a tank full of cucumbers, to fan herself.

"Hello," said a man.

She looked up at a dark-skinned, thin man with short black hair and a curious smile. His yellow jumpsuit bore dirt smears and fluid stains, as if he worked on a real farm.

"Oh, hi. Sorry. Just looking around."

"Figured." He offered a hand. "I'm Sanjay. Don't usually get many people in here who aren't on the team."

"Kerys." She shook hands. "Only been here for three days… well, almost four now."

"Ahh, you came in with the last shuttle. Heard they were bringing in a crew to check out something they discovered outside." He scratched his head. "Was quite a long time ago they found that, wasn't it?"

"Commute was a bitch." She laughed.

He opened his mouth to say something, closed it, tilted his head, and chuckled. "Oh… right. So, checking the place out?"

"Yeah. One of my teammates got hurt, so they decided to cancel the second half of our work today. I should probably be evaluating the images and data from the 3D modeler instead of sightseeing. I guess I'm having some trouble focusing. Starting to feel like I'm a long way from home."

"Heh. That we are. I came out here with the second wave, right around the time they found that hole in the ridge. Been here about three years. Doesn't feel like it."

"Nice little greenhouse you guys have." She turned in place, surveying all the overhead lights, walkways, and fluid-filled tanks. "What's back there in the murky tanks?"

"Meat. Chicken, beef, and pork. Well, muscle tissue grown on an artificial substrate to shape it into layers. From a genetic standpoint, we've all been eating the same three animals for years."

The grilled chicken fought back. Kerys put a hand on her gut. "Ugh."

"Oh, it's actually a lot cleaner than what you get on Earth. No insecticides, no hormones, no contamination of any kind, really. There's no bugs or parasites or anything up here. Plus…" He struck a pose as if trying to amuse a small child. "Fluffy doesn't have to die."

"Well, that's something, I guess. I had this guy in one of my classes… he was so much of a vegan it got obnoxious. We stopped at this place to pick up dinner one night, and he refused to even touch the bag because people had ordered burgers and chicken."

"Wow." Sanjay shook his head.

She turned in place, eyeing a cluster of onions. "Kind of eerie in here, actually. Like the veggies are watching us."

"Maybe they are." He wagged his eyebrows. "Or maybe you've been in a confined space too long."

"Right." She laughed. "This has to be boring as hell."

"Oh, it's got its moments." Sanjay grinned while pointing his thumb over his shoulder at a bank of computer equipment in the back of the chamber. "Whenever I get too bored, I just think about how this room produces the only human-compatible food for thousands of light years. Our survival hinges on a couple of sixty-dollar fuses and about thirty thousand lines of program code. Hope they checked it twice."

Kerys gawked at him.

"Hah. Got you." He winked. "I'm teasing."

She slouched, heaving a sigh of relief.

"The fuses cost about two thousand each," said Sanjay with a straight face.

"That's not helping." She cringed.

He gestured at the south wall. "We've got enough Hydra rations to feed everyone for nine months. Avasar sends out a resupply ship on routine six-month intervals. Usually, they're unmanned, and they drop off things we can't produce here. Certain medical supplies, tools, fuel for the reactor, that sort of thing. If we ran into a critical problem we don't have the parts to fix, we could evacuate on the shuttle in groups of twenty. It's not as dangerous as my teasing implied, but being here makes me feel like I'm doing something more meaningful than farming turnips in deep space."

She held up her hands. "Okay, I'll give you that one."

A beeping noise drew Sanjay's attention to a small screen strapped to his left forearm. "Filter on 11B is acting up. I should check on that. Nice meeting you."

"Yeah, and I should like actually do some work. Same. Nice to meet you."

The packing room felt like air conditioning by comparison to the greenhouse. Kerys unzipped her jumpsuit a little and flapped it against her chest to cool off as she walked. She vaguely remembered seeing a section of cubicles designated for her team, and headed for the stairwell.

As soon as she emerged on the second floor, a woman called her name. Kerys whirled toward the voice. Annapurna strode out from a row of grey fabric cube walls, long black hair fanning out behind her as she hurried over with a look of urgency and concern.

"Yes?" asked Kerys.

"There you are. I've been trying to find you. I wanted to let you know that we've discovered a cavity inside that artifact."

Excitement bloomed in her chest; Kerys felt like a six-year-old waking up to Christmas morning. "How large? Is there something in it?"

"If there's something in it, it's not dense enough to appear on either X-ray or MRI, or some property of that substance is inhibiting our ability to detect it. The 'head'—as people are calling it—appears to be a form of volcanic glass with a high content of a material possessing similar properties to silicon. The cavity is about the size of a cantaloupe. Before you become overly excited, this may well be a simple gas bubble trapped within before it cooled, and not a hidden chamber deliberately made by the xenos."

"Oh. Are they going to allow the artifact inside?"

Annapurna offered a noncommittal shrug. "It's not my decision exclusively, but so far I haven't found anything that would lead me to worry. Mr. Braxton is keen on having it admitted, as is Captain Chen, so I imagine it'll be approved. Doctor Mardling is the most hesitant. Unfortunately, he doesn't have any specific proof beyond what he calls 'a bad feeling' about it. Likely superstition."

"I see." She fidgeted, thinking back to the ominousness that hung over her when she made 'eye contact' with the statue. Crazy as it sounded, she almost felt as if it dropped on Marco deliberately out of spite, then glared at her for disturbing it. But... stone. *Definitely* a statue, not a severed alien head. It couldn't be aware of its own existence.

"What do you think of it?" Annapurna tilted her head. "Certainly a unique discovery."

Fear gave way to delight. Kerys grinned. "I'm thinking it's probably like a bust. A statue, like the Romans put Nero heads all over the place. To me, it looks like a face with four eyes. Doesn't have an evident mouth, so perhaps this species doesn't eat the way we think of eating. They could absorb electricity for nourishment, or photosynthesize, or even have 'mouths' elsewhere on the body."

"Interesting." Annapurna smiled, shifting her demeanor from professional to casual. "Would you mind if I asked you a personal question?"

Here we go. She tensed. "I suppose. About Will, isn't it?"

"Yes. I've noticed he's been on edge since you've arrived. I know you have some history with him, but something is not right with him. I... don't mean to pry, but if you ever need an ear to bend, I'm willing to listen."

Oh, whew. She's not going to push. "Thanks. We dated a while ago. It didn't work out, so I broke up with him. He never got over it. It's not a problem, really. I guess he's not coping with the shock of seeing me."

"I can tell you that's true," said Annapurna. "He's been muttering to himself when he thinks no one can hear him. He's... not happy you're here, but he seems more like he's afraid you'll get hurt. Not that he's angry with you personally."

Kerys sighed, adding an eye-roll. "Back home, he didn't even want me driving. I'm a girl, so I run the risk of fatal injury doing anything but being pretty."

She smirked. "I never pegged him for that manner of chauvinist."

"Oh, he's good. He hides it well. You probably won't see that side of him unless you wind up moving in with him. It's not so much he thinks women are delicate, it's just *his* woman he thinks that way about. I'll give him one thing—he can stay professional at work. He saves the tantrums for where his bosses can't see. He won't let anything get between him and what he wants, not even himself."

"I see." Annapurna shifted her jaw side to side for a moment in thought. "I hope he will be able to stay focused and that your being here won't cause problems."

Kerys twitched. After all she'd been through to get this job, get out here, find the artifact... now this woman had the temerity to suggest they might have to send *her* home if she caused Will's work to suffer. "If Will screws up, it's *his* fault. You can't pin it on me if he can't hold himself together and—"

"Kerys." Annapurna put a hand on her shoulder. "That's not what I'm saying at all. I understand more about your situation than you think I do. His name is Rajesh, and it's been six years since I've detangled my life from his. If Will cannot function with you being here, it wouldn't be you on the shuttle home. At least, not if I have anything to say about it."

Kerys blinked. *What? Wow. Really?* After a few seconds of shocked staring, she exhaled with relief, shivering off the last vestiges of rage she'd summoned to defend herself. "Uhh, wow. Thank you. Yeah, umm... I'd rather stay away from him as much as possible."

"I understand." Annapurna smiled. "I'll send you the result of the scan. I'm sure you're dying to get your hands on some high-res images."

"Yes!" Kerys bounced on her toes.

"I've got a full modeling suite and some VR goggles. Once we do a full laser-scan on a specimen, you could hold it in the palm of your hand or go walking around on it as if you were the size of a flea."

"I feel like a little kid on my birthday. Is it in the system yet?"

"The scanning is done, but the data is still compiling. It should be ready for a simulation in about ten minutes. Come on, I'll show you where they put your desk."

Kerys grinned. "Awesome. Lead the way."

7

LAMIACEAE ADVENA

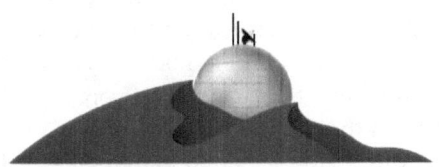

For hours, Kerys wandered the surface of a virtual recreation, exploring the alien 'head' she'd discovered. The simulation scaled her point of view to one-eighth of an inch tall, allowing her to see the material as a dark translucent red around an interior core of black-grey silicon. She could increase or decrease her 'size' by sliding a finger up or down the right side of the VR goggles and kept going back and forth between flea and a perspective roughly equal in height to the head.

The front portion, about where the 'nose' would be, curved downward and back in, somewhat like the shell of a nautilus. At the point where the upward sweep met the main bulk, she discovered a seam, which made her think she'd located the mouth. Whether or not it opened for nutrient intake or served as a means of respiration, she couldn't tell. The more she studied the relic, the more she felt convinced they'd discovered a statue, not a fossilized *actual* alien severed head.

"Well, hello there," said the alien in a strange yet familiar, chirpy tone, its breath fruity.

Kerys froze, staring at it. "What the... Oh. That voice. It's from that stupid cartoon Will liked. I'm dreaming, aren't I?"

Her eyes snapped open, revealing a close-up view of white fabric. She lay on her stomach, both arms hugging her pillow to her face. With the privacy screen on her window closed, the only light in the room came from a single blue LED at the base of her desk terminal, which proved surprising in brightness given its size. She couldn't remember walking back from Annapurna's desk, so she must've spent hours in VR, skipped dinner, and stumbled half-awake to her room.

"Ugh. What time is it?"

Her head felt like a lead weight, refusing to obey her effort to sit up. She yawned and took a deep breath laced with a strong scent somewhere between lavender and peaches. "What is that"—she sniffed—"smell?"

As consciousness spread over her brain, an odd sensation of being watched came on. She froze, breathing the flowery-fruity air for a few minutes while listening to total silence. The little blue dot at the base of her terminal cast tall shadows from small objects around it. She looked around the left side of her room at the chair, desk, and e-pads before spotting her jumpsuit, shoes, socks, and underwear on the floor. Except for her stint in cryo, she usually slept nude, but couldn't remember undressing. Of course, she couldn't remember walking back from Anna's desk either.

She pushed up from the mattress enough to get a look at a small green clock display on the desk, which read: 6:19 a.m. Kerys closed her eyes and moaned into the pillow. Her team got started officially at nine. If she allowed for a shower and breakfast, she could squeeze in at least another thirty minutes of sleep.

Creak.

Again, she went as still as a mouse in the gaze of an eagle. That sense of not being alone grew stronger. After another minute of listening to herself breathe, she shifted her weight up onto her hands and poked her head out from the cubbyhole containing her bed.

A shadowy human form sat against the wall by the door, two eyes glinting in the faint glow of the blue LED.

"Sorry if I woke you," whispered Will.

Kerys clamped the bedding over her mouth and screamed into the fabric. She kicked at the sheet, scooting away from him toward the interior wall while gasping for breath, managing to get one foot on the floor before gathering her wits. Shaking, she fought the urge to leap out of bed since she had only a blanket on, and scurried back into the coffin-sized space, wrapping herself to the chin. "W—what are you doing in here?"

His head tilted slightly to the side. "Watching you sleep. I wanted to make sure you were safe."

"I... I..." She debated screaming louder, but chickened out, worried he'd make it look like she'd gone nuts if she caused a scene.

"Nice to see you still wear the same pajamas."

Warmth rushed to her cheeks.

"You must've been exhausted. You didn't even crawl under the blanket. Hope you don't mind that I covered you."

She broke out in a sweat, clutching the bedding tight to her chest. Any number of bad scenarios played out in her mind. Did he come to take revenge? Her friend Ashley had been convinced he'd show up and kill her for leaving him. *She didn't know him. She only heard me bitching about him all the time. He wouldn't… would he?*

"How long have you been in here?"

A line of teeth appeared in his silhouette, a smile tinted blue. "A little while. I couldn't sleep. It always did make me feel better listening to you breathe at night. You don't know how much I've missed that."

She tucked her feet under her and sat up, still clinging to the blanket. "I locked the door."

"Are you sure?"

"Umm." She glanced at the door. An indicator over the handle displayed 'locked' on a red field. Rather than safe, it made her feel trapped with him. "I… don't remember."

"It's all right. I got it for you."

He sounds so comforting, but… so would a spider. "What's that fruity smell? Are you drinking alcohol? Did you spray me with something? You shouldn't be in here. People will get the wrong idea. Fraternizing is against company policy."

"Don't worry, hon. I've got friends back in LA. They won't fire you if I ask them not to."

Fire me? He's the one that broke into my room. Kerys shook with fear and anger. "You should go before anyone notices you were here."

Will drew his legs in and stood, his back sliding up against the wall. "It's been so long. I've been thinking about everything you said that last day. You were right. I didn't give you enough credit. I can see how you thought I was suffocating."

She absentmindedly scratched at her leg, gripping her ankle to stop her hand from moving. "I didn't *think* you were suffocating. You *were* suffocating."

"Babe, please calm down. Stop shaking. I'd never hurt you."

"Sneaking into my room in the middle of the night and just sitting there staring at me… that's not normal, Will. Calling me twenty times a day for months after I couldn't take it anymore…"

He tapped a panel on the wall, activating the room lights, but keeping them dim enough not to blind her. She stared at his green jumpsuit, open halfway down the chest, exposing a sweat-stained tank top, the clothes he must've worked in all day.

All night he's been in here… Kerys glared at her clothes on the floor. *How long did he stare at me before pulling the blanket up?* She cringed, feeling sick to her stomach and livid.

"I know it seems a bit unusual of me to be here right now, but not a day's gone by since you left that I haven't thought of you." He stepped closer to the bed, gaze down, posture apologetic, but a faint smile nonetheless. "I had to make sure you were okay."

Kerys leaned away, gaze locked on his stomach, unable to look up into his eyes. She flinched when his thighs touched the bed. The opening blocked everything above his pectorals. He lingered for a second before lowering himself to sit on the edge, head bowed forward under the sleep chamber's ceiling.

"I'm fine, Will. Thanks for checking on me, but you really should go back to your quarters before someone sees you in here." She edged away until her shoulders hit the cold metal above her pillow and peered past her blanket-covered knees at a smile she hadn't trusted for years.

"Everyone already expects us to get together. You're dealing with the trauma of being out here all alone and find one familiar face among a hundred." He glanced down at something in his hands emitting a faint light. "People aren't wired like that, babe. Something about isolation makes us realize how precious it is to have someone. You know that Vickers woman? Built like a tank? She's got Hellerman wrapped around her finger. Heard she's a real girly girl."

Kerys swallowed, hating the wall at her back for being solid. "H-Hellerman?"

"He's the IT guy here. Runs all the tech stuff. Good people."

"Is that how you got my door open?"

Will reached over and put a hand atop her right foot. "I've missed you so much, babe. I came out here not really caring if I returned. It's dangerous."

"Too dangerous for me, right?" Indignation chipped away fear.

He smiled. "Too dangerous for anyone with a future. Anything could happen. We could die in five minutes. Five days. A year. I know things didn't work out before, but I'm in a different place now, mentally. It's been what, six years, not counting our cryo? You'll see things are different."

"Popping into my room in the middle of the night isn't the right way to change my mind." Her fingers dug into her leg from her effort not to tremble in front of him. 'Shouting and kicking stuff' Will had been scary, but he had nothing on creepy 'watching her sleep for hours' Will.

"So, there's a chance." He caressed her ankle through the bedding. "I see the doubt in your eyes. We can make up for a lot of lost time."

"You're seriously asking for sex now?"

He looked her in the eye for a long moment before hanging his head and gazing at whatever object he held out of sight. "I'd kind of been hoping you felt the same way I did."

Kerys twitched, flashing back to the night he'd become so upset when she said no. The rage that had taken him convinced her to get out and not look back. He'd only hit furniture, but that's always where it started. She eyed the door, teetering on the point of not caring if she had to run off into the outpost stark naked to get away from him. She could do that... or she could let him do what he wanted and then tell someone, but who would they believe?

"I'm not ready, Will." She cringed ever so slightly, bracing for the explosion.

He sighed, but not with the disappointed huff she'd come to expect. The resignation in his breath caught her off guard. "I understand." Will tossed a clear plastic rectangle on the mattress, a holographic photo of the two of them leaning on a fence, both wearing Berkeley sweatshirts. Someone she didn't recognize ran by in the background in a football uniform. Her twenty-year-old self smiled at the camera, one arm around Will, who made a goofy face. "Remember that?"

Before he showed me his true colors. A tear ran down her cheek. *Why couldn't he have stayed like he was then? What happened? Did he change, or did he trust me enough to drop the act?* He hadn't always been an ass. "Yeah. You talked me out of studying to go to the game with you."

"Still got that A, didn't you?"

She sniffled, the urge to laugh crashed into her fear, dying to a weak smile by the time it reached her mouth. "Yeah. Barely."

"You had fun that night. This is the face I see in my mind every time I think of you."

She looked down. "It wasn't me who changed."

"Things could've been done differently, but that's the 'us' I cling to." He withdrew his hand, lacing his fingers together, elbows on his knees. "So, what did you think of the site?"

"We've only scratched the surface. There's at least seven more chambers we haven't been able to access yet." She shifted to the side, tucking her legs under her butt near the wall, out of his reach. "Hopefully, we'll get farther in today."

"Sounds exciting. More exciting than picking flowers." He chuckled.

An awkward silence lingered.

He sucked in a breath and clapped his hands on his knees, making her jump. "Right, well. Let me know if you change your mind." He stood and started for the door.

She kept quiet, staring to the right so he didn't catch her looking at him. On the desk beside the terminal, a small plastic cup held a bizarre flower that hadn't been there before. It reached about ten inches tall with seven incrementally larger rings of tiny florets that resembled neon violet broccoli in tiers a finger width apart.

"Will?"

He stopped. "Hmm?"

"What's that?"

He turned to face her. "What's what?"

Kerys pulled one arm out from under the blanket to point at the flower. "That. Is that what I've been smelling?"

"Oh, just something I found that I thought you'd like."

"Where did you get it?"

He smiled. "The forest. It's a bit of indigenous flora tentatively recorded as lamiaceae advena."

"Did it go through quarantine?"

"I'm going to suggest they officially name it Lamiaceae Kerysinia."

She furrowed her eyebrows. "Will. Did that go through quarantine? How did you get an indigenous plant in here?"

"Well... that would've actually required submitting it to the quarantine process."

Kerys gasped and covered her mouth and nose. After two seconds, she felt foolish since she'd been breathing it for however long he'd been here. "I've been inhaling that all damn night. We don't know what the hell it is!"

He held up a hand. "Relax, babe. Studying these plants is what I do here. Trust me. It's fine. I'm in here breathing it too, right? You know I would never do anything to hurt you. It's just a pleasant fragrance like any other flower."

She slipped out of bed, keeping the blanket wrapped around herself to the armpits, and padded over to the wall panel. A swipe of her finger brought the lights on to full strength, revealing a purplish tint to the entire slab of transparent amber material serving as her desk.

"It's shedding spores or something. Pollen? What's all that dust?"

"That particular flower reproduces via sporelike particles. Please relax. It's not going to sprout in your lungs. I spent months studying every aspect of this species, and it's completely benign in terms of reactivity to humans."

"I thought you said you snuck it through quarantine? If you've been studying it for months..."

He grinned. "I was referring to that particular sample. We haven't had lamiaceae advena in inventory for a year. You might want to keep it quiet that it's here. Certain people might not react well to undocumented specimens being in your quarters."

Wow. This is new. Trying to make up with me and threatening me in the same night? What's he doing? She glared at him. "I don't understand you at all anymore, Will."

He stepped closer and grasped her by the arms, a gentle touch, but it locked her body rigid nonetheless. "I'm only trying to keep you safe, babe."

She stopped breathing, expecting him to swoop in for an unwanted kiss, but he only winked before backing off. Noticing her foot landed in spore dust, she edged to her left. He paused at the door long enough for a brief smile before slipping out into a dim hallway and closing the door behind him.

Kerys stared at the door for a full minute before her brain thawed out. She rushed over to re-lock the door before bundling her blanket and tossing it onto the bed. Seething, she paced back and forth while casting the occasional glare at the strange plant. Every breath saturated her senses with the strong blended fragrance of lavender and peaches. What started as pleasant grew cloying. The bottom of her right foot darkened as if she'd stepped on ink.

"Dammit."

"Will, you moron..." She lifted her leg and brushed at it, transferring the violet smear to her hand, then studied the stain on her fingertips. "What did you do?"

Sighing, she raked her clean hand over her hair, scratching at her scalp. Of course, if she said anything, he'd claim *she* snuck it in. The first time she attempted to tell someone about his craziness, he'd totally made it sound like *she* went off the deep end. It worked for a while, making her fearful of trying to talk about him to anyone else. She already dropped a stone head on Marco's foot. The bosses have to at least be questioning her. It wouldn't take him much effort to make her look even worse. Dread at losing what she'd worked so hard for, plus panic at waking up to him *in her room*, sent her mind spinning off in a blurry spiral.

No... I have to hide it. I can't tell anyone he was in here.

She searched around for something to put it in, not trusting the flower at all. Her quarters had a small closet with a three-drawer cabinet on the lower right. In one, she found a tall, clear box with a black endcap. From the shapes cut out of the foam inside it, she figured it the packaging her terminal came in. She popped the end off, dumped out the foam, and set the end cap on the desk.

With as much care as if she transferred the nuclear payload of a warhead, she held her breath, grasped the cup of black dirt holding the flower, lifted it three inches, and moved it onto the square. After lowering the clear plastic box over the flower, she resumed breathing.

If anyone asks, I'll say it's some kind of decoration I've had since school. Wait, no... that's stupid. It's obviously a plant from this planet. She took a few deep breaths in search of calm, trying to think straight past her panic.

Annapurna knows about Will. If anyone finds this, I have to tell the truth. I'm done making excuses for him. But... no one's going to find this.

She threw on a bathrobe, ran to the women's room at the north end of the hallway, and wet a towel. It both surprised her and didn't to find cloth towels instead of paper. More expensive, but on the other hand, paper towels couldn't be reused. She cleaned up the spore dust as best she could, and sink-washed the cloth until it merely looked like it had endured a bizarre cosmetics incident. Since no one had seen her scurrying about, she tossed it in the laundry bin and hurried back to her room. With any luck, no one would trace the purple towel back to her.

Once again behind a locked door, she collapsed sitting on the side of her bed and held her face in her hands. Tears came unbidden, driven by anger and terror. Could Will get into her room whenever he wanted? Did he take photos of her while she slept naked? Did he *do* anything else? Shaking, she fell over sideways and curled into a ball.

Dammit! Why the hell is he here? She thought about Anna's offer and bit her lip. *That'll blow up in my face. Who knows what he'll do if he doesn't get his way? Six months... I only have to make it six months before I can get out of here.* All her excitement to come here had, in one fell swoop, become desperation to leave as soon as possible. She hated Will even more for doing that to her.

Frightened, and feeling more alone than she'd ever felt in her life, Kerys stared at the door, clinging to the couple of minutes remaining before she had to leave her little sanctuary and go to work.

8

ADVANCED CIVILIZATION

The ghost of scrambled eggs and bacon bubbled up in the back of Kerys's throat.

Rushing through breakfast plus anxiety guaranteed she'd be tasting it for the next hour or two. She opened her locker in the ready room by the airlock. So far that morning, she'd avoided eye contact with anyone, ducking into the cafeteria after the rest of the crew already finished eating. It took longer than she expected to compose herself enough to step outside her room again, but a quick text message to Don about not feeling well bought her a half hour. She didn't exactly have to 'punch in' at nine on the nose so she could clock out on time and go have fun with friends.

She ignored a few people getting ready behind her and stepped into the e-suit. Reaching for the fasteners gave her more of a stretch than her body wanted to tolerate, but she managed to secure two with a bit of squirming before Annapurna walked over.

"Would you like a hand with the suit?"

Kerys exhaled, nodding while bowing her head to avoid meeting the woman's gaze. "Yeah, thanks."

The clips at her shoulders squeaked one after the next, compressing the suit tight to her front and back.

"There you go."

"Thanks," said Kerys without looking up. "Are you going out too?"

"Oh, no. I was only down here to bring a firmware update to Chris. It came in last night, and the remote station systems really need it. It should speed up the sample analysis by at least twenty percent. Saw you attempting yoga and figured you could use a little help."

She laughed. "Yeah." *Damn.*

"Something wrong?"

"I'm that obvious?"

Annapurna sat on the bench, smoothing the fabric of her emerald jumpsuit over her legs. "Is it something you feel comfortable talking about?"

Kerys kept quiet until she felt confident her voice wouldn't tremble. "I don't want you to do anything yet, but maybe it would be better to stop holding this in." She sank onto the bench as well, still staring at her heavy metal boots.

"If it's something I can in good conscience keep to myself, I will."

"Will visited me in my quarters last night," she whispered. "Okay, maybe 'visited' isn't the right word. He let himself in while I was sleeping. I woke up and he was right there, watching me."

Annapurna gasped, covering her mouth with one hand.

"I... he wanted to... but, I said no and he backed off." Kerys tapped her gloved fingers on her knee. "Last time I said no, he flipped out and started kicking things. I don't know what to think that he just... that he didn't flip out. I-I was so sure he'd lose it, but I said no and he left."

"It is only because you have asked me to keep your confidence that I'm going to let you handle this at your own pace, but entering your quarters like that is inexcusable. I strongly suggest you immediately file a report with HR."

Kerys looked up at her, reassured by the concern on the woman's face. "He said I forgot to lock the door. I mean... it's possible. I don't even remember walking back to my room from your desk."

"That's not an excuse, and you know it." Annapurna reached over and took her hand. "If you need someone to go with you to HR, I'll be there for you."

"There's HR out here?" Kerys chuckled. "Wow. On Copernicus we had to send a SFT and wait months for an answer—if they bothered to read it."

"Of course. Keith is quite fair and open minded."

"I don't know. We're so far out. What can they even do? Will would be stuck here for months waiting for a transport and it would just make everything worse. I don't want him back, but I'm going to wing it. Let him think I'm reconsidering until the next shuttle's here in six months, then I'm out."

"But what about your work?" Annapurna gestured at the airlock. "Doctor Bouchard mentioned he thinks there may be an entire temple structure in that mountain. This could be the find of a lifetime... of an age. Are you going to let that man chase you away from that?"

Hearing it put in those words made her plan feel too much like surrender. Kerys clenched her hands into fists. An e-suit offered far more confidence than being naked under a blanket. "No. No, you're right. I'm not." She stood and grabbed her helmet out of the locker. "Being vague in hopes he leaves me alone will only be playing with his head. That's dangerous. If he doesn't back off, I'll tell him there's no chance."

"That is probably wise. Leading him along could make things worse in the long term. He's with the botany team, so he shouldn't have any reason to be around you. If he pulls a stunt like that again, you promise me you'll do something."

"I will." Kerys tucked her hair up and put her helmet on.

"Or talk to Gensch. The man looks quite intimidating, but he is a gentle soul. I am sure he is more than capable of convincing Will to keep his distance."

She cracked a smile, not quite able to reconcile the concept of 'gentle soul' with the white-haired soldier she'd seen. "I'm sure he would."

***

DUST SWIRLED IN THE AIR WITHIN THE MAIN CHAMBER. FREESTANDING LIGHT posts illuminated the walls, casting the ruins in a dull blue-grey sheen. A maze of thick cables crisscrossed the floor, most connecting to the lights, while two went to short-range excavator lasers dangling from the exo suits' grip. Kerys stepped over the cables, some as thick as her wrist, making her way over to the rest of the team. Ellen and Lars flanked the stone door on the east wall while Don and Paula examined the area on either side of it with handheld devices, mini microwave scanners. Corporal Mitchell sat on the corner of the huge case that held the 3D modeler, her rifle resting in her lap. Every ounce of her body language screamed boredom.

Kerys approached Don. "Sorry I'm late."

He looked back at her, smiling past a layer of fog on his visor. "I hope you're feeling better."

"Yeah. Didn't sleep well over that incident with Marco." She bit her lip. *Not a total lie. I do feel awful about that.*

"He'll be fine. He's parsing our scan data from the comfort of his bed."

"Hello," said Marco over the comm. "Got a screen set up with everyone's camera feeds. Couldn't miss all the fun, right?"

"How's your leg?" asked Kerys.

"Fine. As long as I don't try to move." He chuckled. "Other than that, it hurts like hell."

She sighed. "Sorry."

"If you apologize one more time," said Marco, "I'm going to fill your quarters with styrofoam packing peanuts."

"Okay, okay." She peered around. "Got a spare scanner? I could check the walls of that other room."

"Besides, how many guys can say they broke their leg from a woman giving them head?" asked Marco.

Lars whistled. "Anyone who's ever been with Ellen."

The big woman punched him in the shoulder, knocking his exo suit two steps to the left and making him laugh louder.

"Mr. Trem. Please," said Don, exasperated. "Despite us being at a remote site, this is still technically a work environment."

Paula pointed at one of the open cases. "In there. I'm reading some kind of mechanism in the wall here that I think connects to the door, but I can't find any way to access it."

"If you want that door open, just say the word." Lars hefted the excavating laser. "This thing'll get through it in about twenty minutes."

Kerys walked up to the door and brushed her hand over the stone. "It might be something like wireless. Maybe sound activated?"

"You've been playing too many fantasy games," said Marco. "Like some wizard speaking a command word?"

"Or musical notes," said Kerys. "The aliens might communicate using tonal modulation rather than words."

"If they speak in a range we can even hear at all." Paula tapped at the screen of her e-pad. "Until someone finds recordings or something of that sort, we have nothing to base any projection of spoken language on."

"Or shifts in electromagnetic radiance, or pheromones." Don adjusted a setting on the scanner. "We don't even know enough about them to understand how much we don't know."

Marco chuckled. "Maybe the Atlanteans use, like, telepathy?"

Paula sighed. "I'm not sure what bothers me more between your continued insistence on calling them 'Atlanteans' or your suggestion that phenomena such as telepathy could be real."

"I'm hesitant to condone a destructive method of entry here, but it doesn't seem we have another option." Don collapsed a probe antenna on his handheld and made a 'be my guest' gesture to Lars and Ellen. "Do try and confine the cutting to the door itself?"

"Sure, Doc." Lars and his massive exo suit clomped over. He took a knee and pointed the excavator at the left bottom corner of the door.

Ellen aimed hers at the other side. "All right. Laser time." A secondary visor closed over their helmets, much darker than the normal one. "You all might want to look away. The beams are bright enough to cause permanent damage to the retina without protection."

"Good thing I'm never without protection," said Marco over the comm.

Everyone except Don and Paula chuckled.

Gina shook her head. "That guy just doesn't know when to quit, does he?"

Kerys grinned.

"No one who quits easy would be on this rock," said Ellen, still glaring at Lars.

Except me. She fidgeted, feeling called out over how close she'd come to chickening out simply for finding Will here. In truth, she'd had about an eight-minute window in which she might have been able to run back to the shuttle and demand to go home... but she'd missed it. Nothing to do now but press on, but did that count as 'not quitting' if she had no choice?

Don handed Kerys his handheld. "Might as well check the 'head room.'"

"Sure thing." She gave a resigned sigh. *I can't let Will ruin my life. I won't.*

Brilliant shimmering blue light erupted from the laser units along with a loud droning buzz.

"One good thing about workin' out here in these suits. We can't smell a damn thing," yelled Lars over the noise.

"That is the only reason I'm able to stand so close to you," said Ellen, adding a laugh to the end.

Lars straightened to look over at her. "Aww, come on. I showered already this month."

Kerys shivered, afraid he might not be joking, and hurried to the north tunnel. The secondary chamber remained as they had left it with the metal panel open and the 'head room,' as Don referred to it, exposed. The place felt ten times eerier being alone. She stared at the pedestal, which appeared to be made of the same volcanic glass/silicon mix as the head without the maroon tinge. An unsettling feeling sent a tingle down her back, as if someone or something else stood in the room with her, watching.

Now I'm being silly. It's just a creepy abandoned alien temple. Bah. We don't know for sure it served as a temple. She switched on the scanner and held the probe near the wall, moving it up and down in slow, even passes while focused on the wireframe model on its tiny display screen. If the scanner detected any hollows or changes in material density, they would appear in 3D.

Her nerves prickled. Every minute or so, she glanced over her shoulder expecting to find Will standing there creepily staring at her from the shadows—or some alien ready to pounce on her out of nowhere, but each time she looked, the room remained empty. Inch by inch, she took readings around the exterior wall of the head chamber. Aside from a channel of loose dirt near the northwestern corner, rendered as a sandy texture on the screen, the walls scanned as either solid rock fronted with cut bricks, or had open space behind them.

A soft scrape close behind her made Kerys whirl around with a gasp, raising her arms to defend herself—but the room remained empty. "What the...?"

The footstep-like scratch repeated. Now that she faced the entrance, the noise seemed more like a strange echo from the outer room. *The acoustics in here are weird.* A few minutes later, she ignored a third scuff as well as a metallic *clank* that followed—until a shadow moved on the wall. Kerys let out a yelp and spun around.

Gina froze in the doorway, wide-eyed. "Hey, easy... it's just me."

"Shit, you scared. Me." Kerys let her head hang for a second or two while she caught her breath. "This place is creepy."

"Abandoned tombs like this always are, especially if you're alone." Gina wandered closer, twisting left and right to stare around at the walls and up at the pyramid-shaped vault ceiling. "Wow... this almost looks like a missile silo... if they made missiles square."

Kerys laughed and got back to scanning the wall. "Yeah. I think it was ceremonial, but I haven't made up my mind yet between tomb or place of worship. It's creepy. Before you got here, it felt like something was watching me. Almost as if this place was angry we'd disturbed it."

"Oh boy," said Marco on the comm. "Here we go with the voodoo."

Gina put her back to the wall and aimed her assault rifle around the chamber. "I got nothin' on thermal. Don't feel anything weird either."

"I'm sure it's just my overactive imagination. Being alone in a place like this lets the mind play." She edged to the right, raising and lowering the scanner, grateful for having some company.

After another few minutes of the same boring blankness going by on the screen, Don's voice came over the comm channel. "Kerys, have you discovered anything interesting in there?"

She frowned at the handheld. "I'm about three-fourths of the way around the chamber, and so far, I'm only seeing rock and some loose dirt. The aerial scans didn't show anything beyond this point, so I'm thinking this is probably a dead end."

"You can get back to that later if you'd like to see this," said Don. "They're done cutting on the door."

"Be right there." Eager to get out of the creepy room, she hurried back down the tunnel to the secondary chamber and paused at the corridor leading to the outer area. A thick pall of dense smoke now hung in the outer room, making it difficult to see much more than a few feet in any direction. "Whoa."

Gina stopped close behind her. "Wow, that's a lot of dust."

"Mind your step," said Paula.

Kerys made her way cautiously across the large chamber to the east wall, placing her boots with care to avoid tripping over wires she couldn't see. Soon, the wavering beams of shoulder-mounted spotlights became apparent in the mist. She stopped beside another e-suit, not knowing who it was until Paula turned to look at her. Kerys smiled at her, then leaned forward for a better look at the door. A one-inch-thick gap went all the way around, the stone still glowing faintly orange at the top where the two lasers had converged.

Ellen and Lars bored holes in the center of the slab, then inserted expanding hooks, which they opened to lock in place. Finally, they secured heavy ropes to the eye loop at the end of the hooks and hauled the former door—now a stone monolith—back from the doorway, the exo suits making it look easy.

Don stepped past it into the next chamber first, followed by Paula.

"Whoa," said Marco over the comm.

"My word." Don coughed. "Will you look at that?"

Kerys darted around the slab.

The next chamber matched the outer room in size, but had six square columns in the center, all banded with the same engraved pattern at the midline. Each corner held a hexagonal stone pillar covered in pictographic characters like the ones from the buttons, only a far more varied assortment. Low-lying slabs sat between the obelisks against the north and south walls, about the size of dining room tables, but only at knee level up from the ground. Another door occupied the center of the eastern wall, directly across from the cut-open passage. Six familiar symbols adorned its center.

"That's the same word." Kerys advanced to the center of the chamber, pointing east. "The marks on that door. I found thirty-seven examples of the same 'phrase' on Copernicus. It has to be important. The name of their species, the name of… I guess a company, maybe? Or their god?"

"Interesting." Paula approached the door and studied the marks. "They're quite precise. Laser cut."

"If the Atlanteans had access to technology like that, why are they still carving up statues and building stone temples?" asked Marco.

"Mister Trem," said Paula in a loud voice before lowering it again, "will you *please* cease referring to these beings as Atlanteans? It's distracting and it creates conjecture that we are light years away from even suspecting, much less proving." She shook her head and continued complaining to herself while holding her e-pad up to the writing.

Kerys squatted by one of the slabs. The top had evidence of abrasive wear, deeper in the center. After a little while of studying it, she blinked. "I… think these might've been seats."

"What?" Don rushed over.

"Look." She pointed at erosion forming a shallow bowl-like depression in the slab. "All of these large rectangular platforms have similar wear patterns, and they're not identical. They weren't designed that way. The Atla—aliens may have used them like chairs."

"My, my." Don took a knee. "That could offer quite a bit about their anatomy. These platforms are low to the ground and quite large, suggesting the beings who lived here possessed serpentine or slug-like bodies."

"Maybe they had stumpy little legs," said Gina.

Kerys grinned.

Don held his arms out. "The dimensions of this slab suggest a creature longer than its height, again like a snail, slug, or serpent. Assuming, of course, your theory of these being chairs of a sort is true."

"If these surfaces had regular contact with the aliens, there might be traces of DNA in the stone." Kerys took her hand off it.

"So, stone benches and stuff." Gina wandered over to one of the obelisks. "This kinda looks like Ancient Egyptian writing. Think your Atlanteans built the pyramids too?"

Paula groaned and bonked her helmet into the door.

Gina winked at Kerys. "What if all them stories are wrong? You know, all those sci-fi things where the humans are outgunned by real advanced aliens? What if *we're* the advanced civilization and the aliens are still learning how to make fire?"

"Then," said Lars, "the galaxy is fucked."

"How… eloquent," muttered Don.

Lars twirled his hand around, the actuators of his exo suit whirring, and rendered a formal bow.

"It's definitely an oddity." Kerys got up and wandered over to stand by Gina, leaning close to the obelisk to examine the symbols. "If our alien friends were slug-bodied, how did they cut writing on a twenty-foot-tall stone pillar? These markings look too precise to have been made with hand tools." She shivered with excitement. Visions of giving presentations at universities and interviews with the media flooded her thoughts.

"Maybe they had wings too," said Gina.

Marco laughed. "They might've been gaseous. Like living balloons.

Maybe they could float? Those slabs might've been landing pads instead of seats."

"The most obvious answer to that," said Kerys, "is they did the carving with the columns laid out horizontally, then lifted them into position. Or they had lifting platforms. Same way humans install lights on a twenty-foot ceiling."

"Kerys, why don't you help Paula catalog all the markings on those obelisks, generate some virtual tablets out of them. I'll start on a biomatter sweep of these... 'benches.'" Don opened a case and unpacked several boxes to get at something near the bottom.

"Sure." Kerys held her scanner up to the obelisk, focusing on an intricate glyph composed of swoops and whorls as thin as grass blades. According to the device, the pillar consisted of solid stone. The details within the carvings looked so perfect they appeared more like computer-generated graphics than a real object. "The markings do look laser etched. They're far too precise for hand tools... but I'm not reading any evidence of melting and recrystallization."

"Which suggests no heat," said Marco. "Maybe they weren't cave-aliens after all if they can manipulate matter like that."

Kerys grinned. "I think we're going to wind up being here longer than six months. This is big." For no other reason than already being close enough to reach, she hugged Gina. "This is what I've been hoping for ever since I graduated."

"Looks like these Atlanteans are an enigma." Marco started chuckling even before Paula gasped in frustration.

"How long are you going to insist on calling them that?" Paula stared at the ceiling.

"I dunno. How long is it going to get on your nerves?"

Kerys bit her lip to keep from laughing.

"Besides," said Marco, "Atlanteans sounds better than AV494-i-ans."

"I formally object to using that term in any documentation." Paula pointed at Don. "It's misleading and it's going to make people take our work less seriously."

Don looked up from a bench, the front of his helmet lit green in the glow of a mapping laser. "She has a point there. For brevity's sake, note them as UAS—unidentified alien species."

"Hey, why not Kerysians?" Marco snickered. "Give her some overdue credit."

She rolled her eyes. *First Will wants to name that flower after me, now this.* "Uhh, pass. Having a race of giant space slugs named after me isn't exactly flattering."

"We don't know they're slugs yet," said Don.

Laughter filled the comm for a few seconds.

She stared up at the obelisk. "Ellen, Lars, you guys have any scaffolding or ladders or something so I can reach the top of this thing?"

"Yeah, not here though." Ellen started for the exit. "Back in about twenty."

"Thanks," said Kerys.

Lars followed her out.

"The ladder's that heavy it takes both of you?" asked Kerys.

"No." Lars twisted back to look at her and pointed at Ellen. "Buddy system. It's against the rules for anyone to be alone while outside here."

"Oh. Okay. That makes sense."

Kerys retrieved a laser modeler from a case and opened a new, blank file. Recording the obelisks would likely involve assembling multiple separate sections into a single, large rendering. Despite facing days of tedious work, her body vibrated from the sheer thrill of it.

This is it. We're making history.

9

SPOOKED

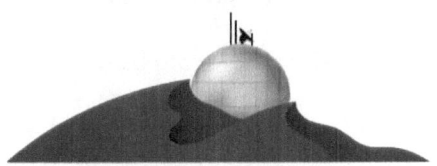

A little after eight that night, a machine spat out a portion of roast chicken cut into little cubes, mixed with mashed potatoes and gravy. Kerys carried her tray to a seat in a mostly empty cafeteria. Still flying on a wave of excitement, she proceeded to devour her meal as well as a pair of small rolls.

AV494 had no moon, which made the night hours pitch black, save for the occasional sparkle of starlight on the regolith. She gave up on the window and hurried her meal along, eager to get back to her quarters and start stitching 3D models together.

"Wow, what did they put in that?" asked Annapurna, from behind.

"Huh?" Kerys glanced back at her with half a mouthful.

Annapurna sat next to her on the bench, facing away from the table. "You're inhaling your food like it's going to be taken away from you." She smiled. "Glad to see you found an appetite."

"We made some promising discoveries today." She swabbed a dinner roll in the gravy mixture and took a big chomp out of it.

"Excellent. Speaking of discoveries, I wanted to give you an update on that 'head' you found."

"Mmm?" Kerys looked up, pausing in mid-chew.

"I found evidence of microbial life inside it. Petrified microorganisms. We're still attempting to verify their age, but the cells are long dead."

"Mmm!" Kerys rushed to swallow and wound up coughing. Once she collected herself, she rasped, "That's amazing... what were they? Bacteria? Plant cells?"

"The specimens are distorted due to being desiccated. It appears whatever species lived here previously might have sealed them in that object as a means of preservation, but I believe such a great amount of time has passed, even being encased in stone didn't protect them. I'm hopeful they were preserved enough it's possible for me to perform gene sequencing and build a digital model, simulating the organism's behavior in the computer to see how they may have looked and behaved while alive."

Kerys bounced. "Alien life..."

"Their structure is similar to single-celled organisms like amoeba, but it could be a form of algae as well. Perhaps you found something akin to a seed store."

"A what?" Kerys glanced down for a second to scoop more gravy on a roll.

"This organism or plant or whatever it is may have been a vital component of their existence, so they created a bunker in the mountainside to store it in case something cataclysmic happened."

"Oh. But there's that forest. Do you think this planet got wiped out?"

Annapurna smiled. "That's a little out of my wheelhouse, but Proxima Flora is the only major collection of biological life we've discovered here so far. Granted, we haven't touched the oceans yet. That's projected to start in about six years once we've exhausted terrestrial research."

"Proxima Flora?" asked Kerys with a hint of a chuckle. "Doesn't that basically mean 'nearby plants?'"

"That's the official name for the 'forest' north and west of us. It's about 270 miles from end to end and thirty-four miles across at its widest point. Thus far, we've documented 118 individual species of plant life, most of which have characteristics similar to fungus."

"Oh. You must be so excited to find something here that isn't a plant." Kerys grinned, dropping her fork on the empty tray. "I know I'm orbiting the moon at what we've found. I don't think I'm going to sleep much tonight."

Annapurna pursed her lips. "Yes, but..."

"What?" Kerys leaned closer.

"I shouldn't discuss it. There's already some improprieties going around. A rushed approval process, carelessness. Some samples were lost."

"Oh." Kerys grimaced. "Hope it wasn't too bad."

"Doctor Bhatia?" asked a younger man in a green jumpsuit, hanging in the cafeteria door. "Do you have a moment?"

Annapurna stood. "Be right there, Ethan." She smiled at Kerys. "Oh, just a small sample. I'm alarmed to have something go missing like that. None of my team knows what happened to it."

"Who would steal research samples?" Kerys blinked. "What would they do with them? Not like they can run off and sell it."

"That, my dear Kerys, is the question that's going to keep me up tonight." Annapurna sighed. "How's your situation?"

"Will?" Kerys shrugged. "I haven't seen him since. Going to work in my room tonight instead of the cube to stay out of sight."

"You have my EIN. Please comm if you need anything."

"Thanks." Kerys frowned at her empty plate. "I think I might spoil myself. There's a donut over there with my name on it."

STREAMS OF WARM WATER FLOWED OVER KERYS'S FACE AND DOWN HER BODY. She stood in one of eight shower stalls arranged around a circular room with a single drain in the middle. Partitions of hospital-white plastic separated each station, but didn't offer much cover. Most of the female staff tended to shower in the early morning before their shifts, which gave Kerys the room all to herself. She found it amusing how she'd avoided organized sports in college, mostly out of fear of group showers, and wound up stuck with that reality on Copernicus. Of course, the military would've been worse.

At least this place separates men and women into different bathrooms.

She spent a moment standing there enjoying the rinse before reaching for a bottle of cleansing gel set in a small recess. A small squeeze dispensed a portion of neon blue gel into her hand. The soft *clunk* of a locker door closing came from the only doorway out of the shower pod.

Damn. So much for having the room to myself.

"Hey," said Gina as she entered.

Kerys twisted left, putting her right arm—and the handprint Will left on it—out of sight nearer the wall. She smiled at Gina, who held eye contact for only a half-second before looking down with an expression like a child about to be scolded for doing something wrong.

The slender, dark-skinned woman didn't have the physique Kerys expected of a soldier, her limbs more sinewy than bulky. She crossed the room to the third stall on the right side, opposite from her, and turned on the water.

Kerys resumed washing herself, trying to stand such that Gina couldn't see her bruise. She rubbed the hand-shaped mark, scowling at the memory of Will grabbing her in the hallway because she dared to walk away when he 'hadn't finished talking' yet. *That* had been the man she left. She didn't at all trust 'nice Will' who'd showed up in her room.

Nice guys don't break into rooms. She shivered at the thought of lying naked in bed with him staring at her for hours. Who knows how long it had taken him to cover her with the blanket. Had he done that before or after taking pictures?

At feeling watched, she peered back. Gina seemed too casual.

Did she see the mark? Again Kerys covered it, ashamed of herself. The spike of humiliation faded in seconds, and she worked a lather into her hair. Moments later while rinsing her head, she caught a glimpse between her arm and body of Gina, who had turned to look at her.

Why is she watching me?

Kerys didn't react, continuing to run her fingers through her hair. *Do they suspect I'm trying to get back with Will? Do they think we're screwing?*

"I wish they'd give us something different. I'm so sick of this honeysuckle soap." Gina's voice echoed around the mostly empty shower room.

"Yeah," said Kerys into the wall. "I'm not sure I trust using the same soap for my hair as everything else."

Gina laughed. "Saving money wherever they can, right? This stuff is supposed to be good for hair."

Gina's reflection in a patch of light gleaming on the wall peered back for an uncomfortably long few seconds. Worry welled up in Kerys's gut. Though young, the other woman *was* part of the military detachment here. *They have separate living quarters and showers. Why is she in here?* Kerys felt like a random cop had decided to follow her, hoping to catch a misdeed.

Her eyes shot open wide. *Do they know about the flower? Someone found the towel!*

Kerys rushed the rest of her shower, skipping the washcloth and running soap over her body with her bare hands. When she turned to rinse her back, Gina startled, hurriedly turning away and again looking too innocent. Kerys kept her gaze on the floor, afraid if the younger woman stared into her eyes, she'd know all about the forbidden flower. Or maybe the people in charge here suspected her complaining about Will had been a cover to allow for them to break company policy. Will had seemed truthful when he claimed others in the outpost ignored that rule.

A slender foot stepped into her view, dark brown against the impossibly white floor.

Kerys's breath caught in her throat. She looked up at Gina, close enough to hug, holding an empty plastic bottle pinched between two fingers by the cap.

"Hey." Gina wiggled the bottle. "You done with the soap? I'm out."

"Uhh yeah." Kerys twisted around behind her, grabbed the bottle from the little cubby in the wall, and handed it over. "This one's almost new."

"Sorry." Gina bit her lip. "I didn't mean to make you uncomfortable. I'm used to the USIC barracks, fifty people in the same shower. Guys too. Kinda loses its awkwardness after a few months." Playfulness glinted in her large brown eyes. She tossed the near full bottle up a few inches and caught it. "Thanks."

"Sure."

Gina walked back to the stall she'd left running.

That's... odd. There are six other empty stalls with bottles... Kerys blinked. *She's... Oh.* Relief pushed the weight of guilt from her shoulders. *I'm not under investigation... she's got a crush on me.* She turned under the spray for a final rinse, debating mentioning the flower. If Gina *did* 'like' her in that way, a little bias in her favor might prevent Will from manipulating appearances. Question being, would it be worth the resulting crapstorm?

Nah. Just keep your head down, girl. Anything goes wrong it could cost you big again. She scowled at the smug grin Doctor Furroughs had given her when she realized they'd stolen the credit for her work. *That's not happening again. I will not let Will screw this up for me.*

She killed the water and hurried out to the adjacent locker area. After drying off, she slipped into a clean tee shirt and sweat pants.

Gina walked over to the locker area, her expression mostly neutral with a touch of disappointment.

"Sorry for running off so fast," said Kerys. "I've got *so* much work to do. We just found some writing in the dig site and it's all I can think about. My head is spinning."

"Oh, cool." Gina took a clean set of underwear from a bag but stood there holding them, smiling. "It say anything interesting?"

Kerys sighed out her nose. "That's what I'm hoping to find out."

"Right on." Gina stepped into her underwear and pulled them up, watching Kerys the whole time.

Not wanting to send the wrong message *or* hurt the woman's feelings, Kerys grumbled about having had so much work dumped on her, waved, and jogged back to her quarters. As soon as she got inside, she hit the button to lock it and stared at the small red screen on the control panel.

"This time, I *know* I didn't forget."

Kerys's dream of being interviewed about everything her team found on AV494 took on a surreal quality when the host's perfume grew overpowering. Purple mist poured out of the microphone. Reality blurred as she gagged on the taste of peaches. Everything went blank.

She squirmed in bed, fidgety and uncomfortable trying to sleep in sweat pants and a tank top. Not since she'd been in high school had she worn anything to bed, but after Will's surprise visit, she didn't feel secure enough to sleep nude here.

At the realization she'd awoken, she pushed herself up off the mattress ready for a fight. She gazed out at her room, but it remained empty of other people. The privacy screen over the window by the desk glowed grey, the sunlight strong enough to overwhelm the little blue LED at the base of her desk terminal. The clock read 6:52 a.m., eight minutes before the alarm would've gone off.

With a groan, she shifted around to sit on the edge of the bed and rubbed her eyes. The interviewer's perfume hung in the air, so strong she tasted peaches.

Kerys shifted her gaze to the clear plastic box. The flower stood exposed on the black square pedestal, the transparent shroud set aside next to it—open. Furious, she leapt to her feet and glowered at the door, but it still showed 'locked.'

"Did he do that before?"

She approached the desk, unable to recall if the flower had been uncovered when she returned from her shower. Again, she'd stayed up too late working on the 3D models of the obelisks, and didn't pay much attention to her room before crashing. Sporefall tinted only the black base lavender; none had spread beyond onto the desk.

"Asshole." She covered the flower, removed her T-shirt, and draped it over the box to hide it. "He thinks he's being cute, but it's seriously creepy."

A tingle spread over her sinuses for a few seconds. She froze, waiting to sneeze, but the sensation faded.

"Ugh. Please tell me I'm not getting sick." Her mind momentarily ran away with itself, feeding her a waking nightmare of alien mushroom spores growing in her sinuses, filling her skull with giant purple mushrooms. She shook her head to dispel the crazy thoughts. "Get a grip, girl."

She shoved her sweatpants to the floor and lifted them to her hand with a toe grip. *Should I ask Anna about this flower? I hope jackass isn't trying to hit me with a 'love potion.'* Fidgeting from nerves, she tossed the pants over the back of her chair and changed into a clean set of underwear and a fresh blue jumpsuit. Guilt grew stronger, dread over getting in trouble and losing everything she'd worked for. *I shouldn't tell anyone about this thing... yet.*

KERYS ENTERED THE CAFETERIA A LITTLE EARLY. A LIGHT CROWD POPULATED
the rows of tables with ample seating available between them. The only
familiar face, Marco, sat on the far-right end of a bench, his cast-
enshrouded leg stuck straight out into the aisle by the wall.

She collected two ladles of eggs, two sausage links, some toast, the
largest coffee available, and carried her feast across the room to sit near
him. Men and women paused in their conversations, staring at her as she
went by. Moods ranging from suspicion to overt hostility greeted her.
Kerys looked around, feeling like she'd walked into the wrong bar in the
wrong part of town.

"Hi... morning," she muttered randomly.

People continued glaring at her.

She scurried to Marco's side and climbed over the bench. "What's
going on?"

Marco shrugged. "Beats me. Caught a few snips here and there.
Captain Chen was screaming at her terminal last night, sending an angry-
ass message off to someone, but no one knows any details."

"Oh. I wonder what that's about." She stabbed at her eggs. "Has
everyone been glaring at you, too?"

He shrugged. "I dunno. Haven't really been noticing much but the
blinding pain in my foot. Thanks for that."

Kerys froze, staring at her food. "Umm."

Marco grunted, shifting his weight.

She glanced to her right. Sweat covered his forehead. "You know I'm
sor—"

"Stop apologizing. Bad enough you laid me up for days and I'm not
out there with the team; the whiny good girl thing isn't helping."

What's going on? Kerys slid her jaw side to side, thinking. Deciding
against making things worse, she slumped in place and ceased trying to
talk to him. She ate in silence for a while, Captain Chen's name rising out
of the murmuring around her every so often. It seemed rumors of the
commander being angry enough to scream had set the entire crew on
edge. Everywhere she looked, people glared at each other.

Eventually, she couldn't take the staring anymore. "What do you want
me to say?"

Marco cringed and massaged the bridge of his nose. "I'm... sorry. The
pain meds aren't doing anything for me and I'm just snapping at people.
It's not you. Can't seem to shake this bad mood. Every little thing is setting
me off—and I think someone gave me their cold too."

She managed a weak excuse for a smile. "You think we'll ever find a cure?"

"Nah." He dumped a jelly packet out on his toast and mashed it with a knife. "If it was curable, they'd have done it by now. Doctors don't even think anymore. Like everyone else, they just push goddamned buttons and let the damn computers do all the work."

Kerys leaned away from the hostility in his voice. She ate, content to avoid talking or making eye contact with anyone.

"Knock that shit off!" yelled a man three tables in front of her.

She snapped her head up. A tall, pale guy in a grey jumpsuit sprang to his feet, one hand gripping the shoulder of the crewman next to him, the other cocked back in a fist. They stared at each other for a few tense seconds before the bigger man seemed to forget what had annoyed him so much, and sat back down.

Soon, the murmuring resumed. The tone of simmering anger shifted toward confusion.

"Something's not right here," whispered Kerys.

"Yeah." Marco gestured at his leg. "My goddamned foot's busted."

She stared guilt into her eggs.

"At least it's Saturday and I won't be missing anything." He slugged down a quarter-mug of coffee in one gulp, clenching his jaw at the heat. "Doc thinks I'll be good to go Monday."

"Saturday?" She blinked. "So? They didn't care about weekends on Copernicus."

"Oh, sorry this isn't your fancy pants expedition." His lip curled in a sneer. "Maybe someone with your *prior experience* can work on a weekend if you want."

Will made her nervous, but the glint in Marco's eyes offered a peek at real violence, the way a man might look at her in a dark alley right before driving a knife into her heart. At his worst, Will had never given her such a frightening stare. The unbridled malice flickered away in a second.

She stiffened. "That's not... I mean... it's not like we can go anywhere."

"Ehh." He waved about dismissively. "It's all psychobabble stuff. We need time to recuperate. Normal people can't handle working seven days a week for six months."

Kerys let all the air leak out of her lungs in a slow sigh. "I suppose there's the holographic beach."

"Course, normal people don't spend three years as an ice cube on a fuckin' starship to come out here." Marco went to take another drink of coffee, found the mug empty, and glared at it. "Son of a—" He drew his arm back as if to throw the mug across the room, but changed his mind and pounded it onto the table. The slam brought silence to the din for a few seconds.

Kerys hurried the remainder of her breakfast and stood, still scooping eggs into her mouth. "Gotta check on something."

He muttered something she didn't catch and waved goodbye as she hurried past him.

OVERTIME

A middle-aged woman in a grey jumpsuit bearing the nametag 'Nakamura' glared at Kerys as they passed in the hallway. She shifted sideways from the intensity in the stare, expecting a sucker punch, but the maintenance worker kept going, shaking her head and grumbling to herself in Japanese.

Urgency hastened her stride; Kerys rushed to the office section in search of Annapurna. Moments later, she stopped at the woman's empty cube. Three unfamiliar men plus Christopher Mardling, all in green jumpsuits, stood in a group off to the right, staring at her, their expressions a mix of shock and disdain. She felt like a filthy vagrant walking into an exclusive restaurant.

"I'm looking for Anna… anyone know where she went?"

"Probably huffing more incense while listening to that racket she calls music. Like a pack of wailing cats." Chris turned away, focusing on his terminal again. "No bloody idea."

Two of the men continued glaring, leaning toward her as if on the verge of bodily removing her from their work area.

"Think she went to the lab," said the fourth man. His expression remained hostile, though his tone sounded confused. "Terminals are locked, by the way. There's nothing for you to snoop on."

Kerys raised her hands. "Hey, relax. I just want to talk to her. Why is everyone so moody today?"

"Because we're being bloody audited," yelled Chris. "Sod it. It's Saturday and we're stuck here combing over piles and piles of data."

"Sorry." She backed up. "I didn't know."

The Middle Eastern-looking man scowled at her. "Someone's real interested in the data about that cursed head you found. If you hadn't brought that thing inside, we'd all be relaxing."

"*She* should be doing this, not us," said a pale man.

"Sorry." Kerys darted out before the hostility level rose further.

She raced down the stairs to the ground level and cut across the dome, running past a handful of others. Most shot her dirty looks, three cowered away from her as if guarding the most valuable secret in the universe they didn't want her to see, and one older man screamed in terror at the sight of her, then took off running.

"What is going on?" Kerys paused to look around at everyone. No one offered anything beyond suspicious or hostile glowers, so she bowed her head and hurried along.

Near the south end of the dome, the corridor split left and right at a door labeled 'Battery Relay 2.' Arrows on the wall indicated a left turn went to the labs, while going right led to a storage pod and the primary power station. She headed for the labs. A short hallway connected to an interlock, where more of the semi-rigid hamster tubing linked the dome to the closer of the two external laboratory pods. The walkway bounced and clanked under her, making the whole tunnel undulate.

The tube bent around a ninety-degree turn and plugged into the west-facing wall of Lab Pod 1. Clear plastic didn't do much for her feelings of safety, but it did give her a nice view of a mild dust storm swirling around the area between the outpost and the excavation site. The tumult had enough density to block the mountains behind a thick charcoal-grey curtain. Bits of the regolith gathered in clusters like swarms of locusts, before falling away from the wind to pelt the metal shell of the lab pod in a surging hailstorm.

Kerys hurried to the end and mashed the button on the wall to the right of the hatch, eager to escape the plastic tube that felt so much like a deathtrap under a rain of daggers. Much to her relief, it opened. She ducked into a hallway with gleaming white walls separated by long sections of window that looked in on laboratories. Some contained simple tables and desks, small pieces of scientific equipment arranged among them. Others had elaborate machines she didn't recognize, as well as huge devices with armholes and robotic hands inside sealed chambers to allow technicians to work with dangerous substances.

Whoa. What are they doing here?

She jogged forward, swiveling her head side to side at each window. About halfway down the hundred-meter-long pod, the hallway pulled a ninety-degree right, becoming an alcove with a break room and two bathrooms. South, a passage led to a link ring where a hamster tube connected to Lab Pod 2. Another corridor continued east, passing between three large labs on the left side and a handful of small workstation rooms on the right.

From the break room, she spotted Annapurna in the center lab on the left. She appeared to be in panic mode, walking back and forth with a hand in her hair. A Chinese man she hadn't seen before, Will, and two pale women stood around her. Will seemed amused, though the other three had the hangdog expressions of employees about to be written up or fired by their boss.

Kerys ducked back into the break room before Will looked in her direction.

Shit! What's he doing there? She balled her hands into fists, feeling stupid. *Duh. He works on her team. Dammit!* She couldn't discuss the flower with her right in front of him. *I'll find her later.* Defeated, she trudged across the lab and returned to the dome. The view of the landscape outside from the hamster tube made her entertain the idea of going out to the site alone in defiance of Saturday, but by the time she'd made it halfway to the locker room, she remembered Lars talking about the 'buddy system.'

After dropping the head on Marco's foot, she didn't want to get in trouble for breaking rules. Especially with the contraband flower in her room. Anything Will could use to allege a pattern of bad conduct would bite her in the ass.

Fuming, she stormed down the hall to the fitness center. Hideous red-orange floor covered a room shaped like one-quarter of a pie, filled with various exercise stations, some lockers, and two private shower rooms. Swirling dust blanketed the world outside the giant, curved window along the outer wall, exacerbating the sense of being 'trapped in a box.'

Unexpected sponginess underfoot made her look down at a strip of rubbery black. A two-lane wide jogging track ran around the perimeter. Two women and three men using treadmills, free weights, and a stationary bike gave her cursory glances as she walked in, going back to what they'd been doing without any odd behavior. They paid her little mind as she took a water bottle from a cooling cabinet and headed over to a padded bench by a rack of small dumbbells and a pull-up bar.

After stretching out for a while, Kerys jumped up to grab the bar. Three years of cryo had an effect, and she managed only five before she couldn't pull herself up again. She took a seat on the bench and used a six-pound hex dumbbell to keep her arms moving. Three sets of fifteen with each arm later, she drank a few mouthfuls of water and headed for one of the treadmills, hoping a light jog would keep her mind from wandering into dark territory. She'd loved running while in school, almost enough to try out for the track team, but that whole organized sports locker room thing had embarrassed her away from the idea.

Granted, back home, jogging also included fresh air and sunlight.

She closed her eyes and settled into a rhythmic stride. In her mind's eye, she pictured the streets around her mother's house. Imaginary sunlight warmed her face, and the *thump thump thump* of her shoes on the treadmill blended with her heartbeat. Neighbors walked by, waving. That coppery-colored dog that always ran after her for two blocks zipped out from between parked cars and gave chase once again. White-glowing e-cars cruised by, so silent she never heard them coming and jumped every time one passed.

Thump, thump, thump. She picked up speed, throwing her consciousness into the daydream, away from this place, away from Will. Her run took her past a small enclosure where tweens played baseball. The glowing orb never left the boundary of the park, steering itself to the ground whenever someone hit it too hard. Kerys cornered left, ducking a low-hanging branch in front of the little coffee shop she'd gone to every day from junior year of high school until she'd left Earth.

When she ran past it, Mrs. Finlay, the owner, gave her a bewildered look. At least she imagined the aging hippy would've given her such a look if she went by without going in. The flavor of their coffee, and the woman's handmade chocolate biscotti came to mind. Kerys got homesick out of nowhere, a feeling that worsened when she took the final left turn back onto her street and saw her ten-year-old brother waiting on the porch for her.

As soon as Jaden waved, she opened her eyes, returning to Wayfarer Outpost. Kerys slapped the console to stop the treadmill and hopped off, lightly winded and pleasantly sore from head to toe. After a series of cool-down stretches, she finished off the water and glanced at the shower stall. She hadn't planned on working out and doing so in her jumpsuit left her feeling sticky.

Kerys refilled her bottle and took a seat near the giant window to watch the dust storm. She swished water around, sipping it slowly to avoid brain freeze, letting her heart rate fade back to normal. Looking at the clock—barely past eleven—annoyed her even more. *Ugh. This is such a waste of time to be sitting around doing nothing.* She flicked her nail at the bottle, debating how much trouble she'd get in for going outside alone.

Shouting echoed out of a ventilation duct nearby in the ceiling, too distant and distorted to make out specific words aside from a random curse every so often. The others in the fitness center looked up with confusion and unease on their faces. The yelling faded in a few seconds, and the other people resumed exercising.

Screw this. I need to get out of here.

She sucked down the last of the water and stood. Before she could take a step, a tall man with a flattop afro stormed in, heading for a weight bench. His random grumbling gave way to a long, malicious stare as soon as he locked eyes with Kerys. He slowed his stride, giving her a look that made her want to run out of the room as fast as possible.

The man pulled his glare away only after reaching the weight bench. He slammed metal discs into place on a bar, banging the equipment around and startling everyone else in the room to silence. Kerys crept back to the stand of hex dumbbells and grasped one of the small six-pounders. No one seemed to notice, so she kept it tight to her chest and hurried out. The way everyone had been giving her the evil eye all morning, she felt better having solid metal in her hand.

She clung to the weight like the handle of Excalibur while creeping from hallway to hallway on her way to the lockers by the garage airlock. Almost everyone she passed, regardless of the color of their jumpsuit, shot her nasty looks as if she'd somehow offended them. A woman in a yellow hydroponics uniform kept getting in other people's faces, as if itching to start a fistfight.

The one man who didn't give her a dirty stare appeared ready to collapse. He couldn't have been forty yet, but walked in the hunched posture of an elderly man. She approached, but he waved her off with a weary smile.

"Headin' to my quarters. Stay the heck back unless you want Flu-zilla too."

She avoided him and hurried down the remaining length of hallway to the ready room. Perhaps a flu or cold had been going around and the people who'd been here for a few years blamed the newcomers for introducing it. That would certainly explain the annoyed glares, but not the outright *malice* in some. Head down, she dodged eye contact and rounded the corner into the ready room.

Don hummed merrily to himself while suiting up across the room from her locker.

"Don?" Kerys opened her locker and set the chrome-plated weight on the top shelf next to her helmet.

"Oh, hello there." He smiled back at her.

"You're suiting up?"

"Too much to do, no interest in any of the movies they have." He shrugged. "Guess I'm a workaholic."

"What about that 'buddy system'?" She sat on the bench and traded her low-top sneakers for boots.

"You're here. I suppose that renders the issue moot." He chuckled.

"Yeah. I suppose it does." After tossing her 'inside shoes' in the locker, she put on her military-style boots, stepped into her e-suit, and eased the metal neck ring over her head.

Don walked up behind her and helped secure the fasteners. After giving each one an exploratory tug to confirm it had closed, he turned to let her return the favor. Neither spoke as they put on their helmets, checked seals, and headed out via the airlock. It struck her as odd seeing only two names in the comm list, but with all the strangeness going on inside, the quiet calm would be welcome.

"May as well take one quad. I don't think those things like me." Don gestured at one of the four-wheelers. "If you don't mind."

"It's fine." She climbed on, waited for him to mount behind her, and hit the power button.

Driving in the dust storm with only about thirty feet of visibility tested her nerves, but the downward slope and artificial lights in the fog ahead helped guide her to the ridge. She stopped a few paces from the door and shut the quad down.

"You're getting better at driving these things." Don patted her shoulder and climbed off. "Almost didn't seem like you were frightened."

Kerys laughed. "Thanks... I needed that. I never did like driving in bad weather, though California rain has nothing on this place."

Don led the way into the alien site, but paused to open one of the large cases in the first chamber. She headed straight back to the obelisk she'd been working on when they'd made her call it a night on Friday. Lars had positioned a two-story tall portable scaffold by it, which made reaching the upper end a simple matter of climbing a ladder to a raised platform. She wasted no time resuming the 3D imaging where she left off.

"Has Paula had any luck figuring out what any of these characters mean?"

"If she has, I haven't heard about it," said Don, "but she does seem to be quite occupied with the effort. Hasn't answered any of my emails today."

Kerys turned at a loud clatter by the entrance. It bothered her that Paula ignored Don, and Marco went from being all smiles and 'don't worry about it' to angry with her for dropping the head on his foot.

Don hummed and whistled like an old farmer tending his field. He left the chamber for a few minutes, returning with a pole mounted device in one hand and a case of electronics in the other, which he set up by the door they hadn't yet opened. "Figured I'd give this thing a whirl while I scrape the slabs for DNA."

"What is it?" Kerys resumed scanning, staring at the handheld's screen, showing the obelisk's surface rendering in 3D. The hardest part of the work entailed keeping it steady enough not to ruin the composite image.

"A deep penetration imager. Ultrasound resonance. It should be able to give us an idea of what's on the other side of that door. Basically, it is a larger version of what you were using the other day."

"Oh. It's so weird being on a team that has a real budget."

He chuckled.

She kept working for a while, tuning out the muttering and clattering of Don setting up the imager. Eventually, he left it to run and resumed examining the 'benches' with a handheld unit. They worked through lunch without stopping, Kerys losing herself in the joy of discovery and the anticipation of what their work could mean for them, for science, and maybe even for humanity as a whole.

After finishing her scan of the northeast obelisk, she climbed down from the scaffold, sat on the steps, and frustrated herself trying to type with two thumbs on the little device in an effort to email herself the files. Once they went back inside, she planned to spend the rest of the day piecing the scan data together into a rendered model. That would allow Paula to study the entire obelisk at once in VR from the comfort of a desk.

"Argh!" She leaned back and growled at the fifth 'invalid address' error.

"Kerys?" asked Don.

"I can't type in these gloves…" She laughed, let out a playful growl, and corrected the typo. "There!"

The ultrasonic unit by the door chirped.

Don ambled over to it. She stood, clipped the 3D scanner to her belt, and tried to drag the scaffold across the room to the northwest obelisk, but it refused to budge.

Damn. Gonna need Lars or Ellen to move it for me. Crap. She glanced to the northwest, then to the southeast where Paula had been doing the scan. *Wonder how far she got?*

"Oh, look at this." Don beckoned her closer with a wave.

"Hmm?" She hurried to his side, huddling close to peer at a display screen inside the armored case on the floor next to the pole.

The system showed a 3D wireframe of the space beyond the door. Eight structures lined the left and right walls. Details remained blurry, though the overall shape suggested pads or tanks with an adjacent pedestal.

"Hmm. Those look like stations." Kerys stooped lower to the screen. "Do you think this could've been some kind of hospital?"

"I suppose it's possible. To our way of thinking, the setup does bear similarities to a bunch of auto-surgeons for massive beings. Then again, we don't know what these creatures really looked like." He laughed. "Maybe those are office cubes."

Kerys smirked. "I thought they were supposed to be more advanced than us."

"You've a wonderful sense of humor. I'm glad you decided to take the position." Don fiddled with a slider bar on the touchscreen, zooming the image in and out a few times before rotating it. "I'm afraid taking guesses based on this information isn't going to get us anywhere. We'll still need to get that door out of our way."

"Yeah." She stared at the image drawn in yellow-on-grey lines. "Not sure we can manage that ourselves."

"I don't know. That excavator isn't too heavy. They've even got a portable power cell." He stood and faced the door."

Kerys straightened. "Have you noticed people acting odd today?"

"Hmm? Oh. Can't say I have." He stepped over the case and approached the door, jabbing his finger at the pictograms. "Damn this miserable hunk of rock. How did you get those buttons to light up? These aren't working."

"Those aren't buttons. They're just carvings."

"Well, then they're useless." He picked up the excavator laser. "Stand back, Kerys. This door needs to come down."

"Whoa, Doctor Bouchard." She ran over and grasped his arm. "Why don't we wait for the rest of the team to be here? Leave the cutting to the pros."

He whirled toward her with a penetrating stare that threatened to melt the thin layer of fog on his visor.

"Doctor? You don't like cutting up dig sites. The laser might go straight through the door and destroy something irreplaceable."

"Oh…" The extreme focus in his eyes evaporated; after a few seconds of bewildered blinking, he looked down at the excavator. "You're right. Hmm. I suppose some of your youthful enthusiasm has rubbed off on me."

I have to be dreaming. Is everyone *going crazy?* She patted him on the back. "Right. I'll, uhh, get started on the base of the other obelisk. Are you going to finish checking the benches for DNA?"

"I need to do that." He put the laser down and scratched at his helmet. "How did I forget I hadn't finished it? We're not even ready to go into the next chamber. There's still so much work left to do in here."

She stood like a statue, watching him retrieve the handheld and return to the wide stone slabs lining the sides of the room. *Something's not right.*

Don resumed humming and seemed like his usual self after a few minutes.

Kerys stepped over wires on her way to the northwest obelisk. She glanced at Don, half-expecting to see him going for the laser again, but he remained content to hunt for scraps of biomatter on the stone. After opening a blank file, she took a knee and started the scan.

"This is going to be a *long* weekend."

OFF LIMITS

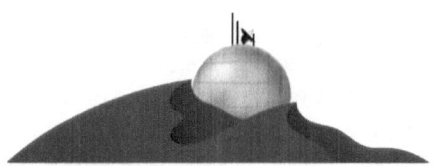

B uzzing dragged Kerys out of a heavy sleep. She groaned, rolled onto her back, and huffed to blow hair off her face. Overcome with fatigue, she rested her arm across her forehead and tried to silence the alarm with sheer force of will. It took a few minutes to summon the energy to move, despite Monday morning beckoning her to work. The irritating buzz-chirp hammered her brain, causing the beginnings of a nasty headache to pulse in time with the electronic audio assault. Kerys sighed, and her nose filled with the scent of peaches and lavender.

"Dammit, Will. Now I *know* you broke into my room."

Kerys flung the blanket to the side, further irritated by having to wear a shirt to bed. She'd skipped the sweat pants, relying instead on her underwear for modesty in case of 'Creepy Will'. The air hit her like a blast of ice, startling a gasp out of her and setting her teeth chattering. In seconds, her throbbing sinuses unleashed a waterfall of snot from her nostrils.

"Ugh... shit." She swung her legs over the edge, took a breath, and stood.

Sure enough, the lamiaceae advena had been uncovered once more. She stormed over to the desk for a tissue. After blowing her nose, she, mashed the alarm to silence it, then placed the clear box over the flower before sweeping the case up in both hands. For a few seconds of manifest rage, smashing it into the wastebasket felt tempting, but she hesitated.

Someone will find that in the trash and start asking questions.

She set it back on the desk and covered it with a shirt again. Will had been in her room, and she knew beyond any doubt she'd locked the door last night. She'd spent all of Sunday in her quarters except for off-hour trips to the cafeteria to grab meals. Thinking of him in here with her while she slept got her blood boiling.

I should be freaking out, scared out of my mind. She scowled. *Is that what he wants?*

Kerys paced around for a few steps, sniffling to test how stuffy her head had become. *This is a 'call out sick if I have something fun to do at home' kind of cold.* Sniff. *Not that bad.* She peeled off her T-shirt, wiped her face with it, and changed into clean underwear and a fresh jumpsuit. The scent of lavender and peach saturated the fabric.

"Son of a bitch." She held her arms out, staring down at her outfit, but couldn't find any trace of violet spores. "What is he doing? Oh, the hell with it. People will think I'm wearing perfume or its body wash."

Too angry to think straight, Kerys stormed out of her room and headed to the cafeteria. The ground floor of the residence pod smelled like soap and steam, likely from the twenty or so people trying to cram themselves into eight stalls to shower in the morning. She disregarded an argument echoing out from the bathrooms that reminded her of an eighth-grade locker-room fight.

Midway along the hamster tube connecting the residence pod to the dome, a man in a green jumpsuit leaned against the wall, bowed forward and coughing. When she passed him, he snapped his head up, glaring at her with bloodshot eyes. Wild light brown hair sprayed in all directions. Sweat dripped from his nose, and every breath came wheezy and dry.

"Chris?" She blinked. "Chris Mardling?"

He covered his mouth before coughing phlegm onto his fingers. "The bloody feck do you want?"

"Uhh…" She backed up.

"Go on then. I'm *sick,* unless you haven't noticed. I—" He lapsed into a coughing fit, spraying dark yellow glops on the wall. "What're you starin' at then? Sod off."

Kerys darted forward into a jog, racing past the dome entrance and crossing the open area beyond to the cafeteria. What had Captain Chen been upset about? *Did everyone else in this place but me get some bit of horrible news that put them in a shitty mood?*

She stopped at the entrance to the cafeteria, preparing herself to witness Armageddon upon walking in. The low murmur inside worried her with its normality. *Huh? Maybe I'm the one who's stressing out.*

A peek past the wall revealed a room packed with Avasar employees. People gathered in clusters of similar-color jumpsuits. Her team, the only blue in the room, collected about halfway in near the right side. All the little round tables by the windows were full. Everyone seemed to be absorbed in their breakfast or muttered conversations. She caught snippets on her way to the automats from people discussing work projects as though nothing at all unusual had occurred over the weekend. Even the freakishly tall man who'd stared at her in the fitness center like he'd wanted to tear her head off appeared to be laughing at something the woman next to him said.

Opting for French toast instead of the scrambled eggs she'd had three days straight, Kerys collected a tray of food, grabbed a coffee, and headed over to sit between Paula and Corporal Guillen.

"Morning."

Guillen muttered past a full mouth, nodding. Paula gave her a weary 'I don't want to be awake right now' look.

Don slurped up a spoonful of oatmeal before smiling. "Good morning, Kerys. Hope you're ready to get back to it."

"Yeah." While dumping syrup from a small plastic packet on her French toast, she eyed the people at the next table over. At least half of them looked exhausted, but no one acted strange. "Where's Marco?"

"Infirmary," said Paula, sounding half-awake. "He mentioned something about the pain in his leg getting worse."

"I thought Doctor Sekhar said he should be walking again by now?" Kerys attacked her meal like she hadn't eaten in days.

"Whoa." Corporal Guillen grinned. "What, you have a normal meal once every winter solstice or something?"

"Is that necessary?" asked Don in a raised voice. "You know it's impolite to criticize a woman's figure."

Paula glanced up at the unexpected tone. "Don, I don't think he meant anything by it."

"No... I'm happy for her," said Corporal Guillen. "Past couple times I've seen her eating, she's barely touched her food. Must be feeling better."

Kerys chuckled and sniffled. "Got a little bit of a cold I think."

"Me too, and more than a little bit of one." Paula massaged her sinuses. "Worst headache I've ever had."

"I saw Chris back in the tube." Kerys stuffed a wad of French toast in her mouth. Everyone waited for her to chew. "Mmf. He looked really bad. Severe flu bad."

"Problem with a contained environment like this. We're all breathing the same air and there's nowhere to go." Corporal Guillen sipped water. "One person gets sick, we're all going to share it."

"And for the record"—Kerys stabbed another piece of toast on her fork —"I don't have an eating disorder. I just have no appetite when I'm nervous. What we're finding out there is beyond any expectation I could've dreamed up. I'm thrilled."

"Dammit," yelled Lars, two tables away and to the left. "Why is everyone so damn loud? I've got the worst damned headache."

Ellen, sitting next to him, glared a challenge at people nearby. She gripped the table, her lips curling into a snarl.

Am I imagining this? Kerys eyed the tall, muscular woman wearing a Hello Kitty amulet and whispered, "Does anyone else notice people acting odd?"

"I've been too busy to really watch people." Don scraped the last of his oatmeal from the bowl to his mouth.

Paula sat with her face resting in her hands, muttering.

"Seems like people are getting short with each other," said Corporal Guillen. "Right after that rumor started going around about the captain sending a nastygram back to Earth."

Well, I was thrilled. Since Lars yelled, the tone of the cafeteria simmered in silent discontent. The more she looked around at people glaring at each other, the more she wanted to get out of there before a spark lit off an explosion. "Once they move that platform, I'll be able to finish scanning Obelisk C today."

"I found something on the slab," said Don, "Sent it to the bio people for analysis. It might've been moss or lichen. I don't think it was alien skin cells, but who knows." He stood.

His motion sent a wave of fidgeting over the crowd, spreading outward like a ripple across a pond that continued all the way to the walls. Kerys inhaled the last few pieces of her French toast and hurried to toss the tray in the collection bin on her way to follow her team out. No one spoke on the walk down the tube to the ready room near the garage.

Don, Paula, Lars, Ellen, and Private Foster went to the lockers holding their e-suits.

"Hey Foster… where's Gina?" asked Kerys.

He spun around and grabbed her jumpsuit, hauling her off her feet and shoving her back against the steel doors. "Why? What the hell do you care? We're just fuckin' grunts to you. Why's Miss College askin' about dumbass soldiers?"

Kerys screamed.

Don stomped. "Young man. Put her down!"

Lars chuckled and muttered something, which caused Ellen to growl and push him into the lockers.

Foster leaned close, bloodshot eyes wide and vibrating with rage. His lips curled back, exposing teeth; a trickle of blood ran from his lip. She grabbed his wrists as his knuckles dug in to her chest. Lars growled and took a swing at Ellen, who flung open her locker door to block. The *bang* of his fist denting the steel door startled Foster. He threw Kerys aside and pulled a knife from his belt, facing Lars and Ellen.

Kerys scurried away from him and ran to her locker to grab the little six-pound dumbbell she'd left there on Saturday. She spun to put her back to the wall, clutching her 'weapon.' Everyone else froze, watching Lars and Ellen.

"Goodbye, kitty." Lars swung a left-handed haymaker at her face.

Ellen ducked and lunged, tackling him flat. They rolled over twice, Lars winding up on top. He drew his fist back, but she shoved with her leg, hurling him face-first into the lockers before he could swing down on her.

"Knock it the fuck off right now," bellowed a deep, authoritative voice.

Sergeant Gensch, half-in an e-suit, stood at the entrance of the ready room with Corporal Guillen right behind him.

"What in the shit-eating hell is going on?" Gensch set his hands on his hips, glaring at Lars.

Ellen snarled.

"Don't think I won't knock you senseless either." He pointed at her. "I'm an equal opportunity asshole. This is my station and you shit-slingers are going to keep a modicum of order here, or there's going to be a giant goddamned problem."

"She thinks we're worthless," yelled Foster, pointing at Kerys.

Gensch shifted his eyes toward her.

"All I did was ask him where Corporal Mitchell was. She usually goes out with our group."

"Mmm." Gensch advanced into the room. His white brush cut seemed to glow from the LED bulb above him. "Wanna try that one again, Foster?"

"She... she..." Private Foster leaned against the lockers, head back, arms slack at his sides. "I dunno. Just the way they all look at us, Sarge. You know they think we're just dumbass meatheads who couldn't get a real job."

Ellen picked herself up from the floor, gaze locked on Sergeant Gensch.

"Come on, do it." Gensch leaned at her, chin thrust forward. "You want to ride this train, you go right ahead, but make damn sure you can afford the ticket." When she made no move, he gave her a smirk of casual dismissal and looked around at everyone else. "The lot of you need to unfuck whatever the hell's going on here, and do it right now."

"Everyone just calm down," said Corporal Guillen.

Paula fell into a swoon on the bench, a hand to her face. Seconds later, she collapsed to the floor. Kerys clung to the dumbbell, wanting to run to her side, but the woman had landed right next to Private Foster. The young soldier looked down at the unconscious woman and laughed.

"Oh, dear." Don took a knee and checked Paula's pulse. "She's fainted."

Sergeant Gensch pointed at Lars and Ellen. "You two. Quarters, now."

"Attention all personnel." Captain Chen's voice came over the PA system. "Until further notice, I am suspending operations outside Wayfarer Outpost. Everyone is to remain inside at this time. Repeat, no personnel are to go EVO."

Kerys looked up at the ceiling. "What? Can she do that?"

"She just did," said Corporal Guillen, with a subtle shake of the head. "Somethin' ain't right."

"You're just noticing that now, shithead?" snapped Lars.

Paula sat up. "Alan? Where's Alan?"

"Who is Alan?" asked Kerys.

"My son. He was... Oh." She rubbed her forehead. "I was dreaming."

Don looked at Kerys. "Help me get her to the infirmary?"

"I don't need to go to the infirmary, Don. I've got a magnitude-nine migraine and got light-headed. I do think I'm going to take the day off and rest."

"We're all taking the day off." Kerys squeezed the dumbbell, her gaze jumping from person to person. Hiding in her quarters with the door locked seemed like a wonderful idea.

Sergeant Gensch grabbed Foster by the chest of his jumpsuit, pulled him close, and swiped the sidearm from his holster. "Get your ass to Doctor Veltmann."

"I ain't fuckin' nuts, Sarge. I don't need a goddamn head shrinker."

"Well, *private*... if Doc V tells me that, then I'll believe it." Gensch loomed over the smaller man. "Now, you can walk there, or I can kick your insubordinate ass down the hall, up the stairs, and straight into his room."

Private Foster's expression shifted from sheepish to angry to murderous and back to sheepish. "Copy that, Sarge." He hung his head and trudged out.

"I'm going to my quarters." Paula stood with Don's help.

"Oh, grand." Don smiled. "Suppose we should get back to work then."

"Don?" Kerys looked up at him. "Haven't you been listening? Captain Chen shut down all outside work. We can't go outside."

"Oh. I wonder why." He blinked. "Hmm. I think I'll go have some tea." He walked off, back in the direction of the cafeteria.

Corporal Guillen twisted to watch Don as he went by. When he faced the room again, he seemed about to say something, but turned his attention to Paula instead. "Do you need assistance, ma'am?"

She groped blindly at him until she found his arm, grabbed it, and nodded. "Thank you... I just need to get to my quarters."

Kerys pushed her locker closed and stood there while everyone else left. "Oh, please tell me this is some kinda twisted dream." The empty ready room offered a sense of comfort compared to the idea of crossing the station and running into other people. She glanced up at the airlock doors, picturing the excavation site a little more than half a mile away. All her hopes and dreams hung on what they might find in there, but amid the inexplicable craziness, the luster had faded.

Gripped by the claws of homesickness and regret, she stared at the hallway, too frightened of what might happen to her if she ran into any people. *I can't just stand here all day.* Eyes closed, she took a few deep breaths until determination overpowered fear.

Kerys ran back to her quarters, refusing to make eye contact with anyone.

CABIN FEVER

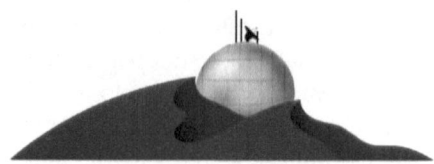

Fear had lessened to worry before evolving into boredom a few hours after Kerys locked herself in her room. To occupy her mind away from whatever chaos spread over the outpost, she tucked close to her desk and pulled up her completed 3D model of Obelisk A. While the pictographic writing remained a total mystery as to meaning, comparing them with images from the Copernicus site convinced her the same species existed in both places.

The obelisk character forms differed in minute ways, suggesting a refinement over many years. Or perhaps they had been made by a machine, like putting handwriting next to a printout. *Could those obelisks have been mass-produced?* She brought up the partial scan she'd gathered of Obelisk C, about eighty percent of the base to as high as she could extend her arms. The fragment on the screen looked like an ancient bracelet, a hollow C with uneven sides.

She spent a while positioning it side by side with the other obelisk, but couldn't match the symbols.

"They're not identical... so it's got to be one long message. But which one is first?"

A heavy *thud* shook the pod seconds before angry shouting echoed in the ventilation duct. Kerys reached a hand toward the desk, curling her fingers around the dumbbell while staring at the slatted hole in the wall to her left. The screaming tapered off to indistinct muttering and silence.

Why did Chen lock down the outpost? Keeping everyone inside is going to make it worse. Pressure builds.

Kerys exhaled, listening to silence for another minute before releasing her grip on the steel weight. Staring at meaningless pictograms twisted a knot of frustration in her gut. She could be sitting on information capable of changing the course of human history, but not even Paula had been able to make sense of it yet.

She switched screens and opened the SFT message client to compose a video to Jaden. Wearing a smile and trying to conceal her nerves, she told him about the exciting stuff she'd found so far. The enthusiasm leaked out of her voice a few minutes in, and she looked down with a sigh.

"Look, kiddo. I'm... I wanted to apologize. I know you've been nothing but supportive about this whole thing, but maybe it was selfish of me to disappear out of your life for so long. I know, too little too late, right? By the time I get back, you'll be halfway through high school... not a kid anymore."

An angry scream leaked from the vent again.

That is, if I get back... She closed her eyes. *Don't think like that. People are just stressed out.*

"Anyway... How's life treating you, li'l bro? Tell me what's going on back home, huh?" She winked. "Almost out of time on this message... so I'll talk to you again soon."

She tapped the button to stop recording and confirmed sending. The screen estimated the message would arrive on Earth in twenty-nine days and some hours. Staring at that large number, despite it being remarkably fast for such a distance, made her feel even more isolated.

"I'm an idiot." She curled over the desk, head down on crossed arms, and sighed. What good was finding alien relics that could inscribe her name in the history books if everything died here with her? She thought about a story she'd read in college, an explorer who'd found a fortune of gold in the jungle, but got trapped in the vault with it. For a few days, he'd become the richest man in the world, but all that wealth didn't help him survive.

As tears formed in her eyes, she sucked in a breath and sat up straight. "Okay. Stop. Fear is the mind killer and all that. You're overreacting." She sniffled, coughed, and wiped her cheeks. "At least I'm not getting sicker." A sigh triggered two sneezes. Kerys grabbed a tissue and blew her nose.

Plum-colored snot made her squeak in surprise.

"T-that's not blood." She cringed, staring at it. Once her initial revulsion wore off, she leaned closer to the tissue, studying the mucous close. She sniffed at the air, but her stuffed-up nose couldn't smell anything. Her glare fell on the boxed plant, which remained sealed. *Great. I've got sinuses full of spores.*

She twisted in the chair to look at the door. *I should go to the infirmary and get that checked.*

Of course, visiting the doctor would require leaving the safety of a locked door in a remote outpost full of people snapping at the slightest provocation. She changed her mind and opened the 3D scan of the alien head. Her attention gravitated to the grapefruit-sized hollow at its center. Could it have been some kind of seed vault like Annapurna theorized? The hollow could have been accidental and maybe those microbes got in unbeknownst to the aliens. No mention of a container existed in the notes. If the aliens deliberately stored a sample of something, wouldn't they have put it in a bottle?

"Get outta my face!" shouted a woman somewhere outside. A dull *thump* struck the wall seconds later.

Heavy footfalls raced past her door.

Kerys grabbed the dumbbell again. An eruption of sincere regret at her decision to take this job blossomed into a crippling abdominal cramp. She doubled over, arms braced across her gut, moaning. The room spun under a wave of dizziness, and a dull headache started at the back of her skull. After a few minutes of rocking herself while sipping air between her teeth, the sensation of a spiked ball in her stomach changed to simple (but strong) nausea. She traded the dumbbell for the wastebasket and put her face over it, expecting to have French toast fly out of her nose any second.

"I hate being sick…"

She took air in shallow, even breaths for a little while more. Eventually, the imminence of vomiting retreated. Prickles and jabs in her gut continued, fanning the fires of worry.

"Okay, screw it. I gotta see the doc."

With the six-pound weight in hand, she crept up to the door and examined the hexagonal nugget on the end of the dumbbell. *This'll hurt someone.* She took a few slow-motion practice swings against an imaginary attacker. Years had passed since she'd attended any self-defense classes, and none of the instructors ever introduced weapons. Mashing a blunt object into someone didn't seem like the most complex self-defense technique out there, so she decided to risk it.

I can do this. Just keep walking. Don't make eye contact.

She put her finger on the slider to unlock her room, for a second feeling as if the button could kill her. Forehead against steel, she listened at the door for a while. Distant voices continued to shout here and there from people arguing. A surge of pain in her stomach doubled her over with a loud groan.

"Ugh. Right. I can do this."

Click.

Kerys stepped into a hallway devoid of people, but littered with bits of clothing, small appliances, and one teddy bear. It looked as though her neighbors had gotten into a war of throwing things at one another. After locking her quarters behind her with a badge scan, she clutched the dumbbell tight to her chest and hurried to the right.

An unconscious man lay face down at the bottom of the ladder between floors. She gripped the side rails and slid down, careful to avoid stepping on him. A little blood leaked from his nose and mouth, but not so much she worried for his life. She started to stoop to check on him, but the sudden fear he'd attack her if he woke made her back off.

Fear worsened the sour feeling in her stomach. She pressed her left hand to her belly and jogged down the hall to the hamster tube linking Residence Pod 2 to the dome. Angry screaming emanated from the closed door to Residence Pod 1. Without looking, she ran past it. Three men loitering in the open area between the tube connection and the cafeteria shifted to face her and started walking toward her, muttering.

She didn't even look at them, picking her pace up from jog to run, and flew into the stairwell some forty feet away. More shouting echoed out from the second floor, someone arguing about a misplaced e-pad, convinced his friend stole it. Kerys swung around the landing and took steps two at a time to the third floor. Hurrying to the infirmary, she peered left and right in the windows of offices and the command room, finding all the desks empty. Most of the chairs in the control center lay askew. She pictured Sergeant Gensch and other soldiers storming in like cops breaking up a bar fight.

This is seriously getting freaky now.

It didn't occur to her until she set foot in the infirmary corridor that with so many people getting sick, she might've been heading into a crowd —but much to her surprise, the medical area looked abandoned. Large windows revealed no one in any of the beds in the recovery room. *Where's Marco?* She crept forward a few steps, enough for Doctor Sekhar's desk to slide into view on the left.

Kerys stared through her reflection on the giant window at the empty chair, glowing in flickering colors from the unattended video game on the monitor. Her heart sank. She started to turn back, but hesitated when a shadow moved on the wall.

"Doctor Sekhar?" whispered Kerys.

She advanced to the door, eyed the two empty auto-surgeons, and looked to her left.

The doctor, in a white jumpsuit, stood in the corner, facing the wall like a misbehaving boy sent to time out. He held his hands at his sides in a posture reminiscent of an Old West gunslinger having a staredown. Even his trigger finger twitched.

"Doctor?" asked Kerys. "Is something wrong?"

"I'm not sure," said Dr. Sekhar, eerily calm. "What are you doing in here?"

She hid the dumbbell behind her back and took another step in. "It's the infirmary, and I wasn't feeling well."

He spun around. Aside from an irritated glower and a layer of sweat on his brow, Doctor Sekhar seemed relatively normal. The intensity in his eyes tightened her fingers on the steel weight, but his expression softened after the span of a few breaths. "Oh. Yes. Not feeling well. How so?"

She scratched at her jumpsuit over her stomach. "Nausea. I keep going from feeling like I'm about to throw up to like I swallowed a ball of nails."

"There seems to be an influenza outbreak on the station." He smiled an unsettling smile, as if the suffering somehow amused him. "It's rather cutting into my game time. Please, hop up on the machine and I'll check things out."

Kerys slid the dumbbell into her jumpsuit's thigh pocket. The doctor didn't move, forcing her to squeeze sideways between him and the desk. His presence behind her scooted her up to a jog. The doctor didn't take a step until after she'd climbed up on the machine and reclined. She picked at the cushions, shivering from nerves as he approached the console on the left. After a couple of beeps from the screen, the egg-shaped dome in the ceiling split open. A trio of robotic arms descended, positioning a boxy device over her stomach. It slid back and forth in a diagonal several times, as if measuring the area between the base of her ribs and crown of her hip.

Doctor Sekhar walked back to his desk, sat, and resumed his video game.

Seriously?

The armature moved to hover over her right hip, and proceeded to perform a series of side-to-side passes, ticking toward her feet by half an inch each time. She lifted her head enough to peer at his screen, unable to believe he seemed to care more about a 'space marine' cleansing a starship corridor of monsters than a live patient.

Two minutes later, the arms retreated up into the egg, which closed. She lay still for another five, but the doctor made no move to peel himself away from the computer. Kerys tapped her fingers on the soft cushions. *Is he going to flip out on me if I say something?*

A digitized explosion accompanied his screen flashing red. Somber music started seconds later.

"Dammit!" yelled the doctor, while pounding his fist on the desk. "I hate this level. Why can't they design games to be challenging without having to make them cheat?"

She stared at him. *Maybe he won't notice me if I just get up and walk out.*

The auto-surgeon creaked when she sat up.

Doctor Sekhar whirled around, sneered at her, and approached the console, grumbling.

Kerys stuffed her left hand in her pocket, grasping the tissue with the spore-laden snot. "There's something else you should see."

"You've likely got a garden-variety cold. The scan results are perfectly normal. Nothing seems wrong with you."

She swung her feet over the edge. "I've been having stomach cramps all morning."

He snapped his head toward her. "Are you telling me that I don't know what I'm talking about?" His voice rose to a near yell. "That you know more than I do? Which one of us spent nine years in medical school and four years in residence at a shithole hospital in Detroit?"

A fleck of spittle flew from his lip and landed on her cheek. She cringed away from the outburst, hands up, and slid to her feet, half-yelling, "Sorry!" before lowering her voice. "I'm sorry. That's not what I meant."

He squared his shoulders at her; again, his trigger finger twitched.

She pulled the tissue out of her pocket. "Doctor, can you please take a look at this?"

He narrowed his eyes. "You're determined to waste more of my time, aren't you?"

"I think I was exposed to something… an indigenous plant with spores. I blew my nose a little while ago and it's purple."

Doctor Sekhar's expression softened. He crossed to a counter full of diagnostic equipment, opened a drawer, and snapped on blue exam gloves. She stood there, holding out the tissue, waiting as he tugged the gloves in place and put on a paper mask. He used tongs to take the tissue from her hand, carried it back to the counter, and examined it.

She opened her mouth to say it looked like spores suspended in mucous, but bit her tongue, not wanting him to go off on her for insinuating he couldn't figure that out.

"Oh, I've seen this before. It's nothing to worry about."

Kerys blinked. "You have?"

"One of the botanists came in with something similar over a year ago. The spores didn't exhibit any interaction with human tissue; they were merely trapped in the mucous membranes. They will pass out of your system via normal excretory processes in about three months or so depending on the level of saturation." He laughed. "Mr. Braxton had a lavender bowel movement." He kept snickering for a long, uncomfortable minute, before going stone-faced in an instant. "It's harmless."

That sounds like Will. Trying to prank me with a purple turd and making me freak out.

"Thank you, Doctor." She took a step back.

His expression darkened.

Kerys offered a polite, but forced, smile, and ran for the door.

She sprinted the length of the corridor to the stairs, rushed down, and skidded to a stop in the atrium between the cafeteria and the access tunnel to the residence pods. The outpost hung in pregnant silence, not a trace of humanity visible. She turned in place, feeling completely alone on an alien world. The instant her brain registered the meaning of 'cafeteria,' the painful nausea in her stomach shifted to hunger.

A few steps brought her close enough to peer into the empty cafeteria. Meal trays, cups, and plastic utensils littered the tables as though thirty people in mid-meal simply vanished. A repetitious whirring emanated from one of the machines behind the counter, the only sound competing with her breathing.

I want to go home... She looked around again, feeling like a thief about to break into a house. Seeing no one, she swiped a plastic-wrapped sandwich and two bottles of water from a cooler cabinet before scurrying out.

The junk in the tube leading to the residence pods had thickened with more random debris scattered about: a chair, a lamp, someone's collection of plastic action figures, and a plate... but no people. She ran to Pod 2, grabbed the side of the door to the corner without falling over, and hurried to the ladder. The unconscious man was gone, only a few drops of blood remained on the floor where his face had been. She climbed at an excruciatingly slow pace, terrified of causing even the slightest sound. Total silence in the upstairs hall made her wonder if everyone decided all at once to ignore Captain Chen's order and rush outside.

Navigating storage cartons, a broken chair or two, clothes, and burst-open boxes that had been hurled against the wall, Kerys crept back to her quarters at the northwest corner. Locking the door behind her brought a small measure of security. She set the sandwich and water bottles on the desk, the dumbbell next to them, and collapsed in her chair, cradling her head in both hands.

"Everyone's losing their minds." Kerys peered between her fingers at the terminal screen showing the alien head model, which seemed to be gloating at her. She couldn't help but think about those old stories going around Berkley regarding the Egyptian pyramids and pharaoh curses. She didn't believe in anything like that... primitive people blaming 'curses' for scientifically explainable things like deadly mold. Yet, the way the statue head stared at her, even from virtual reality, sent a chill down her back.

"How long do I have before I snap like everyone else?"

13

DISINTEGRATING

For hours, Kerys lay in bed, staring at the ceiling of the cubby containing her mattress. Her gaze traced the seams in the plastic over and over again while she imagined tiny racecars going around a track. The malaise in her gut spread out to everywhere, leaving her achy and uninterested in moving. She slowed her breaths, searching the air for traces of lavender/peach, but it had either dissipated or she'd grown so accustomed to the smell, her nose refused to detect it.

A daydream of taking Jaden to the aquarium, two days before she boarded the ship that brought her here, filled the corners of her eyes with tears. She'd been too excited about becoming famous to see the sorrow in his face. He'd acted happy for her, but he didn't want her to go.

Kerys wiped her cheeks. "I'm imagining things now. He was more excited than me." His voice spoke in her mind, going on and on about how he'd tell all his friends about his sister the big important space-archaeologist.

Guess fame is contagious.

A growl came from her stomach. She rubbed it, grimacing. As soon as she'd eaten that sandwich, hunger slam-shifted back to nausea. Hours later, a dull ache settled in her gut that could've been either. The heaviness in her sinuses didn't feel as pronounced either, though the feverish ache in her bones remained.

"I'm not really hungry."

Another few minutes passed, the room quiet except for burbles emanating from her stomach.

"Okay, okay, fine."

She got up, put her shoes on, and grabbed the dumbbell. Walking around with a weapon out might provoke, so she concealed it in her pocket, keeping a hand on it. The hall outside held the soft din of recorded audio. A few familiar lines coming from the left told her someone watched a movie. If not for the random junk thrown about, the relative quiet made it feel like an ordinary afternoon. A glance at her arm showed the time at 6:02 p.m.

Damn. Where'd the day go? Did I fall asleep? No wonder I'm so hungry.

Kerys emerged from the ladder alcove on the ground floor and almost walked into two men wearing camouflage jumpsuits. She backpedaled with a gasp.

"Where are you going?" asked the one on the left, the name 'Santiago, M' over his breast pocket.

"Cafeteria," said Kerys. "Why, is something wrong?"

The other man, 'Edwards, R' according to his uniform, shook his head. "There've been some incidents. Make sure you return directly to your quarters after eating."

A trickle of sweat ran down Santiago's face. His eye twitched.

Kerys shied away from the 'I could kill you if I wanted to' stare emanating from him and looked down. "All right. I understand."

They brushed past her, walking astride and peering at any open door.

This keeps getting stranger and stranger.

Santiago twisted to look at her, his brows knitting together. "You're still standing there."

"Sorry." She rushed to the tube, eager to put a wall between herself and the soldiers.

A small woman in a grey jumpsuit knelt by an open panel on the left side of the tunnel, mumbling to herself in Spanish while poking at the electronics inside. Kerys slowed, curious.

"Fuse went." The woman pointed up and left at a section of LED tubes that didn't glow. "Trying to find the one that needs replacing."

"Oh." Kerys smiled. "Sorry for staring."

A few steps into the dome, a high-pitched wail arose from the right. Kerys pulled the dumbbell out of her pocket and dropped into a jiu-jitsu stance, but relaxed when she recognized Annapurna running toward her with a terrified expression.

The woman grabbed her shoulders, shaking her and ranting in Hindi at such a pace one word blurred into another.

"What? I'm sorry, I don't understand. What's wrong?"

Annapurna jabbed her finger at the stairway, shouting more unrecognizable words. Her eyes seemed ready to burst from their sockets.

"You're trembling. What happened? Anna? I don't understand that language." Kerys reached to take her hand, but the woman jumped back.

She paced in a figure eight, gesturing with both hands while rambling and muttering. Her body language would've fit witnessing a murder. Annapurna kept pointing in the direction of the elevators.

"Something upstairs? Okay… let's go."

The woman backed up, shaking her head so hard her long, black hair flew into a tangled mass. *"Nahin! Nahin! Baahar jao! Yah surakshit nahin hai! Hum marchuke hain!"* She took two more steps away, staring wild-eyed.

"What are you saying?" Kerys offered a hand. "Anna? What's happened?"

Annapurna whirled on her heel and sprinted off, screaming in a beckoning tone like someone shouting for the police. She stopped at the stairs, waved at Kerys while shaking her head, and raced out of sight.

The stunned fog in Kerys's brain faded, allowing her to process the sound of people in the cafeteria. She took a step toward the stairs, but stopped. *Anna didn't seem to want me to follow her.* A sharp cramp clenched her stomach at the same time a wave of lightheadedness came on, strong enough to weaken her knees. Kerys swallowed the saliva gathering in her mouth.

"I'll eat quick and check on her."

A handful of people sat scattered among the tables, no two close enough to converse. The automats all displayed empty messages. Whoever had the job of reloading them appeared to have taken the day off. She trudged to the racks of Hydra trays and selected one at random, Salisbury steak. Forty seconds later, the freeze-dried hockey puck in the octagonal tray came out hot and juicy. The smell of buttery mashed potatoes overwhelmed her, and she grabbed a stale muffin that had likely been sitting since morning as well.

She took a seat at a small, round table near the outer window that allowed her to put her back to a brace in the wall and keep most of the room in sight. Outside, the dust storm continued to swirl, obscuring the view of the mountain ridge. Flickering lights and indistinct boxy shapes hinted at the shuttle pad in the distance.

Abandoning decorum, she tore open the thin plastic covering and attacked her food. After three forkfuls, she slowed a little, her gaze alternating between watching the other people in the cafeteria and staring out the window. Everyone slouched over their meals, quiet and somber. One man shivered between body-wracking coughs.

My head's a little foggy, but I'm not that sick. Am I the one who brought the flu here? Is that why everyone's staring at me like they want to kill me?

She savaged the rehydrated meal, then began nibbling on the muffin.

Motion outside grabbed her attention. Two figures in e-suits to the east by the top of the hill emerged from the swirling silt and grabbed at each other while stumbling in circles. At first, they seemed to be struggling to keep each other upright while making their way to an airlock, but after a few spins, the one on the left took a swing at the other, who staggered away.

Kerys gasped. The half-eaten muffin fell from her hands and plopped into the empty tray between her elbows. *What are they doing? Idiots!*

Both figures grappled in the shifting black sand, twisting around and around. One fell, the other pouncing on its back. She leapt to her feet and pressed against the window. Watching the top figure twisting at the helmet of the other suit got her legs shaking. She couldn't bear to watch, but couldn't turn away.

The suit on top went flying to the left as the one on the ground rammed an elbow into its side, sending the figure rolling. Both people got to their feet in seconds. The helmet-grabber charged again, but the other person raised a metal rod. Despite the suits being fairly sleek for e-suits, she couldn't tell who the people were, or even man from woman.

Kerys yelped as the armed figure swung the rod at the other person's head. Helmet-grabber ducked, backpedaling. The crystalline regolith tripped them up after a few steps, causing them to fall on their ass, arms raised in a feeble defense against the four-foot metal rod bearing down. The attacker pounced, bashing the prone figure in the helmet again and again before they both tumbled out of sight down the hill, vanishing into the dust storm.

She backed away from the window, tears streaming from her eyes.

"Hey, asshole," said Marco. "Watch your damn step."

Kerys whirled.

Marco, still propped up on a cane, glared at Private Foster. Sweat beaded on the young soldier's forehead. His eyes looked sunken and dark with the far-away quality of a serial killer. Marco vibrated in a constant twitch, like a human version of a Chihuahua hopped up on caffeine. The men stood an arm's length apart in the entrance of the cafeteria, exchanging glares.

"That's it. You're done." Foster pulled a knife.

Marco snarled, not a trace of fear in his eyes. As the younger man lunged in, he smashed his cane across Foster's wrist, knocking the knife from his grip, but losing his balance in the process. He let off an agonized growl of pain as his broken leg gave out, dumping him on the floor. Foster kicked him in the gut, sending him sliding a few feet into the cafeteria. Marco rolled onto all fours, crawling toward a cart of steel folding chairs. Whistling like a janitor at work, Foster recovered his knife and stalked up behind him.

Kerys yelled, "Look out!"

Private Foster glared at her and pivoted on his heel, heading straight at her. His lips curled into an anticipatory grin, chilling the blood in her veins. She grabbed the dumbbell in her pocket, but before she could pull it out, Marco rose up behind Foster and walloped him across the shoulders with a chair.

Foster stumbled forward with an "Oof," and collapsed on his chest.

Marco, balanced on one leg, raised the chair, manic rage in his eyes. He limp-shuffled closer, staring at the stunned man's head.

"Marco, don't!"

Corporal Guillen flew in from the side, tackling Marco. Two unfamiliar men and a woman in camouflage jumpsuits followed, pouncing on Private Foster, who went red-faced from his unsuccessful effort to throw them off. It took all three soldiers to hold Foster down, and they seemed to be barely managing it.

Others in the cafeteria continued eating as if nothing happened.

"I'm okay, I'm okay," muttered Marco. He let Corporal Guillen take the chair without protest, and curled up cradling his leg. "Son of a bitch pulled a knife on me."

"He did," said Kerys.

Guillen retrieved the cane and handed it to Marco. "That looks pretty bad. You should head to the infirmary."

"Yeah, I'll get right on that." Marco hobbled over to the counter, cursed at the empty automats, and sifted among the available Hydra trays. "Doc's being a bitch today."

The trio of soldiers dragged Private Foster out. He continued struggling, kicking and ranting about the "Goddamn eggheads have already killed us."

Kerys couldn't look away from the struggle until Corporal Guillen stepped up in front of her. She shifted her gaze to him. That perfect face of his looked weary and in need of a shower, but he radiated genuine concern. No trace of any bizarre anger lingered in his eyes, as if he, too, had been spared from the mysterious… curse. *Wow, am I really thinking we set off a Pharaoh's curse?* "Do you have any idea what's going on?"

"I don't know. We got a complaint from Lab 1, but I can't read whatever language that is so I have no idea."

"Piece of shit!" roared Marco, raising his cane at the Hydra. "What do you mean 'seat tray fully'? It's fucking seated as fully as it can seat."

"Maybe it's backward?" asked a tired-sounding woman nearby.

"It's a damn octagon. It can't be backward." Marco fumed, removed the tray, put it back in, and punched the button.

Corporal Guillen gave him the side eye. "So, what happened?"

Kerys recounted the men bumping shoulders, Marco calling him an asshole, and Foster pulling a knife. She pointed at the window. "Two men outside were fighting by the hill. One had a pole or something... I think he killed someone." She chided herself for sounding like a frightened girl, even if she did have a front row seat to murder.

"What? Where? Who?" Guillen looked over her shoulder at the window. "I don't see anything out there now. What are people doing outside? There's a lockdown."

"How should I know? They had e-suits on. I couldn't tell who they were at all. Can't even say if they were men or women, and they fell down the hill. Why is everyone so touchy?"

"Your guess is as good as mine. Tempers are getting short all around. I heard Chen sent another screamer off to Earth last night. *Something* happened, and command isn't sharing it. Two people outside, fighting?"

She nodded, pointing. "Yeah. I was sitting at that table and they were maybe fifty yards away before they rolled down the hill."

"All right. I'll check on it." He squeezed a mic near his shoulder. "Hey, Sarge. Got a report of unauthorized EVO, two individuals on the east side. Possible assault."

"Copy." Gensch's voice crackled from a little black dot on Guillen's collar. "I'll have Cortez meet you at the southeast airlock."

"On the way." Corporal Guillen grasped Kerys's shoulder and looked her in the eye. "Are you going to be okay?"

"Yeah." She sank into the seat by her tray. The aroma of Salisbury gravy struck her as revolting. She clasped a hand over her mouth, suppressing the urge to throw up. "You should hurry—maybe whoever had their helmet bashed on isn't dead."

He muttered, "On the way," into his shoulder mic, and strode off.

Marco limped over to one of the long tables near the center of the room with his steaming Hydra tray and sat, still grumbling about the machine. Kerys pulled her legs up, hooking her heels on the edge of the chair, her arms wrapped around her knees. More than ever, she felt trapped in a place she wanted no part of anymore.

Minutes later, two people in e-suits bearing assault rifles walked into view outside. One glanced toward the window, faced away, and pointed at the ground where the downhill grade began.

Kerys shivered at the sight of the swirling grey dust devouring Corporal Guillen and his squad mate. In seconds, both men vanished amid the cloud. She extended her legs to the floor and pulled herself to her feet.

I'd better check on Anna.

14

OMNIS MORIAR

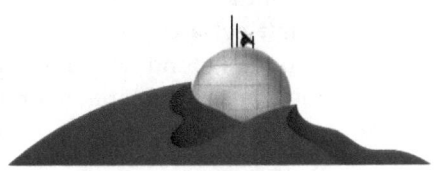

Kerys rounded the stairwell onto the dome's second floor, driven by worry for whatever had rattled Annapurna to such a degree she'd lost her ability to speak English. She gripped and released the dumbbell in her pocket, wary of every moving shadow.

An eruption of shouting ahead stalled her in place. Multiple men and women screamed at each other about being incompetent. A shrill female voice accused someone named Jun of sabotaging her work.

Kerys gulped. *Maybe I should go to my room? No, I have to check on her.* She took three steps deeper into the corridor.

Bang!

At the sound of a gunshot, she screamed and hurled herself against the wall to her left. A man cried out in pain; a woman screamed in rage. Two more shots went off in rapid succession, followed by a heavy *crash* of metal. The floor shuddered underfoot seconds later with the unmistakable rumble of a distant explosion.

Chris Mardling backed out of a side corridor a short distance ahead of her, a handgun aimed at something out of sight. "What was that about British food, mate?" He fired twice, orange muzzle flare bursting like camera flashes. A manic laugh escaped his throat. "There's your fish and bloody chips!" He shifted his eyes to the left. Two seconds later, his head rotated toward her, revealing a spray of blood across his face.

She clutched the dumbbell and screamed.

"Oh, if it isn't you." Chris swung his arm around to aim at her, the gun hanging from a limp grip. "No worries, lass. I've got plenty of ammo left.

Sharing is caring." He fired, the bullet leaving a gouge in the floor a few feet in front of her.

Kerys snapped out of her terrified daze. She pushed off the wall and sprinted, screaming incoherently as she raced for the stairs. Another gunshot slammed the air in her ears, but nothing hit her, so she risked a peek back.

Chris walked after her, smiling. "Lucky ducky you. Bye bye."

"Help!" shouted Kerys as she dove to the ground.

A spark burst from the wall inches to the left of her face. She clambered on all fours into the stairwell, sliding down to the first switchback before somersaulting against the wall at the bottom. Chris appeared at the top as she rolled to her feet, but didn't get a chance to fire before she jumped down the second set of steps to the ground floor. Blind panic drove her to a run. Clattering and slamming in the cafeteria accompanied screams of fury. Food came skittering out on the floor along with trays and loose chairs.

She skidded to a halt, twisting around to stare at two corridors, a hamster tube, and three doors.

"Is it my breath?" Chris emerged from the stairway. "I almost get the idea you don't want me to shoot you."

"I don't!" she yelled, backing up. "I didn't do anything."

"Of course you didn't." He chuckled. "It wouldn't be random violence if I shot you for doing something specific, now would it? Go on, I'll give a few seconds to run."

"Why!" shouted Kerys. "Please don't."

"Because I am bored." He grinned like a silly drunk. "I find this highly amusing."

Marco popped up from behind an orange sofa and hurled his metal cane at Chris. It hit the man in the side of the head, causing him to flinch and fire another bullet off in a harmless direction. Marco speed-limped closer, flailing his arms. Chris tried to bring the gun to bear on him, but Marco closed in too fast, and tackled him.

"Security!" Kerys screamed. "We need help!"

The gun went off again, striking a panel near the cafeteria entrance and setting off a shower of sparks. A bank of LED bulbs in the ceiling went dark. Marco grabbed for the gun, bashing Chris's arm into the floor.

She started to run over to help, but pivoted at a howling scream from behind. A gaunt, pale man with short blond hair, a yellow jumpsuit, and blood all over him came charging out of a doorway at her. She got her arms up in time to catch his chest as he leapt on her. His weight knocked her back a few steps, but she held her balance.

Nose to nose, she stared into blood red eyes. Not a trace of white remained around his pupils.

He growled like a dog, biting at her face.

Kerys leaned back, trying to drive her knee into his groin while pushing him away. Behind her, Marco and Chris continued grunting. The Brit laughed with glee while Marco wailed in pain.

"Oh, that bum leg's a toss, innit? Does it hurt if I do this?"

Marco screamed again, his bright-red face awash with swollen veins.

"Get off me!" yelled Kerys.

The man moaned. When he let go with one hand to punch her, she shoved him hard, remembering to trap his leg with her heel. Her takedown worked, slamming the scrawny man flat on his back hard enough to knock the wind out of him. He stared up at the ceiling, gasping for air, disoriented.

A dull *thunk* came from behind.

"Argh, bastard!" roared the Brit.

Kerys whirled. Blood on Mardling's nose and mouth matched a splat on Marco's forehead. He brought his good knee up into Chris's gut, knocking him aside. Before she could summon any words, Marco twisted the handgun out of the man's grip. It went off again, muted by body and fabric.

A spray of blood burst like a geyser from Chris's back, smearing across the floor. He gurgled and fell limp.

Kerys edged away from the dazed man who'd grabbed her, but didn't fully trust Marco, either. "What's going on?"

"Everyone's gone to loopy town." Marco grunted and pushed himself up on one knee. "Like that moron." He shot the dazed man she'd thrown to the floor in the head.

Kerys screamed.

Marco tilted his head at her. "What?"

"You just killed two people!" She clutched the dumbbell, shaking.

"No, I didn't." Marco casually shot Chris in the head. "*Now* I killed two people." He gestured with the gun toward Kerys, making her squeal and duck. "That bastard was trying to bite you on the face like a damn zombie. What did you want me to—?"

Boom.

The right side of Marco's head exploded in a shower of bloody bits in time with the crack of a rifle from deeper in the corridor. His twitching body collapsed forward onto his chest. Kerys stared at him for a hair more than a second. At the motion of a shadow in the hallway, she sprinted for the hamster tube that led to the residence pods, vomit trailing off her lower lip. The sounds of gunfire, screaming, and metal banging on metal surrounded her. Four steps later, she stopped.

There's tons of people in there… I'll never make it.

Rubberized boots squeaked on the metal floor of the hall leading to the main stairwell, drawing closer. More gunfire erupted in the distance, a rapid, random barrage of pops and chatters. Worse, whoever shot Marco came for her. Kerys ducked into the door from which the feral man appeared, running past a handful of small offices, two of which contained brawls. Her legs almost gave out when she reached the corner thirty feet later and found a dead end.

Hope came in the form of a ventilation intake near the floor. She rushed over, tore the vent cover off, and crawled in before pulling the flimsy aluminum grating back in place behind her. The shaft led only to the left, toward the center of the dome. She shimmied a few feet deeper, far enough that no one looking in could see her, and curled up on her side.

Hidden in the dark of the ventilation duct, she trembled, listening to the sounds of utter chaos. Every time a gunshot went off, someone screamed—or laughed maniacally, she jumped. Putting her hands on her ears didn't help. She caught herself sobbing, wishing Corporal Guillen would show up to protect her. Of course, reality wouldn't be so perfect. Will would probably be the one to find and 'save' her. Salisbury steak crept into the back of her throat at the idea.

Oh, he'd adore that. He always thought I was helpless. Condescending bastard. Anyone with tits is an eternal child incapable of fending for themselves. She shivered at the images her brain conjured in response to the noises. The vent echoed with screamed obscenities, clatters of metal, ripples of gunfire, and wet gurgling that could only mean death.

I've got nowhere to go.

She stifled a gasp as someone ran by the vent. A fleeting shadow leapt across the aluminum shaft. A moment later, the illusion of safety afforded by concealment let her resume breathing. She curled tighter, trying to control her shaking, lest someone hear the duct rattling. Every time she closed her eyes, Marco's face exploded again.

This isn't happening… This isn't happening.

Stuck in a metal box containing the only breathable atmosphere within thousands of light years and surrounded by insanity at every turn, Will didn't seem like such a nightmare after all. She stared glassy-eyed at the wall, afraid to blink, afraid to make a sound as a storm raged outside.

15

THE LAST ONE

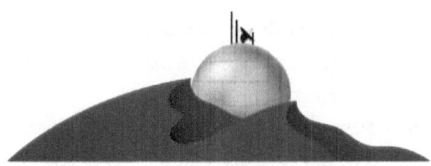

The sudden realization of silence startled Kerys. Somehow, she had fallen asleep against her will. She lay on her side in the ventilation shaft, the whisper of her breaths echoing. Wayfarer Outpost had gone still, save for a repeating electric chirp. For a while, she kept motionless, convinced the slightest movement would create enough noise to attract danger.

She counted to a hundred before risking a shift of weight. Her watch read 1:18 a.m. A momentary pall of disorientation came on, making the world blurry for a few seconds. She swallowed dryness and massaged the front of her throat.

At 1:30, she decided to crawl to the vent cover and peer out. The chirping seemed to be emanating from something under the desk in an office across the hall. Kerys eased the slatted panel aside and peeked out. Seeing no one, she crawled out, turned, and replaced the vent cover before standing and creeping back the way she'd come.

Marco remained where he'd fallen, as did the men he'd shot. Six more unfamiliar corpses had joined them, heaped about like giant discarded dolls. Bloody splats and smears crisscrossed the stark white floor between the bodies. Broken LED light tubes dangled on wires from the ceiling, masked behind a few inches of hovering smoke. She averted her eyes and clenched her teeth, biting back the urge to scream. Even the crunch of broken plastic bits under her sneakers made her cringe.

She crossed the room to the habitation tube entrance. Blood spattered all over the walls as well as the tube's clear upper half, but fortunately, no bodies lay between her and her quarters. Trusting the silence, she hurried down to the door of Residence Pod 2 and peered in the narrow window. Broken furniture, a few mattresses, and clothing littered a corridor smeared with gore, but again, no corpses lay anywhere in sight. Someone had closed the door at the end of the tube. Kerys crept up to it and peered in the window. No people, living or otherwise were there, only more debris thrown around. Still staring in the window, she fumbled around by feel for the button.

At the pneumatic hiss of the door opening, she cringed. As quiet as could be, she advanced into the pod, heading for the ladder. A scrape to the left drew a gasp from her lungs and made her spin to put her back to the wall. The noise came from strips of plastic dangling from the ceiling, swaying in the air blowing from a vent. She stood in place, shaking, unable to look away from the ripped-up room.

Once she collected her nerve, she navigated the debris to the ladder shaft and climbed until she could peek over the floor. A man's arm protruded from a room six doors away to the left, but her room waited to the right. Nothing made a sound, save for her breathing and a faint rattle coming from a fan somewhere. Once she felt alone enough, she climbed a few more rungs and eased herself out into the hallway.

Sorry. It didn't seem right to see a dead person and not express some degree of consolation, even if she spoke only in her head.

Kerys jogged to the north, trying to make as little noise as possible and refusing to look into any open doors. She kept her gaze down until she reached her quarters. A man's bloody handprint on the wall by the access panel stunned her rigid, but the sight of the lock still engaged allowed her to relax. She swiped her ID and ducked inside, locking the door again as fast as it closed.

Safe in her room, she crawled into bed fully dressed, pulled the emergency hatch closed, and curled up under her blanket. The cubby held the strong fragrance of lavender and peach, but she didn't care anymore. Will liked the smell. He wanted her to like it too.

"Damn flower…"

Huddled in her bed, she stared past the transparent barrier at the door, dreading at any moment the red 'locked' message would turn green.

———

AT SOME POINT KERYS COULDN'T RECALL, WEEPING TRADED PLACES WITH unconsciousness.

She startled awake and lost a moment to scatterbrained fear. The closed hatch made her feel like a cat stuck in a glass cage. She grasped the handle to open it, but hesitated, glancing at her desk. *Should I send Jaden a message?* Would it be crueler to tell him people have gone crazy, and she's maybe the last person left alive on the whole station, or might it be kinder to disappear without word?

Kerys checked her watch: 7:04 a.m.

She didn't remember sleeping much—mostly staring at the door. Urgency in her bladder provided the last scrap of motivation that stopped her from lying there doing nothing until starvation set in. She pushed the emergency hatch open and crawled out of the recessed bed. After a glance between her terminal and the door, she sat at the desk and brought up the SFT message client.

"Hey, kiddo. I gotta stop picturing you as a little kid. You're thirteen now. Every time I think about you, I see this smiling ten-year-old. Hope Mom isn't being her usual self. Look, Jay. I... Something's happened out here. I don't understand what's gotten into people, but there's been a situation. Everyone seems to be losing their minds and starting fights. I'm trying to keep my head down and stay out of it, but, oh hell." She bowed her head. *He's not that little anymore.* "Jaden, there's been some deaths. For all I know, I'm the only one left. The company sends ships every six months. It'll be boring as hell, but I'm going to survive to come home. I just have to wait for the next ship. Hopefully, five months and three weeks is enough time to teach myself how to use the communication system. Promise me something, kid. Stay on Earth. Don't ever take a job like mine. Space is not worth it. I swear if I make it home, I'm never doing anything this reckless again. I'd rather be alive than famous. Love you."

She hit send, and forced herself to stand.

"One good thing about having a room all the way at the end...."

Kerys slipped out of her quarters and walked a short distance farther north to the bathroom. Blood trickled out from under the door of the men's room, but the women's looked clean. She crept in, bracing herself for a horror show, but an empty stark white bathroom greeted her, about as welcoming as an abandoned mental hospital. She ducked into the nearest stall, shoved her clothes out of the way, and took a seat.

Elbows on her knees, she cradled her face in her hands and tried not to freak out too much as her bladder emptied. The nearest she'd ever been to a dead body had been the occasional funeral: grandparents, distant cousins on Mom's side, and so on. In the span of mere hours, she'd not only been close enough to touch fresh corpses, she'd watched three men die. Maybe four, but she didn't know for sure what happened to the person outside.

Squeak.

She stifled a gasp and lifted her legs, bracing her feet against the stall door. Fortunately, the chem toilets didn't have a pool of water, so her inability to stop peeing wouldn't give her away from sound.

Footsteps squelched on the tile outside. A shadow drifted over her stall door, continuing to the right. Kerys covered her mouth to keep quiet.

The footsteps ceased a short distance away, leaving the sense of someone close by outside clear in the air. She concentrated on not moving —not even breathing.

Go away. Whoever you are, go away.

She sat still for several minutes after finishing. The person outside hadn't moved either. With her legs on the verge of going numb, she moved one heel up to the front edge of the toilet seat and pushed herself up, then brought her other foot to the seat and stood. After righting her underwear and closing her jumpsuit, she eased herself up to her full height and peered over the top of the stall.

Paula slouched forward, leaning on the sink counter. Bloody handprints stained the back of her blue jumpsuit. Her long, semi-curly black hair, streaked with grey, hung wild across her shoulders. A steady *pat pat pat* of dripping echoed over the stillness. She convulsed, emitting a weak retching noise.

Kerys stepped down from the toilet and opened the stall door. "Paula?"

"Mmm."

"It's so good to see you're okay." Kerys crept closer. "Are you hurt?"

"Headache," muttered Paula. "Still sick."

Kerys reached out and put a hand on the woman's shoulder. "Marco's dead." She sniffled and choked up. "Have you seen Don?"

"Kerys…" whispered Paula. "I… please. I'm hearing voices. Something is very wrong with me."

She leaned back. "No…"

Paula straightened and turned around. The left half of her face hung loose, a flap of skin over her collarbone, the eye dangling on a nerve inches out of the socket. A deep gouge near the middle of her forehead welled with dark blood.

Kerys stumbled back, screaming.

"He had a hatchet…" Paula swooned to the side, catching herself on the counter. The middle and ring fingers of her right hand were missing.

"No!" Kerys sobbed. "No… Paula… Who?"

"Soldier." Her former boss gurgled. "I… kind of want to kill you, but I don't have the energy."

Kerys blinked. "What?"

"Wait, no. I remember you. The shower. I told you about my kids." Paula twisted her head to the left and rasped, "Stop that. Be quiet."

Instinct told her to run, that this mangled woman had ceased being the same person. At any second, she might snap and go violent... but she couldn't give up on the chance that a trace of her remained somewhere in there. "Paula, it's me, Kerys Loring. We're on the archaeology team with Doctor Bouchard."

"Have you seen Don?" asked Paula. Blood from the dent in her skull dripped off the end of her nose.

"No." Kerys considered trying to push the skin flap back in place, but didn't trust getting close to her, nor did she really want to touch it. "What do you mean voices?"

"They're talking. Won't stop. I just want some quiet. They don't care I've got a pounding migraine." She grasped her head wound and grunted. "Not much time left. I'd ask you to tell my kids I love them, but you're not going to see Earth again either."

"Six months. We just have to hold on for six months. Come on. Hang in there; we can get to the infirmary."

Paula tilted her head, making the dangling eyeball wobble. "This is bizarre. I can still see out of it. So dizzy."

The woman teetered forward.

Kerys lunged in and caught her, guiding her to a gentle landing on the floor. "Hey, don't quit."

Paula gurgled. "Addison and Alan. Silly, huh? Both A names."

Cringing, Kerys grasped the loose eyeball with three fingers and tried to put it back in the socket.

"Ngh!" Paula's hands shot up and closed around Kerys's throat. "Urghh."

Kerys jumped back, slipping out of the feeble grip with ease. Paula's intact eye focused on her for a second. She barked out a laugh, convulsed, and her head lolled to the side.

"Paula?" Kerys rubbed her neck where she'd been grabbed; her hand came away bloody.

When Paula didn't move, Kerys crept closer and pressed two fingers at the side of the woman's neck.

No pulse.

Kerys rocked back, seated on the floor, hand over her mouth. Their brief chat about stretch marks came to mind. Even if Paula had been a bit of a prig about the whole Atlantean thing, Kerys liked her. Marco died. Now Paula. Two people she'd liked. Two people who'd never go home, never see their family. Again, she pictured Jaden as a ten-year-old waiting for her in the front window. The bizarre violence, and the reality of being stranded on some planet years away from Earth crashed into her. She burst into tears and took hold of Paula's arm, checking at the wrist for a pulse.

Still nothing.

After a while of staring at Paula, the gore went so far beyond anything she could handle, it left her numb. *This isn't really happening. I'm stuck in a bad dream. An entire crew doesn't all go insane at the same time.* Her conversation with Paula in the shower aboard the *Avasar 4* replayed in her mind. Stretch marks. Two grown kids who'll never see her again. The older woman looked so wrong with her eye dangling out. It would be horrible if her son and daughter saw her like that. She couldn't do anything more to help, but it bothered Kerys leaving her in such a state. As if on auto-pilot, she mushed the eyeball back into the socket and adjusted the dangling flap of skin over the exposed muscles as best she could.

Seconds later, abject disgust came over her at touching an eyeball. She scrambled to her feet and got her head over the sink before an explosion of vomit launched from her mouth. Clinging to the counter to keep from falling, Kerys threw up twice more before sinking to her knees. Little but bile came out, and the taste made her dry heave again.

I can't leave her on the floor. There's got to be some kind of morgue here.

She stumbled out of the bathroom, intent on searching the infirmary for a stretcher or something similar enough to serve as one. The idea seemed sound until she made it halfway down the ladder to the residence pod's ground floor. She looked up, then down.

"What am I going to do, throw her down the ladder?"

Maybe there's a harness somewhere.

As soon as her shoe touched the landing, a hand clamped onto her shoulder and hauled her backward. Kerys let off a scream as she stumbled, tripping over her own feet, and crashed into the far wall. She bounced off the metal and stared into the barrel of Private Foster's sidearm, inches from her face.

He glared at her, his eyes devoid of soul and a maniacal smile across his face. Some of his teeth had gone missing, letting blood ooze over his lower lip. He'd smeared some under his eyes like war paint, and his body trembled with ill-contained rage.

Click.

Kerys's knees weakened. She fell back against the wall, barely able to breathe.

He grunted in annoyance and tossed the gun aside before going for a knife.

Air flooded her lungs, and she let off an ear-piercing scream. She leapt to the side, evading a wild sideways swing that gouged his blade into the wall.

"Foster, stop it!" She ran, vaulting boxes and chairs. "Please, stop!"

"Don't run," rasped Foster with a bark of a laugh. "You'll only die tired."

She hurled herself down the corridor, hitting the hamster tube too fast to turn, and crashed into the side. Foster stomped after her, kicking junk aside rather than walking around it. A quick glance back at his utterly psychotic expression chased away any notion of reasoning with him. She sprinted down the tube for the dome. He trotted up to a light run, making whooping and growling noises.

Shying away from the spread of bodies in the first room, Kerys ran straight ahead into the cafeteria. A few more dead people lay slumped over the tables and one of the automats had burned to a black crisp. She skirted the tables, sprinting for the best option in sight: a steel door to the kitchen behind the counter full of vendomats and food displays.

Rather than run all the way around the counter, she flung herself into a dive through an empty vending case, sliding on her chest under a row of heat lamps. Her hands hit the floor first; she scrambled to her feet before hurling herself at the door, bashing it open. Once past it, she spun and slammed it shut, but couldn't find any way to lock it.

"Shit!"

Red metal to her right caught her eye. She grabbed a hand truck and jimmied it under the handle, wedging the door closed three seconds before Private Foster rammed himself into it. Bellowing and roaring, he punched the combat knife into a round pie-sized window, tearing at the plastic. He yanked it free with a tortured squeak, and stabbed it in again. Kerys backed up, mesmerized at the mindlessness of a man attacking a door with a knife.

Her shoulders hit something soft.

She glanced back at a dead man in a yellow jumpsuit, half-draped off a shelf holding trays of unbaked bread dough pre-formed into loaves. Someone had slit his throat, though he no longer bled. From there, her gaze tracked to the food prep area, where at least twenty corpses had been piled on tables and counters. Blood even spattered on the ceiling.

A sharp *clank* made her spin back to the door. Foster continued assaulting the metal with his knife, grunting and howling like a beast. She forced herself to look at the bloodbath behind her and spotted another door in the opposite corner. Foster seemed mindless enough he might continue attacking the door without realizing she left. She swallowed her terror and tiptoed across the blood slick.

The kitchen's rear door opened to the other end of the cafeteria. Foster's rage echoed off the walls, but the curved shape of the serving area kept him out of sight. Kerys ducked, scurrying past the tables while heading for the southwest exit she'd never used. Once she had wall between her and Foster, she sped up to a run, and ducked into a stairwell about ten meters later. The urge to get as far from him as possible pushed her all the way up to the fifth floor.

She stopped where the stairwell met corridor. *What am I doing?* Her eyes narrowed. *I wonder if Captain Chen is still alive?* The woman had sent an angry message to Earth at least a day before people lost their minds. *She had to have known something was going on… and she didn't say a damn word to anyone.*

Kerys stormed down a short corridor. At what she assumed to be the middle of the dome, it went left to a door bearing a sign 'Captain Emily Chen,' opposite a door marked 'Authorized Personnel Only.' Straight ahead, a metal hatch bore a 'Danger High Voltage' sign. She crept around to the captain's office.

The door hung ajar; unlike every other door she'd seen in this place, this one didn't slide into the wall to open. An acrid 'burning plastic' smell in the air made her cough. She pushed the door in, gazing around at an office decorated in muted reds and browns. A five-tiered shelf on the left held six bonsai trees as well as an assortment of e-pads and some books. More bonsai trees flanked the workstation's two monitors. One of two silver-and-maroon chairs in front of the desk lay on its side.

She crept around to get a look at the terminals. The captain's black-cushioned chair had been knocked back into a set of beige blinds over a huge window. The left monitor displayed a 'signal lost' error. The other held the feed from an exterior camera, showing two bodies in e-suits apparently dead on the shuttle pad. She gasped, shivered, and forced herself to lean closer to the screen. Between the suits, the dust, and the distance, she couldn't recognize either one.

Please don't be Corporal Guillen… please. He seemed to be holding it together too.

A wheeze from the left startled her; she turned her head toward an opening in the back of the office. A zigzag burn on the floor nearby connected to a melt line on the metal wall, where a door had been cut away and kicked in.

A quick check of desk drawers found nothing useful as a weapon.

"Who's out there?" asked a woman. "Show yourself."

Kerys crept up to the doorway, peering around the edge into a bedroom about four times the size of her quarters.

Don lay dead on the floor at the foot end of the bed, slumped over an excavating laser. He'd been shot numerous times in the chest. Fluid leaked from his battery backpack into a smoking puddle on the rug. The wall on the other side of the bed looked like someone had scrawled over it with a massive, black crayon, no doubt burns from the laser.

Captain Emily Chen sat on the floor in the corner, propped up against the wall. Her olive-drab jumpsuit appeared so disheveled, she had to have been wearing it for days. A misting of dried blood painted a face devoid of energy. Kerys's gaze went straight to the sidearm dangling from the woman's right hand.

"I know what you want," snarled Captain Chen. "You can't have it."

"Why did you kill him?!" Kerys ducked tight to the doorway, leaving only enough of herself exposed to see the woman. "What happened here? You know something, don't you?"

"I tried. Really I tried." Captain Chen looked down. "I've done all I could, but there's just not enough to go around. I'm sorry. You can't have it."

"What are you talking about?" Kerys clutched the wall, tensing her muscles, ready to jump away if the gun moved.

"I used to have fifty-five."

"What?"

"Three times eighteen, plus one. That greedy old man wanted more than his fair share. He took six."

Kerys couldn't stop shaking, though from anger or fear she couldn't tell. "You've gone nuts too, haven't you? You're not making any sense."

The captain lifted her chin, narrowing her eyes at Kerys. "I know what you want. You're as greedy as the rest of them. I'm sorry, but I'm just not going to give it to you."

"This is pointless," muttered Kerys. "Why did everyone go crazy? You know, dammit. I know you know! Tell me what you sent to Earth!"

Captain Chen smiled. "You're here to steal my last one." She raised the gun.

Kerys ducked out of sight, back flat to the wall. "You're insane!"

"I want to give it to you, but I promised. I can't."

"You're not making any sense," said Kerys.

"Girl."

"What?"

"Look at me."

"You think I'm stupid, don't you? You're going to shoot me."

"I knew it! You want it! No, you can't have my last bullet!"

Kerys blinked. "I don't want your last bullet."

"Liar," yelled Captain Chen. "You all want them. I was happy to share what I had, but you people just kept taking."

Holy shit this woman's gone way off the farm. "Don't shoot me."

"You can't have it, so stop asking for it."

Kerys risked a peek. Captain Chen's arm once again hung limp over her knee, gun pointed at the floor. She leaned out a little more. "I really do not want your bullet."

"Of course you do." Captain Chen smiled. "You all do. I had to give them what they wanted, but I can't do it anymore. Not my last one. It's mine!"

"What was on that message?"

"Girl."

Kerys narrowed her eyes. "What?"

"No one else. I promised. Don't let it out. You can't let it out." Captain Emily Chen's eyes flared wide, bloodshot as her lips curled into a rictus grin. She threw her head back and let off a maniacal cackle. "Don't let it out!"

"I—"

Captain Chen whipped her arm up, put the gun under her chin, and fired her last bullet.

Kerys screamed.

A glop of blood and brains slid down the wall, disappearing behind the dead woman's head.

16

DEGREES OF SANITY

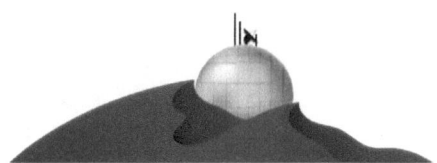

Hallway after hallway passed in a blur. Kerys ran until she reached her quarters. Once inside, she locked the door and collapsed to the floor, bawling. Marco's exploding head and Captain Chen's utterly psychotic stare traded places against the backs of her eyelids. She sobbed into her arms for what felt like hours, unable to process the idea of being stranded here, the one sane rat in a cage full of bloodthirsty animals.

Eventually, she stopped crying, but lacked the will to move. That she didn't sniffle or feel stuffy-headed surprised her. She sat up, rubbing her sinuses. The congestion had broken. It couldn't have been a minor cold that made everyone go insane. If whatever caused this had been in the air, surely, she should've been out of her mind with everyone else. It didn't make any sense for her to suffer only aches, pains, and congestion while everyone else went murderously delusional.

Kerys considered the possibility she might have set off some kind of alien curse that spared her because she'd been the one to touch the head. But that made no sense. For one thing, if she started to seriously entertain the idea of 'magic' as being possible, she'd have to file herself away as 'insane' like everyone else. For another, why would it spare the person who broke the seal? No, she hadn't invaded some ancient Egyptian burial vault. And she didn't believe in curses either.

What was Anna trying to tell me? Maybe there's something on her computer?

Sore muscles, the last vestiges of fever aches, protested her attempt to move, but she wiped her cheeks and stood. A few laps around her tiny room eased the stiffness. She spent a few minutes stretching as if preparing for a workout, grabbed her dumbbell, and approached the door.

Three out of five people she trusted were dead and she had no way to know if the other two, Gina or Corporal Guillen, remained alive or even sane. Whatever happened here had so far spared her. Perhaps others shared whatever genetic quirk she had protecting her and escaped craziness as well. The idea that Foster might *still* be pounding on the door in the cafeteria caused a nervous laugh, followed by a pang of guilt.

I don't know if there's anything out there. If people who die away from Earth go to the same place... or if people who die even go anywhere. Never much thought about that stuff before. She wished for Don, Paula, and Marco to rest in peace, took a breath, and opened her door.

"Okay," she whispered. "Anna works in Lab 1. She knew something was coming; maybe she's okay." *Down the hall to the tube, across the dome to the south, left side tunnel.*

The soft hum of the ventilation system, a sound she never noticed before with people moving around, filled the hallway outside. She crept to the ladder and made her way down, careful to watch for another surprise from behind. No one waited for her at the bottom. She clutched the hex dumbbell like a knight with a broken sword, and made her way to the dome.

Nothing looked different in the flexible tube or the area outside the cafeteria. All the bodies remained as they had been before. The absence of banging proved Foster had gone elsewhere, which got the hairs on the back of her neck standing up. She kept her weight on her toes to minimize sound as she followed the hallway past the stairs to the southern half of the dome.

White noise hissed from a speaker in a small office on the left. Dripping came from a single-occupant bathroom a few feet ahead on the right. She stared at the door, expecting someone to jump out at her. A sudden buzz overhead made her jump back from a fluttering LED tube, evidently damaged by a stray bullet.

"Shit," she whispered. "Just lights."

Kerys glanced side to side at doors as she advanced, unsure if she should be comforted or worried at being in the military section. The barracks on her left looked quiet and dark. Across the hall, an abandoned security monitoring station contained two empty chairs facing a bank of monitors.

"Ooh." She grabbed the doorknob, hoping to get a view around the facility, but the knob wouldn't turn. The panel rejected her ID badge with an irritating warning tone. "Dammit."

She started to go up on tiptoe to peer in the window, but jumped away at motion in the reflection near her head.

Private Foster, only a few steps away, froze when she moved. He'd looked devoid of sense before, but the expression on his face now had become as blank as an android. With all the emotion of a moving corpse, he clenched and relaxed his grip on his combat knife. For three seconds they stared at each other in silence—then he charged.

Kerys spun to the right, grabbing for his leading arm. The knife tore a slice along the sleeve of her jumpsuit on its way into the wall. She grunted and pushed at him. He closed his left hand around the front of her throat, pushing her against the door to the security room.

She scrambled for a second before swinging her arm up and bashing the dumbbell into his forearm. He pressed harder into her neck, lifting her on tiptoe while ripping his knife hand out of her weak grab on his wrist. She gurgled an attempt to scream and drove her shin into his groin. His face reddened; he froze, stooped slightly forward, wheezing. Shrieking in desperation, Kerys swung her right arm sideways, driving the hexagonal nugget at the end of the dumbbell into the side of Foster's head.

He tumbled to the side, collapsing to all fours.

Gagging and choking for air, she took a few steps away, watching him cradle his groin and crawl forward. She glanced at a smear of blood on the chrome in her hand. Foster dragged himself forward another few feet and flattened out on his chest. Blood streamed from his crushed left eye socket. She rubbed her neck, swallowed, and backed away.

Metal clanged and clattered from the end of the corridor where it split in two directions, one to the lab, one to the reactor. Kerys looked around for a place to hide, but hesitated, hoping whoever moved down there might not be crazy. Of course, if they'd snapped, and had a gun, she'd be stupid to stay out in the open.

She started for the barracks door, but made it only two steps before Ellen came tromping up the corridor, wearing her exo suit, her head mere inches from the ceiling. Blood dribbled over the dinner-plate-sized Hello Kitty face on the thick metal chest plate.

The giant woman stared at her the way a Rottweiler might look at filet mignon.

"Hey, Ellen. Good to see you're okay." Kerys forced a smile.

"You're not real!" shouted the big woman. "Get out of my head!"

"I'm—"

Ellen raised her metal-encased arms, gave a furious roar, then rushed at her. The entire hallway shuddered from the mass of the exo suit.

"Shit…" Kerys sprinted back the way she came, her mind racing for any idea of where to go to get away.

"Rrrah!" shouted Ellen before muttering to herself about figments.

At the unusual grunting scream, Kerys made the mistake of looking back an instant before a pink-and-silver armored boot liquefied Private Foster's head. As if enraged by the corpse having the temerity to be in her path, Ellen stopped chasing her long enough to pick the body up by the belt and hurl it into the wall, leaving a dent in the metal. A mushy sack of meat flopped to the ground.

"Argh!" Ellen grabbed her head, bent forward, and let out a scream of pain, then punched a hole in the wall.

Kerys kept running, taking three random turns into unfamiliar hallways before the clanking footsteps resumed following her. She headed for a smaller door labeled 'maintenance only.' Someone had already shot out the access panel, enabling her to pull the door open. Hoping Ellen's suit couldn't fit in there, she crawled in and closed the door. The passage beyond had about half the width of the normal corridors, with bundles of wires and pipes on the left wall. She made it about twenty feet by the time an ear-punishing screech of metal came from behind.

Ellen tore the door clear off its hinges and cast it aside like tinfoil. Her steel-wrapped shoulders and chest slammed against the bulkhead with such a *boom* it seemed the entire dome trembled. "I'm coming for you, figment! I'll kill all of you."

"I'm real, Ellen. I'm not a figment of your imagination."

Armored fingers clamped around the doorframe and ripped it off its bolts, widening the opening.

"Oh, shit." Kerys whirled around and sprinted hard for the right-angle turn up ahead.

Ellen pivoted, leading with her right shoulder, and followed her into the maintenance hall. "Think you're so pretty, don't you?"

"Not really," yelled Kerys as she rounded the corner... and stared at what looked like a dead end twenty feet away. A heavy black grille over a maintenance crawlspace vibrated with a mechanical thrum.

"I don't care what you think of me. I know I'm pretty."

"You are! You're very pretty!"

Scraping metal grew louder from Ellen forcing the exo suit down the passage.

Kerys spun in place, searching for anything. She frowned at the dumbbell. *That woman wouldn't even notice me hitting her.*

"Got you, mouse." Ellen crammed herself into the bend, straining to pull the massive assisted armor past the corner. The inner wall crumpled under the strain.

The exo suit's left shoulder mangled a pipe as she walked, knocking it askew and shearing metal away from bundles of blue wires. The other end of the pipe broke apart from the wall, ripping down a panel covering a narrow passage lined with wires and glowing circuit boards. Kerys ducked, narrowly avoiding a steel pipe to the face.

Caught between a certain crushing death and a possible electrical one, she ran for the only option offering any chance: a smallish grille up ahead. Ellen continued sidestepping down the narrow passage while Kerys ran to the opening and pulled the grille aside. She scrambled into the cramped crawlspace tunnel with Ellen bearing down on her, the giant exo suit shearing more pipes and components off the walls. The giant woman lunged at the opening; metal fingers snagged the thick sole of her shoe. Kerys grabbed a spar crossing near the top of the crawlspace, clinging in defiance of the giant suit attempting to pull her out.

Her body hung suspended between her hands and one foot.

The half-inch bar bowed under the strain. A *pop* came from Kerys's shoulder; a second later, a similar noise emanated from her left hip. She groaned in agony. The exo-suit's metal fingers slipped a little on the hard rubber. If Ellen pulled too hard, she'd lose her grip.

She's not mindless... just psychotic. "Please let go... I swear you're pretty!"

"Got you, mousey mousey," cooed Ellen.

Kerys stared at her failing grip, tears running from her eyes at the pain in her fingers. "Please, don't." She kicked at her trapped shoe, trying to slip out of it, but she'd secured the Velcro too tight.

"Come now, mousey." Ellen thrust her left arm in, pushing at the wall and crushing the glowing components out of her way in a flurry of sparks.

A bright flash preceded a deafening *bang* that slammed the air out of her lungs.

The grip on her shoe released. Kerys lurched forward, landed flat on her front, and slid a few inches. She curled fetal, clutching her hands to her chest. Her palms throbbed with pain as though someone had slashed a knife across them.

Ellen convulsed, emitting a half-scream, half moan that stopped and started in a staccato rhythm. Great blue arc flashes lapped at her suit, springing out from the ruined hole her fingers had torn in the wall. Kerys looked away, cringing from the zapping, buzzing, shrieking mess only five feet away.

In seconds, the screaming ceased, but the buzzing continued. After a moment, she risked a peek. Ellen's head hung bowed, steaming blood and white foam dripping to the duct floor below her. The stink of overcooked meat brought bile to the back of Kerys' throat. Electrical arcs continued jumping from the suit's shoulders to the metal walls.

Even if she had the strength to move Ellen out of her way, touching the suit would probably deliver a fatal shock.

Kerys twisted to look behind her, and let off a gasp of relief at not being trapped between an electrocuted corpse and a dead end. The passage continued about fifteen feet deeper where it split left and right. She glanced back at Ellen and clamped a hand over her mouth and nose in an effort to stop smelling the awful stench of cooking person.

Sniffling and coughing, she crawled to the junction. Left only went a few feet to a cabinet full of circuit breakers. The other direction extended much farther, with bundles of blue wire diverting off here and there into tiny conduits. A mesh panel at the far end appeared to be a way out, or at least might be thin enough to kick down.

She headed in that direction, but slowed at the sound of men muttering.

"You tell me. You're the damn tech," said Sergeant Gensch.

Another man replied, "Something blew up."

Gensch chuckled. "Is that your, uhh, professional opinion?"

"Cut him some slack man," said a third voice with a Scottish accent. "With everything going on, that could've been anything."

"Hey," said voice two, "someone's cooking. Smells like steak."

Kerys threw up a little in her mouth, and spat.

"Nope." Gensch heaved a throaty sigh. "Someone humped an electric outlet. That's fried dead idiot."

Voice two dry heaved.

She crawled up to the mesh screen and peeked out into the space beyond. Three men sat on the floor behind an improvised barricade of boxes, chairs, and two desks. She recognized Sergeant Gensch, but not the exhausted man next to him. Both he and the beefy ginger on his other side wore grey jumpsuits. *MacLeod... The facilities manager.*

"This is all kinds of fucked up," said the black guy. "Everyone just freaked the hell out all at once. Goddamned Munoz tried to stab me."

"I had to kill Jodie." MacLeod hung his head and swallowed a lump. "Hell with Munoz."

"At least she went out knowing you loved her." Gensch adjusted a bandage on MacLeod's right bicep. "I'd have shot the bitch *before* she stabbed me."

MacLeod wiped tears.

Kerys pushed the hatch open.

Gensch whirled on her with a gun poised.

MacLeod's sorrow receded. He raised a giant wrench like a broadsword. The other man drew a pair of combat knives.

"I'm okay." Kerys raised her hands. A droplet of blood trickled down her palm from where the bar she'd been clinging to cut her fingers. "I'm not crazy."

"Come on out of there nice and easy," said Gensch.

She slithered out, pulling herself onto the floor, and stood with her hands in the air.

"Who's that?" asked MacLeod. "Don't recognize her."

"Blue jumpsuit." The black man shifted his jaw side to side. "From the new team. The archaeologists or some shit."

"Yeah. I'm Kerys."

Gensch stared at her, hazel eyes unwavering, but also full of sanity. "What's ninety-four times 206?"

"Uhh, not sure." Slow and easy, she tugged her e-pad off her belt and opened a calculator app. "It's 19,364."

Sergeant Gensch chuckled and lowered his gun.

"She cheated," said MacLeod.

The nameless man put his knives away and swatted at him. "Someone who lost their shit wouldn't think to use a damn e-pad." He smiled at her. "Louis Hellerman."

"Oh. Right." MacLeod nodded at Hellerman and relaxed.

"Guess we're plus one." Gensch lowered himself to sit once more. "Have a seat."

Kerys eased herself down and rubbed her shoulder. It didn't feel dislocated, but remained sore. "Wait... *Hellerman*? Did you hack my quarters for Will Braxton?"

Hellerman's smile became far too innocent.

"You did. Son of a bitch." She grumbled.

"Wait... he said you two were gonna get married, but he had to take this job out here. Wanted to surprise you by leavin' a ring in your room. I, uhh, didn't think it, umm...."

"He can be quite convincing." She frowned. "For the record, I was on the verge of being willing to marry him, but he had an acute case of asshole. Stalked me for months."

"Oh, shit." Hellerman scratched at his hair. "Sorry. I had no idea."

Sergeant Gensch shrugged. "Sounds like a complaint for HR, but I think they're kinda busy at the moment."

"So, uhh... what's going on?" She glanced at the barricade.

"Bunch of Gensch's former buddies decided to do a sweep and clear." MacLeod pointed out bullet gouges on the walls around them. "We made a last stand here."

Two assault rifles lay on the floor behind him, likely out of ammo.

Kerys worked her leg back and forth, trying to get her hip to stop hurting. "I meant in general."

"Beats me. The crew all hopped the same shuttle to planet batshit." Sergeant Gensch took a long pull from a vape inhaler. "Most of my people are dead, some are missing, and I can't get a response from the captain."

"You won't. Chen's dead." Kerys shivered at the memory. "She shot herself."

MacLeod took a grey plastic packet from a box and tossed it to her. "Hungry?"

"Not really, but I should probably eat something… it's been at least a day. Please don't be any form of steak."

Gensch gave her a pointed look.

"Ellen Vickers. She thought I was a figment of her imagination and tried to smash me. I wound up in that passage trying to get away from her. She had an exo suit on and tried to climb in behind me, put her hand into something and… zap."

Hellerman shook his head. "Aww damn, girl. Shit. What'd you do to ya'self?" He flung himself down with a defeated look on his face.

"Dammit," MacLeod grumbled. "I hope she didn't overload the primary. If that melted, we're going to have a real nasty time of it."

"Can't we bypass Bank 1 and filter everything 'round the auxiliary capacitors?" asked Hellerman, his lip quivering.

"Yeah, but that's gonna require a lot of crawling into places my ass ain't fittin' in." MacLeod crossed his arms.

"What are you talking about?" Kerys sucked some vaguely chicken-flavored orange goo from a silver packet.

"If Ellen broke into a line carrying enough juice to fry her, I'm inclined to believe she ate a rapid discharge from the primary capacitor. Basically," said MacLeod, "she used up a couple days' worth of juice in a few seconds. It'd be a miracle if the capacitor units didn't melt. Everything runs off the external power pod. The dome doesn't have a reactor of its own—just solar arrays, which aren't set up because we have the reactor module. All these space buildings are modular."

"The lights are still on," said Kerys.

"True." MacLeod gazed up. "Could be we got lucky."

"Whatever happened here hasn't affected the computers, but the communications system isn't responding." Hellerman pressed a fist to his chin, cracking his neck. "I can probably fix it, but I think the problem is with the transmission array itself… and to check it, I need to go outside."

"Where is it?" asked Kerys. "There's gotta be suits left."

"On top of the dome." Hellerman switched fists and popped his neck the other way. "Pretty easy to get to, 'long as we don't run into no more crazy sons of bitches tryin' to kill us."

She nodded at him and huddled up against a box, cradling her meal packet in two hands. Not being alone anymore charged her with hope. Whatever drove the crew mad didn't seem to work on everyone. Sergeant Gensch sucked another pull from his vape wand, exhaling a strange, sweet fragrance. A small fault appeared in his hardass exterior. For an instant, the look he gave her almost seemed pitying.

Kerys managed a weak smile. She'd always loathed it when Will treated her like a damsel, but she didn't get the same feeling from the sergeant—more a sense of empathy for someone without combat training stuck in the kind of awful situation only soldiers should wind up in.

"So, what now?" asked MacLeod. "Sittin' here on our asses ain't gonna do anything. And what the hell am I sniffing?"

Gensch exhaled a thick stream of vapor from his mouth and nose. "Whiskey and cigar." The right half of his mouth curled into a grin. "Flavor's called BAMF."

Kerys cringed, and squeezed a large portion of chicken stew paste into her mouth to distract her brain away from imagining what 'whiskey cigar' tasted like.

"Figure we give it another few hours, stay away from people who might be contagious, let the nuts kill each other off. Should make it easier to do what we need to do." Gensch glanced at Hellerman. "'Less you got a better idea."

"Not really." He looked down. "Figure it don't much matter now. Damn, Ellen…"

MacLeod patted his shoulder. "Hey man. Losin' your girl is serious bad, but don't go givin' up. Whatever whacked out crap did this spared your sorry ass for a reason."

Hellerman shrugged.

"All right." Gensch slapped the box he'd been leaning his elbow on. "Next supply ship will be in orbit in five months and three weeks. This outpost's designed to support a crew of 150 for seven months. We had ninety-four. Down to four—most likely. MacLeod's the head of the maintenance team. He knows every fuse and toilet drain in this place. Hellerman installed every damn computer, electronic lock, and camera. Ain't no question of *if* we make it to see the shuttle. We just gotta do it."

"Yeah," said Hellerman, raising a water bottle.

"Aye." MacLeod held up a bottle.

Hellerman tossed a bottle of water to Kerys.

She raised it. "Sounds good."

Sergeant Gensch grinned. "That's what I like to hear."

17

ON EDGE

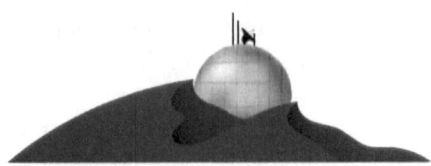

The security of no longer being alone afforded Kerys a chance to nap.

A merciful lack of dreams ended at the jostle of a hand on her shoulder. She startled awake and grabbed at her pocket for the dumbbell she'd forgotten in the tunnel. Sergeant Gensch held her seated until the instinctive urge to leap to her feet faded.

"Almost time." His deep, scratchy voice permeated her consciousness, soothing her fear.

Kerys exhaled, relaxed, and summoned up a weary smile from the deepest depths of her foggy brain. "All right. Thanks."

He maintained a steely face, though snuck in a wink as he shifted back to sit in his usual spot. She looked down before she felt too vulnerable. A required psych course or two got her thoughts circling around her absent father. Professor Robertson's words nattered on in her imagination, claiming the instant sense of trust she felt toward the aging soldier had to come from some inner longing for the father figure she never knew.

Freud got high and stayed there.

She finished off the last few gulps from her water bottle and stretched.

MacLeod and Hellerman knelt on either side of a cube-shaped cargo box, huddled over an e-pad. They pointed at its screen, muttering about the locations of power couplings and water lines.

"Once the ladies are done checking out the map," said Gensch, "we're gonna make for the armory. Might be a rifle or two still locked up. Then, we sweep the place from corner to corner. See if we got any more survivors or any other poor bastards dead on their feet."

"Be quicker if Scotty here'd stop hoggin' the map." Hellerman jabbed his finger at the e-pad.

MacLeod threw an empty water bottle at him.

Sergeant Gensch chuckled.

"Knock that shit off." MacLeod tore open another case and sucked down a whole bottle of water in one shot.

"You shouldn't let that get under your skin, man." Gensch toked on his vape, his next words came written in fog. "Name o' MacLeod, working in engineering, come on."

"Both of ya can go straight ta hell." MacLeod drilled his finger at the e-pad, dragging the image to one side. "Figure we check the spot where—"

"Stop hoggin' the goddamned screen!" Hellerman yanked a knife off his belt and jammed it into MacLeod's chest.

The big guy wheezed and collapsed over sideways.

Kerys backed against the wall. As Gensch went for his sidearm, Hellerman pulled and threw another knife, forcing the older man to dive to the floor. He cross-drew a third knife and pounced on Kerys. She got her arms up to catch his wrist before the blade bit into her. They struggled for control of the knife until Gensch aimed his weapon from the ground. Hellerman dragged her away from the wall, flipped her around, and grabbed her from behind with a blade at her throat.

Gensch shoved himself up to his knees, aiming high. "Louis, what the fuck?"

"Ungh," wheezed MacLeod, feebly grasping at the knife sticking out of him.

Hellerman ducked, keeping his face at the back of her head. "There's a ship. That's what Chen was screaming about. They shuttin' the place down, right? She ain't wanna tell no one nothin'. We all laid off. Screwed again." His breath blasted warmth down the back of her neck. "I'm gettin' on that damned shuttle."

"You cut her, you're a dead man," said Gensch.

"Kill the bastard," muttered MacLeod before groaning and passing out.

"Outta my way, old man," muttered Hellerman into her hair.

Gensch's finger twitched. Kerys closed her eyes, bracing for a bullet slicing the side of her head. Four seconds felt like four hours.

"Do it, man." Hellerman edged to the left, dragging her. "They're tellin' me the ship's here."

"They who?" asked Gensch.

"All them whisperin' dead. Everyone who died here. They're talkin' to me now, even Ellie."

Kerys slid her arm up.

Gensch flicked his gaze at her creeping hand and pushed his gun forward, raising his voice. "It's waiting for you on the shuttle pad. Just let her go and I won't stop you."

"Bullshit man." Hellerman shied away from the weapon, hiding behind her. "You just sayin'—"

Kerys grabbed his forearm with both hands and yanked it down while shoving her right elbow up to force his arm over her head. Twisting toward him, she slipped away and flipped him by the arm to the floor.

Bang.

She jumped back from the spatter of blood, staring at Gensch in shock. "Y-you shot him."

"Yeah." Gensch holstered his gun. "Were you expecting him to get un-crazy?"

"Umm." She brushed her fingers at her throat where the knife had been. "Guess not."

"Nice move."

Kerys paced. "I haven't even thought about jiu-jitsu since I was a freshman in college."

"Must've had a good instructor, then. Muscle memory never forgets."

She cringed away from the dead Hellerman. "Never thought I'd really need it… only took the classes 'cause yoga put me to sleep."

"Yoga puts me to sleep, too. Whenever I see someone doing it." He took a knee to check on MacLeod. "Hmm. It's bad, but he's not dead yet."

"Infirmary?"

Gensch rubbed his chin. The scratch of silvery stubble filled in a short pause. "Haven't seen the doc since it hit the fan."

"Everything's automated. Even the damn shuttles. It's probably only a few buttons. We have to at least try." She sighed. "So much for being lucky."

He hauled MacLeod upright, looping the man's arm across his shoulders. "You got a strange definition of lucky, kid."

"I'm not a kid, I'm twenty-eight."

He gave her a flat look. "You're a kid."

Kerys picked up the knife that had been at her throat and moved past the barricade. "I was trying to understand how everyone lost their minds, hoping Annapurna's terminal might've had an answer, but I didn't make it to her office. When I found you guys, I thought maybe it's got a genetic component, like the way mosquitos like some people and never bite others, or that one friend who never gets sick. It's gotta be something we can't see… some kind of microbial—" She froze in shocked guilt, staring at the wall.

"Hmm. Don't think that would'a hit everyone all at the same time. Don't those kinds of infections need a cut or somethin'?" He glanced at the knife sticking out MacLeod's left pectoral. "Andy's got a bit of a nick."

"Holy shit... the head."

Gensch's eyebrows crept up. "No, it's in his chest. Hey, why'd you stop?"

"It can't be... Anna said the organisms were dead... dried up." Kerys shivered, but got moving again.

"Gotta go a little slower for this old man to keep up, and I mean the explanation. You could walk faster. I'm sure Andy'd appreciate it."

She jogged out of the dead-end where they'd taken refuge, looking left and right at a T intersection. *Crap, where am I?* "Which way is closer to the stairs?"

"Right, then the first left."

MacLeod woke for an instant, gurgled, and passed out.

"We discovered a stone head in the cavern. It had a hollow space inside that they found these dead microorganisms in."

"Think it's in the water?"

Kerys jogged to a door by the stairwell and held it open while Gensch carried MacLeod past. "I don't know. It spread so fast..." *How much more time do I have before I snap like Hellerman?* "I want to go to the lab after the infirmary. Maybe Anna found something."

Gensch grunted with the effort of hauling the big Scot up two flights. "Could be someone else out there, batshit crazy, ready to kill anything that moves."

"Yeah, but we have to do *something*." She exited the stairwell at the third floor, glancing left and right down a frigid, dark hallway. "Shit. The lights are out. It's not supposed to be this cold, is it?"

"It's been pretty quiet in the dome for a while. Haven't checked the lab pods yet." He loped out behind her. "Come on. Keep moving. Andy doesn't have time for us to dick around."

"I mean after. And didn't your plan include a full sweep? If we gotta live here for six months..."

"Yeah, yeah..." Gensch grunted. "Andy, you need to ease off on the damn donuts."

MacLeod emitted an incoherent murmur.

Kerys got her bearings and headed down the hall to the right. By the time she reached the empty command room, her breath appeared as fog. Four conference rooms away, stark white light glowed from the passage on the right that led to the infirmary. The huge wraparound windows that had once lined the corridor covered the floor as a thick layer of glittering bits.

Kerys shivered in the over-cranked air conditioning. Staring at shattered glass that looked so much like snow only made her colder.

"Watch out. Glass all over the floor here."

Gensch grunted. "It's safety glass. That black shit outside is more dangerous."

"Right..." She took a hesitant crunching step. "Kinda sounds the same."

"Get a move on, kid. MacLeod's not in great shape."

Kerys clenched her fists and jogged over the glass to a four-way intersection, and went left. The infirmary sat at the end of the next hallway like a single light left on in a dark house. She bee-lined for the room with the auto-surgeons, finding Doctor Sekhar's desk empty. Aside from a couple of bullet dents in the supply room door at the rear left corner, the area looked pristine.

The lack of blood anywhere reassured her.

Gensch hauled MacLeod in, the unconscious man's boots squeaking over the polished floor. He placed him seated on the edge of the nearer surgery table, and Kerys helped ease him back to recline. The man's shirt had become saturated with blood, his injury no doubt made worse by being carried up two flights of stairs.

Kerys rushed to the console, exhaling into her hands for warmth.

Items on the main menu included: diagnostic, trauma, preventative, chronic.

She tapped 'trauma.'

A submenu offered a long list of options. She tapped 'penetrating injury: chest.'

Sergeant Gensch's white caterpillar eyebrows rose when the egg on the ceiling split open.

The console buzzed and displayed, ‹patient position fault.›

She lifted MacLeod's dangling right arm to rest on the cushion next to him. The error went away. A robotic armature swooped down and projected a blue scanning laser over his body, zeroing in on the protruding knife in seconds. Three additional robotic limbs descended, focusing on the area, while four tiny 'spider legs' extended from the edge of the table and pierced his arm with needles. Vital signs appeared on the screen, reading a measurable heartbeat. Another sub-window offered a computer-generated model of the wound channel, showing the knife had pierced the lung.

"How bad is it?" asked Gensch.

"I don't know." Kerys shrugged. "I'm not a doctor... I think the machine is feeling optimistic since it's doing stuff."

The screen emitted a *boop* noise with the text: ‹Tension Pneumothorax detected. Patient lung deflated. Script ready. Operator: remove foreign object now.›

She threaded her arms between the robotic limbs, grasped the blade with both hands, and took a breath. After a second to psych herself up, she yanked the knife straight up out of MacLeod. Moving at the speed of blur, robot arms peeled away clothing around the wound while another suctioned up blood welling out of the hole. Two thin probes extended deep inside the wound cavity. On the little screen, a magnified view showed the tips poking around severed blood vessels in the top of the lung.

"Anyone out there?" Corporal Guillen's voice crackled from a little black box on Gensch's belt. "Repeat, is anyone listening?"

Gensch wandered away from the whirring auto-surgeon and squeezed his shoulder mic. "Copy, Corporal. Gensch here. Go ahead."

"There's something going on at the excavation site. I'm picking up some kind of activity inside I can't explain."

"What's your status, Corporal?" asked Gensch.

"Are you reading, Sarge? Got activity in the ruins. I'm gonna check it out."

"Stand down, Corporal. Stay clear of that place. Where's Cortez?"

Kerys bit her lip. At least the electric heartbeat chirps coming from the auto-surgeon sounded like a normal speed.

"Dead. Cortez is gone. So's Murano and Bax. Looks like they killed each other. I couldn't do anything for them. Gonna head inside and see what the hell all that light is."

"What *what* light is?" asked Kerys. "Is he serious? Activity in the alien site?" She remembered feeling watched in the 'head room.' Had they somehow awakened the locals?

"Son of a bitch," muttered Gensch before squeezing the mic again. "Corporal Guillen, do *not* go in that ruin. Return to the airlock." He listened to the hiss of a dead radio for a few seconds before looking at Kerys. "He's either hallucinating or someone's in there jacking off with a laser excavator."

She nodded. "Yeah. Heh. Aliens... right."

"You stay here." Gensch trucked out of the infirmary like someone had lit his pants on fire.

I would not want that man angry with me. She edged up to the console, mesmerized by the microscopic feelers dancing on the 3D image. It looked like the lung had already been closed, and another long arm suctioned blood out of it.

"Hey..." She patted his leg. "That thing seems to know what it's doing. You gotta promise me you won't go crazy on us, okay?"

Kerys stared at the screen for a little while more before shifting her attention out past the broken windows. *There's no way we woke up aliens.* Her lip quivered at the idea Guillen had succumbed to the madness as well. "This isn't fair…."

"What are you doing?" whispered a man.

She started to turn, but something struck her across the back of the head, knocking the room into a smear of color. The next thing she knew, she stared across the floor at the side of a desk, her cheek on icy metal.

"You're not authorized to operate that." Doctor Sekhar crouched down, his face looming close to hers. He thumbed one of her eyelids wider, smirked, and let go.

The room slipped away into a tunnel of blackness.

18

MALPRACTICE

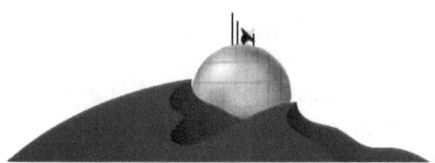

Merry humming seeped into Kerys's consciousness, along with a sharp pain in the back of her head. Soft padding under her body caressed her cheek and tried to lure her back to sleep, but the odd singing needled at her with a sense of wrongness. She attempted to sit up, but her body refused to listen. A pall of dizziness made her feel like she flew among the clouds, twisting and spinning on her cushioned pedestal.

A man whistled and hummed. Wet squishing noises preceded a gooey *slap* on the other side of the room.

Fake leather met her fingers when she squeezed.

I'm on a surgery machine…

Her eyes fluttered open. She lay on the second station, a few feet away from MacLeod, whose skin held a deathly pallor. The injectors that had been in his right arm had retracted. His head faced away from her, and he didn't seem to be breathing anymore. She looked past him at blood sprayed all over the wall. She tried to scream, but the sound occurred only in her mind.

Doctor Sekhar, his white jumpsuit spattered red from collar to knees, withdrew his hands from inside the man's chest cavity, cradling a meaty lump.

"Beam me up, Scotty!" cried the doctor, before hurling the organ upward.

It struck the ceiling with a *slap* and stuck. He cackled with glee.

The dull red lump peeled away a second later, falling to the floor.

Splut.

Kerys shrieked.

Doctor Sekhar jumped back, grasping his chest and hyperventilating. Paralytic shock in his eyes flashed to rage. He rushed at her, grabbing her arm and leaning his weight on it, pinning her to the cushions while cinching a black nylon strap tight around her left wrist. She struggled to shake the fog in her mind, but her free arm flopped about as if packed with lead.

"No!" she screamed. "Get off!"

The doctor seized her other arm in both hands and forced it down to the cushion. Kerys thrashed side to side, but couldn't overpower him. She drew her leg back, trying to push him away, but he leaned too close for her to get it between them.

"Stop fighting. You're in need of medical attention. You shouldn't even be conscious right now given how hard I hit you."

She squirmed her hand away from slippery, bloody fingers and raked her nails at his face. He cried out and jumped back. As soon as she reached over to grab the strap binding her left wrist, he dove across her body, fighting to control her free arm.

"Get off me!" she roared.

"Oh, I remember now. You're the patient complaining of a stomach issue. No matter, I'll just remove the whole thing. That way, it won't cause any problems."

She screamed past clenched teeth, but her post-blow-to-the-head body couldn't find enough strength to stop him from pushing her arm down once more. He broke eye contact to search for the second strap.

Kerys swung herself up and smashed her forehead into his nose. The impact left her seeing stars, but the doctor jerked upright, away from her. She planted her shoe against his chest and kicked as hard as she could.

He wailed, lost his footing in the blood all over the floor, and crashed against the counter of medical devices, dragging two of them, plus a basket full of little plastic bottles, to the ground. Grunting, she sat up and grabbed at the strap around her wrist, fumbling at the release catch.

"Patient is exhibiting pronounced violent behavior," muttered the doctor past the hand bracing his bleeding nose. "I'm afraid we'll need to use restraints."

The strap came loose a split second after he lunged to his feet. Kerys rolled off the table, leaving him diving onto empty cushions. She tried to run, but blood took her shoes out from under her, dumping her flat on her chest; a noise like a barking goose came out of her on impact. An irregular fleshy lump of light purple striated with blood vessels sat on the floor inches in front of her face. She recoiled and forced herself up.

To her horror, pieces of MacLeod lay all over: on the floor, on the counter top, stuck to the walls, in the sink... everywhere but inside the man they belonged to.

Doctor Sekhar shambled to the counter and opened a drawer, rummaging for a small bottle before going back for a syringe. "Now, now, this won't hurt."

She surged upright and ran at him, stomp-kicking the drawer closed on his hand. He screamed, grasping his right wrist and tugging at his arm.

"What's wrong with you!" shouted Kerys, leaning as much of her weight into the drawer as the slippery floor allowed.

He braced himself against the counter, pulling at his arm in an effort to free his hand from the drawer. Her left foot slid backward. She eyed the desk. The edge of Hellerman's combat knife gleamed in the light from the screen.

Clattering plastic snapped her attention back to the doctor. He pulled a used syringe out of a sharps container, holding it like an icepick while glaring at her ankle. Before he could stab her, Kerys jumped back, slipped, and fell on her ass. The doctor rolled away from the drawer, cradling his wrist to his chest, his gaze wild.

"It's good that Avasar has a full medical plan. I'm going to need to run a few hundred tests on you."

She scrambled to all fours and crawled for the desk. The doctor roared and jumped on her back, wrapping his arms around her. He grunted, straining to haul her upright, but he stepped on a hunk of MacLeod that took his right foot out from under him and sent them both spilling to the side. The doctor wheezed on impact, but his grip tightened.

She drove her elbow backward into his chest over and over again until he let go and stumbled back cradling his gut.

"Patient is extremely psychotic," said Doctor Sekhar.

"Look in a damn mirror, doc." She rolled into a crawl, putting her hand down on something squishy, but ignored the awfulness, focusing only on her effort to reach the knife.

"This treatment is mandatory, I'm afraid."

Kerys reached Sekhar's desk, grabbed the top, and pulled herself to her feet. The computer screen, despite a spattering of blood, still displayed the space marine video game, paused. The knife she'd taken from Hellerman lay between it and the keyboard.

Doctor Sekhar picked himself up. "Get away from there. I've only gotten to that boss twice. Damn you people and your constant interruptions! Now, stop fighting and let me do what I have to do so I can get back to my god... damned... game."

She eased her arm forward, curling her fingers around the knife handle. Head bowed, she peered between her arm and her side, watching him approach. The instant he raised his hands to grab her, she let off a war cry, spun, and drove the blade into his chest.

The rage in his eyes melted to confusion. He looked down at her hand, back at her, and laughed before collapsing away from the knife. Kerys stood motionless, staring down at him for a few seconds before she lowered her arm. Blood dripped from the blade to the floor by her shoe.

"That's a mortal wound." Flat on his back, Doctor Sekhar laughed so hard he cried. "I'm dying! I'm going to die for real. Funny. I always thought it would hurt more than this." He looked up at her and snickered. "Damn, I hate how these games cheat."

For his last few seconds of life, he laughed uncontrollably.

When he went still, she looked down at the knife in her grasp. She might not have killed Private Foster; the man was most certainly alive before Ellen stepped on him. The doctor, however, she had no doubt.

I killed someone…

Kerys tossed the knife onto the desk like it would burn her and wiped her hand on her jumpsuit. She paced in circles, cradling the back of her head where a little blood matted her hair. Touching the spot reawakened a headache. Between that and guilt, she dropped to her knees and retched until she couldn't move. Not having anything inside her to get rid of seemed to make her body try three times as hard to puke. When the convulsions finally stopped, she gasped for air, a thread of bile connecting her lip to the floor.

"He would've killed me." She wiped her mouth on the back of her arm. Thinking of the smiling doctor she'd first met for a routine physical brought shivers of guilt. "What happened to you? You're a doctor! You must've figured out something. Why is everyone going insane?" She sniffled, unable to stop crying. "I killed you…" She swallowed hard. "I didn't have a choice. You would've killed me. You *did* kill MacLeod. Why did you kill him? He was going to survive."

She gingerly took hold of the knife again. Picturing Jaden smiling at her let her rein in her tears.

"I'm not going to quit. I am going home." She huddled under the desk, clutching the blade close. *I'll stay out of sight 'til Gensch comes back… what if he doesn't?*

"He's gotta…" Kerys bowed her head, shaking from adrenalin.

19

NOT CUT OUT

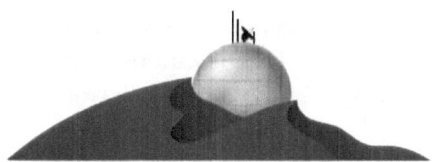

Kerys hid in the space beneath the desk for a while in silence, staring at a hunk of something that used to be MacLeod. That she didn't feel any compulsion to look away from the piece of organ worried her. She waited, listening to every creak from the walls, every phantom scrape echoing in the vents. A crinkle of plastic floated in the wind—or did crazy still lurk the halls of Wayfarer Outpost?

Come on, Gensch. Where the hell are you?

She imagined him finding Corporal Guillen outside and an argument blossoming into gunfire. Or maybe the man hadn't been hallucinating and something *did* wake up in the excavation. Her team had certainly been making enough noise. *No. That's silly. If there'd been aliens in there... this outpost has been here for years. Why did they wait until now?*

"The vault..." Her mind leapt back to her pushing the buttons, finding the head. Could she have set something in motion? "No. I can't believe that. Aliens? *Live* aliens here?"

She glanced to her right at the table holding MacLeod's remains. A long, foggy exhale left her mouth. *It's as cold as a morgue.* The thought got her teeth chattering.

"I can't leave him like that."

MacLeod's left arm slipped from the table and dangled.

Kerys yelped at the sight of a dead man moving, banging her head on the underside of the desk with a startled jump. She stared at him for a few minutes, ready to run like hell if he moved again... but he didn't.

"We tried." She choked up. Fresh tears slipped down her cheeks. "I'm sorry. We tried."

After crawling out from under the desk, she tucked the knife in her jumpsuit pocket and retrieved a pair of blue exam gloves from the drawer in the counter. She gathered the various bits, hunks, and blobs, depositing them one by one in his open chest cavity. At first, she tried not to look, but forty minutes and dozens of pieces later, it didn't bother her anymore.

Each time she put something back, she whispered an apology.

Eventually, she ran out of parts in reach. The rest of MacLeod stuck to walls too high for her to get to. Kerys pulled the knife from her pocket and advanced on the supply closet door. She yanked it open, ready for someone to attack, but the room held no people.

A sleeping bag, a cluster of water bottles, and a stack of hydra trays sat on the floor in between two shelves of various medical supplies.

"Doc was watching us the whole time... bastard waited for Gensch to leave."

She dragged a stepladder out and used it to recover the rest of MacLeod's internal parts. After a bit of poking around the auto-surgeon's menu, she found an autopsy command menu and managed to get the machine to stitch him closed.

That, she didn't watch.

Tromping boots overpowered the whirring-clicking of robotic arms. Kerys readied her knife and ducked out of sight against the wall by the door.

"Kid, you still here?" said Gensch.

Kerys wanted to melt into a puddle from relief. "Yeah. What happened?"

"Thing almost done with him?" Sergeant Gensch walked in, put his hands on his hips, and smirked. He glanced at the wall and tracked his gaze around at all the gore. "So, looks like there were complications with the surgery?"

Her lip quivered. "MacLeod's dead..."

Gensch started toward her, but stopped when he noticed Doctor Sekhar. "You okay?"

"No. Not really. The doctor was hiding in the closet. As soon as you left, he jumped me from behind, knocked me out. I woke up... MacLeod was already dead. He... umm..."

"Yeah. I get the picture." He took a step closer, shaking his head.

Kerys leaned against him, not quite hugging him. He didn't embrace her back, but he didn't really have to. She figured for a man like him, this equated to an uncharacteristic show of emotion. "Outside?"

"I couldn't find him. Heard Mitchell on the comm a few times, but I think she's gone loopy. Kept ranting about 'it' coming for her. I must've run around the damn complex four times. Couple of jackasses by the landing pad were playing tag with bullets. Figured I'd join in. Been awhile since I had a good match. Other than that, no sign of anything."

She cringed. "What about aliens… that light?"

"I think Guillen saw Deering running wild with an excavator laser. Found him and his exo suit shot to shit in the cavern. Could'a been Guillen. Looked like APEX."

"Huh? Apex? Deering?"

"Lars Deering, and APEX is the standard-issue ammunition for our rifles. It's 'grunt speak' for armor-piercing explosive. Each bullet has a microsecond fuse, designed to punch a hole in armor and explode inside where all the soft bits are." Gensch pulled his vape wand from his pocket and took a hit, grinning. "Think ol' Lars might've scared the corporal. Counted at least twenty holes in that exo."

Kerys sighed, gathered her composure, and stopped leaning against him. "Thanks."

"Mmm." He took a step and booted Doctor Sekhar in the head. "That's for Andy."

Kerys peeled the exam gloves off and tossed them across the room onto the counter. "So now what? I'm an archaeologist; you're a soldier. Is this place going to run itself for six months without MacLeod or his team to maintain it?"

He chuckled out a cloud of vape fog. "Either that or we better learn to hold our breath." He tipped the inhaler at her. "You're a smart one. I'm sure you'll figure any of that technical crap out with the user's manual."

"I can try." She rubbed her hands up and down her arms for warmth. "What about MacLeod? Does this place have a morgue… or something?"

"Ehh… I suppose we'll eventually get around to burying the dead. Haven't tried to dig outside, but we got the excavation site. Damn place looks like a tomb. We can use it for one. Before we deal with that, we need to secure the area."

"All right."

"Hungry?" He raised an eyebrow.

"Not really."

"Great. Me neither. Come on." He tucked the vape wand in his pocket, drew his sidearm, and walked out.

Kerys followed him close, the squeak of rubber soles on metal floor echoing in the stillness. A distant *thud* made her jump. Gensch halted and aimed down the hall. She all but stopped breathing. A moment later, he lowered his arm and moved on. They crept across the third floor and descended into warmer air. By the time they reached the first floor, she almost had feeling back in her fingers.

"Is it possible for it to be that cold upstairs without a problem? Please tell me that's not a sign we're losing air."

Gensch shrugged one shoulder. "Got me. Ask MacLeod."

Damn.

A door on the right creaked open a short distance ahead, swinging out into the hall. Gensch whipped his arm up to aim. Kerys clutched her knife. Ten seconds later, Gensch made a 'wait here' gesture with his left hand, then advanced. He swung wide to the left, angling on the doorway, but dropped his arm once he got even with it.

"Wind," he muttered.

She started breathing again.

Gensch led the way to the cafeteria, and a short while later, they sat with rehydrated meals steaming in front of them. He peeled his open without hesitation, attacking turkey in gravy. She stared through the clear plastic covering at fried chicken fingers, corn, and mashed potatoes.

Five minutes of watching him devour his food while smelling hers got her to open her Hydra tray, and she forced herself to eat. To get the image of MacLeod out of her mind, she pretended none of this space stuff had been real. In her mind, she made herself think she'd only gone jogging, and sat inside Mrs. Finlay's coffee shop having a snack.

Neither spoke during their meal. Once they finished, Gensch stood, grabbed the empty trays, and tossed them in the trash box. The act struck her as funny.

"What?" He gave her a confused look.

"It's not really funny, but... we're basically in hell and you're still putting trash in the bin."

He laughed. "Ain't no reason to give up on cleanliness. We still gotta live in this paradise for another six months. Might as well treat it like home."

She cringed at the word 'home.' The notion she could've ever been *excited* to be here seemed ludicrous. He headed for the southwest exit, away from the residential pods. Kerys followed, not questioning where he went until he wound up right back at the barricaded dead end where she'd first found them.

"What?"

"Figure we could both use some rest. It's almost midnight." He grabbed Hellerman's body by the back of the jumpsuit. "Be right back."

She sat on a clump of plain, grey blankets. Hellerman's legs slid out of her field of view as Gensch dragged the man off. "Where are you putting him?"

"Infirmary. Nice and cold up there."

"Okay."

She sat there dreading some future day when she and Gensch had to gather up all the dead bodies and transport them to the alien site. He had a point. A hollowed-out chamber in the mountain *did* seem like a tomb. As much as it pained her to contaminate a site of xenoarchaeological significance, she couldn't summon the slightest bit of interest in discovering its secrets. Better to put the bodies out there than keep them inside where she'd be living for the next five months.

Eventually, she paid a visit to a one-person bathroom at the midpoint of the dead-end spur. After flushing, she checked herself in the mirror. A quick wet-towel pass cleared blood from her face and hands. She wanted to grab a clean jumpsuit, but it didn't seem worth risking a walk across the outpost alone. Prodding fingers tested the lump on the back of her head, which didn't seem to be as large a wound as the pain it gave off might indicate.

Sergeant Gensch returned a few minutes after she wrapped herself in blankets. He sat with his back to the opposite wall, arm balanced over a knee, silver vape wand dangling between his fingers. Kerys stared at the spot next to him longingly, blushed, and looked away. The whoosh of him sucking on the inhaler filled the silence and faded. She looked back at him. He flicked a glance at the floor beside him. His expression seemed to say 'if you want.'

"So, how'd you wind up here, kid?"

Kerys buried her face up to the nose in the blanket and sighed. "I went out with another expedition a couple years ago. We found a significant amount of non-human artifacts, some major pieces too. I was the most junior person on the team, so I got overlooked. Almost everyone else involved had their faces on the news, magazines, archaeological journals…

"Not me. I guessed correctly about something and the project lead was furious at me for this fresh-out-of-college kid upstaging him. Fast forward a couple years, someone at Avasar finds my name on the crew roster, vids me. I talked to her for a bit and the next thing I know, I get offered this contract. She sent photos of the primary chamber here, said they think the 'complex' had between eight and ten rooms. I couldn't believe it. My mouth said yes before my brain could react."

"Suppose about now you're havin' some regrets." He smiled.

"Yeah. My brother was only ten when I left. I shouldn't have come here."

He raised a bushy white eyebrow. "You two close?"

"Kind of. Jaden came along real late, and we don't have the same father. My dad disappeared before I was born. I never knew him. Mom got into a 'no strings attached' arrangement with someone at her work and got pregnant at forty-three. I'd been so pissed off at her for so long, I didn't really see much of my brother 'til he was about nine. One day he went from avoiding me to adoring me." She choked up.

"Now what's a mother gotta do to get their kid pissed off like that?"

She wiped her cheek on the blanket. "I guess it could've been a lot worse. Mom was more like an employer than a parent, about as affectionate as a lump of steel wool. Kept me in extra-curricular activities so she didn't have to watch me when I was small. Rode me all the time about grades as I got older. 'Oh, you have to do well to get into this school. You have to get into this school to get a good job' and so on."

"Mmm." The vape tube hissed and gurgled. He blew a fog ring, a bigger one after it, and shot a fast tiny one through both.

"I met Will at Berkeley. He seemed like a nice guy at first. Everyone loves him when they first meet him. There's just something about him that makes people want to trust him. I lived with him for two and a half years, and spent like ten months of that time trying to psych myself up to leave. He's such a domineering, manipulative bastard."

Gensch chuckled.

She blinked. "Wow… did I just really say that? I mean… I've thought it, but I've never been able to tell someone the truth like that before."

He waved the vape wand about. "Near-death experiences have a way of diminishing inhibitions."

Kerys looked down at the lumps her shoes made under the blanket. "Yeah… so, what about you? Why'd you come out here?"

He exhaled a long plume of vapor. "Figured my ex-wife's lawyers couldn't find me here."

She cracked up laughing.

"Eh, bad joke. Don't mind me." The vape wand gurgled, loud against the oppressive silence, as he took another pull, apparently fighting a smile. "Never had a wife. USIC didn't leave me much time for that mess. Enlisted within an hour of turnin' eighteen, never looked back." He stared off into nowhere, fog leaking from his nostrils. "Figured I ain't cut out for that whole 'family' thing."

Kerys crossed the hall and sat beside him. "I dunno. I think you would've been an okay father."

"Is that so?"

She ducked under his arm and leaned against him. "Don't take my word for it. I'm no judge of fatherhood. I've never even met mine."

He chuckled. "Well, *kiddo*, try and get some rest."

"Yeah, right." Kerys rested her head on his shoulder.

"I draw the line at bedtime stories." The vape tube hissed, cutting off with a sputter. "Don't get your hopes up. That ain't happenin'."

She smirked. "Night, *Dad*."

RECKLESS

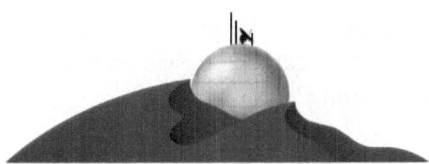

A hard sneeze shocked Kerys awake. She sneezed again, tried to breathe in, but her nose refused to admit air. The attempt caused her to cough to the point of gagging. Sensing imminent vomit, she lurched over sideways, mouth open. A little saliva dribbled from her lip, but after a few labored breaths, her stomach calmed. She gave it another few seconds in case a surprise occurred before sitting up and wiping her face on her sleeve.

Sergeant Gensch leaned away, right eyebrow high.

"I'm not nuts yet. Shit, thought I'd gotten over this cold." Kerys leaned back against the wall and focused on breathing for a little while. Within a few minutes, the congestion went away. She sniffled. "Ugh. Guess I'm just allergic to morning."

"In high school, I couldn't stand mornings. USIC cured that little hang up." He tossed her a ration pack.

She squeezed cheeseburger-flavored paste into her mouth, barely chewing before swallowing, and emptying it in under a minute.

"Ready?"

"Yeah." She shed the blanket from her shoulders, stood, and stretched. "I need to get to the lab."

He got up with a grunt. "Been quiet all night."

"Did you sleep?" She blinked.

"A little."

Sergeant Gensch led the way down the corridor, turning left where the dead-end met another hall, and taking a right about ten feet later into a long stretch lined with doors. Faint clattering surged and ebbed like wind-driven hailstones against the windows at the far end. He advanced with his body canted sideways, left shoulder leading, hand on his pistol. He stopped at the corner and peered around to the right.

Kerys tucked up behind him. "Why'd you stop?"

"Thought I heard something moving." He peered back at her. "Might've been wrong."

A metal crash echoed in the distance behind them, like a pile of cafeteria trays falling over.

She leapt against the wall, knife pointing down the hallway to the rear. "That wasn't the wind."

"Even the crazy get hungry." He stared toward where the sound came from. "You think whatever's eatin' people's brains is gonna kill 'em, or are we gonna need to go hunting?"

"No idea. That's why I want to go to the lab."

"Mmm." He slipped around the corner, heading south.

Kerys backed after him, keeping her eyes locked on the noisy hallway until she put solid wall between her and being seen. Her breathing slowed to small sips of air; her heart pounded.

"Coming?" muttered Gensch.

"Yeah." She jogged to catch up. "My hands are shaking. I wish I could be calm like you."

"I'm fuckin' terrified," he said, deadpan.

She let out a nervous giggle, covering her mouth to keep quiet.

He pointed his gun around a left turn, swiveling after it and aiming at four distinct points before relaxing. "Damn. Poor bastards."

Five bodies lay in the antechamber where the hamster tube connecting to the lab pod met the dome. All wore green jumpsuits, riddled with bullet holes. The nearest body didn't have much of a head anymore.

He stooped to pick up an assault rifle, but discarded it with an annoyed grumble. "Three things cause people to fire on full auto: idiocy, panic, or bein' crazy. Looks like Miller had the trifecta."

She shrugged.

"Come on." Gensch ducked to enter the tube and jogged ahead.

At the eastward bend, about a third of the way to the lab pod, a faint hissing became noticeable. Blood coated the wall to the right in a spray pattern. Three bodies lay slumped close together, a woman and man in camouflage jumpsuits next to a large man in a grey one. Faint sizzling came from up ahead, as if someone in the lab cooked up burgers, though the air carried no appealing smells.

Gensch hurried to the dead, rummaged the bodies, and took a pistol magazine from the woman's belt.

"What's that hissing?"

"Bullet cracked the window." He pointed at a starburst in the plastic. "Air's going out like a leaky tire."

"Oh, shit." She backed up.

"It's not too bad. Air pressure's not that much different. Least it's in our favor. Bad shit ain't comin' in."

"What do we do?" She gulped.

"Check the lab for any survivors, nut jobs, or usable supplies... then I'm gonna seal this tube. We won't need the damn lab sittin' here waitin' for a ship."

She nodded.

Kerys jogged ahead to the opening at the west end of Lab Pod 1. She stepped in and looked around at dimly lit empty labs, each one surrounded by glass like enormous fish tanks. Here and there, computer terminals provided some light from desktop backgrounds or lock screens. One monitor played a movie with spaceships trading laser fire. Gensch entered behind her, handgun up.

He swept his gaze across the area and relaxed. "Guess they took the day off."

"What day is it, anyway?"

"Tuesday." He shrugged. "I mean. It's Tuesday on Earth right now, in LA. Avasar uses California time out here. This dirt ball's got somethin' like two-point-four days to one Earth day, so it'll be dark on Sunday and Monday, lit all day Tuesday and Wednesday, and some of Thursday..."

"Suppose it's easier to use fake time without exterior windows."

Kerys tried to remember the way she'd gone before, when she'd been intent on asking Anna's opinion on the flower but chickened out at the sight of Will in the same room.

Will. Oh, no... I haven't seen him since everything went to hell...

A pang of almost-sorrow hit her at the thought of him dying. He'd been an asshole, but she had once loved him. The same way she let the good moments keep her hopeful and sticking around far longer than she should have, she dwelled on a somber sense of loss. After so long, she'd finally accepted that he'd been abusive, but despite that, she didn't feel right *cheering* about his death. Worse, the idea he'd probably died gave a sense of relief she felt horrible for appreciating.

Floor tiles shifted and clanked underfoot from Gensch walking up behind her. She put Will out of her mind and marched on. Black spaces on the floor up ahead, missing tiles, exposed a sunken space full of wire bundles. A handprint smeared in blood suggested someone tried to crawl down there to hide, but didn't make it.

Near the door to Anna's lab, a man lay dead against the wall, most of his jaw missing as well as a significant portion of skin on the front of his neck and chest. A large glass flask lay inches from his right hand. Whatever liquid had spilled from it ate a hole in the floor.

"Damn." Gensch shook his head. "That had to hurt."

She cringed and scurried past the body.

Three more corpses sat in a stack by the left wall inside the lab: two men, their skulls bashed-in, lay next to a slim Asian woman with a large hole in her chest, bigger than what a bullet would've left.

Gensch looked around, again with his weapon high. "Someone moved them after they died. We might not be alone."

"I'm going in. Cover me."

He almost chuckled. "What?"

She walked toward Anna's desk, the same place she'd spent hours in VR exploring the virtual alien 'head.' "That's what you military types always say, right?"

"Only in movies."

Kerys sat at the desk and tapped the keyboard. With a chirp, the screen lit up to a desktop. "Lucky… Anna forgot to lock her workstation."

She dove into the file system hunting for research notes. Gensch paced around, keeping his attention on the giant windows and other labs.

Squeeeeeak.

Kerys looked back over her shoulder.

Annapurna emerged from a tall storage cabinet, her eyes wide in a manic stare. A blood-soaked white lab coat hung half off her shoulders. Her bra peeked out from the ripped front of her jumpsuit, three fingernail scratches clear on the skin above her breast.

"Anna!" Kerys jumped to her feet. "You're alive!"

"What are you doing?" asked Anna. "That's my research."

No! Kerys sniffled, hand over her mouth. Grief crashed into her like a speeding car. "Anna… Are you still you?"

"Get away from my research!" screamed Annapurna.

Behind her, Gensch muttered, "Shit!"

The enraged scientist charged at Kerys, raising a pry bar coated in dried blood. Kerys dove to the side, landing on all fours and scrambling upright as the hook end gouged the desk mere inches from the keyboard.

"Anna, please stop!" Kerys gave Gensch a pleading look. "You've caught something that's made you sick. You're not being rational. Something's infected people, and we need your help to figure out what's happened."

"Wasting your time," muttered Gensch.

Annapurna didn't seem concerned with the handgun aimed at her face; her wild glare never left Kerys. "You're a liar. This whole time you've been cuddling up to me to get my research. That stuff with Will was a lie to make people feel sorry for you. I'm a fool to have ever believed it. He's such a sweet man. Now I see what you're really like."

"No, Anna. You're delusional from whatever's infected you." Kerys raised her hands, staring at the crowbar. The straight end had a foot or so of blood caked on it. She shot a brief look at the dead woman, assuming the large hole in her chest came from the pry bar. "Think about it. You found microbes in the statue, right?"

Anna lunged, swinging high. Kerys ducked left, yelping as the bar ripped a strand or two of her hair out.

"Son of a…" Gensch charged up behind Anna, grabbing her in a bear hug and pinning her arms. "She's gone, kid. Ain't no comin' back."

Annapurna thrashed, screaming, "You can't steal my research! I've already sent it all back to Earth. They know it's my work! Lying, scheming, backstabbing bitch!"

Gensch shifted her to the right and gave Kerys a 'where do you want this?' look as if he held a piece of furniture. "This one's past her expiration date."

"No…" Kerys looked down. "She's my friend."

Annapurna whacked at his leg. He grunted and tossed her, flailing and shrieking, over the desk.

"Anna! Stop!" yelled Kerys. "Please help us!"

The woman sprang to her feet, crowbar held high. Gensch aimed, but hesitated at the pained expression on Kerys's face.

"Please, Anna." Kerys offered a hand. "Please listen."

Annapurna lowered the crowbar, twitching, her eyes blinking with a spasmodic tic. She walked around the desk, staring at Kerys.

"Come on, Anna. You're still in there. You did great work. It's all yours. I know what it's like to have your efforts stolen. I'd never do that to anyone else."

"You're looking for information…" Annapurna glanced off to the side, muttering in Hindi.

"What did you try to tell me? You were so terrified."

Annapurna walked up to her, craning her neck to stare around at the ceiling. "I said something about my research. It's going to kill you. It's killing everyone."

"What is?" Kerys grasped Anna's left hand. "You found it. Tell me."

"I…"

Gensch raised the gun.

Kerys shook her head. "Please… tell us what you found."

Annapurna lolled her head around once before locking eyes with her. Her expression of placid calm shifted to sorrow. "We're already dead."

"No, we don't know that yet. There might be a cure... or maybe it wears off."

Her expression twisted with sudden rage. Annapurna leapt at Kerys, shrieking a war cry, and dragged her to the ground. Kerys landed on her back, fighting to grab hold of the crowbar. They rocked side to side in a battle of strength for a few seconds before Kerys shoved her off and rolled onto all fours to crawl away.

Anna jumped on her, pulling the crowbar tight across her throat. Kerys grabbed it with both hands and forced herself upright, kneeling. She tried to yell for Anna to stop, but couldn't breathe.

Bang.

Kerys yanked the crowbar away from her throat as the woman trying to kill her slumped forward, dead weight on her back. She dropped it, coughing, cradling her neck and desperately gulping air.

Sergeant Gensch put Anna's body over by the others, arranging her flat on her back with her arms at her sides.

It's not right... it's not right. Shaking her head, she covered her face in her hands and cried.

"Sorry it happened that way," muttered Gensch.

Kerys sniffled. "It's not your fault. Thanks for the help."

"Just a matter of time before that's us." He walked a few steps to the next desk and flopped in the chair. "At first, I thought whatever did this was takin' longer to affect people with more body mass. You know, fit, healthy people. Most of my soldiers seemed to be stayin' sane, but they only lasted hours more than the eggheads." He scratched at his stubble. "Maybe I'm wrong though. You're still holdin' it together."

"Gee, thanks." She rubbed her neck again.

He chuckled. "You ain't no little twig, but you're no Ellen either."

"Ugh." Kerys shivered at the last memory she had of that woman. That awful scream. That awful, awful smell. "She was so close... I could hear the electricity sizzling under her skin."

"Damn shame. Never know it lookin' at her, but she's all into that frilly shit."

"Hello Kitty."

"Huh?"

Kerys pushed herself upright and sat by Anna's terminal. "That white cat face she put on everything." She traced her fingers across the VR helmet and cried more. "It's not fair. All these people are dead. Why?"

"Dunno," muttered Gensch. "Isn't that what you wanted to come here to find out?"

She stared at Annapurna's body via reflection on the monitor. "I'm so sorry... I know you didn't mean any of that. Something affected your mind."

After offering a moment of silence for her friend, she resumed her search. A while later, she opened a file containing a lab report about 'alien microbes.' According to the parts that didn't fly over her head, Anna's team had been experimenting with the desiccated microbes found in the alien statue. They attempted to rehydrate them and succeeded in 'reanimating' a sample, which they'd kept in isolation. A video clip showed a man in a full protective suit standing by a clear-walled box. He had his arms in holes, manipulating robotic hands inside. Other attached images depicted capsule-shaped bacterium with long, thin hairs waving around. Anna's notes indicated she believed the hairs allowed them a 'degree of mobility never before witnessed in single-celled organisms of this size.'

"Oh, shit..." Kerys swallowed hard. "That's got to be what happened."

"Care to enlighten the grunt?" The vape tube gurgled.

"That stuff'll kill you."

He drew a harder pull and winked. "If this won't, something else will. Surprised I made it this long."

"You *want* to die?" She stared at him.

"Nah. Just ain't afraid of it. I figure the universe gives us each a set amount of time, and when it's up, it's up."

"Didn't peg you for religious."

He blew vape rings again. After seven, he shrugged. "Didn't grow up that way. Maybe I still ain't, but when you have a hundred some odd shitheads throwing bullets at you at eighty rounds per minute, ya kinda start hoping there's somethin' waitin' for ya after this whole mortal life thing."

"That statue head we found contained dead alien bacteria. This file says the scientists here managed to rehydrate some of them and brought them back to life."

He shook his head with a hollow chuckle. "Alien apocalypse, just add water."

"I don't know how it got out, or how bacteria hit everyone so fast... They worked on it in an isolation box. Maybe it's just coincidental? Maybe we found something else too and didn't see it." Thinking back to the feeling she'd gotten in that chamber made her shiver. *Or we tripped a curse.* Aliens and ancient Egypt collided in her brain. *Yeah right...*

She pored over file after file, most of which contained bio-pharma jargon she could barely follow, interspersed with numerous pictures of plants, cells, spores, and fibers. An hour or so later, she ran out of files and decided to check the email system.

A row of red exclamation points drew her attention to the subject line: "I want this careless idiot off my team immediately!"

"Oh, shit," she whispered while tapping the screen to open the message.

CAPTAIN CHEN,

As you know, the sudden onset in most of the crew of inexplicable flu-like symptoms is getting worse. I have been trying to analyze some of the blood samples Doctor Sekhar sent over, and I made a most disturbing discovery. The patient's blood contained live AM-3 organisms, which I had believed existed only in my lab. Upon reviewing the attached security feed, I discovered the reason.

Will Braxton's carelessness has endangered this entire station and everyone on it. Not only did he mishandle a dangerous, unknown sample, he failed to notify anyone of his ineptitude. Now that I think about it, he made a request for me to bring a firmware update over to Mr. Mardling around this time. I'm sure his intention was to get me out of the lab so he could gain access to the secure cabinet unobserved. I believe he wanted to steal the team's work and take sole credit for it, but his carelessness may have put us all at risk. Worse, he attempted to conceal the accident as though it never occurred. His callous disregard for the safety and welfare of everyone on this station is beyond incompetent. It is criminal.

With all due respect, captain, I will not tolerate behavior like this among my science team. I am formally requesting his termination, and I would like your security detail to have him detained until he can be sent back to Earth.

-Annapurna Bhatia, PhD.

KERYS SQUEAKED. "OH, YOU IDIOT... WHAT DID YOU DO?"

Sergeant Gensch stood and walked over.

The video attached to the email contained a ceiling-eye view of a laboratory space full of cabinets and boxes. Will walked into the frame from the right, dressed in his usual green jumpsuit, reading an e-pad. He crossed the room at a casual gait, stopping by a storage cabinet labeled 'Level 3 protection required.'

"You're an idiot!" rasped Kerys.

Will glanced around, opened the door, and retrieved a clear capsule about the size of a beer can with metal ends that appeared to hold a small quantity of blue sand. He started to walk away, but his elbow bumped the cabinet door, knocking the sample from his hand.

The tube shattered on contact with the ground, bursting in a puff of azure mist. Kerys slammed both fists on the desk in time with it breaking.

"Dumb ass mother..." Sergeant Gensch grumbled the rest under his breath.

Will grimaced. After another look around, he rushed to sweep up the glass bits, dumped them in a trashcan, and scurried out of the room as though nothing happened. The video ended a few seconds later.

"You careless goddamned idiot!" yelled Kerys.

In seconds, she became so angry rage tears ran down her cheeks.

All the times he'd been a shit to her paled in comparison to this.

"Jackass! You've always been an arrogant, careless, inconsiderate, self-important bastard... but *this?!* What kind of idiot opens a level 3 cabinet without wearing *any* protective gear? How could you drop a Level 3 container and just pretend nothing happened?"

Sergeant Gensch squeezed her shoulder. "Poor shithead was at ground zero. He got the full blast. Probably the first one gone."

"Dammit." She looked around for something to smash, found nothing, and settled for pounding her fists into the desk a few more times. "I don't know whether to feel messed up over his death or pissed off. If he's dead, I can't kick his ass."

Gensch chuckled.

"I have to send a warning to corporate. We can't let people walk in here blind." She shivered, gripped by a new terror. *What if they see that and just leave us to rot?*

He nodded. "Yeah."

"What if they leave us here?" Eyes closed, she forced herself calm. "No... I have to tell them. It might get back to Earth."

"Hey, maybe it died again. Them little bastards might not breathe our air."

Kerys opened the SFT client on Anna's desk and started a new message. She attached Anna's email to Captain Chen, and the file about the rehydration of alien microbes, then recorded a brief explanation of what she believed happened. "I'm sure it's in the air. He just dropped the capsule and the stuff has spread over the entire facility. So far, it hasn't affected me, or Sergeant Gensch. There may be other people who have some kind of resistance to it... or maybe wherever we were at the time it got out shielded us by some freak fortune in the design of the vents.

"We're going to try and stay alive until a ship arrives. I don't want to be left here, but I had to warn you about possible contagion. It should be safe for us to stay in e-suits and go straight to cryo back to quarantine medical treatment on Earth. I'm no doctor. I don't know if it's infected us and hasn't shown signs, or if we're clear. I hope you give us the chance to find out."

She pushed the 'send message' button.

The little orb spun around and around as it always did whenever the system uploaded to the space fold transmitter. After a few minutes, it displayed: ‹Transmission error, retry?›

She tapped the 'yes' button.

Twenty seconds later, the same error appeared.

"Dammit." She looked up at Gensch as if he could make it work by the mere wanting of it. "Why isn't it working?"

"Hellerman thought the antenna array went down."

Kerys drummed her fingers on the transparent amber desk. "So, let's check on it."

"It's on the roof." He pointed at the ceiling. "Outside."

"There's e-suits… there's gotta be technical manuals in the system somewhere, like you said."

Sergeant Gensch frowned at his vape wand, tilting it to study a tiny bit of fluid left in the reservoir. "What the hell. Not like we're gonna break it more."

21

BREATHLESS

K erys tried not to think about Annapurna lying dead on the floor back in the dome.

A brief search of rooms in Lab Pod 1 found nothing critical worth collecting. Sergeant Gensch sealed the airlock where the hamster tube connected to the pod. The hissing out in the tunnel hadn't worsened, but it got under her skin. She gazed past the white scuff on the window at the glimmery regolith, the blue-indigo sky, and the distant strip of giant 'trees.' Having only a half-inch-thick layer of polycarbonate resin standing between her and a toxic atmosphere made her clench her hands from anxiety.

Fortunately, Wayfarer Outpost's atmosphere processing system hadn't been damaged. Where the e-suits contained a small canister of cyanobacteria to re-oxygenate the air, the outpost had a huge living colony. The e-suit capsules ran out after a while, but the station's massive biomass filter could reproduce effectively to sustain itself indefinitely. Assuming nothing else went wrong, they'd at least have breathable air for as long as it would take the next starship to pull into orbit.

Gensch startled her out of her stupor by grasping her shoulder and urging her to walk. When they reached the end where the tunnel connected to the dome, he hit a button. Two halves of round door emerged from the sides, sealing off access to the labs.

She stood a few seconds in silence, unable to hear the hissing.

"Where should I look for those manuals?"

"Probably engineering or the command area." He shrugged.

Kerys jogged down the hall toward the stairs. "We've seen the command area is empty."

"Easier for us. No crazy bastards in our way."

She grimaced.

He followed her to the middle of the third floor. Kerys shivered at the cold by the time they reached the command and control center for the whole outpost. She brushed a few nuggets of broken safety glass from a red cushioned chair, and sat.

"D-damn, it's freezing in here," whispered Kerys.

Sergeant Gensch looked around at the emptiness. So many rooms had wraparound windows, even if the glass hadn't been shot out, they would've had a clear view across the entire floor, except what the giant wall of monitors blocked off. "Seems quiet here. Think you'll be all right for a few minutes?"

She swiped at the screen, hunting for a path to systems information. The idea of being alone, even for a few minutes, terrified her—but it *had* been hours since they saw anyone other than Anna. "Yeah. Don't get lost."

"I'll keep that in mind." He winked and jogged out.

It took her a few minutes to find the technical documentation for the space-fold transmitter. After reading for a little while, the idea of marching into the excavation site and translating the alien pictograms felt like it would've been a more productive use of time. She gravitated to pictures of the hardware, a cluster of metal boxes with seven rods of varying length protruding from the top. Three held a ring-shaped structure above the 'primary focuser,' the thickest rod.

"Any luck?" Gensch walked back in and set a cup of coffee on the desk beside her, steam wafting between his fingers.

It smelled a touch on the stale side, but all things considered, she'd take having coffee at all as a win. Kerys clutched the cup in both hands, ignoring the blood dried into the creases of her knuckles, sipping while staring past the blurry text on the screen. "I never did too well at math."

"Well…" Gensch lowered himself to sit with a grunt. "Hellerman thought he could get it back online, and he mostly handled the computers and network stuff. How hard could it be?"

"Never ask that." She sighed.

Kerys studied the 'user manual' for what amounted to a nine-million-dollar radio, focusing on a diagram depicting how the major components connected. Gensch scratched at his gut and grumbled.

"Well, that only took two days. Be right back. Got a matter of some importance I need to discuss with the plumbing."

"Thanks for sharing." She leaned her head in her hand and kept reading. At least the techno-jargon kept her mind off having killed a man.

Gensch headed out into the hall and went to the right.

She held the coffee close to her chin, absorbing its heat. She debated asking him to turn down the air conditioning, but with bodies piling up, the cold became a blessing. Minutes passed, all the words and diagrams turning into a meaningless blur. She caught herself skimming, and backed up to re-read a whole section she'd glazed over.

"…ck in range…" Gina's voice came from the ceiling, wrapped in static. "… canister's about had it. Don't… don't think I'm gonna reach…"

"Gina?" asked Kerys. "Where are you? Can you hear me or do I have to push something?"

"I'm." Gina wheezed. "Filter's done. I"—squelch ate a few seconds of her voice—"Runnin' outta air."

"Come back inside!"

The woman's voice regained some strength. "No goddamn way… I'm not going in there. It's in the goddamn air. I ain't breathin' that shit!"

"Gina, you have to come inside… You're gonna suffocate out there. I think it's gone already. I'm still here. Gensch is sane too." *Fuck it.* "I'm coming. Hang on!"

Kerys pulled the combat knife out of her pocket and sprinted out into the hall. Snowy glass bits sprayed away from her boots when she hit the swath of broken windows. She grabbed the wall, cornering into the stairs at a full run. *There's spare filter pods in the locker. I'll bring her one. That'll be faster than dragging her inside.*

She raced out of the stairwell on the first floor, heading right toward the atrium, where the entrances to the cafeteria, garage area, and residence pods converged. Repetitive metal grinding came from somewhere up ahead. Kerys jumped over Marco's body, zoomed past the cafeteria, and headed down the tube to the garage airlock. By the time she reached the ready room, the scraping sound had ceased.

Come on, Gina… you can make it.

Her locker hung open, but aside from a bullet hole in the door, it hadn't changed from how she'd left it. Her heart almost stopped at the sight of the finger-sized opening in the steel, but as soon as she got a good look at her undamaged suit, and a row of eight filter pods at the bottom, she relaxed.

After tossing the knife onto the shelf by the helmet, she pulled the suit out and got into it as fast she could. She squirmed around, trying to reach behind her back to secure the clamps. The hip ones proved easier, but she got the shoulder fasteners closed part way by hand and finished them off by slamming her back against the next locker.

Kerys grabbed her helmet and a filter canister before running for the airlock. She tucked the gel pod under one arm, packing her hair and seating the helmet on the run. Within a second of the ring around her neck sealing, a man came out of nowhere, howling and shrieking nonsense. She didn't even have time to turn before he tackled her. The cylinder bounced out of her grip and went sliding across the room.

She screamed in shock, but her cry of fear changed to a snarl of anger before her lungs emptied.

The man grabbed her by the shoulders and bashed her helmet onto the floor.

"Don't... worry 'bout me..." said Gina, a dim yellow light winking on by her name along the left side of the HUD.

Kerys growled. She threw herself to the right in a twist. The man groaned as the e-suit's backpack rolled over his chest. She flung her arms for torque, slipped out of his grip, and landed on her hands and knees beside him, searching around frantically for the gel pod. As soon as she spotted it on the other side of the room, she scrambled into a crawl. A shift of her gaze to the blank line logged her in to the comm system. "Hang on, Gina. I'm almost at the airlock."

The man howled into a cackle. He lunged, wrapping his arms around her giant metal boot, and dragged her backward away from the filter capsule.

"Dammit! Get off me!" she shouted, while stomping blindly to the rear.

Thump.

The meaty smack cut off his horrible whooping and left him curled on the floor cradling his head. Kerys hurried to the capsule, scooping it up as she got to her feet. She walked sideways toward the airlock, glaring at a Middle Eastern man in a grey bloodstained jumpsuit.

He snapped his head up, growling, his jaw crushed in and oozing blood.

"Go away! I don't have time for your shit right now." She ran into the airlock, crossed to the outer door, and slapped the screen to start the cycle.

"Ngh!" The man wobbled to his feet and shambled after her.

Kerys flattened herself against the outer door as flashing yellow lights came on around the inside hatch. The idiot charged between the closing doors, heedless of the warning. She brought her hands up, ready for him. "Oh, you're a damn genius."

He leapt at her, grabbing for her helmet and chest, but she held him away, keeping her back against the wall so he couldn't reach the clips... not that he had enough mental capacity left to understand how the suit worked.

Manic eyes widened at a sudden loud hissing, though he kept trying to claw at her. He raked a hand down her visor; his nails caught at the bottom and tore away from his fingertips inches in front of her eyes.

Kerys roared in disgust and smashed her helmet into his face, knocking him into a backward stumble. She shifted her weight, preparing to kick him, but hesitated as he wobbled down to one knee, clutching at his throat. For the four seconds the airlock existed in vacuum, his expression seemed to reclaim reason. He scratched at his chest, giving her a pleading look, as if she had a gun to his head about to pull the trigger.

She eyed the control panel; she had a few seconds to abort, but that would kill Gina... and this man had gone beyond any help she could give him.

"I'm sorry." She looked down, wracked with guilt. "You're already dead."

The doors behind her opened with a blast of not-air that ruffled his jumpsuit and knocked him over. His eyes bulged as his body sucked in a huge instinctual breath. A second later, he lapsed into a convulsive fit, raking at his chest and screaming like a man burned alive. Blood oozed from his mouth and nose. Kerys looked away as he slumped over on his side, twitching.

"Gina, where are you?"

"Mmm..." A weak moan came over the comm.

"Gina!" shouted Kerys.

'SSG Gensch' appeared in the comm list with a faint chime. "Dammit, girl, what's going on? Leave you alone for a few minutes to take a dump and—"

"Gina's outside. She's running out of air. I can't find her!"

"Son of a bitch," muttered Gensch. "Hold on."

Kerys crossed the garage, descended the ramp, and took a few steps on the surface. The regolith crunched under her boots; all around her, it shimmered and glinted like flakes of black ice.

A *boop* sound filled her helmet as a yellow arrow blinked into existence at the top center of her vision.

"Found her transponder. Set a waypoint. Looks like she's about 308 meters north, northeast of you."

Kerys rotated to her left until the yellow triangle pointed straight up. "Okay." She started to run, but stopped. *I'm an idiot.* After doubling back to the garage, she pounced on a quad, twisted the handle, and backed up into a rack of tools hard enough to knock it over. Muttering curses, she pivoted the handlebars toward the door, leaned forward, and cranked the accelerator.

Fat, knobby wheels squeaked on the steel floor for a half second before they caught traction, launching her across the garage. The quad bounced down the ramp onto the shifting regolith, kicking up a spray as she hauled it around a left turn to face the waypoint. Once lined up, she accelerated more than she'd ever dared to before. The quad reported fifty-four MPH, the distance counter ticking down too fast to read the last digit. About sixty meters from the garage, she steered for a gap between a pair of large, boxy machines, catching a glimpse of a yellow 'high voltage' lightning bolt on one.

She blew past them, emitting an uneasy wail at the narrow channel, and cruised across the huge hexagonal landing pad, the grind of gravel replaced for a few seconds with the banshee wail of knobby tires on metal gridding.

The quad devoured an incline on the far side of the landing pad with ease. Cresting the top of the berm gave her a much better view of the surroundings. Blue-teal 'forest' painted the horizon in front of her with an ominous presence. Without a dust storm, endless black dunes filled in everywhere else, except for the silvery-grey mountainous ridge behind her to the right. She twisted the handle more, gaining speed on the downhill slope. The quad buzzed a warning as it hit sixty-four MPH. Kerys ignored the alarm, focused on the distance readout to the waypoint counting down.

At sixty-two meters, she made out the dullness of an e-suit's dark armored panels against the shimmery ground.

"Keep going," said Gensch, "Forty meters... twenty... fifteen... ten..."

Kerys jammed on the brake, throwing another wave of sharp rocks into the air as the quad skidded to a stop. Gina lay face down at the end of a long trail of footprints that seemed to come from the forest several miles away.

"Gina!" She hopped off the quad and rushed to the woman's side, grabbing and shaking her. "Say something!"

Corporal Gina Mitchell didn't move.

Kerys rolled her over. The young woman stared into space, her mouth open. Rigid arms clung to a compact assault rifle; a glowing red ammo counter read: '32.' Fog on the inside of her visor glittered blue in the cloud-filtered sunlight. "God dammit..." She shook Gina with a two-fisted grip on her chest. "Don't die! You're not allowed to die!"

Gensch's thick sigh leaked over the comm. "Uhh, kid... her vitals aren't there. Come on back inside. You did all you could do."

"Dammit..." Kerys squeezed the gel capsule in frustration. "I brought this out here for you, and I'm going to damn well give it to you." She shoved Gina back on her chest and opened the hatch at the bottom right of the backpack module. The old capsule's gel had turned pale white. Usually, the 'dead' ones still had a little cyan tint to them. "I brought you a new one." She tossed the spent one aside, rammed the fresh one in, and slapped the hatch closed. "There."

Kneeling in the glittering regolith, Kerys bowed her head, too distraught and angry to cry. The tiny list of names at the left of her vision made her think of her first time setting foot on this planet: two soldiers eager to get out of here and go home, two others looking forward to an adventurous new tour of duty, ninety some other people she never met.

Her whole team had already died. Scraps and flashes of memory came back and faded. She pictured Marco smiling, frazzle-haired Don trying to figure out if his food was chicken, and Paula's smile when she talked about her kids.

"I probably shouldn't fill this damn helmet up with tears, huh?" She sniffled. "C'mon. I'm not going to leave you out here to be forgotten."

Kerys dragged Gina's body to the quad, draping her over the back end before climbing on. She eased on the accelerator, steering toward the outpost while driving at a running pace. Gina might be dead and unable to feel pain, but she still didn't want to drop her.

In somber silence, she drove over the hill and across the landing pad, steering for a narrow passage between giant metal boxes full of machinery.

Sudden motion from the right startled her as the quad exited the gap on the far side. A person in an e-suit bowled into her hard enough to knock her clear off the quad, which kept on going. Screaming, Kerys landed sliding and tumbling, unable to get a grip on anything to stop herself. Dark blue sky and glittery black ground traded places too many times to count.

She stopped rolling on her back, still sliding down a hill.

The other e-suit jumped on top of her again, straddling her thighs, one hand on her shoulder.

Kerys gazed up into the face of Corporal Guillen. Bubbled plastic surrounded an inch-wide gap in his helmet, from his jaw to his missing left eye, likely melted away by an excavating laser. Violet ichor oozed from the empty socket, dripping over a cheek studded with small undulating pods nestled in thumbnail-sized cavities. Skin and muscle at the jawline had been incinerated, leaving only blackened bone and teeth where the laser hit him.

"Gah!" she screamed.

Corporal Guillen's remaining eye held no trace of familiarity. He raised a combat knife over his head while pushing her shoulder into the ground. Scratching at the back of her helmet sounded like a dozen little razor blades slicing at the metal.

"Shit!" yelled Kerys.

She struggled, but couldn't move him.

The knife came down and glanced off the top of her helmet with a loud *clack*.

"Aaaah!" She punched at the arm pinning her, barely fazing him.

Corporal Guillen jammed the knife down again, striking her in the chest. The point gouged the rubber-coated metal plate above her left breast, but didn't pierce.

Primal fear overrode disgust; Kerys thrust her arm up and dug her thumb into his empty eye socket. He twisted his head toward her grip. She gouged and pulled until he let go of her shoulder and wrenched himself away.

"Gensch! Guillen's trying to kill me!" The regolith shifted under her boots when she tried to stand, taking her feet out from under her and sending her sliding down a steeper section of hill.

"Uhh, that's not possible…" A static pop preceded a few-second pause in Gensch's voice. "His vitals are flatlined."

Guillen grabbed her by the backpack. She flailed, but couldn't turn enough to get a hand on him. He hauled her into the air, raising her horizontally over his head. She kicked and thrashed, causing him to topple over before he could slam her into the ground. Losing balance, he hurled her at the last second before he fell over.

She landed in a bouncing, tumbling roll, flipping over and over again before winding up on her chest, facing uphill while sliding down. Kerys grabbed at the ground, but failed to stop herself… the thick fingers of her e-suit gloves raked grooves in the loose material, doing little to slow her. Guillen stood with the slow deliberateness of an android, rotating side to side, searching. Her slide came to a stop about thirty meters from the top of the ridge; she remained still.

Maybe he won't see me if I don't move?

He stopped twisting back and forth, staring straight at her.

"Or not."

Gensch tried to say something else, but his transmission garbled into static.

Guillen, or whatever he had become, walked toward her.

Kerys shoved herself upright and ran. Twice, she tried to head for the outpost, but the shifting ground beneath her boots nearly tripped her, forcing her to keep going down the hill to avoid wiping out. Between the cumbersome e-suit and the uneven terrain, she had to put more effort into staying upright than moving fast. *He's going to catch me if I try to go uphill… The dig site! There's gotta be a laser in there.*

He grasped her backpack.

Kerys screamed and twisted away, forcing herself to pump her legs faster despite the heavy boots. Every breath reflected from the visor, fogging it and washing back over her face. Building claustrophobia and burning lungs made her feel as though she drowned.

Again, Corporal Guillen seized the backpack, pulling at her.

Kerys roared and twisted away, stumbling when her boots collided with a loud *crack* of metal striking metal. Arms flailing, she kept her balance, wheezing and babbling in an attempt to yell for Gensch. Her breaths turned gaspy, her throat dry and raw. Heavy crunches kept at her heels, Guillen closing in, urging her forward.

The bright glow of lamps up ahead gave her a second wind. She leaned into her stride and sprinted for the narrow strip of level ground by the base of the mountain. A last, desperate surge of energy pushed her out in front of Guillen, and she homed in on the dig site entrance. She got her hands up in time to catch herself on the silicon-silver wall, before shoving off and staggering into the hallway.

Lacking finesse, Guillen ran straight into the stone behind her, bouncing away and landing flat on his back. She spared only a half-second to look at him, then rushed inside.

Little appeared different in the first chamber from when she'd last been here, but the inner room farther east made her gasp. The scaffold she'd been using lay about in pieces, smashed into slabs of steel and loose pipes. To her horror, three of the obelisks had been sliced apart, each chunk having a precision-laser finish on the cut surface. The remaining one in the southwest corner sported numerous divots from bullet strikes.

Lars lay on his back near the boxes of the team's equipment. The left leg of his exo suit twitched from a malfunctioning actuator, though the sheer number of bullet holes in him left no hope that he remained alive. Sparks spat from multiple points where the riddling of gunfire had shredded power lines.

A hard impact to the back knocked Kerys into a stumble. She tripped over an obelisk fragment and landed in a somersault. Corporal Guillen pivoted like a soldier doing drills, stalking around the huge piece of stone. She rolled to her feet and darted to the right, keeping the car-sized chunk of obelisk between them.

The lifeless expression on his face chilled the blood in her veins. His one remaining eye fixed on her with the singularity of a machine bent on destruction, a remorseless killer the likes of which the military could only hope to train. The dozen or so little eye-like pods embedded in his left cheek all seemed to focus on her too, twitching back and forth. A thin, black vein—or root—descended from his mouth, disappearing into the neck of his suit.

"Rick? Are you still there?" She edged around the stone.

He faked to his right and charged the other direction, coming around the edge the same way she'd gone. Kerys bit back a startled scream. A snap decision borne of panic caused her to spring *at* him. She planted her hands on his chest and shoved. He scrabbled at her helmet but couldn't get a grip before he flew over backward.

"Guess not..."

A patch of periwinkle blue on his leg grabbed her attention. A glop of bubbling foam swelled out from a hole in his thigh, plugging a wound the same diameter as the excavator laser beam.

The mass undulated... moving. A clump broke away and slid down his leg, leaving a wet trail.

That looks like the stuff in the canister Will dropped.

"Oh, shit. Oh, shit, oh, shit."

"Kerys?" yelled Gensch. "I'm comin' out the airlock. Where the hell are you?"

"Ruins!" she yelled. "Guillen isn't Guillen anymore... that alien shit is inside him. I... I don't even know what he is. H-his helmet's breached and he's still moving. He shouldn't still be alive!"

"He *isn't*," said Gensch. "His vitals are gone."

Kerys gulped. "Uhh, someone needs to tell *him* that."

Guillen sat up, grabbed the hunk of obelisk, and pulled himself upright. Again, his lifeless stare bored into her.

She darted to the left and grabbed a long section of pipe, raising it in two hands. "Come on, thing. Whatever you are."

He crept closer. Kerys pushed her memory of the old Corporal Guillen aside. He'd been so handsome, so confident, humble, honorable—everything Will hadn't been. Perhaps after a couple of weeks around him, she wouldn't have been able to stay away. But that man was dead. This *thing* only looked like him.

Somewhat.

With a roar, Kerys swung the pipe around, smashing it down on the left side of his head. A loud, resonant *ding* reverberated across the chamber. He lurched a step to the right, head tilted to the side at a frightening angle. She jumped back, evading a grabbing hand, and howled again as she swung. Guillen made no attempt to avoid her strike.

The pipe hit him on the shoulder with a dull *clank*, but he didn't react, continuing to walk closer.

He grabbed the pipe before she could pull it away, starting a tug of war that dragged her stumbling side to side.

Damn, he's strong!

Guillen jerked the pipe from her grasp and swung it at her. She leapt backward and ducked as the metal tube passed over her helmet with a *whoosh*. The fog on her visor thickened, plunging the chamber into a blurry mess.

Her deteriorating ability to see terrified her, making the already claustrophobic ruin close in on her. She ran to the left, dancing among smaller hunks of obelisk on her way toward the dead Lars.

Clank!

The former corporal drilled her in the backpack with the pipe, launching her into the air. She landed a few feet from Lars, a spray of saliva painting her visor. The excavator laser under his right arm wound up directly in front of her in clear view. Kerys crawled for it, but stopped short as Guillen stepped on her leg. She twisted around and raised her arm to defend her face.

He brought the pipe down with a two-handed swing onto her left forearm, drilling it into her helmet and knocking her into a slide that came to a crashing halt against the fallen exo suit. A lightning bolt of pain shot from her elbow to her fingertips, numbing her whole arm.

Guillen's half-face remained expressionless as he stalked closer, raising the pipe again. The pods in his cheek widened like a nest of eager little eyes.

Kerys twisted to her left and grabbed the handgrip of the excavator laser, but the weight of the exo pinned it to the floor. "Shit!"

A burst of gunfire roared from above and behind her.

Three holes appeared in Guillen's chest. A split second later, a blast of gore flew out of his back with a dull *whump* as the bullets inside him detonated.

He staggered to the side and fell to one knee, syrupy dark red liquid striated with blue leaking from his mouth.

Another person in an e-suit rushed over, pointing an assault rifle at Guillen's back.

"Cut that a little close, sarge," whispered Kerys.

The helmet turned toward her, revealing a young woman's large brown eyes. Gina attempted to smile, but didn't quite manage it. "I ain't no sergeant yet."

Guillen lunged upright, rounding the pipe in a silvery blur that caught Gina in the face. She flew almost ten feet before landing on her back in a sliding tumble. Evidently forgetting Kerys existed, he walked after the young soldier.

Kerys rolled onto her knees and shoved at the exo suit.

"Shit!" rasped Gina.

A burst of gunfire went off behind Kerys. She strained at the giant silver laser while pushing Lars's dead exo suit with her shoulders. Her left arm throbbed, but she gritted her teeth and dragged the laser free.

Gina ran around behind Lars, pausing a second to fire another burst. "Gah! He's still moving."

"He's dead." Kerys hefted the cumbersome excavator. *Oh please still have power.*

Corporal Guillen staggered toward Gina, oozy periwinkle blue glop filling in the fist-sized holes in his back from her explosive ammunition. She fired again, spraying blood, flesh, and blue slime into the air, but it didn't slow him down much.

Kerys clicked the trigger.

A thick beam of whitish energy struck Guillen in the lower back, penetrating his front and going into the wall. He turned on her; for the first time, a trace of emotion showed in his half-face: anger.

"Remember this thing, don't you?" She dragged the beam up to his heart. "Bet it hurts."

Sergeant Gensch jogged in and aimed his handgun at the flailing not-Guillen.

Kerys kept the beam on him for three more seconds, until he erupted in flames like an alcohol-soaked rag. Tiny comets of flaming goop burst out of him in all directions, hitting the ground and burning green. She edged away, trying to catch her breath as the once-humanoid figure withered into an unrecognizable burning blob.

"Uhh, got a little problem," said Gina.

Kerys looked over.

The woman's visor had cracked.

"You have to go inside." Kerys dropped the laser and ran to take Gina's hand.

The nineteen-year-old looked terrified, but nodded.

Kerys stared at her, surprised at how happy she was to see the younger woman alive. Her stare held both warmth, gratitude, and the kind of tenderness Will could never possess. Before her mind could wander too far along a strange new path, she took hold of Gina's hand and dragged her down the passage out of the ruin, shocked to find a pair of quads right by the entrance.

"Thanks for leavin' me a ride." Gina jogged to one and got on. "I think... I think..."

"Gina?" Kerys ran over as the woman slumped over the handlebars.

"Go!" yelled Gensch. "I'll catch up."

Kerys hopped on behind Gina and reached past her for the handlebars. A spray of little black crystals flew out from the wheels when she cranked the accelerator, showering Sergeant Gensch. Pushed to its top speed of fifty-five, the quad cleared the distance back to the garage in a little under a minute. She drove across the room straight into the airlock, squeaking to a halt and leaving glittering black dust trails on the steel floor next to the dead man.

Gina coughed and wheezed.

Kerys jumped off the quad and slapped at the control panel, initiating the airlock cycle. When the flashing lights came on, she returned to Gina's side and held her hand. The outer doors closed. Seconds after they sealed, the toxic atmosphere drained and breathable air replaced it. As soon as the red dot vanished from her HUD indicating the air clean, she fell to her knees.

Adrenalin faded, and all the exhaustion of running for her life hit her at once.

"Holy shit, I'm alive," muttered Gina.

Kerys didn't want to get up. "I second that statement."

Gina cradled Kerys's helmet and lifted her head to make eye contact. Red droplets spattered the inside of the woman's visor. "Coughin' up a little blood, but I'll take it. You look like hell."

"Used to run a lot back home. Every day if I could." Kerys gagged on a dry throat. "Never did a three-quarter-mile in twenty-pound boots before, but I had some great motivation."

Gensch pounded on the outer door. "Knock, knock."

"Just a second," muttered Kerys. "My legs have quit for the day."

"Clearing the lock, sarge." Gina pulled her upright and helped her out of the airlock so Gensch could cycle it and come in. "C'mon. Let's get the hell out of these damn suits."

22

DADDY ISSUES

Kerys awoke curled up on a cushioned bench by the left wall of the command room. Her eyes fluttered open to a blurry view of grey fabric blotched with dried blood. Gina had taken another couch that sat catty-corner against the south wall. She hadn't even brushed all the glass bits away before flopping face-first and passing out. Sergeant Gensch sat at a steel table near the center rear of the room, hunched over a mug of coffee with his back to her. The rhythmic *snap... snap... snap...* of bullets clicking into a magazine filled in the silence. She found it oddly reassuring.

It took her brain a few minutes to dredge up the memory of being half-carried up here from the locker room by the garage. She groaned and sat up, rubbing her sore legs.

"Ugh. How long was I asleep?" She yawned, stood, and struggled to stretch. Pain in her muscles made her shiver as flashes of Corporal Guillen chasing her came back. She forced herself not to think of him standing beside her, trying to play the gallant military man, showing 'the new girl' how to use an e-suit.

Head bowed, she lost a moment to grief with her hands clasped over her mouth. *A ship is coming already. They're here every six months. We will go home.* Idle hope that a shift in the wind might've knocked the transmission array back online pulled her across the control room to a seat at the console.

Again, she recorded a message with the SFT client, using the two-minute video to give a detailed summary of everything as best she understood. She held her finger over the screen, hovering millimeters from the send button.

"Come on, please…"

‹Transmit Error.›

"Damn." Kerys scowled. "I'm going to the roof."

Clack.

Kerys jumped at the sudden, sharp metallic noise. She twisted to her right to peer toward the source.

Sergeant Gensch's left arm extended to the side, hand atop his sidearm where he'd set it down hard on the table.

A long, awkward silence stretched out as he remained motionless. His arm trembled.

"Sarge?" whispered Kerys.

"You should kill me." Gensch bowed his head a little, emitting a strained grunt.

"No… Sarge… this isn't funny." Kerys eased herself upright.

He shook his head as if in slow motion. "I ain't tryin' to be humorous. Take it. That shit is in my head. S'pose I'm not as tough as I act."

She trembled, a lump in her throat as big as if she watched a father she never had dying before her eyes. "I…"

Gensch chuckled. "You know I was hoping Vickers backed off. She probably would've kicked my ass."

"You're just saying that. Come on, Sarge…" Kerys took two steps closer.

Gina popped awake, yawned, and sat up. "What time is it?"

"Time to do what you gotta do." Gensch grimaced; he seemed to be trying to pull his hand away from the gun, but it stuck as if glued. "It's in my head. The voices. Drill Sergeant Monroe… wants to kill you. Kill everyone."

Kerys sniffled, tears streaming out of her eyes. "No no no no no…"

Gina sucked in a breath. She snapped upright, going from dazed to petrified in an instant. Eyes wide, she stood as rigid as a statue.

"Mitchell. Secure that rifle and uphold your…" Gensch cringed, stifling a scream. He pounded his right fist on the table. "Oath. I'm… losing this one."

"You gotta hold on," said Kerys. "We can get to the infirmary. Maybe I can get the machine to do something…"

"Take the gun!" roared Gensch. "Now!"

Kerys rushed forward, grabbing it as well as his hand. He twisted his head to look at her, cheeks bright red, all the veins in his forehead prominent. His body shuddered. Jaw clenched, he lifted his grip away from the weapon like his arm weighed a hundred pounds. She kept holding his hand in both of hers, shaking her head.

He grasped her hand, and their eyes met. In an instant, the regret of a life unlived flickered over his features. A leaden weight pressed heavily on her heart. He seemed to read the emotion on her face and bowed his head. In a mere day or so, he'd become more of a father than she'd ever known.

"Come on, Gensch. I can't do this without you."

"Ngh." He winced as if in the throes of a stomach cramp. "You can. And you gotta. Don't get all soft on me now 'cause you think I'm your old man. I ain't cut out for bein' no one's pop."

She squeezed his hand, begging him to be okay with a stare. Her lip quivered and the room went blurry under a layer of tears. "You're a good man. I'd be happy to call you Dad."

Gensch started to chuckle, but wound up grunting. His head twitched in an erratic shiver as he muttered, "They're not real," a few times before looking up at her. "Take the gun. Let me go out when I'm still me."

Kerys reluctantly released his hand and picked up the weapon. "Please don't make me do this...."

"Mitchell," gurgled Gensch.

Kerys twisted her head to the right, staring at the sofas. Gina had disappeared. "S-she's gone...."

He bounded upright into a spin, dog tags swaying from his neck. Kerys let out a yelp of surprise and almost pointed the gun at him, her hand shaking.

Gensch grabbed the weapon and her hand, pulling the barrel to his forehead. His thick brush cut seemed much whiter against his bright red skin. "I'm losing this fight, kid. I always figured this black ball of shit planet was gonna be a one-way trip for me." He squeezed her fingers into the gun. "It's been twenty-nine hours, but you gave me a chance to feel like—"

She tried to jump back as he screamed past a clenched jaw, but couldn't get her hand away from his grip.

"Do... it," he rasped, eyes bulging.

Her heart throbbed as she fingered the trigger, staring over the sights at his hair. "I..." She sobbed. "You're...."

Seconds felt like hours. She couldn't kill the father she wanted so badly.

Gensch snapped his head up. His veins receded, as did the redness. Something had changed in his eyes. The sense of comfort he'd once projected had gone away. Malice stared back at her.

Kerys opened her mouth to speak, but he shoved her hand, driving the gun into her jaw and knocking her backward, stumbling. Some part of him must've remained, as he didn't try to take the gun away. He loomed at her, hesitating. She grabbed it in both hands, pointing the shaking weapon at his chest. Her breath came in ragged gasps.

I can't…

He roared and rushed at her.

She screamed, darting to the right as he went by. Her escape jerked to a halt seconds later when fingers clamped around her trailing hair. Knuckles dug into her back as Gensch lifted her off her feet by a fistful of jumpsuit and hurled her airborne. She landed on the steel table, slid across it, and tumbled to the floor on the other side, taking a chair down with her.

Growling, he stomped after her.

"Dammit." She scrambled to her feet and aimed at him again. Fear overrode guilt, and she squeezed the trigger, but nothing happened. "Uhh… shit…"

Before he rounded the corner of the table, she sprinted for the door. His boots clomped behind her, his stride advancing up to a jog. At the end of the corridor, she risked a look down at the gun as she cornered left. *What's wrong with—safety! Shit!*

Fumbling to disengage the safety while running as fast as her sore muscles would move her, Kerys headed for the stairwell, Gensch right behind her. When she reached the opening, she whipped her arms around to the rear intending to shoot, but he'd gotten closer than she expected. He swatted her aim aside as the gun went off, suffering a minor nip to the left shoulder, and drove his right palm into her chest. The hit knocked her over and sent her sliding down the first set of stairs on her back.

Kerys fired again as soon as she came to a halt at the bottom. A spark flashed from the bulkhead next to him. He bellowed like a soldier charging the enemy line and stormed down the stairs. She rolled to her feet, her lunge for the next section cut short by a large hand snagging her right bicep.

Screaming, she snapped her arm out and bashed him in the cheek with the handgun. He laughed, a sick, dark voice that didn't belong to any man she knew. An evil smile warped his lips a second before he flung her into the wall. She bounced away and staggered to the right, opting to flee down the stairs, having lost the nerve to shoot him.

Panic drove her to the ground floor, with no particular destination in mind. After a few random turns down dark, empty corridors, she tore open a small doorway she'd never gone through before. The narrow corridor beyond reminded her of the maintenance passage where Ellen cornered her.

Second thoughts died fast when Gensch jogged around the corner behind her, growling. With nowhere else to go, she sprinted forward, ducking to avoid a handful of low-hanging horizontal pipes. The duct bent around to the right after a short run, but turned left again after a mere four paces. She skidded to a stop in a small doorway a few seconds past the zigzag, but it led to a tiny break room with no way out. Four chairs, a little round table, and a hydra occupied the space, along with a dead man in a grey jumpsuit, who lay flat on the floor below a bloody spot on the wall where he'd evidently bashed his face until he died.

Gensch appeared at the S-bend and stared at her.

"Gah!" she yelled, whirling and firing too fast to aim. A metallic *ping* preceded a fleshy *thump*.

He stumbled, grabbing his left thigh. Reacting to pain with an angry grunt, he lunged closer.

Kerys ran. The off-kilter rhythm of his limping gait echoed in the tunnel of metal walls, making them feel tighter, narrower, more confining. Seconds later, the maintenance duct expanded into a small room with four lockers and a black metal trapdoor open over a square hole. A yellow-painted ladder led into darkness.

She jumped down, yanking the trapdoor closed mere seconds before he caught up to her. All her weight hung on four fingers, her legs floundering at the ladder as she tried to find footing. Gensch lifted the trapdoor, and her with it.

"Dammit!" she yelled. "Why?!"

Kerys raised the gun with her right hand, aiming at the expanding space between the trapdoor and the floor. As soon as they made eye contact, she hesitated a second too long. He let go of the hatch, which slammed down with a deafening *clang.*

The jolt broke her grip, and she fell into the blackness.

She landed on a metal catwalk with a resounding *bang.* The metal flexed enough under her weight to spring back and toss her an inch or three into the air. The second time her back made contact with the grating, she slid off into cold water.

In a panic, she flailed, managing to slap her left hand onto the walkway hard enough to numb it, but also catch herself.

"Ow... shit."

Holding onto something solid stalled her fear of drowning. When her body relaxed, her feet found solid ground. She stood in a neck-deep pool. It took a few seconds for her eyes to adjust to the feeble glow from weak rectangular lights every few feet on the ceiling. The underground chamber stretched far off to her left, at least two hundred meters, though the pool stopped less than a third that distance away. Constant dripping echoed off the stone walls. Even the ceiling had the silvery-grey sheen of silicon.

I'm underground...

Gensch's loud grunt emanated from the ladder shaft, startling her. Kerys ducked under the walkway and tried to hold still despite the cold water making her shiver. She clutched the gun in both hands inches above the surface, unable to make her brain accept the idea of having to shoot him.

Boots clunked on metal rungs, getting louder with each step. She squeezed the handgrip, hoping the weapon would still work after its quick bath. Since the ammo counter still gave off its dull red glow, she had hope.

He's not Gensch anymore. He's already dead. He's not my father.

Gensch stepped onto the walkway right above her, rattling it.

She peered up through the grating, holding her breath as he took his other foot from the ladder and set it down. He walked over her, his boot soles lifting off the grating like an army of tiny suction cups popping. She dared not twist to watch him, lest he notice her moving.

When he'd taken a dozen or so steps deeper into the chamber, she rotated to face the far end of the room, slid out from under the walkway, and aimed.

This is our drinking water. Bad idea to leave a body in it. I'll wind up drinking more of the shit that killed him.

She bit her lip to keep from swearing aloud, shifted back under the catwalk, and followed him.

"I know she's down here," he whispered. "No. Do you? If y'ain't gonna help, shut the hell up." Two steps later, he growled. "Same to you, lieutenant."

Gensch whirled around. She froze, barely managing not to emit a squeal of surprise. He stood still for a four-count before resuming his trek. Up to her chin in frigid water, Kerys shadowed him for the length of the reservoir. Near the far end, a continuous mechanical thrum vibrated the ground under her feet, and the source of the dripping came into view: a pair of pipes as big around as her thigh that extended about a foot down from the ceiling. Both dribbled trails of water into the pool, the flow varying between drips and small streams.

Catwalk continued beyond the western end of the reservoir onto solid ground, passing between two boxy metal machines, the likely source of the vibration. She took advantage of the pumps' noise and pulled herself up onto the walkway after Gensch had gone a few meters away from the edge of the water. Killing him here wouldn't contaminate the water.

Kerys raised the weapon in one arm, sighting over it at Gensch's back. She teared up again, and added her left hand to steady her aim, wobbly from the cold. Step by step, she followed him into a low-ceilinged tunnel that made him stoop.

"Tricky, tricky," muttered Gensch, stopping.

"I'm sorry." She sniffled. "It's not fair."

He spun around, murder in his eyes.

Blam!

Blinding muzzle flare and a deafening report filled the underground chamber.

She fired again, unable to see anything but the flash from the first shot burned onto her retina.

Gensch let off a wheeze and hit the ground.

Her vision cleared a few seconds later. Gensch clutched a hand over his chest, blood seeping between his fingers as he struggled to breathe. She crept closer, still aiming at him while crying.

The hostility in his eyes remained. She didn't trust him not to be faking and raised the weapon for a head shot.

His face sharpened in her perception as the gunsights blurred. His expression seemed more like the old Sergeant Gensch. A hopeful gasp leaped past her teeth as she lowered her aim.

"For the record, lieutenant…" Gensch coughed up blood. "You can take that court martial, and stuff it up your ass."

She sniffled. "You got court martialed?"

"Nah." He groaned, pushing himself into a seated position against the wall. "Bastard's sayin' he's gonna court martial me if I let you live."

She wiped tears with one hand while almost keeping the gun aimed at him in the other. "I'm sorry…"

"Hey, kid. You gotta do me a favor." He coughed hard, then swallowed something before grasping his dog tags and breaking the chain from his neck with a sharp yank.

"What?" She nodded. "Anything."

He tossed the two steel tabs onto the ground at her feet. "Survive. Get the fuck off this rock." His eyelids drooped. "Oh, and one more thing… Thanks for… not letting me… kill anyone innocent."

Kerys shuddered with grief.

Sergeant Gensch let out a long, gravelly exhale, and slumped sideways.

She stared at him, wracking sobs shaking her body. Minutes later, she swooned to her knees, both arms draped in her lap. Bad enough someone she trusted, her rock to cling to, died. Worse, *she* had fired the fatal shot.

Still clutching the gun in both hands, she bawled.

DISTRESS CALL

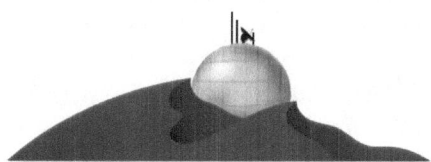

Time lost meaning to Kerys. She wept uncontrollably, kneeling in the dark underground chamber on silt-coated stone, six feet from the body of the first person she'd ever thought of as a father figure, the first man she'd trusted after Will, a man she had killed. So what if alien microbes left him violently deranged? He'd shown her a bit of sensitivity she felt certain few people had ever been allowed to see in him. And now he'd died because of her.

Kerys growled into her hands. No. Not because of her.

Because of Will's carelessness.

For a day and a few hours, she'd almost had a family.

She couldn't possibly carry him up a ladder to the infirmary, but the reservoir chamber felt enough like a tomb already. *Who am I kidding? I'm never getting out of here. I'm probably already infected. Maybe I've snapped and I don't know it. Do crazy people know they're crazy? What if I'm the one that went nuts and Gensch was trying to stop me?*

All the low moments in her life when she'd ever asked fate why she had been denied a father replayed. Eliza came to mind, a childhood friend with an awesome dad who she'd been jealous of. Night after night of shouting matches with Mom followed. Whenever they argued over schoolwork or extra-curricular activities she hadn't been interested in, her mother would always ask the ceiling to send her useless father home to take her useless child away. Mom always called her useless if she didn't get perfect grades or score in the top five percent at whatever activity she'd been forced into. For most of her teen years, Kerys believed it. Even now, deep down inside, she felt useless. Powerless to stand up to the other team who stole her work. Powerless to help anyone here. Powerless to get off this planet. Just like mother said —useless.

Eventually, she dwelled on her college days, specifically how she'd avoided her small circle of friends whenever they started talking about going home for the holidays. She'd rather be alone in a dorm than be around her mother, and she didn't need to hear how happy they all were to go home.

At some point in her high school days, she'd spent futile hours searching for her father online before finally accepting his abandoning them hadn't been *her* fault. More likely, the man couldn't stand Mom.

Kerys couldn't stand her either.

I don't even know if he's alive. She sniffled. *Maybe he's still out there. Oh, stop. I haven't been able to find him before. Not like he'd show up out of thin air if I make it out of here, but I can't leave Jaden alone with The Manager. He's too laid back. That's gotta be driving her nuts. It's only going to get worse when he's older. She's gonna give him the same routine, and he's going to rebel.*

"Oh, why not go for xenoarchaeology?" she said to no one in a bright, cheery tone. "You like that alien stuff. And, it's a small field. Easy to get noticed." *Easy to get dead.*

She leaned forward and grasped Sergeant Gensch's lukewarm hand. "Okay. One last favor right? Get the hell off this rock. I'll give it everything I have. Watch my back, okay?" She set his arm on his leg as if he'd merely sat on the floor to take a break. "Bye…"

Another wave of tears came and went when she picked up his dog tags. A few breaths later, she gathered her tattered scraps of composure, forced herself to stand, and trudged along the walkway over the reservoir back to the ladder.

Kerys climbed, ascending a shaft of pure darkness. No light leaked in around the trapdoor at the top, nor did the weak glow of the reservoir chamber LED lamps help. Every two rungs, she paused, reaching over her head to feel at the dark so she didn't bash her skull on steel. Eventually, her fingertips met something solid. Kerys climbed another rung and pushed, but the trapdoor had no give whatsoever. She felt around until she located a wheel in the middle, which refused to budge when she tried to turn it. With her legs braced on the ladder, she grabbed it in both hands, grunting and straining.

She fought until she ran out of strength, and grabbed the ladder to catch her breath.

"Shit! Did he lock it? Or am I just weak?"

Again she tried, this time trying to turn it the other way. She twisted with her entire body, shoes squeaking on the ladder, but she may as well have been attempting to bend stone.

"No... no... no goddamned way." She thought of shooting it out, but decided against eating a ricochet. "Don't panic. Gina's still out there... and she's on the third floor. She'll never hear me down here."

Twice more, she strained until her arms felt like rubber, to no effect. She climbed down and sat on the walkway with her back against the ladder, listening to the soft lapping of water against the stone beneath her. A part of her wanted to call Gensch a bastard for whatever he did, but she knew it hadn't been really him. *That grunt he made... He just tightened it as hard as he could.*

Struggling to open an over-tightened mechanism would've been hard enough if she could see it. She had no idea which way to spin the wheel; all her effort could've been making it worse.

"Shit!" she shouted, her voice echoing over itself a few times before fading to the chirp of soft, continuous dripping.

"Least I won't go thirsty."

She thought for a while, until the dripping water became maddening.

"Okay. I'm going to go crazy down here."

Doctor Sekhar had told her not to go swimming in it. The idea got her laughing, but she stopped in seconds. *He also said there's a tunnel to the hydroponics pod!*

Kerys bounded to her feet. Again, she walked over the reservoir, this time studying the ceiling for any openings. Gensch remained as she had left him, and she continued on by, muttering another farewell. The metal walkway stopped at plain rock about thirty paces from his body. A short distance ahead, the passage narrowed from the width of the reservoir chamber down to a cramped hallway. Dark grey silt on the walls reminded her of the thrill she'd gotten during the first few hours her team had spent in the alien site. She choked up, but forced her way out from under grief and pressed onward.

Feeble lights continued ahead, every ten feet, illuminating a passageway she'd have nightmares about for the rest of her life.

"Whoa, it's creepy down here."

Minutes later, a bend emerged from the murk up ahead. The air took on a strong earthen smell, tinged with chemicals and sulphur. She walked faster, not trusting her eyes for making her think the distant wall reflected light. The closer she got, the brighter the glare became, pulling her up to a run. She raced around the curve and stopped short at the sight of a ladder standing between two massive control panels full of knobs and glowing lights. Shelves on the right held various bits of pipe fitting, large tools, and plastic boxes of smaller parts like fuses.

"Yes!"

Kerys darted the length of the spur and jumped on the ladder, peering up at an open hatch from which bright light rained down. The stink got worse, but she didn't care, hauling herself up as fast as she could make her limbs move.

She emerged from a hole cut in a plate of red-painted metal, set in the floor of a storage chamber stocked with enormous plastic tanks and shelves upon shelves of briefcase-sized plastiboard boxes. The huge tanks all held dark liquid and bore the label 'Base Fluid - Growth Medium.'

This has to be hydroponics. Whee! I know where I am.

One door at the other end of the closet beckoned her. Kerys crept around the rows of tanks and shelves to the only exit from the storage room. A small, square window confirmed her suspicion as she peered out over the hydroponic tanks full of vegetables and meat slabs.

"Crap. I don't know how to run any of this equipment. We're going to have to harvest anything that looks 'done,' and either freeze it or… ugh."

She mashed the button on the wall and the door slid open with a soft *hiss.* To her surprise, the air outside the storage room stank less. *This place almost knocked me on my ass the first time. Guess it's way worse in the closet.*

Scratching in the distance among tanks slowed her eager stride to a cautious creep. A man gave a soft grunt, then the scratching grew louder.

Kerys pulled the gun out of her pocket and lowered her stance enough so her head didn't peek over the top of the tanks. *Someone's here…* The vats stood in a grid formation. Eight rows at the westernmost end all held meat lumps in various stages from tiny buds the size of acorns to three-foot-long slabs of beef, chicken, pork, and fish. Each tank had an attached platform even with the top, accessible by narrow metal stairs.

A patch of blood on the ground between the tenth and eleventh rows set the hairs on the back of her neck on end. Her feet squished in her waterlogged shoes, seeming as loud as gunfire. She cringed, shortening her steps. Damp cloth clung to her body, easing the overwhelming heat of the greenhouse.

The scratching came again from up ahead, though the way it echoed blurred direction. She aimed around, but spotted nothing moving. A tank farther ahead on the right gave her pause, as the liquid inside appeared too dark. Aiming at it, she crept closer… and regretted looking.

Multiple bodies floated in the growth medium. One man's face mushed against the glass at the end, mouth agape. Another person's arm draped over the edge about halfway down the length of the tank. Blood spattered the floor and the walls of other tanks further down the aisle.

A few seconds later, the smell hit her.

Ugh!

She looked away, burying her face in the crook of her elbow and running for the exit. She caught a glimpse of a bloated dead woman in a tank on the left, and bit back the urge to vomit.

"Gotcha!" shouted a man.

Kerys let off a startled scream as a figure in a blood-spattered yellow jumpsuit sprang off a platform above her. She got her hands up, somewhat catching him as they collided, the impact slamming her into the side of a tank with a resounding *boom*. Softball-sized potatoes inside wobbled around.

He snarled, glaring into her eyes, his mangled nose an inch away from hers. The man looked as though he'd tried to tongue-kiss a shotgun. Most of his cheeks had been reduced to a seeping, tattered ruin.

"You're starving. You need to grow!" The wild-eyed man's facial muscles twitched, likely an attempt to grin. He grabbed her by the arms, dragging her toward the metal stairs leading to the top of the tank.

She struggled, her shoes slipping in a puddle of liquid. The man bore down on her, three shards of glass embedded in his face pressing closer as he pulled her to the side. Kerys cringed away from the bloody, tattered skin. She fought to get away from his grasp, but he overpowered her with ease. Desperate, she tilted her right hand inward and pulled the trigger.

A blast of gore flew out of his left shin. Shrieking in agony, he hurled her down.

Kerys landed hard on her back atop the stairs; the pain of metal edges jabbing into her skin along the length of her body paralyzed her. The gun slipped out of her grip, bounced off a step, and fell between them to the floor under the stairway. The man pounced on her before she could will herself to move, seizing two fistfuls of jumpsuit and hauling her up onto the platform.

He tossed her to the edge, draping her over the side and plunging her up to the armpits in syrupy fluid that tasted like dirt mixed with sweaty socks. Kerys gagged, scrambling to spit the fetid chemicals out of her mouth. Fingers tightened at the base of her neck, holding her under. She flailed and kicked, forcing the man to stumble to the right. She grabbed the platform edge, shoving herself upward as hard as she could. Kerys managed to lift her face out of the fluid long enough to gulp a quick breath before he growled and shoved her down again.

A previously unnoticed cut on her lip flared up with pain like she'd kissed a hot soldering iron. Precious air leaked into bubbles with her scream. She scrabbled at the tank wall, trying to push herself out, but couldn't overpower him.

The more she fought, the worse the cut on her lip burned—but it gave her an idea.

She splashed and slapped at the growth medium, trying to throw it on his shredded face. Seconds before consciousness left her, the man abandoned his grip on her neck. She shoved herself up out of the liquid, gagging and choking, to the sound of horrible wailing.

The slap of a body hitting the floor interrupted the agonized shrieking for only a second.

Kerys retched, crawling away from the tank on her hands and knees atop the narrow metal platform. She alternated spitting to the side and gasping for breath. The syrupy growth liquid streamed off her chin and nose. Her stomach wanted to vomit, but had nothing to get rid of. After the convulsions subsided, she peered over the side at the floor five feet down. The man writhed, clawing at his face, screaming with such intensity she almost felt bad for splashing him.

She grasped the middle railing and slid off the ledge, lowering herself to her feet. The man kicked at the air, howling, his voice growing hoarse and as tattered as his face. She wiped at her burning lip, cringing at the thought of what that liquid had to feel like on such a massive wound.

Kerys ducked to retrieve the gun from under the stairs, aimed, and shot him in the chest. The man went still and silent. She backed up two steps, staring at the body. Once certain he'd stopped breathing, she sprinted to the packing room.

"Okay, so maybe we'll try to get by on Hydra rations. No way am I eating anything in here now."

In her best attempt to mimic how Sergeant Gensch had 'military walked' down the corridors and hallways of Wayfarer Outpost, Kerys crept along the tunnel linking the hydroponics pod to the dome, and headed for her quarters.

She snuck past the door to Residence Pod 1, which had been left open, revealing a hallway strewn with bodies. Most appeared to have been shot, though one man had a combat knife sticking out of his head.

Kerys paused, aiming into the hall. "Anyone in there and still sane?"

A woman's cackling laughter erupted from deep within. Soon, a possibly-Chinese woman in a white jumpsuit stained with bloody handprints and smears emerged from a room. More blood leaked from her mouth—the apparent source a hunk of raw, human meat in her left hand.

"You're not sane, are you?"

The former medic laughed. "Sane? No, I'm Mai. You hungry? There's plenty. Better eat it before it spoils."

She pointed the gun at Mai. "Are you going to try and kill me?"

"Umm." The woman tilted her head side to side, and got into a discussion with several nonexistent people about if it would be a good idea to 'kill that girl' or not since they had a 'full fridge' already.

Kerys shot her in the head.

Mai collapsed with a soft *thump*.

"Sorry."

Kerys resumed her attempt at a tactical walk on the way back into Residence Pod 2. Everything looked the same as it did when she fled Private Foster's ambush, which made her feel a *little* safer that no one alive had been back since. She headed up the ladder to the second floor, raced to her room, and locked the door behind her.

An overwhelming blast of lavender/peachy fragrance hit her, but compared to the hydroponics room, she welcomed it. Her nose and sinuses tingled after a few breaths as if she'd sniffed strong mint oil. She disregarded the sensation and kicked off her shoes before peeling away the bloodstained, torn, soaked-in-nasty-growth-medium jumpsuit, and dropping it to the floor with a *splat*.

I am not putting on in an e-suit with that mess.

Off came her soaked underwear.

She grabbed a fresh pair of panties and a sports bra as well as a clean blue jumpsuit from her closet, then scurried the twenty feet to the women's room naked, carrying clothes in one hand and the gun in the other. She looked away from Paula still lying on the floor, and tried not to notice the smell hanging in the air while rushing a shower to get the stickiness of the growth tank fluid off her skin and out of her hair. Still naked, wet, and dripping, she walked to the farthest sink possible from Paula where she'd left her dry clothing and brushed her teeth to purge the taste of awfulness from her mouth.

After the second repetition of mouthwash, she examined her face in the mirror. Based on the amount of pain she felt while dunked in the tank, she expected a huge gash in her lip, and blinked in disbelief at a small split where Gensch smacked her in the face with the gun.

Pleased at not needing to visit the infirmary for stitches, she got dressed and padded back to her room for clean socks and dry shoes. Refusing to sit down or become idle, lest she continue dwelling on Gensch, she jogged out, intent on returning to the command area on the second floor to find Gina. Having fired a gun three times between two shots in the hydroponic pod and putting Mai out of her misery, she figured if anyone else had been alive (and crazy), they'd have come hunting after hearing the blasts. Abandoning caution, she ran.

Kerys reached the command room a few minutes later, finding only Gensch's unfinished coffee—and no sign of Gina. She scowled at the mug. *Damn this place. I wish I'd never come here.*

"Gina?"

Silence.

She sighed. Gensch had lasted roughly two days before the alien stuff drove him insane. Gina apparently knew about it and feared coming inside—but a cracked helmet didn't give her much choice. Kerys stared at her hands, still baffled at how she hadn't succumbed to the alien microbes eating her brain. What about her was different from everyone else? Her train of thought jumped tracks as the need to warn Earth about what happened here took focus.

Transmitter array time.

After grabbing her e-pad from the desk and stuffing it in her pocket, she returned to the ready room by the garage airlock and climbed into her e-suit. Eerie silence got under her skin. The rattling of the rigid suit seemed to echo down every corridor. She froze, contemplating being alone in this place for six months. She didn't want to be alone, but she also didn't expect Gina would be as lucky as her and somehow prove resistant to the alien stuff.

I've got movies to watch, and Jaden's messages. I can still talk to him.

She sighed, putting the loneliness out of her mind for now. After wriggling around like a bear trying to scratch its back against a tree, she secured the clamps and got the helmet on. *Maybe in four months, I'll trust that I really am the only one left.* She sighed. *Gina looked so damn terrified. Please just be hiding.*

The e-suit gloves made handling the pistol a little tricky, but still well within the realm of doable. She found a holster in Guillen's locker and clipped it to her belt. E-pad in hand, she went to the airlock. Ignoring the quad, she walked out of the garage, heading for the north face of the dome where the schematics had shown a way up to the top.

Sure enough, a ladder enclosed by a cage-like guard ran up the side to the cluster of equipment and vertical rods she'd been staring at for hours on a screen. She didn't bother 'logging in' to the communication channel, leaving the blank [login] line alone. No other names appeared, a morbid reminder of how screwed she would be if she didn't keep her wits.

Rung by rung, Kerys dragged herself up five stories to a small platform. Two doors on the equipment cabinet for the spacefold transmitter were already open, exposing a rack of removable modules about the size of notebooks on one side, each with a red or green light under them. Some had blue ends, some orange, some red. The other cabinet contained a nest of wires connecting sockets in one boxy component to sockets in another around two huge batteries and a main power lead coming up from inside the dome.

Hmm.

She'd expected damage, or sparks, or something catastrophic, but aside from the machinery being open, it looked fine.

Kerys pulled the diagrams up on her e-pad, comparing the pictures to reality.

The wires all look like they're going to the right places. She unplugged and reseated about thirty connectors, making sure none had been loose. *Okay, maybe with the doors open, sharp dust got inside?*

She frowned at the diagram and at the rat's nest of wiring again. Ten minutes of studying it didn't make the arrangement look any less exactly the same.

Okay. Side two.

Aside from color, the modules more or less matched the picture. After staring at them for another few minutes, she noticed that the diagram had all the blue ones in the same group at the top and about a third of the way into the second row, a swath of orange in the middle, and all the red ones at the bottom. Each module had an indicator light under it, but only six of forty showed green.

Son of a bitch... someone moved them around on purpose!

She knelt in front of the cabinet and unplugged all thirty-four modules showing red status lights, stacking the foot-long, inch-thick devices in three piles based on color. Next, she selected a random blue module and plugged it into the first slot. The light remained red, so she moved it one space over. Still red. The seventh slot turned green when she plugged it in.

Bingo. "Tedium I can deal with... My job is *all* about tedium." She grabbed another blue card. "My job *was* about tedium. Xenoarchaeology can go to hell."

Board by board, she inserted and removed them until, the better part of two hours later, she had only one left to seat. As soon as she pushed it into place, a noticeable change in the air occurred above her, a sense of energy that hadn't been there before. All forty lights glowed a bright, lovely green. With reverence due for sealing a ceremonial tomb, Kerys bowed her head and shut the cabinet doors.

It's too important that this works. She snapped her head up. "That's what Chen meant! Don't let it get off the planet... she was talking about the microbes!"

NOT ON YOU

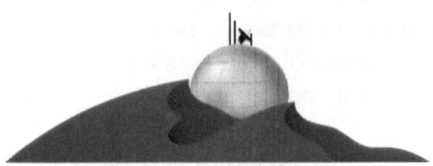

Kerys rushed to the ladder and climbed back to the ground. Forgetting some random crazy person might leap out at her at any moment, she sprinted east toward the garage. At least outside, the odds of someone being around had fallen off to near-zero.

She hoped.

Out came the gun.

What if someone else turned into whatever Corporal Guillen was... She racked her brain trying to come up with an explanation for the bizarre blue algae-like substance that oozed from his wounds. *He'd been outside... The microbes must react differently to the natural atmosphere. Maybe our air weakens or kills them?*

She crept back to the garage, stalking behind her raised firearm as she cleared her way to the airlock. Inside, she tapped her metal boot impatiently after hitting the button, waiting for the machinery to cycle. The two-minute process felt like an hour—even longer when staring at the countdown.

After stowing her e-suit back in the locker, she sprinted to the command room and fell into the chair she'd been using. The SFT client kept a log of 'sent messages.' A folder full of icons popped open, each showing the face of some person in an olive-drab jumpsuit, along with their weekly status reports back to Earth. On the last three icons, Kerys' weary face stared back at her, more forlorn and desperate than she remembered feeling. Those had a red X at the top right corner, indicating errors, while all the others had green dots. She tapped one after the next and poked the 're-send' button.

"Come on… come on… work, dammit."

The error marks went away forty seconds later, but no green dots lit up.

"Oh, now what? Did it transmit or not?"

She hit re-send again and waited. No error came up, but no confirmation message displayed either.

"Ugh. Maybe the messages got corrupted…"

Kerys opened a new message and hit 'record.'

"This is Kerys Loring on Wayfarer Outpost, planet AV494. A dangerous microorganism has been released here. As far as I know, there are only two survivors: myself, and Corporal Gina Mitchell, USIC. I'm no doctor, but whatever this stuff is, it gets into the brain and causes people to lose their grip on sanity. Everyone became mindlessly violent. They spoke of hearing voices telling them to kill. Some people took their own lives. One man drank acid. I know there's a supply ship on the way already, and the fastest anything will get here is another five months and two weeks. I don't know if I'll survive that long.

"I'm not sure why the microbes haven't affected me yet. Maybe the two of us got lucky and our immune systems fought it off. I had a cold and got over it, but maybe it wasn't a cold. I know sending this message might cause you to just write the place off as too dangerous. I want to go home. I don't want to be left here to die, but I have to warn whoever comes here to take precautions. Do not take your e-suits off. I can't say for sure if the air in here is still contaminated or how long those things survive in Earth-type atmosphere. I understand we'll need to be quarantined if you're willing to risk picking us up. That's better than being stuck here. Please send help."

She tapped send.

Forty seconds later, the message appeared as an icon, without an indicator either way. No error, no confirmation.

"What the hell now?"

A scuff came from behind.

Kerys grabbed the pistol and spun, but relaxed at the sight of Gina creeping in the door. The young woman looked like a terrified orphan about to beg for food. With a sigh of relief, she put the gun down on the desk and stood.

"Hey," whispered Kerys. "About Gensch. I… umm. Had to, umm…"

"Yeah." Gina bowed her head. "I know."

"It's okay. I'm not angry or upset with you for running. I ran too." Kerys offered a hopeful smile.

Gina took two steps closer. She kept her arms tight to her chest, glancing around the room as if navigating a lab full of deadly substances. "Gensch was a hardass, but fair. I only served with him for eight months, but felt like I knew him for a lot longer."

"Yeah." She stared once more at the screen, fighting the building need to cry. She had other things to deal with before surrendering to grief. "We need to come up with a plan. He wanted to, uhh, what did he call it? Sweep and clear the place. Check for other survivors or threats. I've never even gone to the reactor area or the storage pod. There's a leak in the tunnel to Lab 1, but we never checked Lab 2. Hydroponics is a bloodbath. Not sure I trust any of that food. Once we're sure there's no one else left, we have to do something about all the bodies."

Gina crept closer, hands folded in front of her. "I was right."

"What?" Kerys put a hand on her shoulder. "About what?"

"It's in the air. Whatever's making people lose their shit."

Kerys' heart sank. *No...* "It can't be in the air. I'm fine. You're fine... we're going to get out of here."

"I can feel it." Gina lifted her head; tear trails glistened on her dark brown cheeks. Her emotion made her look even younger than nineteen. "My head's getting foggy. Startin' to see shit."

"No." Kerys choked up. "Please, no..." She pulled Gina into a hug, wracked with fear and sorrow. "Fight it."

Gina sniffled, clinging to her. "It's okay. You didn't know you'd kill me by bringing me inside. Thought I could keep myself safe if I stayed out at the forest site. Damn shuttle didn't have any more filter pods. I scavved a couple from dead people, but...."

"You're not dying." Kerys pushed her out to arms' length, gripping her shoulders. "Shuttle?"

"Yeah." Gina shivered. "There's a shuttle over there. They were using it to haul the big machinery from the outpost to the campsite. Won't do you any good, though, unless you want to starve in orbit. Need a starship to get back to Earth. And you ain't no pilot."

Kerys took her by the hand and stared into the young soldier's frightened eyes. Grief and guilt threatened to shut her brain down, but she fought it off. *Useless*, said the voice of her mother. She couldn't afford to be useless anymore. Her mother lied. *Why* did the stuff leave her alone but kill everyone else?

Sniffling, Gina rubbed her face. "My sinuses are on fire."

Memory of sharp tingles spread through her face—as soon as she'd smelled the lavender-peach aroma. Will's words replayed in her mind: *I'm only trying to keep you safe, babe.* At the time she'd thought it merely a ramble of his narcissism. How could he keep her safe by insisting on smuggling a flower into quarters—unless…

"Son of a bitch."

"What?" whispered Gina.

"It sounds crazy, but trust me." Kerys tugged her toward the door.

"It's not your fault." Gina held her ground. "Visor was fucked. If I didn't go in, I'da died out there. Hell, I was so scared shitless out there of every little thing, maybe I had it already. Thought I saw people hunting me in the forest, but no one was there." Tendons on the sides of her neck tensioned and released as her jaw locked for a second. She twitched, her expression shifted to furious and melted back to innocent. "Not now. Not now."

"Gina… please, at least let me try." Kerys dragged the smaller woman a few feet closer to the door.

"Ain't gonna help. I seen how these people went. One way trip. I'm dead already." She twitched, eyes darting left and right. "Damn things are whispering at me."

Kerys kept pulling. "I'm not giving up. Don't quit, Marine!"

"I ain't no Marine. I'm USIC. Interstellar Corps. Not quite the same. Marines don't leave Earth." Gina giggled, scowled at the corner of the room for two seconds, and jumped away from Kerys, holding her face and growling. "Son of a bitch."

"Gina…?" Kerys clenched and released her hands, feeling helpless. "I… can't just do nothing and watch you die."

"Not on you, babe." Gina eyed the pistol on the desk. "I know I'm done. Second I breathed the air in here, I was doomed. Look…" Shuddering like a zombie, she forced her head around to make eye contact. "'Fore I check out, I gotta confession to make."

I let Gensch down. He didn't want to succumb… With tears leaking from her eyes, Kerys edged around Gina, who rotated to keep facing her, and grasped the gun. Gina's lips flickered to a smile for an instant.

The small woman leaned forward in as aggressive a posture as her frame permitted. A repetitive tic twitched her face, eyes fluttering. "Before I die, I gotta tell you how I feel. Had a crush on you since I first looked you in the eye, but my ass was too chickenshit to say anything."

"I'm flattered, but… uhh."

Gina chuckled. "Not into women. Yeah, I figured when you didn't pick up my signals in the shower. S'all good. I just wanted you to know."

Kerys looked down. "But, hey, I dunno. Never tried dating a girl before. We gotta live with each other for a couple months. Fight that crap. Let's try the auto-surgeon. You fight that off and we can give it a shot, okay?"

"Not sure it works that way." Gina's cheeks darkened with a blush.

Kerys stared at her. The idea of dating another woman never really came to mind before, but also didn't seem repulsive. *That I'm even considering it must mean I'm not as straight as I think.* She bit her lip, unsure if these feelings truly came from within or due to extreme stress. The unusually powerful grief she'd experienced upon thinking Gina dead—and subsequent elation at discovering she survived—made sense if she contemplated it deeply enough. "Maybe it's not the way I mean it."

"'Preciate the effort. Y'already saved my skinny ass once. Nothin' you can do for me now. I'm 'bout to lose it. Got all sorts of chatter in my head tellin' me to do awful shit to you, an' a headache like... damn."

"No... I can't kill you, too. No way." *Why is it not driving me crazy too?*

"Not on you, babe. The *shit* killed me. Do it. Don't let me hurt you."

Kerys stared down at the gun limply in her grasp as Gina twitched like an android with bad actuators. She reluctantly lifted it to aim—but stopped herself. There had to be a reason the alien microbes hadn't eaten her brain yet. A faint tingle in her sinuses set off an explosion of ideas. She went wide-eyed. "No. I have to try something."

Gina shuddered, tears streaming out of her eyes. Enough of her remained to give hope.

"Come on. Trust me. Fight it. You got yourself out of that bad foster situation. You survived worse than some xeno germs. Don't give up."

After a few seconds of staring, Gina's tears slowed and she nodded once.

Kerys dragged her out of the room, racing across the outpost to the residence pods. Gina intermittently yelled 'go away' or simply cried out as if startled, but managed to keep up. Kerys pulled the younger woman on like a backpack and carried her up the ladder to the second floor, then continued carrying her down the hall to her quarters.

"Are you serious?" wheezed Gina. "You're taking me to your room? I..." She chuckled. "I gotta admit, I daydreamed about this."

Kerys badged open the door and rushed inside. "There's way more chance of us ending up in bed together than me ever getting back with Will."

"Heh." Gina scrunched her face up. "What the heck is that smell? Did you bust open a bottle of perfume in here?"

"No, it's a plant." Kerys rushed to the desk and uncovered it. "I've been trying to think of why this stuff hasn't affected me... and..."

"And?" Gina grabbed her head, woozy, and sank to sit on the edge of the bed.

Kerys paced. "Will... he snuck this thing into my room. He said something about wanting to protect me. It's almost like he knew what was going to happen." She growled. Math had never been her favorite subject, but two plus two did not equal five. Will put the flower in her room *before* he fumbled the reanimated microbes—and before he could've even known about the microbes. Perhaps she *had* gone crazy and didn't realize it. His 'trying to keep her safe' might have had nothing to do with the flower, but it's the only thing different about her compared to everyone else—having it in her quarters. Breathing its spores every night while she slept. The idea this strange flower protected her made more sense than a lucky genetic anomaly.

Gina squeezed the edge of the mattress. Already, the diminutive woman had broken out in a heavy sweat. She stared at Kerys with the gaze of a cornered feral cat, seemingly preparing to leap into an attack at any second.

"You okay?" whispered Kerys, the corners of her eyes tingling from imminent tears.

She *couldn't* kill anyone else who still had enough of themselves left. Gensch had been hard enough. This young soldier nearly died to her air purifier running out. It seemed far too cruel to save her only to be forced to kill her afterward.

"My throat's on fire and my whole damn head feels huge." Gina grasped her neck. "I'm kinda getting super angry at you, but I know it don't make no sense. Shit's got me. The hell are we doing in here?"

Kerys eyed the bed compartment, specifically the emergency hatch. "Scoot back. Lie down."

"You serious?"

"Yes, but I'm not talking about having sex with you."

Gina started to move back into the bed, but hesitated—then leapt at her.

"Gah!" Kerys dropped the gun to free her hands, catching Gina and holding her back from biting her face. "Stop it! Fight!"

They wrestled for a moment before Gina went limp, gagging and choking. The slight woman grabbed her head in both hands and screamed in pain. Sweat beaded on her skin. In seconds, violent convulsions wracked her body.

Kerys scooped her up and put her on the bed, then grabbed the alien plant. She shook it over Gina, creating a visible cloud of purple spores in the air—then shut the hatch door on the bed cubby, then wedged the chair under the lip, turning the bed into a literal cage.

"It's crazy… but… I can't shoot you." Kerys sank to sit in a ball, staring through the glass at Gina, who seemingly lapsed into a seizure.

Moments later, Gina stopped twitching, but her chest still rose and fell with breathing.

Kerys glanced down at the little plant in her hands. It may or may not matter, but a crazy, outside chance beat the alternative. She momentarily felt foolish for distrusting it simply because Will gave it to her... then raised it to her face and took a big sniff.

HOPE, HOWEVER FAINT

Kerys stared at the blank white wall of the shower stall as hot water cascaded over her head.

The soft patter of bare feet came up behind her.

She turned, gazing back at an equally naked Gina, who stared at her the same way Gensch did right before he lost his battle for sanity. An empty shower stall on the other side of the room sprayed water on the floor.

"Do it," whispered Gina.

The bottle of soap gel in Kerys's right hand had become Gensch's gun. Gina grasped the weapon, lifting it to put the barrel against her sternum.

"No," said Kerys. "I won't let it win."

"It already has." Gina stared into her eyes. "You know you have to do it. We're all going to die."

Kerys tried to pull her hand back, but the surprisingly strong nineteen-year-old held the gun firmly in place over her heart.

"Do it."

"No."

Gina's eyes turned completely black. Her cheeks erupted with dozens of deep pits dotted with alien eyeballs. Her sudden inhuman roar caused Kerys to reflexively squeeze the trigger.

Blood and blue gunk sprayed out from the younger woman's back, spattering all over the floor and walls. Gina's eyes shifted back to normal an instant before she collapsed in a gangly heap, a look of peace on her face.

"Not on you," whispered Gina.

Kerys dropped to her knees and took her hand. "I'm sorry. I'm sorry. I'm sorry."

Gina's jaw twitched, but no sound left her mouth. A second later, she stopped breathing.

Sobbing, Kerys gathered Gina's limp body in a hug. Warm shower water continued raining on both of them. She swayed with her until the waves of anger and grief subsided minutes later.

Damn you, Will. You careless, arrogant, son of a bitch.

She eyed the gun laying a few feet away in the bloody water, thankful Will had vanished since everything went to hell. If he'd been within sight, she might've shot him without a word.

"I'm dreaming. This is a damn dream."

Kerys glanced down at Gina's body—which promptly disintegrated into a writhing pile of periwinkle blue worms with black pincer mandibles.

SHE WOKE UP SCREAMING.

Kerys found herself on the floor of her quarters. The lamiaceae advena lay on the carpet inches in front of her face. She sat up, relieved to find Gina still trapped inside the 'emergency survival' bed chamber behind the foggy transparent hatch window. Kerys shifted up onto her knees and crept closer, peering inside. Gina had stripped out of her camo jumpsuit, which lay in a ball at the foot end of the bed, now mottled with vomit stains and snot. She remained unconscious, dark fluid leaking out of her nostrils. It didn't look enough like blood to freak Kerys out. The young woman continued sweating far more than she should have given the temperature. Her tank top and briefs appeared as wet as if she'd worn them to shower.

She's still alive.

It seemed ever so slightly wrong to keep her locked in a chamber like that, but Kerys preferred it to murder. Her idea about the plant having an effect on the reanimated microbes sounded unbelievable, but it's all she could come up with to explain her continued sanity—assuming she did, in fact, remain sane. She'd been breathing the spores for several days, so she'd at least give it a full twenty-four hours before she risked opening the hatch and letting Gina out.

I can't leave her in there that *long. She needs water, food... bathroom.* The need to take care of and protect this woman grew into an overwhelming compulsion.

HOPE, HOWEVER FAINT | 221

"Be right back. Gonna get you some water and food."

Kerys picked the plant up, put it on her desk uncovered, and let herself out into the hall. A trace of blood on her arm clearly not her own gave her pause. It must've come from Gina when they struggled. She winced, fearing it may be infectious... but then again, the dangerous organisms had been (or perhaps still remained) in the air.

I should've been exposed to this shit, too. Why am I still here?

Her heart grew heavy with guilt at surviving. She found herself not caring if someone ambushed her on the way down the hall to the cafeteria. If Gina didn't make it, Kerys would be the only living human for a couple thousand light years in every direction. The thought created a whole new level of alone. The idea of being attacked by an insane person momentarily appealed more than spending five months here alone. Gina may or may not survive.

Those convulsions... haven't seen that before.

The unusual reaction gave her some hope. She debated making a deal with the universe and seeing where things might go with Gina romantically if they survived, but gave up on the idea after only a moment. It wouldn't be fair to Gina. Kerys never really thought much about women in that sense, though in hindsight, did have an unusual fixation on this girl Averie Lawson in tenth grade. At the time, she'd thought her classmate unbelievably pretty, but chalked it up to envy even though it didn't feel at all toxic or make her feel inferior.

If these feelings came entirely from the stress of being in an impossibly dangerous situation, Gina would have to settle for having a big sister. The more Kerys thought about the future, the less weird it struck her to consider dating. *Okay, wow. I'm either seriously desperate or I'm learning new things about myself.* Already, she heard her mother joking about Will being such an asshole he turned her off men, but that wasn't true either. She'd fancied Corporal Guillen... though could never again picture his movie-star handsome face without seeing a hundred tiny alien eyeballs in his cheek.

Shuddering, she put thoughts of him aside and walked faster.

Alas, thoughts kept swirling around the impossible choice between shooting Gina or leaving her trapped in the bed cubby to starve if the woman remained permanently out of her mind. Starving to death definitely counted as cruel, even if Gina lacked the mental faculties to understand what happened.

Her decision to commit a mercy killing if necessary solidified, Kerys cried the rest of the way to the cafeteria. The only question remaining was how long to wait before giving up hope Gina could be saved.

As humid as it looked inside the bed cubby, no amount of body heat or sweat would make a Hydra meal edible. Taking the prepacked trays back to her quarters wouldn't do anyone any good. She also had no idea how long it would take for Gina to wake up... *if* she did. However, cold food would be far more edible than the rock-hard dehydrated form, so Kerys grabbed two meals at random. She stuck them in two different Hydras, hit the buttons to start the 'cooking' process, and went to the other end of the serving lane to grab bottled water.

A faint squeak of shoe rubber on smooth floor came from behind her.

Kerys spun, barely processing the sight of a man in a camo green jumpsuit before the knife he'd thrown at her embedded itself into her left arm a hand's width below her shoulder. She gasped in shock, not yet feeling the pain. Processing that her sudden turn likely saved her life freaked her out too much to do anything for a few seconds.

He tilted her head, staring at her as if unable to understand why she hadn't died. His gaze shifted to the knife sticking out of her arm. It took him a moment to evidently realize what happened. As soon as he started toward her, Kerys snapped back to her senses, yanked Gensch's gun out of her jumpsuit pocket, and shot the man twice in the chest.

The former soldier let out a gurgle of a wheeze and toppled over forward.

"Son of a..."

She gritted her teeth as the pain set in.

"Guess food's going to be a little cold." She scowled at the blade. "Gotta deal with this first."

Having yet another crazed brain-rotted person come out of nowhere like that reawakened her fear of every shadow. Kerys hurried as fast as she could manage without making too much noise to the stairway, intent on going to the infirmary. Every creak, groan, or unexplained thud made her jump and point her gun into the dark.

It didn't help when she found another soldier dead on the stairs. The man hadn't been there the last time she'd come this way with Sergeant Gensch. Too much blood made it difficult to tell *how* he died, though she felt quite certain she'd discovered a corpse. Much to her surprise, she set squeamishness aside and helped herself to the two handgun magazines on his belt. His weapon was missing, which worried her.

Hope he dropped it somewhere and whoever killed him didn't take it. She glanced at the magazines. *Why take the gun but not the ammo? Doesn't make sense. Yeah, he probably dropped it.*

Kerys stuffed the extra magazines into her pocket and kept going up. She stepped into the frigid third-floor air, and caught herself wondering if it would be better to succumb to the microbes and go insane or spend months alone here surrounded by dead people. The thought brought a pang of regret at killing Mai. *She seemed a little saner than the others. Okay, cannibalism aside.* Kerys sighed. *She would've killed me in my sleep as soon as she got hungry.*

She crept out from the darkened hallways around the command room to the bright-white hospital area, squinting from the harsh change. Hellerman's body occupied the chair at the desk, posed with his legs up and arms folded. Gensch had even put Sekhar's sunglasses on him. A reminder of the old soldier's dark sense of humor got her maudlin again. MacLeod remained on surgery table 1, in the same position as before—an attribute she found reassuring for a corpse.

Wow. Maybe I am slipping. I keep expecting him to sit up.

Kerys stepped over Doctor Sekhar's corpse to the second surgery machine. She selected trauma, followed by an option for 'laceration, external' before opening her jumpsuit's zipper.

The words 'patient position fault' scrolled out on the screen.

"Yeah, yeah. I know. Give me a second."

Somewhere, she'd heard that pulling a knife out of a wound would only make it bleed more... but she'd already gotten herself to the infirmary. If the machine shot her up with something to knock her out, she wouldn't be able to remove it... and might end up stuck there, kept under anesthesia while the robo-surgeon waited for a nonexistent doctor to move the knife out of its way.

Jaw clenched, Kerys grasped the handle of the knife, held her breath, and yanked it out. A jolt of pain brought involuntary tears and nearly dumped her to her knees.

Oh, fuck, that was in the bone. Ow...

Once the initial paralysis of sudden pain lessened, she opened her jumpsuit, pulled her arms out, and shoved the garment down to her waist. Standing there with only a sports bra on from the waist up in what amounted to a freezer brought instant chattering to her teeth. The console beeped a warning tone. She hopped up on the table, gasping at the cold cushions touching her back, and rested her arms neatly at her sides. A pleased beep came from the console.

The egg in the ceiling split open, and an array of robotic arms descended. A boxy device at the end of one swept wide across her body before homing in on the stab wound. The other arms followed it to the injury site.

Kerys closed her eyes and rotated her head away so she didn't have to watch. She twitched in surprise when three needles jammed into her right arm, but forced herself to keep still.

The next thing she knew, she lay in a silent, freezing room, her head foggy and all the robotic arms gone. A chirp emanated from her left thigh pocket. Sharp pain in her left arm had diminished to a dull ache.

Damn thing did *knock me out.* Kerys didn't really like having spent however long unconscious in a room with dead people, but at least she survived to wake up. She exhaled and raised her right hand to wipe her face. Tiny needle dots on her arm reminded her of why she lay on an auto-surgeon, and freezing cold air on her exposed skin helped her push past the inertia of post-anesthetic lethargy.

"Ugh…" Woozy, she sat up and examined her arm. A thin line of pale skin denoted where the knife went in. She pressed her hand over it, testing the area with a gentle rub. The wound had closed, but the muscles remained tender. *Marco said something about it taking a day or two for synthetic stem cells to work…* "Fuck this planet!"

The wave of anger that hit her at remembering Marco surprised her. She pulled her jumpsuit up and zipped it before wrapping her arms around her knees and curling in a ball for warmth, staring across the room at the bloody handprint Doctor Sekhar left on the drawer.

"No… I'm not going to die in this place. If those miserable little fucking bugs don't get me, I will make damn sure people know what happened here."

Electronic chirping came from her thigh pocket. It took her brain a second or two to process the meaning of the noise: someone called her e-pad. Kerys slid her hand into her pocket, grasped the device, and pulled it out. The contents of the screen caused her brain to shudder to a screeching halt.

The words: ‹Incoming call from: Braxton, Will› floated over a picture of him flashing a giant shit-eating grin.

PRIMITIVE CREATURES

Kerys slipped off the auto-surgeon to her feet, e-pad in hand, staring in disbelief at Will's picture. Her body felt numb, but not from lying half-exposed in the freezing infirmary for however long she'd been out. She watched it ring, dreading the call from a dead man may be the first sign the tiny aliens had gotten into her brain at last.

"I'm hallucinating this. I've got to be."

It stopped ringing, and she sighed with relief.

"As soon as I realize it's in my head, it stops. Shit. I guess that means I'm—"

Her e-pad started ringing again, startling her into almost dropping it.

She caught it to her chest, clinging as she hurried out of the infirmary, down the hall, and to the stairwell in search of warmer surroundings. It continued ringing the whole way. She debated going to the hydroponics pod to bask in the heat for a few minutes, but dreaded what a 102-degree chamber would smell like with decaying bodies in it. She still needed to get food and water for Gina... assuming the woman remained both alive and sane.

I'm going to have to deal with that eventually... Or not. Maybe I can just seal the place off and live on Hydra packs... if there's enough.

Will called again.

"Shit. I can't be imagining this." She tapped the green 'answer' box. "H... hello?"

"Hey," said Will, though the screen remained dark. "About time you picked up. Look, I need you to go right away to the storage pod and give me a hand with something."

"What? Are you serious?" She glared at the device. "Who are you giving orders to? You know, Will, the most infuriating thing about you is that you *still* don't understand why I left. Everyone exists for your benefit and everything that goes wrong is always someone else's fault to you."

He started to sigh, but grunted in pain. "Sorry. You know how I get when under stress. I'm under stress right now... as well as a few hundred pounds of metal. Will you *please* go to the storage pod?"

I should put a bullet in your damned face for what you've done. Stupid, careless, idiot. Kerys sighed. "Fine, but if this is some kind of trick...."

"No bullshit. Promise."

"Where's the storage pod, anyway? I haven't been there before."

"Check the map," said Will. "It's southwest, between the dome and the reactor. Take tube four."

"Okay, fine. Be there as soon as I can."

He grunted. "Great. Take your time. Not like I'm bleeding or anything."

Asshole. She hung up.

"Well, that figures..." She stared at the lump the gun made in her jumpsuit pocket. "He *would* be the last person left alive with me here. Of all the people on this god damned place...." Kerys paused. "C'mon, Gina. You can't die. I don't want to be here alone with *him*."

Not fully trusting his story about being trapped under metal—and not particularly concerned if he really was, since he didn't sound too desperate —Kerys made her way back to the cafeteria, walking with her gun up. Except for twitching at shadows and wasting a bullet on a fluttering piece of plastic hanging from a hole in the ceiling, the journey from infirmary to cafeteria proved uneventful.

Both meals she'd cooked felt slightly warmer than room temperature. She hadn't been unconscious for *too* long. Considering she had a finite amount of food, wasting any sounded like a horrible idea. She scarfed down the attempt at chicken nuggets as fast as she could chew it, not caring much about the taste. Once finished, she grabbed two water bottles and the other meal before running back to her quarters.

Gina remained unconscious, still curled up in a fetal position as she'd been earlier. Dark purple... something leaked from her mouth and nostrils. Kerys knocked on the hatch. Gina didn't stir. She stared nervously at the woman, afraid she might attack as soon as the hatch opened. Eventually, she felt reasonably sure unconsciousness wasn't fake. Gingerly, Kerys de-wedged the chair away from the bed and set it aside before twisting the handle on the 'lifeboat' door.

A blast of humid air saturated with the scent of a sweaty body, peach, and lavender washed over her in the wake of the opening hatch. She couldn't call the combined aroma pleasant, but it definitely beat the reek of death—or other bodily fluids. Kerys set the water bottles and Hydra tray on the bed, collected the vomit-stained jumpsuit, and put a clean one in its place. She gingerly grasped Gina's tiny wrist and felt for a pulse. The woman's skin seemed hot, almost feverishly so, but her breathing appeared to be normal.

"Hey," whispered Kerys while wiping the purple muck off Gina's face. "Something's happening... I think it's a good sign. You're gonna be okay. We're going to get off this planet. Just gotta take care of some stuff first."

She bit her lip, aware of tingling in her sinuses. *Is this plant fighting the microbes I've been inhaling?* She glanced at the strange violet flower, and decided to give Gina another generous dusting of spores before closing and securing the hatch again.

"Sorry for shutting you in there, but I gotta know if you're still you first." Kerys took a few deep sniffs of the plant, put it on the desk again, and picked up the vomit-stained jumpsuit. She didn't expect the laundry crew to work anymore—due to their likely being dead—but getting the stink of puke out of her living quarters wasn't negotiable. Eventually, she'd figure out where the laundry machines were and do it herself. But for now, she had bigger problems, like Will.

Grumbling, she flicked open a browser client on her e-pad and accessed the Avasar information site, which had a link to a facility map. A square about two-thirds the size of the vehicle garage located due west of the lab pods southeast of the outpost, bore the label 'storage – authorized personnel only.' The map showed a length of tube linking the storage building to the dome, as well as a second tube connecting its far corner to the reactor.

"Guess they don't wanna move radioactive fuel through the main building." She chuckled for a second and frowned. "Shit. I hope that damn reactor can run itself for five months."

As much as it galled her to think of being stuck here with Will, having another person around *did* make her feel a little better. Grumbling, she clenched her fists at her sides and headed down the corridor, following the map. The walk reminded her of following Gensch to the labs, and spun up her emotions into a swirling storm of anger and guilt. Everyone who died in this place ultimately came back to Will being an idiot. She had no way to know if anyone could've stopped it if he admitted his error right away rather than pretending it never happened. In typical Will fashion, mistakes no one caught him committing never happened.

But Annapurna *had* caught him... too late.

She reached the link ring where the hamster tube connected the dome to the storage pod. The sight of the round door being closed caught her off guard. All the other tunnels (except for the lab Gensch sealed due to the air leak) had been locked open. The narrow strip of window on the left half of the circular door offered a view of a tunnel strewn with bodies. At least eleven corpses lay about as if an out-of-control brawl had come to a sudden stop. One man gripped another by the throat, frozen in the act of choking him. A woman still clutched the handle of a knife rammed into a man's ribs. Another man in a camouflage jumpsuit lay on his side, the butt of his assault rifle smeared with blood. Close to where he'd fallen, a woman with a bashed-in face sprawled on the floor.

Kerys recoiled in horror. "Shit...."

Red light drew her attention to a tiny two-by-two-inch screen at the center of the door showing a flashing red dot with a white X on it. The warning message indicated the tube between the dome and the storage pod had no air in it. Her gaze shot back and forth from the screen to the window a few times.

Someone blew the air while they were rioting...

A touchscreen panel on the wall to the right of the link collar contained a series of controls for air management, hatch operation, and interlock activation. Beneath it, an open hatch revealed three valve wheels and two large levers—likely a manual backup in case the power failed. She approached the screen, which confirmed the tube was presently in a state of vacuum and ready to be flooded with exterior atmosphere in preparation for disconnection. Buttons offered her the options of re-pressurizing the tube or opening vents to the outside—as well as turning the lights off.

After a moment's hesitation, she pushed the large green rectangle for re-pressurization.

The floor vibrated along with a mechanical whirr. Loud hissing came from beyond the sealed hatch; hair on several corpses fluttered. Less than a minute later, the red X on the door's screen went black. The button she'd pressed changed caption to depressurize. Beside it, a new button appeared marked 'door open.'

She pushed it. Two door halves with interlocking trapezoidal 'teeth' slid apart, vanishing into the walls. Kerys braced for stink, but a breeze of stale air carried only the smell of metal.

Huh... oh, I guess they wouldn't rot in a vacuum.

Cringing, she fast-stepped around the bodies down the tube to a westward bend. Four more corpses lay on the ground past the corner, all apparently shot to death. She crept up to the door at the far end of the tube, but hesitated before touching the button to open it.

I don't know that he's still sane. Am I even still sane? Maybe I died in my sleep and all of this is some nightmare taking place in three seconds of real time. Maybe I'm still in stasis dreaming, and we haven't even reached the planet yet. She rubbed her arm where the knife hit her. Still tender. "Ow." *No... at least they always say pain proves you're not dreaming.*

Kerys slid her hand into her pocket, squeezing her fingers around the rubberized grip of Gensch's sidearm. A moment of doubt came and went. She pulled it out, wondering if she had any bullets left. A thumbnail-sized screen on the left side above the trigger displayed: 06.

Reassured, she slid the weapon back in her pocket, but didn't let go.

Okay... time to deal with the asshole.

She reached across with her left hand and hit the button, causing the door to open with a pneumatic whoosh. Beyond it lay a warehouse-like room of floor-to-ceiling metal shelves containing metal cargo boxes of varying size. Some looked large enough to hold bathtubs, while the smallest were perhaps a foot cubic.

Leaning in, she looked side to side down aisles between shelves.

"Babe? That you?" said Will, his voice echoing over the silence.

She squeezed the gun. "Yeah. And I'm not your babe."

"Awesome. I'm near the northeast corner. It's safe. No one left in here but me, or I'd be dead. Have trouble finding the place? It's been a while."

"Not too bad," she muttered. "Only had to kill one person." *And check on Gina. You can definitely wait for her.*

The array of boxes on four levels of shelving held hundreds of shadowy spots between them. She drew the gun, not trusting anything about this place.

"I don't hear you walking," said Will.

"Because I'm not," she said, raising her voice. "I'm beyond bullshit, Will. I don't trust this at all."

He remained quiet for a moment. "Okay, I can accept that. I'm not trying to trick you, babe. Remember that little cat keychain I gave you on our second date? Had LEDs for eyes that lit up when you squeezed it? You named it 'Bill.'"

A lump started to block off her throat, but she swallowed it. "Okay, so maybe you're not as crazy as everyone else."

"You don't sound crazy either, hon."

"Don't call me that, either. Outside of your own private little world, we're not a *thing* anymore."

He sighed. "I know. Just hoping you'll give me the chance to make up for screwing that up. I never got over you."

Kerys advanced, wary eyes searching the shadows with each step. "I got that feeling from you calling me twenty times a day for months."

"Sorry. Look, can you please move a little faster? My leg's gone numb."

She kept the same cautious pace down the aisle up to an opening on the right, where black skid marks on the steel floor swerved. Staying mostly hidden behind the corner of a shelf, she peered around a box labeled 'Dehydrated meals – 1000 CT.'

Will lay on the floor facing away from her, pinned up to the chest under a section of shelf that had collapsed. A pistol sat on the ground near his hand, the slide locked back. *He's out of bullets.* To his right a short distance, a dead man slumped over the controls of a forklift crashed into the destroyed shelf. Another dead man sat on the floor, his back propped up against a still-intact shelf some fifteen or so feet away from Will. He appeared to have been shot five or six times, all over his chest, one in the shoulder, and one in his hip.

"Okay, so maybe you're not full of shit." Kerys slipped the gun in her pocket to keep it out of sight, leaving her hand on it.

Will sat up enough to bend his head backward, staring at her upside-down. His face had a few bruises and dried blood clung to his lip. He looked like he'd gotten into a fight and hadn't exactly walked away the winner. "Hey. Wow. You're so damn beautiful. Like an angel."

"How'd you wind up there?" She walked closer, stopping a good five paces away.

"Shithead in the lift tried to impale me. He swerved when I started shooting at him, but he hit the damn shelf and… well, here I am."

"How long have you been stuck like that?" She raised an eyebrow.

"Not sure. Couple hours." He gave a weak chuckle.

Kerys walked to the left, keeping enough distance in case he faked being stuck.

"Hon, relax. I'm still me."

She smirked. "That's what I'm afraid of. And if you don't stop calling me 'hon,' I may leave you there."

He squirmed, tugging at his legs. "I'm really stuck."

Kerys squatted, examining the warped metal. The right leg of his green botanical jumpsuit had gone dark red from the knee down. Enough metal pressed into him that she opened her mind to the idea he might really be trapped. "I should leave you there, anyway."

"What?" He blinked at her in disbelief. "How could you say that?"

"I've had to kill two people who I considered close friends. I almost died both times because I couldn't bring myself to do it without hesitating. I don't think I'll have the same problem if you crack."

He let out a nervous chuckle. "Well, good thing for me I'm not nuts."

"I ought to leave you there." She lunged to her feet, shouting, "How could you be so damn careless! You dropped that shit and you didn't warn anyone!"

Will cringed, making a face like a boy who'd been caught doing something he'd been told not to. "Uhh... look, I had no idea how dangerous the stuff was. Anna was being all secretive about it. You know me... I guess I couldn't live without being the one who made the breakthrough discovery. I just wanted to examine the stuff myself to see if I could—"

"Steal her work." Kerys tapped her foot. "And take all the credit."

He let his head fall on the steel with a soft *thump*. "Yeah. I'd spent years in this place, studying all these plants and molds and fungi, but none of it turned out to be useful to Avasar. The bosses back on Earth were hoping for something with medical applications or maybe a way to improve the CBPs for the e-suits. Alien life, even if it had only been plants, offered so much promise... but when we got here, it had no value."

"What about scientific value, a better understanding of the universe beyond Earth?"

He rolled his eyes. "There's no money in that. Avasar came out here to make a profit."

Kerys frowned. "And so did you."

"Yeah." He looked away in shame.

"You should have told someone you dropped it."

"I panicked. Thought it was just some crummy little algae or something. Everything else we found here has been useless." He rolled his head left to stare up at her. "Look, if I could go back in time, I'd never touch the stuff. I've lost everyone I've worked with for the past four years. It's not just you who's had to deal with that. Think about how *I* feel, knowing they're all dead because I'm a careless idiot."

She looked away as his lip started to quiver. *Just like Will. Always about him. Of course, I'm the selfish one for not caring about how he feels.*

"I'm sorry. My leg's kinda messed up. Please get this shit off me? You don't want to spend the next six months alone, do you?"

"How do I know you're not going to snap in a day or a week? I'm tired of finding people I think are okay only to have to kill them hours later." She shed a tear for Anna and Sergeant Gensch, then bit her lip in worry over Gina. Another tear formed for MacLeod, even though she hardly knew him. "I get you out of there and you try to kill me tomorrow."

Will reached toward her. That irritating smile he always had on his face, regardless of whatever happened around him, flattened to the most serious expression she'd ever seen him make. "I would never hurt you."

"Hurt has more than one definition, Will." She let her hand slip from the pistol and folded her arms.

"I'm not perfect. I'm far from it. You know what my dad was like. Kinda like your mother actually, now that I think about it. All business. Be confident, go after what you want, and take it."

"I'm not an 'it' to be taken. You never could accept me as a person, and I am not some bit of swag to decorate your home with."

"I got caught up in the job. Think about that first year we had together. *That* was me. I promise you when we get back to Earth, if you'll give me a chance, I can be that guy again. I'll quit Avasar. I'll find the most stress-free job I can think of. Maybe I'll teach yoga."

She blurted an unexpected laugh. *Am I starting to believe this bullshit, or am I just that desperate not to be alone here if Gina doesn't make it?* "I'm so damn angry with you for dropping that phial. All these deaths are on you."

He looked at the ceiling. "I know. I have that to deal with for the rest of my life."

"The way things are going, that might not be long." She crept closer and stooped to grab the shelf.

Will put a hand on her back. "Hey, don't talk like that. Envision what you want to happen and hold that in your heart, and you'll get it."

"This isn't a corporate goal, Will. Blowing sunshine up my ass won't help. That motivational shit..." She grunted, straining against the shelf, but couldn't budge the warped steel.

He opened his mouth to say something, but kept quiet.

"I... dammit." Kerys looked down at him. "Not strong enough to—" Blurry orange at the top of her vision caught her eye. She looked up at the forklift. *Damn it. Why do I always go scatterbrained around him?* "Duh."

He smiled.

Kerys stepped over him and approached the dead man. Blood spattered on the console to the right, indicating Will shot him after the crash. She gritted her teeth, pulling the body out of the seat and guiding him to the floor. The instant she disturbed him, a powerful stench rose into the air, making her gag and spit bile to the side.

Eyes blurry from the stink, she climbed into the lift and fumbled with the controls. When she located the 'on' button, a labored mechanical whine came from the forklift. Her attempt to move the loader caused a howl of pain from Will. She let go of the control stick as if it burned her.

"Sorry."

He grunted. "Forgiven. I probably deserved that."

No probably about it... and you deserve worse. "Will?"

"Hmm?"

"Why are we still sane? How did the things not eat your brain since you got the first dose?" She narrowed her eyes. Though she suspected the strange flower had something to do with it, she didn't want to mention it. He'd certainly take credit for 'protecting' her if she admitted to being in his debt.

He raised his hands and lowered them in the best approximation of a shrug a man could accomplish while pinned under a shelf. "Best I can figure is it's probably luck. Something about our physiology that the little bastards didn't like. Or maybe it was the massive dose of antibiotics I took when I felt a flu coming on. I didn't want to lose any time working."

Damn, he's so full of shit. She pictured him standing in her room the night he brought the lamiacaea advena. *No one smuggles a specimen past procedure to give a girl a flower. Doctor Sekhar said Will had the same purple snot years ago. He was one of their lead botanists… but how could he know the spores would do anything to a microbe he didn't even know existed? Ugh. Maybe I'm wrong and it's freak luck I'm okay.*

Kerys hated how being around him always made her second-guess herself on everything. If she guessed wrong about the spores, she basically only prolonged Gina's suffering. However, none of the other people who started to lose their grip convulsed, collapsed, or leaked purple slime. *Something* significant happened. She couldn't be completely off the mark.

While her mind wandered around possible explanations, Kerys tugged on a different stick. The forklift crept backward, making an ear-splitting screech of metal on metal. Once the tines came free from the shelf, she played with the controls enough to get a feel for how to raise and lower it, as well as steer. "I didn't take anything."

"Okay, so maybe for me it was the meds, for you… biological luck?"

Kerys shimmied the forklift back and forth, lining up the left tine within a few inches of his leg. She nudged the lift forward, positioning the forks under a shelf containing grey jumpsuits. Raising the lift pushed the metal up, away from Will's leg, with a groaning shudder of stressed steel. Heavy thuds and slams came from the other side as boxes fell off the top of an adjacent—still standing—shelf. She looked around at the echoes.

Well, if there's anyone left alive out there, they heard that….

He moaned, feebly attempting to drag himself backward.

Kerys slid down from the seat, grabbed his arm, and dragged him away from the twisted metal, then frowned at his bloody right leg. "I honestly don't know why I didn't let you stay there."

His smile returned. "Because you are an angel, and I hope I can prove to you that I'm serious about The New Will."

I'm not holding my breath. For the first time in her life, she didn't have any hope of 'getting him back' like he used to be. What she'd said to Gina earlier rang true. She'd sooner experiment with dating a girl than trust him again. Her mother warned her 'men like that' always say things to get the woman to trust them, then go right back to their same old ways. Times she agreed with that woman she could count on one hand. Of course, the idea of being stuck here with him in a bad mood scared her more than what Will might do if she went easy on him.

"Come on. I've been working on my medical certification." She threaded his arm around her shoulders and helped him stand.

"Huh?" He put all his weight on his left leg, hopping for balance. "Seriously? You've been going to medical school?"

"In a manner of speaking."

"For how long?"

She helped him across the storage pod to the tunnel, and past the bodies. "About ten minutes. I can probably get the auto-surgeon in the infirmary to fix that leg... at least stop the bleeding."

He blinked as if the idea hadn't even occurred to him. "Oh. Yeah, good idea. Guess the doctor is out."

Kerys cringed. "Yeah... *way* out. He's dead."

Will glanced at her. "You saw him?"

Her gaze fell to the floor. "I had to kill him."

He let out a soft whistle. "Sorry."

Kerys supported most of his weight as they made their way up the stairs to the third floor. He groaned and grunted in pain the whole time.

"Heh... This hurts like hell, but it's so good to have my arm around you again."

"Will?"

"Hmm?" He hopped to a halt beside her, hope on his face.

"Shut up."

WHAT IFS

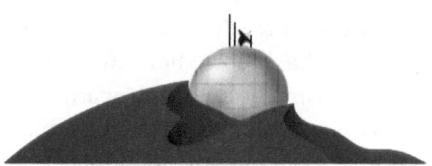

U pon entering the infirmary, Will winced at the blood-smeared walls.

He gave a muffled cry of shock when MacLeod and Hellerman came into view. He shifted his weight off her shoulder and grabbed his face in both hands after a long stare at the enormous stitching down the center of MacLeod's chest.

"Just lie down on the open table. The machine does all the work."

He hobbled over to the table. She helped him up to lay flat on the cushions.

"So you figured out how to run this thing?" Will shied away from the robo-surgeon dome above him. "Doesn't that take like years of medical school?"

Kerys moved to the control screen, hunting for an option that seemed appropriate for a crushed leg. Sadly, the auto-surgeon had no setting to fix 'misogynistic shithead.' "Doctor Sekhar seemed to think it did." She pushed 'internal injury' and looked at the sub menu. "I was trying to save MacLeod over there, but the doctor objected to me touching the equipment. He hit me over the head from behind. Woke up to find him tossing body parts at the walls to see how long he could make them stick."

Will gurgled and lurched over sideways, but didn't throw up.

"Lie still." She chuckled to herself. *Should be good at lying.*

He flattened out again, staring up at her. A placid smile replaced his nauseated expression. "The worst part of the past few days was not knowing if you were okay. It's so good to see you."

Internal injury… crushed limb… leg. Wow, this thing. Why do we even have doctors anymore? She glanced at a panel presenting 'recommended dosages' of various complicated sounding chemicals and asking for user confirmation. *Okay, that's why.* In a perfect world, she should probably compare the meds with any list of known allergies or interactions with anything else Will might be taking… but had neither the expertise, the data, nor the time. *Uhh. I'll trust the defaults.* She clicked 'accept.'

The egg split open and the 'scanning arm' lowered.

"Whoa… you turned it on," said Will.

"Yeah. I've been getting too much practice lately." She backed up.

The machine could take care of him by itself. Being around him had been uncomfortable enough already. Any longer, and he'd surely start trying to weasel his way back into her life. Surprisingly, she didn't worry about caving in this time—she didn't want to deal with what he'd do when she said no. Will could be volatile in normal circumstances, but out here? She couldn't even begin to imagine what the extreme desperation of being stranded on an alien world with an invisible killer would do to his personality. The less time she gave him to try talking to her, the better for both of them. Besides, she wanted to go check on Gina.

He pressed himself into the cushion as if trying to escape from the mechanism. "So, umm…"

"Just relax. It might give you something to help with the pain… maybe knock you out while it looks at that leg." She turned away. "I'll be back in a bit. I need a moment."

She hurried out before he could say anything, initially running with no destination in mind other than 'away from Will.' Hallways and stairs passed in a blur of emotion, and she found herself heading toward the residence pod, drawn both to the illusion of safety offered by her quarters as well as concern for Gina. She'd refused to let the young soldier die out there on the planet's surface, and she doubly refused to let her survive near suffocation only to die to the goddamned microbes.

Kerys didn't look down the hallway to Residence Pod 1 to avoid having to see Mai's body. She paused long enough to close the door, and ran the rest of the way to Pod 2.

The air smelled like death, which made her remember Paula in the bathroom at the north end of the second floor. They'd have to deal with the bodies before the stench of decay could contaminate the air scrubbers and fill the entire outpost. The thought of moving dead bodies around horrified and disgusted her, but no one else would do it and… it had to be done. Better to touch the dead than breathe them.

The longer we wait, the worse it will be.

Honestly, judging by Will's reaction to the infirmary, *she'd* have to deal with the bodies. He couldn't handle anything remotely disgusting.

Kerys sighed. "Nothing an e-suit and transport cart can't fix."

Her room smelled like a peach meteorite crashed into a lavender grove. Compared to the building rot outside, she took a deep breath of it, making her sinuses tingle. Feeling 'safe' in her quarters, she closed and locked the door before pacing around, kicking at dirty clothes. Gina had moved, now mostly on her back with her knees bent, feet flat on the mattress. Dried trails of the purple ooze marked her face by her nose and mouth. Sweaty handprints on the transparent hatch indicated she'd come to and tried to get out.

She crept toward the bed cautiously. One water bottle was empty, the other had been filled somewhat less than half with a dark purple liquid. It took Kerys a few seconds to logic out that Gina must've drank both bottles... then had to go to the bathroom.

Dark purple piss? Ack. That can't be good. Or... can it? She bit her lip. Doctor Sekhar told her Will complained of a purple stool. Thus far, Kerys had not experienced a similar effect, only some purple snot when she'd been sick. She stared at Gina breathing in her sleep. Her underwear didn't cover much, giving Kerys a mostly unobstructed view of her body. No sign of any alien mutations appeared on her skin. Her expression seemed so peaceful it infuriated Kerys all over again at how Will could be so careless. This girl was just that—a girl. Nineteen. In sleep, she looked even younger, stirring a similar protectiveness to what Kerys felt for her little brother.

"Please be okay." Kerys pressed her hand to the transparent hatch atop one of the prints Gina made.

Her desperation to save at least *one* person from the outpost brought her to tears, as painful as it was ridiculous. She had no training for situations like this. What even made her think she *could* do anything?

I'll be lucky to save myself... but I have to try. She closed her eyes. *I should have left Will there. Sigh. No. I can't. Bad enough having to shoot people the microbes already killed. He might be an asshole, but killing him would be wrong.*

"How can I not want to be alone at the same time I don't want to be on the same planet as him?"

Her mind swirled with random thoughts and too few answers as she paced around for a while.

Eventually, she sat on the desk, head in her hands. *The microbes are obviously in the air. They should've made Will sick by now. They should've made me sick by now.* Kerys peered between her fingers at her desk, her gaze settling on the strange purplish-blue flower. The floret rings seemed less vivid than before, though remained pretty.

Someone had traced a heart and 'Love you' in the spore dust beside it.

Seems to be doing okay without water... Kerys blinked. *Will? How the hell did he do that while stuck under a shelf?* Gina couldn't have done it and gotten back in the bed cubby with the chair wedged against the hatch. She pictured the scene where she'd found him in the storage pod. It seemed legit, and if he had been running around the whole place avoiding her before, why would he all of a sudden need to lure her into the storage room? *No... he really got stuck. But if he's up to something, that couldn't have been part of his plan. What the....*

She stared at the flower, then at the closed bed hatch.

Does he know about Gina? No... he had to have missed her. The hatch is so fogged up he probably didn't even see her. He'd definitely have said something nasty if he saw a mostly naked girl other than me in my bed.

"Yeah..." Kerys sniffed the flower again. "It *has* to be the spores... it's the only thing we were both exposed to that no one else was." She touched her fingertips to her face, beside her nose. The image of a tissue full of purple snot came to mind. Crouching, she leaned close to the flower, gazing into the intricate lattice of tiny florets. "What did you do to me? I've been breathing you for days... what are you?"

The flower, being a plant, did not reply.

"He kept opening the case to expose me to the spores." She snarled. "He knew something. He knew this thing would... protect me? His crap turned purple. Like that pee in the bottle... was Will exposed to the microbes before?"

Both Gina and Will experienced discoloration of excreted waste. Kerys hadn't. Gina definitely suffered the effects of the alien microbe infection. Logic said she'd discovered proof the spores could both cure it as well as essentially 'vaccinate' a person from it. Since she hadn't left anything purple in a toilet, it must mean she'd never been fully infected. Her stomach did a flip at the realization he must have known about the microbes before she even got to this planet. But how? No one here saw the alien writing on Copernicus... and they had to drill into the stone head to get at the microbes inside it. There had to have been another source— perhaps out in the forest somewhere. But... the discovery of a potential first source hadn't destroyed the entire colony.

A scenario played out fast forward in her mind: Will experimenting on plants, somehow gets simultaneously exposed to the microbe as well as the spores from the lamiacaea advena. Maybe the microbes started to affect his mind and he recovered thanks to the spores?

"He put the damn flower in here for a reason." She cradled it in both hands, feeling like an idiot for ever wanting to get rid of it. "If I'm right, little guy, you saved us."

She inhaled. Strong lavender-peach flooded her senses. Pins and needles within her nostrils spread up into her sinuses and brought involuntary tears to her eyes. The fragrance struck her as wonderful and fruity. Savoring it, she breathed in until her lungs could hold no more air.

Reassured by her reasoning, Kerys removed the wedged chair and opened the bed hatch. She dusted Gina with another cloud of spores for good measure, replaced the plant on the desk, then collected the urine bottle. Being stranded in a deadly situation was no excuse for being disgusting when unnecessary. After hurrying to the bathroom a few doors down the hall to dump the bottle out in a toilet, she returned to her room, righted the chair, sat in it, and activated her terminal.

It no longer seemed necessary to 'lock' Gina in the bed. If, as she hypothesized, Will suffered the same microbial infection and recovered, she would, too.

A few seconds' worth of exploring the Avasar intranet site brought her to a directory listing. She located Will's room on the ground level of Pod 1, seventh door on the left. Forgetting her guilty need to avoid seeing Mai's body, she raced out the door, down the ladder, and around to the other residence pod.

Mai remained dead in the doorway where she'd fallen, still clutching a decaying hunk of human muscle—with a bite out of it. Kerys jumped over the body and skidded to a halt a few meters later by Will's door. He hadn't locked it, so she barged in. The room stood in perfect order, far neater than normal for a man. No clothes on the floor, nothing in the wastebasket, bed made and folded.

There, on the desk nestled among plastic bamboo plants, stood a sprig of the same flower he'd given her. *Why don't I smell it in here?* She walked closer and stared at it. Dark spores came away on her fingertip from a light touch. "Probably because I took a giant damn sniff of it a minute ago."

A small case next to the computer terminal had violet fingerprints on the lid. She lifted the lid, exposing a box of dust. Concentrated, the spores took on an iridescent indigo sheen. The empty glass to the right of the monitor had a faint lavender tint from dried liquid.

"He's been... milking it for the spores." She shifted her jaw side to side. "Is he overdoing it, or should I give Gina a spore cocktail?"

Kerys curled forward, speechless from a sudden attack of grief. She had it in her room the whole time. Had she not let herself get so freaked out by what went on, had she stopped to *think*, Sergeant Gensch, MacLeod, Hellerman... maybe even Ellen might still be alive. A new torrent of guilt brought wracking sobs. Her stupidity killed people. No, not stupidity—she'd lost herself to emotions and panic.

Gina's gonna make it. I'm not a complete idiot. She's gotta make it.

After a while, she calmed, staring at the flower while sniffling.

"Shit... is this me going nuts? Crying over a damn flower?"

Kerys leaned back and wiped her face. A spot of yellow on the monitor announced an unread message. She tapped the keyboard and got a password prompt.

Damn. Eyes narrowed, she typed: I@mUnst0ppa3le.

And got in.

Arrogant son of a... She'd thought the password conceited years ago, too. He'd used the same one on his computer at the apartment they'd shared. Being too rattled to think clearly didn't count as stupid, even if it could be argued people died because of it. Using the same password for almost a decade *did* count as stupid.

The message client showed one new text-only message from someone named 'Broussard, A' next to an Avasar Biotech logo.

WILL,

It's been a while since you sent a status update, and the group is becoming concerned. We need your full report on how the Wayfarer Personnel reacted to the experimental substance. We need timelines of morbidity from exposure to cessation of life, preferably correlated to their psych profiles for a full evaluation of weapons potential of AM-3. Please provide an update as soon as possible.

REGARDS,

ADAM H BROUSSARD.
   Vice President of Research and Development
   Avasar Biotechnology – Military Application Division

"YOU... BASTARD..." KERYS COVERED HER MOUTH. SHE SCROLLED DOWN TO previous messages in the thread, reading them in reverse chronological order.

ADAM,

THINGS ARE A LITTLE OFF THE RAILS, BUT IT'S UNDER CONTROL. THE ENTIRE crew has been exposed to AM-3 as planned. Everyone except myself and Kerys are

*infected. The antigen in the lamiaceae advena sample appears to be working
exactly as my tests showed it should. She didn't trust the plant, so I had to take
some extra precautions to ensure she got enough in her system. I never had the
chance to get her to ingest the derivative agent, but it seems that breathing the
spores in a confined space over a series of days works just as well. Not as practical
for our needs though.*

*My one area of concern is that after I released AM-3, symptom onset was more
rapid than anticipated. Some of the crew succumbed to violent episodes within
mere hours of exposure. We may have issues with distribution and controlling
target areas. On the upside, now that Kerys was able to recover the large store of
the agent for us, we're having success growing AM-3 in the lab. It should be
highly possible to weaponize it.*

WILL BRAXTON
  Senior Project Lead
  Avasar Biotech – Wayfarer Expedition
  - - - - - - - -
  Will,

*THAT IS GREAT NEWS! YOU WERE RIGHT WHEN YOU SAID SHE WAS SMART. USE
her for an antidote control test. Unless you're willing to arrange an 'injury' so
severe she gets sent home by medical order, anything I do from this side will be
suspicious. Have a little faith in your research on those spores. You trust your own
life to them, but not hers? Grow a pair, man.*

ADAM H BROUSSARD.
  Vice President of Research and Development
  Avasar Biotechnology – Military Application Division
  - - - - - - - -
  Adam,

*I CAN'T BELIEVE IT. HER FIRST DAMN DAY IN THERE AND KERYS OPENS THE
vault. I'm not sure what shocked me more, that no one questioned the silt we
sprayed on the walls or that she managed to get it open so damn fast. The project
is going ahead of schedule now since we budgeted a few months for them to figure
out how to gain access to the hidden chamber. Guess they were all too gobsmacked
at the alien stuff to wonder how dust built up on the walls of a sealed cavern.
Hilarious how advanced scientists can be so damned stupid sometimes.*

Since we have plenty of extra time, can we come up with a way to get her out of here before moving to phase two?

WILL BRAXTON
    Senior Project Lead
    Avasar Biotech – Wayfarer Expedition
    - - - - - - - -
    Will,

DON'T WORRY ABOUT DOCTOR BHATIA. CAPTAIN CHEN IS AWARE THAT THE TRUE mission of *Wayfarer Outpost is weapons research. Why else do you think there's no civilian administration personnel on site? We've told her that most of the civilian scientists are not aware of this for security reasons. She's on our team. I almost feel bad for her since she doesn't know she's in the test pool.*

ADAM H BROUSSARD.
    Vice President of Research and Development
    Avasar Biotechnology – Military Application Division
    - - - - - - - -
    Adam,

OKAY, OKAY... I MANAGED TO GET ANOTHER SAMPLE OF L.A., AND PUT IT IN HER *quarters. Might be an issue getting her to keep it. She doesn't trust it, but I'm trying. I think Doctor Bhatia is becoming suspicious of our true motives for coming here. She's been on my ass like a damn hawk. Who had the bright idea for me NOT to be the damn boss of the botanical group, anyway? You put ONE person technically over my head and of course, she's a problem. I think she's got Chen's ear. If what we're really doing here gets back to the USIC, we're all going to be fucked.*

WILL BRAXTON
    Senior Project Lead
    Avasar Biotech – Wayfarer Expedition
    - - - - - - - -
    Adam,

. . .

OFF THE RECORD, YOU'RE AN ASSHOLE. I DON'T KNOW IF I CAN DO THIS.

WILL BRAXTON
  Senior Project Lead
  Avasar Biotech – Wayfarer Expedition
  - - - - - - - -
  Will,

IT COULDN'T BE HELPED. WHAT CAN I SAY? WE POSTED A JOB, SHE ANSWERED, and she had the qualifications. Best part was, she got the shaft so hard at her last job she jumped at the contract, didn't even balk at the initial salary offer. The group wants the largest chance of success. Now isn't the time to get sentimental on us, Will. There's too much money at stake, remember? Do what you're being paid to do. Oh, and if you're confident enough in the counter-agent, wouldn't your little girlfriend make an ideal test candidate for the control group? Every experiment needs a control group. If you feel that guilty about it, maybe you can share some of your bonus with her. Avasar's saving a lot of money not having to fly everyone home.

REGARDS,

ADAM H BROUSSARD.
  Vice President of Research and Development
  Avasar Biotechnology – Military Application Division
  - - - - - - - -
  Adam,

WHAT THE HELL IS KERYS DOING HERE? DO YOU HONESTLY EXPECT ME TO GO through with this project now? When we ran into that snag finding more samples and I asked for some people who could make sense of that alien shit, that did NOT mean send my goddamned girlfriend up here. Everything is on hold until she's off world. No way. I'm not putting her in the middle of this. You can't offer me enough money for her life.

WILL BRAXTON
  Senior Project Lead

Avasar Biotech – Wayfarer Expedition

KERYS LEANED BACK IN THE SEAT, FEELING A DEEP, CAVERNOUS HOLLOW expand where her guts should be. She stared at the screen, mouth agape, before scrolling back to the top and reading it over again.

"They knew… they goddamned knew the whole time." She jumped to her feet, knocking the chair over and screamed, "You fucking bastard!"

She yanked the handgun from her pocket and stormed out of the room, heading for the infirmary. His hesitance at exposing her to danger became a tiny thread holding up a ten-ton steel weight. If not for that, she'd have shot him as soon as she laid eyes on him. By the time she reached the third floor, her arms shook from pure rage. She marched over the snowfield of glass bits, rounded the corner past the command room, hooked right into the bright hallway leading to the infirmary, and swooped in the door with the weapon pointed…

At an empty table.

Kerys stood like a statue, moving only her eyes to scan around for where Will had gone. Not wanting a repeat of the doctor, she checked the supply closet first, breathing a small sigh of relief when he didn't jump out at her.

The auto-surgeon emitted an irritating buzz-chirp.

Lowering the gun, she approached the screen. Red text scrolled across the middle: ‹Procedure hold. Patient position fault. Progress 01%›

He left before it did anything. He was faking. No wonder he seemed afraid of the auto-surgeon. Breath caught in her throat. Her heart raced as she gazed out over broken windows and a dozen empty rooms.

"What are you up to now?"

N O

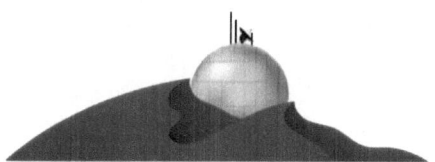

T he third floor of the dome seemed infinite in its darkness compared to the infirmary area. Here and there, light glinted back at her from chrome furnishings or broken glass. The shadows of desks, cabinets, and chairs surrounded her. Kerys backed into the counter and gritted her teeth in anger at MacLeod's body. She *did* have the means to save him and Sergeant Gensch. If only she'd known, if only she'd not been so freaked out by Will being here and could *think* straight.

She'd been so consumed with worry at getting in trouble over having an undocumented specimen in her possession, she didn't stop to consider *why* he really insisted on exposing her to it. Gensch's last few seconds replayed in her mind, bringing a fresh wave of regret and tears.

"Can't change the past..." She sniffled, wiped her face on her arm, the cold steel of her handgun brushing over her forehead. "I can affect the future. My future... Gina's future..." Kerys narrowed her eyes. "And the bastard's future."

An argument swirled around her head. Half of her wanted to hunt him down like a dog; half of her hesitated at his strange drive to protect her. No situation that played out in her head over the next few minutes presented a rosy outcome. If she killed him for what he did, the supply ship that picked her up would probably be expecting to find only Will. Or, she could act like she hadn't found his email and play innocent... and hope for a chance to expose Avasar after returning to Earth. That, of course, meant allowing Will to think she had feelings for him again. And what of Gina? Would Will try to get rid of her?

Kerys bit her lip. *He knew the whole time. Everyone on this outpost except for him was supposed to be a test subject. The company planned on them all dying. Except... the military didn't know. Sure, they knew it's a weapons project but not that Avasar wanted to kill everyone here as a test. They're going to be pissed. I need evidence... the messages.*

Come to think of it, those text messages did not seem as if they'd taken months to go back and forth... she couldn't remember the last time she'd sent an interplanetary text-only email, if ever. Perhaps the SFT could send a couple words in a matter of hours instead of weeks? Or maybe the military had tech no one else knew about. The technical manual for the SFT had gone in circles about exponential increases in energy cost and transmission time—a couple of bytes of data could make the trip much faster than a large video file.

I never was a good liar. He'll know I'm playing him... Do I trust him enough to go into cryo? I'll probably never wake up. Cryo's not dead, but he has to keep me quiet. He might sabotage our pods, so Gina and I never wake up. Kerys shuddered with hopeful grief. *She's gotta make it. Please, live.*

Squeaking shoes startled her. Before thinking, she stuffed the gun in her pocket, afraid to let him catch her with it. As long as he didn't know she had a weapon, it would be an advantage.

Will strolled in, smiling. "Hey, good news. I made contact. Captain Chen already sent an emergency request. There's a ship on the way. We don't have to wait months."

"Uhh, how long? Your leg?" She stuck her other hand in her pocket, trying too hard to look casual.

"Fixed it right up." He winked. "You're a genius. So tough... so pretty." Will walked up to stand in front of her and put a hand on her shoulder. "If the timestamp on that message is accurate, they should be dropping out of translight soon and sending a shuttle down within hours."

Hours? She gawked. Hope dared to dance inside her soul. "We're not going to be—you're serious? We're... not stuck here for months? We might actually see Earth again?"

"That's right, babe. You know I never let anything keep me away from what I want." He brushed a thumb over her cheek. "So... we got a few hours. Want me to take your mind off our situation?"

"Will..." She grasped his wrist and pulled his hand away from her face. "How can you even *think* about sex after everything? Get real! There are three dead people in the room with us."

He put his hands on his hips. "I guess it's like that old joke about a plane crash or a sinking ship. What else to lose, right?"

Kerys thrust her left hand out, pointing. "That's MacLeod... Andrew I think. I have no idea how old he was, but he didn't deserve to die!

Neither did Hellerman. Doctor Sekhar was a really sweet guy before those *things* ate his brain! Anna is dead, too. So is Marco, Don, Paula... *everyone!*"

"I know." He looked down. "I'm sorry. If I could go back—"

"Bullshit! I know you broke the phial on purpose. It wasn't an accident at all. Who's Adam Broussard? Will... I almost wanted to trust you. I almost wanted to give you another chance, but you're far more of a bastard than I ever thought you capable of." *Shit!* Kerys clenched her jaw. Emotion got the better of her again. *Now he knows I know. Dammit!*

He reached for her shoulders. "Kerys, you're not—"

"I'm not what? Heartless? Focused only on money and to hell with anyone and everything else? You're *just* like your father. You'll step on anyone's throat to get ahead. I'm..." She pulled away, sliding a few feet to the right. "I don't know what to say to you."

"You were in my room."

She snapped her head up, glaring at him. "Gee. Wonder who I learned that from?"

His smile faded to a determined frown. "If you know that name, then you know what I said to him. I didn't want you to get hurt. When I saw you step off the shuttle, I almost passed out. I know you 'left' and I know we're not 'officially' dating anymore, but some guys find that one person and that's it for them. I'll never let another woman into my heart but you. If you won't have me, then I'll die alone."

"You're not a stupid person. How could you be so damned foolish as to release that stuff on purpose? Maybe this thing is what killed the aliens who used to live here? Don thought that complex was some kind of medical facility."

He glided closer, threading his arm around her back. "It's fine. It's completely under control. You and me? We're all the proof-of-concept Avasar needed. Weapon and antidote. It's the best kind of weapon. Why spend ammunition and risk lives when an enemy force can be made to destroy itself?"

"No, Will." She jumped away, yanking the handgun out and pointing it at his chest. "You, and whatever cohorts you conspired with at Avasar, murdered over a hundred people. *Good* people. I... you made me kill people I cared about. Friends. Gina had such a shitty life, and she doesn't deserve to die before she's even old enough to buy a goddamned beer. Paula had a family waiting for her back home. How many other people here had families?"

Will scratched behind his ear. "Ehh, most who came out here were loners. Only a handful really had anyone. When I told you that I accepted this job not caring if it killed me, I was being totally honest. You leaving destroyed me. It made me not care about anything. I couldn't bear the thought of growing old without you."

"Stop trying to manipulate me!"

"I'm not. Truth isn't manipulation when it's true."

She twitched. "That doesn't make any sense. You killed all these people. Sergeant Gensch, Marco... Don...."

Will chuckled.

"It's *not* funny, you sociopath! Because of you, I've shot four people—one with a damned rock-coring laser. I watched a man get dissected. I had someone try to drown me in a vat of burning crap. I thought I was going to starve in the reservoir chamber. I watched Ellen and her giant effing steel suit cook two feet away from me. Dammit, Will, you're laughing?!"

"Sorry." He put on a grim face. "I was just thinking of the irony when you mentioned Don."

"You're really clueless, aren't you? You can't comprehend what you did. What the hell is wrong with you, Will? I'm pointing a loaded gun at you and you're acting like it's not even there."

"Oh, you wouldn't kill me. As much as I could never let anything hurt you."

Kerys narrowed her eyes. "You still set that shit loose with me here."

"I knew it wouldn't work on you. If I wasn't perfectly confident you'd be okay, I would've told Adam to eat a dick." He leaned on the counter by the drawer she'd smashed the doctor's hand in hours ago, smiling again. "You should at least find this somewhat amusing... Old Don thought Captain Chen was in on the project. I don't know how he figured out the AM-3 release was intentional, but he got all kinds of lathered up and stormed in there with an excavating laser. He went there to"—Will chuckled again—"talk her out of it, but she'd already gone so loopy she thought the whole thing was *his* fault because it all started after he got here. The two of them were trying to kill each other; each one believing the other responsible for releasing a biological weapon."

"You're wrong. There's nothing at all funny about that." Kerys bowed her head. "You're wrong about something else too."

He lowered his voice to that cloying tone he always used, as if he spoke to an upset child. "I know you're upset right now, but you have to believe that I never stopped loving you."

"That's not what I mean." She glanced over her shoulder at him, squeezing and releasing her grip on the gun. "You see nothing wrong with what happened here. You're wrong about the spores. I don't think they kill the microbes. They did something to your brain. You *are* insane. The Will I knew wouldn't be so casual about killing 150 people."

"I'm fine. This isn't the result of brain damage from my initial infection.

At first, behavioral changes in the subject are due to chemicals the microbes give off in brain tissue. It takes somewhere between one to three days before the microbes begin to consume tissue and cause permanent damage—that's when the real psycho stuff starts. I, uhh, changed a cyano canister in another site on the north end of the forest. We suspected it contained the agent we searched for, but no one knew it was loose out there. It got into my suit when I popped the canister. But… my work with the plants exposed me to the spores and the microbes didn't live long enough in my body to cause permanent damage."

"Lucky you," deadpanned Kerys.

"I didn't even realize the exposure until after my thoughts cleared up. Took me a few weeks to put together what happened."

She frowned, still pointing the gun at him. "So why am I here? Why did you bring my whole team here to die?"

Will raked a hand up over his hair. "Not my idea. Look, we were hunting for this microbe after finding a tiny sample of it at the other site. We found the ruins in the mountain, which we suspected of being a military installation or something like that. None of us could get that door open and Adam didn't want to authorize using an excavation laser on the wall there for fear it would destroy the stuff."

"So you played us. Pretended you'd 'stumbled' on alien ruins when you knew a lot more than you admitted to."

He shrugged. "Yeah, basically. Relax, babe."

"Relax?" She shouted. "You want me to relax? A man I thought I knew is responsible for murdering 150 people—for making *me* shoot people I cared about. I can't believe you."

He swooped close, grabbing her by the arms above each elbow. "AM-3 microbes have long 'hairs' that let them ride the wind. They get into a host via the nose, migrating to the brain where they replicate. Initially, they give off chemicals that affect brain function. As they multiply, they begin consuming brain tissue. Their activity excites neurons while they're being digested, causing symptoms like hallucinations, vivid memories coming back, voices, muscle weakness, spasms. There's some similarity to amoebic encephalitis, but AM-3 seems intelligent enough not to cause so much damage the host dies directly from the infestation."

"Will. Let go of me."

He moved with her as she tried to back away. "I can't explain what happened to that one grunt outside. There's got to be something in the native atmosphere that caused the microbes to explode in an exponential leap. I think they took over the body after he died. You know, now I'm wondering about it. Maybe the effect we saw in here with the insanity was unique due to our air. I wonder if the purpose of the microbes was to mutate the victim into whatever that soldier turned into... Think you found the aliens' seeds or something? Wait for some other species to find that stash of microbes, and they get to come back from the dead."

"Will!" Kerys pulled back until she hit the corner where the counter met the wall. "Get off me! You went too far. Why did you help them kill all these people?"

He pressed close, pinning her. Stuck nose to nose with him, she froze in panic. That night in the bedroom he almost didn't stop at 'no.' Out here, with no one to get in the way, he could do whatever he wanted.

"Please don't..."

Will leaned closer, but rather than kiss her, he whispered in her ear, "You don't know anything about what happened here. You couldn't understand what I went through after you arrived! You think I wanted to do this? If you hadn't walked out on me, we'd both still be back on Earth and every one of these people might still be alive."

She shoved at him. "This is not my fault! Don't you dare try to put this on me."

"You're so damn beautiful." Will grasped her hip, his eyes half closed as he leaned in for a kiss.

He's crazy! Kerys let off a wild shriek and swung the handgun into the side of his head with every ounce of power a surge of panic gave her. Will made a "gyuhh" noise and crumpled to the floor, unconscious. A trickle of blood ran down the side of his head.

Kerys edged to the door, aiming at his face with a two-handed grip. "He's got it. He's gone nuts. I have to... I should... He's dead already."

Her finger teased at the trigger. Memories flooded back in a chain of images: the beach, him carrying her home after a party, the way his laugh once made her feel so loved and cherished. Her arms drooped. She couldn't do it. Not after Gensch. She couldn't kill a person. Not without *knowing* they were gone beyond saving. Not even Will. He really *could* be this much of an asshole without alien bacteria eating his brain. He hadn't succumbed to the stuff; he'd succumbed to greed.

It's just Desperate Will, close to getting what he wants... and worried he'll lose it. He's... he's not acting like he's hearing voices.

Kerys backed out the door, keeping the gun pointed at him. Not wanting to be anywhere near him when he woke up, she sprinted for the safety of her room.

THIRTY MINUTES OUT

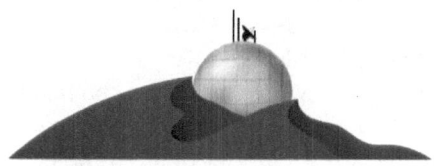

G un pointed at the door, Kerys sat on the floor of her quarters until her butt went numb.

No sound came from the hallway outside, no sign of Will coming after her. *He had to be awake by now. I didn't hit him hard enough to kill.* She shivered, dreading how he'd react when they crossed paths again. Did he lie in wait for her somewhere? What if she'd allowed sentiment to get the better of her and she refused to see that he *had* succumbed to the microbes? The others had resisted the insanity for a short time by clinging to their emotions toward her. Sarge for his protectiveness, Gina for her crush. Walloping him across the head might've changed how he felt about her.

Her vision focused on the tip of the gun, the door beyond blurring.

"What am I doing?" She tried to stop trembling, to minimal success. "Hiding in my room like a scared kid." She pictured Captain Chen telling her not to let it off the planet. Gensch's voice filled in after, ordering her to 'get the hell off this rock.' She gripped his dog tags in her left thigh pocket. "I have to stop him. That shit stays on this planet."

"Agreed," whispered Gina.

Kerys jumped.

Gina pushed herself up to sit. Her eyes remained mostly closed. She seemed wobbly, as if waking up with a massive hangover. "What happened? Did we...?"

"No," said Kerys.

"Darn." Gina chuckled. "Guess it was a dream."

Kerys blushed. "Are you… you? How much do you remember?"

"I… told you to shoot me, didn't I?"

"Yeah."

Gina looked down at herself. "Thanks for not listening to me. The shit's out of my head now. Got a headache from hell, but there ain't no more voices… or hallucinations."

Kerys crawled over to the bed cubby and took her hand, nearly brought to tears by joy. A moment later, Gina sluggishly leaned forward and embraced her before breaking down in sobs. The emotion proved contagious. Kerys cried with her, overcome with relief at not being forced to kill anyone else who didn't deserve to die.

"How are you feeling?" whispered Kerys.

"Like I got hit by a truck. My bones hurt. I can barely move."

Kerys leaned back to make eye contact. "Are you having any trouble thinking? Have you lost any memories or anything like that?"

Gina made a series of contemplative faces. "Kinda in a fog, but I don't think so. It's like I'm coming out the tail end of a wicked flu. Why is everything purple?"

"Everything?" Kerys looked around at the room. "You're hallucinating?"

"No, I mean… snot, pee… spit." Gina held up her arm. "Even my sweat's turned kinda purple."

"Oh." Kerys pointed at the flower. "Your sweat is only purple because you have spore dust all over you."

"Spore dust…" Gina winced.

Kerys sat with her, explaining everything she'd figured out or learned about the microbes, Will, the plant, and their situation. "… and I'm sorry. If I wasn't such a wimp, I wouldn't have needed to shoot Gensch."

"Not on you, Ker." Gina brushed a hand across her cheek. "That man did damage to you. It's not easy to just 'get over it.'"

Kerys looked down. "So they keep telling me."

"What are we gonna do?" Gina sucked in a breath. "You for real about that shit? I'm not gonna die?"

"Do you feel like yourself?"

"Yeah."

"Then, no. You're not gonna die… at least…" Kerys cringed. "Not from the alien stuff. We still have a Will to worry about and… maybe another problem."

"Reactor?" Gina's eyes widened.

"No. There's another ship coming. It's hours away. I don't know what's going to happen. If it's Broussard's people, they're not going to be expecting any survivors other than Will—and possibly me."

The 'scared child' in Gina's face hardened back to the determined expression of a soldier on a mission. "Then we kick some ass, take their shuttle, and get the hell off this piece of shit planet. There's two of us and he doesn't know I'm still here."

Kerys nodded. *She* probably couldn't bring herself to shoot Will unless he had a literal gun to her head. Gina suffered no such hesitation. "I need to get an idea of what's going on."

"Command center?"

"Yeah, something like that."

Gina climbed out of the bed to her feet and peeled her underwear off.

"Uhh…"

"Don't freak out. I'm just changing. They're soaked."

Kerys looked away, blushing. "Right. Forgot. Military. You're probably used to just changing in front of everyone."

"Yep." Gina wobbled over to the cabinet. She'd evidently noticed the redness on Kerys' face and smiled. "Hope you don't mind if I borrow some shit."

"My spare shoes won't fit you, but you're welcome to whatever."

Gina grabbed a set of clean underwear and a blue jumpsuit, which she hurried into. "I'm a bit wobbly, so probably not a great idea for me to get into a fight. Let me get the shit off his terminal, that evidence you mentioned."

"Okay." Kerys stared into her eyes, her hands shaking from emotion. This girl no longer had the fatalistic gleam in her eyes of a walking dead person begging for a mercy killing. She once again looked like herself. "Be careful."

"Don't worry about me. Only thing I'm scared of is that alien shit in the air. If you're right, then I ain't got no worries." Gina bowed her head. "You pulled my ass out of the fire *twice*. I shouldn't be alive."

"You are." Kerys hugged her. "Make sure you stay that way."

"Girl, you keep huggin' me, you're going to start sending the wrong signals."

Kerys laughed. "Maybe they aren't so wrong."

"Now you're messing with me."

"I dunno. This place is messing with me, too. Maybe I'm more open to the idea than I thought or maybe it's just desperate circumstances." Kerys sighed.

"Ever kiss a girl before?"

Kerys snickered. "Honestly? Yes."

"Wow, really?"

"Used to think it was just a stupid dare in high school." She shrugged. "Didn't mean anything. At least, I didn't think it did. This girl named Averie I went to high school with. I, umm… might have had a thing for her and didn't realize it."

Gina fidgeted, her expression brightening. "Oh. Hey, you remember what I said that day?"

"Kinda vague…"

"Heh." Gina nibbled on her lip. "When I told you about growing up with fosters, I said only one's gonna save me is me… but I was wrong."

"Wrong?"

"Yeah." Gina made eye contact, seeming nervous, fidgety. "I was wrong. I used to think no one was ever gonna save me but me, but here you are. Twice now."

Kerys choked up. "For what it's worth, I'm like feeling super protective of you even though you're the badass soldier."

"Heh. I'm not a kid even if I might look like one."

"You don't… not really." Kerys half smiled. "Only when you sleep."

Gina chuckled. "All right. 'Fore this gets any weirder… we ain't got time."

"It's not really weird, but yeah… no time now to talk about it." She picked up the weapon. "Do you want the gun?"

"Nah. You need it more than me. I got some training in hand-to-hand." Gina frowned. "There's a couple more guns out in the hall, but no ammo."

Kerys pulled one of the two magazines she'd found out of her pocket and held it out. "Here."

"Nice." Gina swiped it. "Okay. Let's do this."

"Right. Plan?"

"Information first. I'll get the files off his terminal, then meet you at the command room—might go to my quarters for some shoes."

"Sounds good."

Kerys took a breath for confidence, opened her door, and maneuvered out into the hall, gun raised. Nothing sprang at her. She checked left and right before stepping into the corpse-fetid air. They crept down the hall past six rooms before Gina squatted to pick a handgun up from under the hand of a dead soldier. She rammed the magazine in and let the slide crash forward.

"You care if I shoot his ass on sight?" whispered Gina.

"Umm. Is it wrong that I can't immediately say yes or no to that?"

Gina raised her eyebrows. "Nah, I get how ya feel. Hard to kill someone you love, even if they are a mass murdering psycho."

"But… I *don't* love him. I did. Maybe I *thought* I did… but not now. I haven't for a while. Makes no sense, but I'm more scared of him than anything. Just… every time I see him, I freeze up like some frightened little kid. I hate it."

Gina patted her on the shoulder and squeezed. "I got you, boo."

Does she think I'm interested now? Kerys bit her lip. *Or is that just a friendly term?* That she didn't find herself freaking out at the idea made her wonder if the future might lead to uncharted territory. *They say surviving combat creates bonds unlike anything else. We're definitely gonna be close for the rest of our lives even if it doesn't go romantic.* She swallowed saliva. *Hope the 'rest of our life' is longer than a few days.*

"Thanks," whispered Kerys. "Stay alive."

"You too… and that's an order."

"I'm not enlisted."

Gina gave her an appraising look. "You'd make a decent soldier. Survived this long."

"Luck. If I get back to Earth, the most dangerous thing I'm ever going to do again is walking alone to the coffee place."

"Maybe you don't gotta be alone," said Gina in a soft voice.

"I hate being alone." Kerys squeezed the gun and smiled at her. "C'mon, let's get the hell out of here."

Gina nodded.

On the way to the ladder, Kerys aimed at every open door, expecting Will—or a random infected person—to jump out. At the ladder shaft, she aimed down at emptiness and managed a one-handed climb to keep the gun trained on the opening to the hallway. Gina followed, bare feet silent on the rungs.

Their breaths seemed deafening. Seven steps away from the ladder, an alarm clock erupted, blaring music from a room on the right. Kerys whirled and shot the device, staring at the sparking pile of debris for a few seconds while trying to get her heart to move again.

Gina patted her on the back. "Easy… try not to be so jumpy."

He'd have heard that… "Yeah. Sorry."

Kerys continued down the hall. At the end of the residence pod, she hid behind the corner and peered around. The upper half of the tube consisted mostly of window, offering a clear view of the flexible tunnel that linked back to the dome. No sign of Will. She moved out and headed east, while Gina headed for the other residence pod to access Will's terminal. Time and time again, problems in her life had come down to Will's word against hers. A corporation as big and wealthy as Avasar Biotech would *not* appreciate what she had to say upon her return. Concrete evidence could easily mean the difference between her survival and disappearing without a trace.

At the end of the passage, Kerys pressed herself to the wall, her shoulder pressed to the metal of the link ring where the tunnel met the outside of the dome. Seconds passed as she caught her breath, listening to silence. Will said the ship was mere hours away, but how long had she been dozing off in her room? The residence pods sat close to the landing pad. If a shuttle had come down, she would've noticed.

Will thinks I'm brittle. He might believe I panicked. Okay... I did panic, but I'm back together now.

Kerys slipped around the link ring, aiming into the atrium toward the cafeteria. Once she felt confident nothing waited to ambush her, she advanced and headed for the stairwell. A small door on the right creaked. She swung her arms, gun pointed, and stopped breathing.

A moment later, the door drifted a little on the breeze.

"Shit," she whispered, relaxing her arms. *I can't be jumpy. If Gina startles me and I shoot her, I'll never forgive myself.*

She spun around while creeping toward the stairs, watching in all directions in case he came after her. *He was about to force himself on me. He thinks I'm his... probably going to try again.* Kerys stopped at the opening to the stairwell, her brain stewing on the thought of killing him. She *had* to stop him from taking AM-3 off the planet, but she couldn't put a bullet in a man she'd loved with the coldness of a trained soldier. No, she'd have to at least *try* to talk sense into him—or at least keep him talking long enough for Gina to surprise him. Kerys didn't really want to watch Will die, but better that than allowing him to take such a horrible 'weapon' back to Earth.

This is Will after all. He'll take the microbes back to Earth, lose control of them, kill 98% of humanity, and somehow blame me for it.

Raising the gun high, she aimed at the corner where the stairwell wrapped around at the first switchback. Step by step, she climbed to the landing, hesitated for a second, and whipped around, pointing her weapon up the stairs.

Nothing.

She crept up to the next landing and peered out into darkness. The lights on the second floor were off. Had Will gone in there to hide? Somewhere beyond the ghostly forms of grey fabric cubes, Anna lay dead. Though Kerys hadn't been the one to kill her, she still felt guilty. A minute or so passed in silence, yet nothing within the shadows moved. Disregarding the second floor, she eased up the stairs, careful to set her shoes down without making any noise. The third floor looked empty. It seemed more likely that aside from Gina and Will, everyone else who had been on this planet died already. Perhaps someone lingered, hiding in the vents, their insanity manifesting as severe phobia instead of aggression. With a ship hours away, she didn't have time to scour every inch of the place. Besides, if they'd succumbed to the microbes, the only thing she could offer them would be a bullet. By now, they'd all have suffered irreversible damage from the organisms dissolving their brains. Gina had been lucky. She'd somehow figured out a dangerous substance got loose in the air and went EVO before it got to her. Exposure happened only after Kerys brought her back inside. The microbes hadn't been in her long enough to eat her brain, only poison it.

Searching for any other people wouldn't help them. Doing so would only waste time and possibly cause her to miss the shuttle.

The crunch of glass fragments underfoot in the hall raised the hairs on the backs of her arms and got her heart racing with dread. Every shadow became suspect. She edged to the left against the wall and crept toward the command room with her gun poised. Knowing she had to hesitate shooting anything that moved long enough to make sure it wasn't Gina terrified her worse than anything she'd ever been through before. Even a split second's delay could kill her… but she couldn't bear the thought of shooting the woman she'd worked so hard to protect.

Faint beeping grew louder the farther she went, and by the time she reached the command room, the noise seemed to slither into her ears and slide down her back. One of the terminals on the right, a workstation with a bank of five monitors and a large component covered in switches and dials, seemed to be the source.

Kerys spun around once in search of Will before advancing to the desk. A screen displayed an 'incoming message alert' window. The timestamp showed it came in three hours and fifty-one minutes ago. She touched an orange 'open' button at the bottom right of the pop-up box.

A window opened, containing video of a fortyish man with a thin face, crows' feet, and greying hair. His charcoal-colored military style jacket framed the bottom of the portrait box. "Braxton, you down there? We dropped out of TL about fifteen minutes ago. Getting the team thawed and some coffee in them now. Should be making landfall in about five or six hours. Get your shit together and be ready. We ain't wasting any more time than we have to down there. What's this about a second person? Some girl? Couldn't keep it in your pants, huh, Braxton?" The man chuckled. "See you soon."

She stared at the frozen face. *Five or six hours… close to four hours ago. They're almost here!* A storm of emotions swam from terror to hope, anger, and worry. "Where the hell is he?" She ran out of the command room and jogged across the hall to the security station. Ignoring the dead man in the chair by the bank of screens, she searched the closed-circuit feeds that covered almost everywhere inside the outpost except for private quarters and bathrooms.

Something moved on the ninth monitor in the third row down from the top. Kerys leaned closer to that screen.

In what appeared to be some manner of research area, Will collected beer-can sized canisters from a cabinet and stuffed them into a rigid, foam-lined carrying case. Text at the bottom of the video identified the feed as Lab 4, Unit 1.

"Oh, no you don't..."

She pushed off the desk, knocking the poor dead man out of his chair in her haste, and ran as fast as she could move herself to the stairs, down to the first floor, and to the south end of the dome. Before the tube link to the lab area came into view, the hissing of leaking air confirmed he'd opened the tube Gensch sealed. Seconds later, she rounded the corner past the battery room and rushed down the tube to the lab, slowing to a cautious walk at the end of the tunnel.

Vast windows around each lab made it easy to spot him three rooms in on the right side. Tingling infused her sinuses as she entered, filling her mind with jitters at the idea that fresh microbes battled spores deep in her skull.

Trepidation exploded into anger at the sight of him closing the case over the deadly organism.

Kerys shoved the door marked 4A open, no longer caring about quiet, and shouted, "Will!"

He jumped with a brief cry, and whirled to stare at her.

"You're not thinking. What will those people do with that shit if you give it to them? You have no idea. Once you let it out of here, you have no control. It got everyone in this place in hours. Do you want to be responsible for destroying humanity?"

"Relax, babe. You're overreacting."

She aimed at his head. "Am I?"

"Just a bit." He smiled.

"How long does the organism last in the air before it dies if it doesn't find a nose to climb into?"

"About twenty...."

"Hours?"

He looked down. "Days."

Her jaw hung open.

"Relax—the microbes stay in our system for two weeks, probably longer here given the concentration people in a sealed air system sucked up. However, *our* bodies are toxic to them. The spores kill it in under a minute. You've got nothing to worry about."

"Twenty days! Seriously? How the hell do you expect anyone to use that as a weapon? They can't control it. They drop it on, what, a camp of insurgents somewhere and a month later, the entire country is gone. Two months later, humanity is gone. Okay, so maybe your spore vaccine protects the soldiers handling the 'weapon,' but are you going to vaccinate all the citizens before you drop these things on the target? A few carry off on the wind and we're all dead."

He raised his left hand. "That's not my part of the job. I'm not a combat strategist."

"Braxton..." A voice emanated from his pocket, laced with radio crackle. "We are twenty-eight minutes out. Get your ass to the shuttle pad with or without your bitch. I want to be back in orbit pronto."

"Will, please," whispered Kerys. "Tell them something went wrong... the machine malfunctioned or got damaged when everyone freaked out. Blame Captain Chen even. Just don't do this. Don't bring that evil shit to Earth. Think about the kind of death and destruction that would happen if this stuff got loose. Look what it did here. Do you want to be responsible for that on a global scale?"

"Sure, that *could* happen if someone fucks up... but they know how dangerous AM-3 is. It's worth trillions."

Kerys grasped the gun in both hands. A surge of anger almost made her squeeze the trigger. "Money... What good is money if everyone's dead?"

He smiled. "I get a ten percent commission."

Bang.

Will screamed and dove to his side as a bullet ricocheted around the back of the lab. He crawled behind a bank of heavy test equipment. "You shot at me!"

"That was a warning."

"A warning?" he yelled. "I think you nipped my ear."

"You keep saying you're not the same person. What happened to the Will I fell in love with at Berkeley? Did the stress of an alien world get to you or is it the microbe?"

"Kerys, you're not understanding here. I *need* you in my life. I'm sorry about what happened in the infirmary. I... it's been so long since I'd been close to you, I lost control. I swear it won't happen again. I deserved that bonk on the head, but *think!* Avasar has a two-trillion-dollar contract for this stuff. Ten percent is two-hundred-billion! We will never have to work again... even after taxes."

"I can't let you take that stuff off this planet. Not for that amount of money. Not for any amount of money. You're blind. You always were an opportunist of the highest order. You don't care how many people get hurt. Always what *you* want."

He peered over the top of the machine. "You're not seeing the bigger picture."

"I'm seeing dead people!" she yelled. "Good people who turned into nightmares because of *you.*"

"Kerys—"

"Leave that shit behind. Please… let's get out of here alive and forget this place, and that stuff. If there's anything decent left inside you."

Will stood, hands up, and approached. He didn't even look at the case when he passed it. "Babe… I know what's really bothering you."

"Yeah. That shit in the box."

He smiled. "No, guilt. You're blaming yourself for the whole test, all these people who died here, because you opened that door we'd been stuck on for so long."

No. You're not making this into my fault. "Why did you fake us out with the silt on the walls? Why not just send images of those buttons back for people to look at?"

"They tried that." He sighed. "Your old buddy Doctor Furroughs looked them over and called it fake. Said it was 'too intact' to possibly be real, and wouldn't return our calls. Seemed like a much better idea to let your expedition people feel like they made the discovery themselves, so they took it seriously."

"Bastard," she muttered.

He smirked. "Would it have changed your mind if you saw it before you got the job offer?"

Kerys scowled at him for a few long seconds. "No."

"So, I apologize for giving you a couple hours of work clearing that stuff." He chuckled. "I can't believe those two meatheads didn't slip and say something."

She furrowed her brow.

"Oh, the two lunks in the exo suits. Who do you think sprayed the dust all over the walls?" He snickered. "It's amazing they kept straight faces. Never pegged either one of them for actors."

Kerys grabbed his arm. "We're leaving, and that stuff is staying here."

"It will probably never get used. It might even have medical applications down the line. Don't you want to be so wealthy you never have to worry about getting stuck on a remote planet again?"

Kerys stared at her grip on his arm while tapping her finger on the side of the gun in her other hand. "No, Will. It's too dangerous. And the last people I'd trust something like that with are the heads of corporations like Avasar, or anyone willing to pay that much for something so horrible." She lifted her gaze to meet his. "There's more important things than money. If you had to choose between that money or me, what would it be?"

He brushed a hand over her cheek, his deep brown eyes gleaming with sorrow. "It hurts that you'd even ask that. You. Always."

She almost smiled and looked down. "Maybe Will is still in there after all. C'mon. Let's go home." Kerys glanced to the side and down, close to telling him Gina was still alive and needed to go with them.

Liquid splashed in her face, blurring her vision. Pungent fumes choked her and made the room spin in circles. Gagging, she staggered backward, flailing. Livid, hurt, and terrified, she tried to aim for him, but couldn't tell which blur belonged to Will and which came from the wall. Dizziness worsened, and she fell on her hands and knees, grabbing at her face and her burning eyes.

"I'm sorry, babe, but you're just too emotional right now and I don't want you to ruin this for us. You'll see in time that I'm making the right decision. We'll live like royalty. You'll be safe here until the next ship shows up. There's plenty of hydra packs, and the power system, like everything else these days, runs itself."

"Argh! No! Don't leave me here!" She crawled toward where his voice came from. The scrape of a metal case sliding off a counter made her scream, "No!"

His footsteps grew distant. "Don't panic. That stuff won't sting too long. Only a couple minutes." He sighed. "I really wish you'd have come around. I hate like hell making you wait for the next ship, but a hundred billion dollars each for you and me. Only a fool would walk away from that. I can't let you get emotional and ruin things for us. You'll thank me later when we're living the sweet life."

Kerys scrambled forward trying to chase him, but her head collided with metal, sending a shock straight down her spine to her tailbone. "Shit!" She cradled her skull and whimpered. "Will, please don't leave me here!"

"I don't have to choose between you and money, Kerys. I can have both. I never wanted you to be here, to be exposed to this, get hurt, see all this horribleness... but here you are. I did everything I could to protect you, and I hope you'll understand that and find me in a couple years when you get back."

"Will, please." She crawled at another shapeless blur, and grabbed an empty chair.

"I promise you, I will make sure they get you out of here. I won't give them the samples until you're on Earth."

She sat back on her heels and wiped at her watering eyes. Her vision cleared a little, enough to spot a Will-shaped smear standing by the door out of the lab. He looked… sad. Kerys grabbed the gun and lurched to her feet.

"See you soon, babe." Will slid the door closed and ran off down the hall.

"Dammit, you bastard, don't you dare bring that shit to Earth!" She scrambled to her feet and stumbled into the door. Gagging and spitting on the unknown liquid, she pulled it open and chased him down the hall to the tube link, swaying on rubbery legs, bouncing off the walls.

Will skidded to a halt as soon as he entered the tunnel and swung around to take cover behind the link ring. He reached for the console, and the doors snapped closed before her noodle legs could carry her halfway down the length of the lab pod. Unable to slow down, she crashed into the doors and held on to keep from falling. Her face pressed to the narrow strip of window, she stared in horror as Will pulled on a lever, causing a heavy *thud* to rock the link collar.

The panel on the inside face went red. A flashing warning came up on the inside screen bearing the words: ‹no habitation interlink connected.›

Will pressed his hand to the glass. "I'm sorry, babe. I love you more than anything, but you can be emotional. This is for your own good. You'll see that as soon as we're rich."

"Don't do this!" shouted Kerys, banging her fists on the door.

Will turned away, hesitated a second, and ran.

Kerys slumped to her knees, her head still spinning. He'd pulled the manual interlock open enough to trip the sensor, but not enough to make the tube disconnect. She'd need an excavating laser to open the door from this side. Defeat seeped in, and she slumped against the wall. Her gaze settled on a tiny sliver of green reflecting off the floor to her left. She raised her head, looking toward it.

At the southwest corner of the lab pod, a bright green point glowed from the face of another connector hatch. Kerys jumped to her feet and staggered to where a second hamster tunnel ran west to a tall, cube-shaped pod in the distance. From there, a separate link connected that pod to the dome via a ninety-degree bend. This tube had a wide oval profile big enough for a forklift carrying large objects, unlike the rest, which had been perfect circles.

This goes to the storage pod! I can catch him!

Kerys ran into the tube, blinking away the last remnants of tears from whatever chemical he'd thrown in her face. The clear upper half of the tunnel revealed an angry, dark sky swirling with luminous azure clouds.

She made it about halfway down the hundred-meter-plus long tube before a bright flash of white appeared overhead, followed seconds later by a thunderous roar and a torrent of dust. Tiny black regolith flecks clattered on the tunnel walls. Kerys cringed as a shuttle screamed over the facility and began a lazy descending turn toward the pad in the northeast.

"I'm going, sarge… I'm going." Kerys reached into the deepest reserves of her energy, ignored the stiffness in her legs, and threw herself into a desperate sprint. "Dammit, Gina. Where are you? Get your ass to the airlock!"

They had only minutes, and not a second to spare.

EVAC

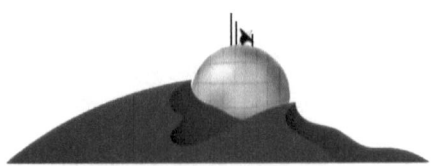

Wayfarer outpost hung in dark silence, save for the repetitive slap-squeak of Kerys's shoes on hard, white floor panels. The roar of shuttle engines had ceased before she reached the end of the tube. She cleared the cargo pod in seconds and ducked into the connecting tunnel. Gasping for breath, she pushed onward, sprinting along the main north-south hallway down the center of the dome's ground floor.

The tromp of boots made her spin, raising her gun at one of the hallways connected to the large atrium. Gina stagger-ran in, seeming once again more like a freaked-out teenager than a soldier. She'd evidently gone to her quarters for boots. They stared—and aimed guns—at each other for a second and a half before recognition set in and they both relaxed, lowering their weapons.

Gina's fear evaporated. "Holy shit. There you are… checked the command room and—"

"I saw Will." Kerys rushed over and grabbed her arm. "He's trying to bring this shit back to Earth."

"Fuck." Gina scowled. "You know what we have to do."

Kerys looked down. "Yeah. Did you get the messages?"

"Yep." Gina patted the breast pocket of her jumpsuit. "Brought our little friends, too." She indicated the tall clear box that had been on the desk, now under her arm. It contained two lamiacaea advena plants. "Just in case."

"Good thinking… C'mon. We need to suit up."

The heart of the outpost had two integral airlocks, not counting the one she'd always used at the garage. Fair bet, Will did not go to the one in the southeast, so she figured he'd have either chosen the northern one, which offered an easier walk to the landing pad, or the garage.

Unwilling to waste time trying to decide, she followed habit and raced to the ready room she always used at the garage. She tossed the handgun onto the bench, then hauled her e-suit out of its locker and scrambled into it as fast as she could. Gina suited up as well. They secured each other's suit clamps, slapping them a few times to make sure they'd closed completely. After grabbing her helmet and gun, Kerys rushed into the airlock that still held the quad plus a dead man. Gina followed, her gait sluggish.

"You still feeling okay?"

"Mostly. Sore everywhere. Little dizzy. Deffo not at my best, but I'll take it." Gina gave her side eye. "This gonna go away or is this the new normal?"

Kerys fidgeted. "I think it will go away. Will got infected and he has no symptoms like that."

"Sweet." Gina put her helmet on.

"Don't log into comms. I don't trust these people," whispered Kerys. *I'm 'Will's bitch' to them… not a good sign.*

Gina nodded once.

Bright light washed over the garage beyond the outer door, no doubt thrown off by the shuttle's engines.

She hurried to the control panel, clamped the pistol between her knees, and seated her helmet. As soon as the seal clicked, the HUD came online with a list of names:

Aaron
Braxton, W
GiantDICK
Harmon, V
Roma, E
[login]

The airlock control panel screen displayed an exterior camera view of the landing pad where a shuttle smaller than the one she'd arrived on perched, its primary wings canted up in the middle like a seagull doing yoga. Four men in pale grey e-suits with bulky rebreather packs stood in a row a few paces in front of the belly ramp. Will faced them from a short distance away, the case of AM-3 clutched in both hands across his chest.

"Come on, let's get out of here," said Will over the comm.

Kerys reached for the button to cycle the airlock, but something in their body language made her hesitate. The four men seemed more like Old

West gunslingers who'd cornered an outlaw than a bunch of guys coming to pick them up and give them a ride home. She eyed the list of names, careful to avoid staring at the [login] line. As long as she didn't link in, they wouldn't know she and Gina listened—or existed.

The yellow gem by 'Harmon, V' lit up; the voice sounded the same as the man from the video message. "You're sure there's no one else alive in the facility?"

Will edged backward a step, almost hiding behind the case. He twisted to his right, peering at the dome. "Uhh… no. Everyone else is dead. Not what I'd hoped for."

You lying sack of shit! I'm not letting you take that crap to Earth. You're not leaving me here!

She raised her fist to slam the button to cycle the airlock, but froze at Harmon's dark laugh.

"There's been a slight change of plans, Braxton. The company wants everything burned."

Yes! She raised her fist over the button again to cycle the airlock.

"What are you talking about?" asked Will. "It was a controlled test. I'm clean. Everything's fine. Talk to Broussard."

One of the four men took a step forward, raising a rifle at Will.

She froze, her knuckle a finger's width away from the touch screen.

Gina mouthed, 'Oh shit' without adding voice.

Will backed up another step. "No. Wait! What are you doing?"

"Apparently," said Harmon, "your little bioweapon is too unstable and too dangerous. The people in fancy suits looked at your results and I guess they decided they can't use it for anything. They need a weapon they can control."

"No!" Will shook his helmet hard. "That wasn't the arrangement."

Kerys moved her hand away from the screen.

"Arrangements have changed," said Harmon.

"Talk to Broussard!" screamed Will.

"Who do you think told us to burn this place?" asked Harmon, his voice icy.

A flickering of muzzle fire lit up the screen, accompanied by a fusillade of dull pops on the other side of the thick doors as all four of the men fired.

Will collapsed backward, silvery-blue spray flying from the case in his hands as bullets shredded it. His howling gurgle flooded her ears. Kerys screamed, not that anyone heard her. She bowed her head, helmet to the wall, and shuddered. Gina put an arm around her as best she could past the bulky e-suit backpack. Kerys had been an inch from shooting him herself, but hoped he'd listen to reason.

Tears pattered the inside of her visor. *Goddamit. Why am I crying over him?*

Harmon walked up on Will, rifle pointed at his face. "You sure there's no one left? You're the last thing alive down here?"

"Yeah." Will rasped, clutching his chest. He twisted toward the dome again, breath wheezing over the comm. "Heh. I came out here to *shuttle* flowers back and forth. Never"—he grunted and coughed—"figured they'd screw me over, too. I'm the last one here."

"You know, in all fairness, I don't think they planned to fuck you from the start," said Harmon. "Just happened that way when you couldn't control your little alien germs." He aimed at Will's head. "But I suppose they don't have a lot of respect for a man who can spend four years smiling at people he knows all along he's going to kill."

Kerys looked away from the screen. Seconds later, the loud *boom* from a rifle made her jump.

"All right," said Harmon. "Let's check and make sure there's nothin' moving around. Ed, you're with me. Dick, you and Aaron start with the residence pods. That's probably where anyone would've holed up. I want the sweep done in thirty minutes, then we're setting up the charge on the primary reactor. Do *not* break the seal of your e-suits or ol' Braxy here's gonna have an eternity buddy."

"Heh," said 'Roma, E.'

"Move it people." Harmon raised his voice. "We're lifting off in forty minutes and not a second longer."

Kerys backed away from the airlock panel. Gina stared at her making a 'shit, now what' face. They'd surely notice the flashing lights if she tried to go out that way. *Shit... shit... shit...* She whipped her head side to side, staring at the walls as if they held an answer of what to do. Those men would shoot her without hesitation. She couldn't sneak onto their shuttle —they would kill her inside just as easy as kill her out here. Or worse, if they thought she'd infected them, they'd all stay behind and ride the nuclear blast to hell.

A soft beep in her helmet accompanied a message box appearing in the HUD. ‹Private Channel Invite: Mitchell, G›

Oh, neat. How'd she do that? Kerys didn't waste time wondering, and stared pointedly at the 'accept' button.

"Hey," whispered Gina. "They can't see this channel. Won't know we exist."

"Nice."

"We're fucked," said Gina.

"No... we're not. Just have to... come up with something."

Gina patted her sidearm. "There are only four of them."

"No." Kerys touched helmets. "They have rifles, are intending to shoot everything that moves without even trying to talk, and... you're a little groggy."

"A little." Gina chuckled. "Now there's the understatement of the year."

"Shuttle..." Kerys gasped. "Shuttle flowers... Will, you son of a bitch." She choked up. *That was a message... He knew I was listening. Or maybe he hoped. There's a damn shuttle out in the forest.* A plan formed. "Got it."

"Got what? The sick?"

"No." Kerys exhaled hard. "An idea. The shuttle isn't important. We need to get to the orbiting starship before they do. They're not USIC."

"Damn straight. Looks like mercenaries to me. Definitely not military."

Kerys took a breath. "Yeah. The suits don't look right and they know about Broussard, which makes them Avasar thugs. Your commanders didn't know about the plan to kill everyone, only that this base's purpose was really weapons research."

"Ain't sure that's much better, but at least the brass wasn't gonna kill us on purpose." Gina hardened her glare. "Just pissed I ain't get the chance to shoot the son of a bitch myself."

"There's another shuttle. In the forest."

Gina's eyes opened as wide as they possibly could. "Oh, shit. You're right. Damn, let's do it!"

Clinging to the hope the military would do the right thing if she could only reach them, Kerys pulled Gina over to the quad parked in the airlock. She hopped on in front with Gina clinging to her. It felt strange to drive *into* the dome, but they had little other choice. Exiting here twenty feet away from the mercenaries would lead directly to a firefight. She did *not* like the odds of two on four, especially when she and Gina had sidearms, neither with a full magazine—and only Gina had training. Running might have been cowardly, but she couldn't risk surviving everything else on this horrible planet only to end up being shot by a corporate mercenary.

Tires chirped on the slick floor as the quad careened across the ready room. They bounced over the link ring into the tube connecting the garage pod to the dome. She flattened herself forward, chin to handlebars, trying to stay below the midline of the wall where solid became window. Electric whirring filled the air. The tunnel sat about two hundred meters south of the landing pad, running about a quarter of that distance before a leftward bend connected it to the dome.

The 'rescue team' would have to walk a fairly long distance before they arrived at the north airlock, which would hopefully give her enough time to reach the forest. *Shit.* She accelerated in an effort to clear the tube before they spotted her, but had no idea where she should go. The dome's southeast airlock might work, but she'd have to drive around the garage into plain sight to go north toward the forest. She could disconnect the south tube and go out the ring, but they would *definitely* notice someone blowing the entire outpost's atmosphere.

"Hey Dick, you see that?" asked 'Roma E.'

"Huh? See what?" said a man who sounded huge, and not much like a scientist.

"Thought I saw something moving in that tube."

"Check it out," said Harmon, irritation clear in his voice. "I had a feeling Braxton might've been hiding something."

"Guess he had a fight with the little lady, eh?" The light next to the name 'Aaron' flickered along with a throaty chuckle.

"Hope she's ugly," said Roma. "Be a damn shame havin' to kill a pretty one."

"Uhh, why?" asked 'GiantDICK.' "You actually look at their faces?"

Harmon snickered. "You're a special kind of fucked-up, Rich, you know that?"

"It's *Dick*," said 'GiantDICK.' "I ain't rich."

All four lights winked on and off with laughter.

Storage!

The storage pod had a big airlock on its south wall to accept cargo boxes. Going out that way would put her at the exact opposite side of the outpost from where she needed to go. She'd have to swing way around west to go north, over open sand. If the men started their search at the residence pods, they'd see her with ease. Still, she'd have to risk it since she didn't have the time to make a careful plan.

Maybe they'll think I'm crazy for driving off. Please let them not know there's another shuttle out there.

She leaned on the brakes to take the sharp left and sped into the atrium outside the cafeteria. Blood on the floor robbed her of steering for a second, the quad more sliding than driving; she ran over Marco, not that the fat tires did any real damage to his body.

"Sorry...."

Tires squeaked when rubber caught a dry patch of floor, making her lurch forward from the sudden slowdown. Gina crashed into her from behind, nearly tossing her over the handlebars. Kerys grunted, holding on, righting herself in the seat with a quick tap of the accelerator. She steered for the passage south and twisted the handlebars to dodge a bench. Walls blurred by as they got up to forty-two MPH in the corridor.

The quad skidded sideways when she tried to turn at the end. Both left tires slammed into the wall, launching her and Gina off the seat. They bounced away from a storage hatch and fell flat on her back. The plants in the clear plastic box popped out of Gina's grip and went sliding. A noise part terror, part pain, and part anger escaped out her nose. Swinging her arms rolled her like a flipped turtle upon the heavy air-scrubber backpack.

Shit! I can't get up.

Gina grabbed her hand and pulled her upright.

"Thanks," whispered Kerys.

Gina grinned, then darted after the plant. Kerys almost yelled at her to leave it, no time, but those tiny flowers made the difference between spending the rest of their lives in quarantine or testing negative for unknown organisms. She hopped on the quad, shaking with anticipation until Gina jumped on behind her.

"Got it. Go!" Gina patted her shoulder. "And don't take turns so damn fast."

"Right…"

Lights came on at the north end of the corridor, along with the warning *buzz* of the airlock cycling.

"Tell me you didn't hear that," said Roma.

"I did," said 'GiantDICK.' "Sounded like a big-ass door slamming."

Damn. They heard the crash.

"Someone's alive in there, and they're not running *to* us. You know what that means," said Harmon.

"Yeah, means Dick forgot his deodorant. I can smell him through the fuckin' e-suit." The light winked on next to the name 'Aaron,' the deepest voice of the lot.

"I don't wear deodorant. It's fulla chemicals and shit."

"Yeah, we know," said Roma, coughing. "We know."

"It means whoever it is, is contaminated… not in their right mind." Harmon chuckled. "A sane person would think we're here to rescue them."

Kerys leaned forward and twisted the handgrip to accelerate. Flashing yellow lights started a second before she drove into the tube that would take them to the cargo pod.

"Split up," said Harmon. "Anything moves, kill it. You two got eight minutes for the residence pods while I'm grabbing the black boxes. Go."

She slowed to navigate the ninety-degree bend, but once she lined up with the storage pod, she wrenched the accelerator down and zipped over the last fifty meters in seconds, catching a little air when the tires hit the link ring.

The quad went into a spin as she tried to pull a hard left around a shelf. Kerys managed to keep from crashing, narrowly avoiding a shelf before finding herself driving way too fast directly at the collapsed tangle of metal and a forklift. She cursed, about to slam on the brakes, but a stack of toilet paper on the left made a far more appealing target than solid steel. She ducked and drove into it, sending cubes of plastic-wrapped paper flying. The shelf above her brushed her rebreather pack, but the hit didn't seem too hard and the scrape hadn't sounded loud enough to worry her.

Gina managed to duck in time to avoid taking a metal bar to the face.

Thirty-two seconds later, Kerys skidded the quad to a halt in the airlock. She hopped off and mashed the button to activate the cycle. At this point, she had no choice but to hope the mercenaries wouldn't notice the flashing lights. The inner door slid closed. She stared out the window at the endless expanse of glittering black ground leading south.

The hill! When she'd run from Corporal Guillen, she couldn't see the outpost from the bottom of the hill. If she drove down there before heading north, the mercenaries wouldn't be able to see them. Energized with hope, she bounced on her toes until the red spot appeared in her visor, indicating a lack of breathable air outside.

She jabbed the button to open the outer door and leapt back on the quad. Gina threaded one arm around her, holding on, still cradling the boxed plants under one arm like a football. The instant the doors parted enough to let the vehicle slip past, Kerys rolled forward. A forklift ramp worked fine for the quad, but her ass left the seat for a few seconds as the front wheels bit into the regolith.

Rocks sprayed behind her when she twisted the accelerator down as far as it would move. The quad gained speed, bouncing and wobbling, but she held on, refusing to fear her ride more than the men coming to kill them.

Crude remarks came over the comm, rating the looks of any dead woman they found, especially from 'GiantDICK.' Harmon kept quiet for the most part, which worried her more. Each time one of the mercenaries got graphic about his sexual remarks in regard to dead women, Gina squirmed. Stranding living people on this planet had to be a rather evil thing to do, but the more the men joked and made disgusting comments about the dead, the less Kerys felt guilty at the idea. After all, they would definitely kill her and Gina without hesitation.

She steered in a gradual left, racing past the southern tip of the Lab Pod 2 and heading straight for the hill down to the excavation site. Every few seconds, she looked back over her shoulder. As soon as she couldn't see the lower two stories of the dome, she steered left again, north toward the forest. Too much could go wrong for her to fixate on any one way to get herself killed. She hadn't been to the remote camp before and had no idea exactly how far away it was or how long it would take to get there. She started to worry about threats, but Gina spent a while out there, and she'd at least kept her sanity until she returned to the main facility. If anyone had gone crazy out there, she'd probably already killed them.

"Which way?" rasped Kerys.

"Left a bit more. There." Gina pointed at a noticeable gap in the distant trees. "Almost a road. We're on course."

We just need to get to the shuttle.

She almost let off the accelerator.

What am I doing? Shuttle? I'm not a damn pilot… Fuck!

Tears gathered in her eyes. To have a chance at survival waved in front of her and taken away felt as cruel as killing her friends. She looked left at the uphill slope, and debated her odds at sweet-talking the Avasar thugs into letting her live. They sounded like a real bunch of charmers. At that moment, a comment from Aaron about one of the dead being 'still hot enough' changed her mind.

"Damn… What am—?" She stared ahead like a deer in the headlights of an oncoming starship.

"Now what?" asked Gina.

"The shuttle… I'm not a pilot."

"Who cares? It's all automated."

Kerys thought back to the flight down to the surface. The lazy pilot doing nothing. *He said they fly themselves… It's gotta be like the auto-surgeon. Shit. If I can teach myself to be a doctor in five minutes, I can fly a ship.*

"Right. Okay." Kerys sped up. "We got this."

"Clear," said Aaron. "Nothin' twitching in the residence pods. Moving to the hydro farm."

"Copy that." Harmon cleared his throat. "We're halfway done with the labs. Meet up in the storage room in ten. Roma, check the reservoir."

"Uhh, boss?" asked 'GiantDICK,' "If we're gonna just nuke this place, why do we have to search?"

"Because, I don't want anyone hitting the off switch on the bomb after we leave."

Confident she'd gone far enough away from the outpost no one would see them, Kerys steered up the hill.

"It's got an off switch?" asked Aaron.

"Just sweep the damn place already." Harmon sighed. "Three years in a damn freezer, it'd be nice to get some target practice. I really want to shoot something."

Aaron laughed. "Yeah."

Kerys bounced off the seat again as the quad crested the top of the hill to level ground. Up ahead, a pathway lined with silver posts tipped with weak lights pointed the way into the forest. Some effort had been made to smooth the dunes into a roadway there, which made pulling fifty-six MPH less nerve wracking.

Her visor fogged from ragged, panicky breaths. The quad wobbled a little, but she had no trouble keeping it on the road. Gensch's dog tags bit into her leg from the e-suit squeezing down on her thigh pocket; she didn't care. The discomfort reminded her of him, almost as if he had her back.

Ahead, the swath of blue-violet-pink foliage rose higher and higher until she felt like an ant in the forest. Some of the trunks looked wide enough to be hollowed out into houses. Low-lying plants mostly resembled spongy mushrooms or glistening lichens, ranging from white to rose-red and shades of blue. Lamiacaea advena sprouted here and there, far more of it than she expected. Seeing it relaxed her somewhat. The deadly microbe couldn't possibly exist in a forest teeming with the thing that killed it.

All the colors passed in a blur.

The trail looped to the right before it snaked left to avoid another massive tree with a periwinkle-blue stalk. A campsite slid into view as she rounded the curve, four tiny inflatable structures reminiscent of the Copernicus mission surrounded a large flat space where another Avasar shuttle perched. The membranous walls of the one-room bubbles wavered in the breeze; one had bloody smears on it, but no sign of a body.

Kerys drove straight into the camp and up the open belly-ramp of the shuttle. The quad skidded when she tried to stop, but she slowed enough to where her crash against the inner wall only bounced it.

Gina crashed into her again but laughed. "Smooth."

"Move your ass, girl!"

"Copy that." Gina got up.

Kerys jumped off the quad, rushed to the most obvious control panel on the wall, and found a button to close the ramp. The interface resembled the airlock controls from the dome, except for the word 'hold' replacing 'airlock.' Cycling it proved a simple matter of poking two buttons. A rush of wind buffeted her, and the red atmosphere-warning dot vanished.

A crimson glow at the center of the wall she'd crashed into shifted to green. Four feet to the left of the quad, a door opened to reveal a spiral stairwell. She didn't bother trying to take her suit off, and rushed up to the second level. The passage at the top led left and right, wrapping around the stairwell toward the rear of the ship. It also continued straight, past a small locker room to the cockpit.

Kerys sprinted to the pilot's seat and fell into it. She prodded the middle screen, gave the flight stick an uneasy glance, and poked another screen. A whimper of surprise escaped her lips when everything switched on all at once.

Gina sidled up next to her. "Everything's automated. Shuttle's as easy as operating a Hydra in the caf."

"I keep trying to tell myself that." Kerys gulped.

The middle monitor displayed a menu of routines as well as the word 'Synching...' with a spinning circle to the right.

‹Transponder signal acquired: *AV-1841 Imperator*. Local orbit. Flight designation: Unspecified›

"It's not a scheduled run... that ship had to be on the way already... they all knew what would happen here." The idea that the six-month supply ship might not even exist since Avasar planned on everyone here being dead brought bile into the back of her throat. Will had almost left her stranded here for good.

"Bastards. God damn. Command is going to lose their damn minds." Gina shook her head. "Hope I get to watch the fireworks."

"Umm. Shit. Where's the 'go' button?"

"Why you askin' me for? They ain't teach me how to do this." Gina gestured at the screen.

"Can't be more complicated than the robo-surgeon, right?" Kerys tapped the screen above the 'transponder detected' line and a bar of highlight appeared over it. An instant later, a sub window popped open. 'Transponder confirmed, initiate flight routine?"

"*Yes!*" she shouted, and drove her finger like a knife into the screen.

Gina blinked. "Okay, that was a lot easier than I thought it would be."

Distant buzzing evolved to a subdued whine. Over the next ten seconds, it built into a roar that made the entire shuttle vibrate. Kerys slid back into the seat and pulled the safety harness on.

"Shit." Gina ran out of the cockpit.

A moment later, a great cloud of dust blasted out from underneath the windscreen, rolling forward. Soon, the ground fell away from the wide viewscreen in front of her.

"All good, I'm strapped in," said Gina over the comm. "Go ahead."

"I'm not going ahead... it's doing it by itself. Probably safer that way."

"Yeah."

Kerys grunted under increasing acceleration, clawing at the armrests as her stomach tried to leave her body via her rear end. Wisps of indigo, cyan, and bright blue shifted before her eyes. A feeling of rotation ceased, and a tremendous *boom* preceded acceleration, pinning her to the seat with a thundering roar so loud she couldn't hear herself screaming. She came close to soiling herself, terrified being at the controls of a shuttle she had no idea how to operate. The screens filled with moving diagrams of lines that looked like old video games, bar charts, and numbers.

Right as she sensed imminent loss of consciousness, the G-forces crushing her abated. All the pretty colors in the windscreen gave way to the infinite void of space and the silence of the primary engines powering down.

Kerys gathered her hands to her chest, shaking with fear, relief, and hope. Proxima Flora felt as if it had been far away from the outpost the mercenaries might not have heard the shuttle take off.

A cheerful beep from the console made her glance at a monitor displaying: ‹signal lock, guidance routine engaged. Handshake accepted.›

The nightmare of AV494 shrank away, vanishing beneath the lower edge of the view-screen.

A HOME SO FAR

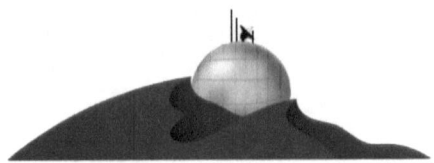

Afraid to move, lest she throw something off, Kerys clutched the armrests and stared out at the stars.

Gina crept into the cockpit again, still fully e-suited. "We... made it."

"Almost there," whispered Kerys. "Space is better than that damn planet."

"No shit."

Soon, a flash of glint stood out against the black. She leaned forward, daring to hope they had a chance. A thin line of silver grew into the oblong shape of an interstellar ship. A somewhat-aerodynamic section at the front linked via a narrow spine and hundreds of smaller scaffold-like struts to the translight drive, which accounted for three-quarters of the ship's bulk.

Small thrusters barked in short puffs and burps. The shuttle altered course, following a route that brought it around and 'under' the starship. She watched the silent ballet occurring between machines and computers in mute awe. An angled section at the underside of the starship's nose opened, two clamshell doors extending to the sides like some massive snake preparing to engulf an egg. The shuttle rotated, sliding sideways as it passed the larger vessel. Once it cleared the nose, it turned to face the huge ship, drifting backward. A few puffs from the maneuvering thrusters pushed them sideways into the behemoth's path and another short blast nudged them down, lining up with a bay large enough to hold a single shuttle.

She tried to bite on her knuckle, but the helmet got in the way.

Without a sound but her breathing echoing in her ears, the shuttle glided into the hangar bay, solid steel walls sliding past the canopy on both sides. More thruster puffs slowed the little ship to a relative halt, the tip of the nose about fifteen meters from the inner wall. Mechanical whirring thrummed in the floor, ending a few seconds later with a heavy *clunk.*

The bay doors closed and the shuttle screen displayed the message: ‹flight routine end.›

A flash of blue from a panel to her right startled her. The side-mounted screen displayed a command interface to the big ship, offering the option to re-pressurize the shuttle bay or open the exterior doors. She tapped the button for re-pressurize. A red 'bay locked' icon appeared at the bottom, along with a heavy *thud* that rattled the whole starship.

Flashing yellow lights came on out in the bay, becoming solid green after half a minute.

Kerys sprung from the seat, raced down the spiral stairway, and opened the belly hatch. Gina ran after her, lagging behind somewhat due to her beleaguered muscles. The layout of the ship matched the one that brought her here enough for her to find her way upstairs. She unclipped the pistol from the e-suit's belt, gripped it, and advanced toward the flight deck. Gina also raised her weapon. Like a pair of cops in an action movie, they cleared the area door by door, passing a room with a table, chairs, and a Hydra unit on the left; a door on the right led to a shower.

In preparation for conflict, Kerys clenched her grip on the pistol as she stepped into the narrow passage connecting the corridor to the flight deck. Surprisingly, she found the bridge empty. The flight that brought her here had two medics, and she assumed at least a two-person pilot crew, but she had never seen anyone other than the medics and the man who'd flown the shuttle. Or at least the man who'd sat there while the shuttle flew itself.

"If this was a secret flight, maybe they skipped the medics?" whispered Kerys.

"Could be." Gina nodded once. "Mercs after all. Cheap. No medic means they don't gotta pay one."

Kerys lowered herself into the central chair, feeling dwarfed by the movie-screen sized view before her of the planet's surface. "Oh, please be as simple as the shuttle..."

She spent a few minutes poking at the console, hunting down command menus. Eventually, she located a menu option that appeared to be a preprogrammed flight path. When she tapped the screen on that line, a diagram came up in a sub window on the main view-screen, showing a translight route plot between AV494 and Earth. Tears of joy came unbidden, gathering against her chin inside the helmet.

She pushed a virtual button marked 'load.' The route plot vanished, replaced with a message:

Commit route plot for Translight (Yes / No):

Origin: AV494

Destination: Earth

Estimated flight time: 02Y 09M 03W 2D 11H

She pushed 'yes.'

The prompt box went black for a second before turning red.

‹Warning: transponder ID in shuttle bay differs from launch configuration. Confirm change?›

She felt evil for only an instant, and hit 'yes.' "Screw 'em. They would've killed us."

"No guilt, boo. No guilt." Gina patted her shoulder.

A pleasant feminine voice filled the room. "Route plot loading. Calculating standard flight path to translight entry point. Estimated time before transition is fourteen hours and nine minutes. Translight initiation can be aborted at any time within the next thirteen hours."

"Umm. No, thanks. No aborting. Bring us home."

Kerys sat there for about ten minutes, basking in the idea that going back to Earth might really happen.

A brilliant white flicker came from a point on the planet's surface, a second before a blinding flash sent an expanding ring rippling across the atmosphere. A globe of energy swelled up like a glowing tick stuck to the side of a cow. It lasted only a second before fading to a localized spot of dull glow. Forty seconds after the blast, if she hadn't seen the explosion, the area of the detonation wouldn't have struck her as notable among the swirls of color.

Shit. Those guys are probably in their shuttle coming back up here.

The blue-black ball slid to the left as the starship broke orbit, shrinking into space at a speed that offered some relief. It seemed unlikely a shuttle had a chance of catching up, and even if it did, the bay had no room for it. Worry the mercenaries might be able to abort her trip via remote pushed her into hunting over command menus until she found an option to lock in the flight routine with a password.

She entered "IgotmyA$$offthatrockSarge" as the password.

‹Password confirmed. Translight program initiation process secured.›

Kerys reclined, smiling at the screen for a little while, watching the controls in case the kill squad did something she hadn't thought of. Gina sat in the next chair, intermittently shaking.

"You okay?" whispered Kerys.

"Fine."

"You're shaking. Cold?"

"No." Gina took her hand. "Can't believe we're alive. I'm excited."

They sat there in silence for an hour or so. Once she couldn't differentiate AV494 apart from all the stars and bright spots anymore, she felt confident enough to leave the ship to fly itself. If the mercenaries hadn't been able to interrupt them by now and recall the ship, they wouldn't be able to. Maybe they'd return to the surface. Maybe they'd shoot each other in the shuttle rather than risk it. On some level, the thought of their fate horrified her, but she could summon up only so much pity for the sort of men willing to murder total strangers for a paycheck.

"Shit. I hope the cryo tubes are automatic too. This is going to be a long flight otherwise."

"They ought'a be," said Gina.

Kerys meandered down the hall to the shower room, checking lockers and storage cabinets. A few contained men's t-shirts and boxers.

Any port in a storm, right?

A storage compartment in the small infirmary held ten plastic body bags, each with an adhesive seal. She took one and headed down to the docking bay. Gina did the same. Standing beneath the shuttle's engines, as close to the bay door's seam in the hull as she dared get, Kerys finally broke the seal of her e-suit's helmet and took it off.

The stink of oil and burnt ozone swam into her senses.

Gina removed her helmet as well.

With methodical care, (and a bit of contortionism) she opened the clasps on her e-suit, got out, and packed it into the body bag.

"You saved my ass, but you might be contaminated. Sorry." She patted the helmet, feeling stupid for getting emotionally attached to her suit. *I will never take another job that requires me to wear a damn e-suit. I'm never leaving Earth again.*

She kicked off her shoes, squealing at the coldness of the bare metal floor, and stripped stark naked. Every bit of clothing, from shoes to socks to underwear, went into the body bag. She considered burning it but doubted she could find anything to light a fire with on a starship, nor did the idea of lighting a fire on a starship seem wise.

"Well, this is… awkward," said Gina, also stark naked and standing beside a stuffed body bag. "Stuck on a ship with you naked is kind of a dream I had."

Kerys chuckled. "I'm blushing but not really embarrassed…"

"I'm not embarrassed but I'm blushing." Gina winked.

Surprisingly, it didn't feel awkward anymore. Being with Gina didn't sound like all that bad an idea, no matter what form it took between lovers or damn close friends who'd survived an impossible situation.

"So… umm, now what?" asked Gina.

"We dump this stuff out into space to make absolutely sure there aren't any microbes following us home... then shower."

Gina smiled. "Okay. Don't worry. I'm too sore and tired to think about suggesting a fun shower. Feels like I could sleep for years."

"Funny you should say 'sleep for years'." Kerys elbowed her lightly.

"Ugh. Didn't mean it that way, but you're right." Gina slouched, looking exhausted.

With everything from the planet's surface—except Gensch's dog tags and the lamiacaea advena plants—in the body bags, she pulled the plastic strips from the adhesive and sealed them. Streaking the shuttle bay proved *quite* cold. Teeth chattering, she and Gina sprinted the hundred yards or so to the stairwell and hurried up to the much warmer crew level, then walked to the shower area.

An idle daydream about being stuck naked with a whole starship to themselves until they got back to Earth made her blush—but not because of Gina being with her. Whoever found them in the cryo pods upon their arrival home would get an eye full. Fortunately, they at least had the boxers and t-shirts the mercenaries' brought with them, even if the garments wouldn't fit well.

She cranked the water up as hot as she could tolerate, then made it a little hotter. She washed the dog tags and set them aside. Wanting to be absolutely sure she had no alien hitchhikers, she lathered up and scrubbed, standing in the flow until she felt like a lobster, using several shower cycles' worth of soap.

Gina washed herself under the adjacent spray, the military-style showers having no privacy screens between each 'stall.' The woman barely looked at her, seeming exhausted from her battle with the microbes and escape from Planet Hell. Showering so close to her seemed nothing more than routine.

After toweling herself dry, Kerys headed over to the locker area to grab something to wear. As expected, the boxers and shirts belonged to men much larger than her and Gina. Still, it beat being found naked in the cryo pods. She took a T-shirt and a set of boxers that wouldn't stay on unless she held the elastic at her hip, then went to the small mess hall. Gina sat next to her, close enough to share body heat. A tray of re-hydrated roast beef and green beans went down like a lavish meal at a fancy restaurant.

Once done with their meal, they returned to the flight deck. Kerys poked around the computer until she found the option to open the shuttle bay doors. A moment later, the body bags containing possibly contaminated clothing and their e-suits tumbled off into space. She sat a while, staring at it getting smaller and smaller.

"Translight cannot be initiated while the shuttle bay is open. Do you wish to abort the designated flight path?" asked the female voice.

The same message appeared in text on the screen. She pushed 'no.'

Faint hydraulic whining in the hull accompanied the doors closing. She put her feet up on the console, ankles crossed, and stargazed for a little while, listening to her stomach squawk and chirp. Gina sat in the chair next to her, also staring out the window with an 'I can't believe we made it' expression.

We're going home. Hands over her mouth, she wept with relief and guilt. Once she regained her composure, she sat up straight, opened a message window in the SFT client, and recorded a video.

"My name is Kerys Loring. I accepted a job from Avasar Biotech to research alien ruins on a planet they designated AV494. What I thought was the find of a lifetime turned out to be a lie. The company deceived us all. They'd found a deadly alien microbe on this planet and decided to evaluate its effectiveness as a biological weapon—using their own employees as test subjects.

"Corporal Gina Mitchell, USIC is with me. She and I are the only survivors from the Wayfarer Outpost."

Gina leaned into view of the camera, not quite smiling.

"We have been exposed to this microbe, but were given an antidote which, according to the botany team's studies, renders our bodies toxic to the organism for a few weeks. Their testing results proved all traces of the microbe die after one hour in the system of a person given this antidote. We will wait at least six hours before entering the cryo pods to ensure no traces of the dangerous organism are preserved.

"I can't say for sure if I had any of those damn things inside me, but I do know I am not suffering any effects of the infection. I should not be contagious, but I can't say with full certainty that I'm not. The microbe behaves like amoebic encephalitis, which is not transmissible from person to person once the infection sets in. We have done everything possible to scrub up. We've shot our clothes and all equipment from the planet's surface into space to prevent contamination.

"I am sending this message to my family, as well as the USIC. I'm on a ship designated the *Imperator*, registered to Avasar Biotechnology. The USIC needs to intercept this ship. If Avasar gets to us first, they'll probably kill us, hoping to keep what happened on AV494 secret. Their operation here was illegal and conducted without the military understanding the true intent of it. I fully expect to be quarantined for evaluation on my return, assuming this ship actually makes it back. I will not resist. I want legitimate medics to check me out. I want to know for sure if I'm clean. I do not want to risk anyone else's life. Too many have died to this already... for no reason other than greed.

"Jaden, I hope you're doing all right. It'll be a while before I can send another message. Gonna take about three years to get back. Make sure Mom watches this. I know I haven't always seen eye to eye with her, but she can get things done. If something happens to me, she'll make sure they all know what happened here."

"Here." Gina handed over a small memory nodule. "All the messages from the bastard's terminal."

Kerys plugged it in, transferring the contents of the thumbnail drive to the SFT message. "I'm attaching messages exchanged between an executive at Avasar and the man responsible for what happened at the outpost."

She bowed her head and sighed.

"Be strong, Jay. See ya soon."

Kerys entered her brother's address as well as her mother's, and three addresses Gina gave her for various command level groups at the United States Interstellar Corps. She hit send, waited for it to come back confirmed, and sent the message two more times to guard against any corruption in the transmission.

A sudden, heavy feeling came over her at the memory of watching Will die. Once upon a long time ago, she had loved him... and despite seeing the real him, despite knowing what he'd done on AV494, some tiny shred of her somehow managed to mourn him.

"Bye, Will." She let out a morose chuckle. "You'd probably think I'm foolish for feeling sad over you after everything you did, but I don't. That's the difference between us... and you *still* wouldn't understand."

"I don't understand, and I ain't no psycho," whispered Gina.

Kerys stood, and her boxers fell to the floor.

"Oops," muttered Gina. "They a little big on you."

"Just a bit." Kerys sighed.

The burden of guilt at having to kill Sergeant Gensch when she might have been able to save him almost made her say 'screw it' and leave them there. Gina's amused smile proved contagious. Kerys stooped to hike her boxers back up. After a short stop at the bathroom, she padded to a small lounge where they spent a few hours bundled together in a blanket staring at movies without really watching them, mostly talking.

Kerys never really had a best friend growing up, her mother being such a taskmaster pushing her into an endless stream of activities. Being with Gina didn't quite feel like she expected it would to hang out with a friend, a sibling, or even a romantic partner—but some combination of all three.

Whatever the future held for them, Kerys looked forward to it.

Eventually, they returned to the mess hall for another Hydra meal, then zonked out on the sofa in the lounge together until the entire starship shuddered with the transition into translight. It had taken the ship six hours and forty-nine minutes to fly on 'slow power' from planetary orbit to the proper coordinates to initiate the main engines.

Finally, trusting that the mercenaries couldn't ruin their trip home, Kerys shut off the TV.

"Time for bed, huh?" asked Gina.

"Yeah. Though it's almost tempting to stay awake. I like being with you. Never really had anyone I could talk to like this before."

Gina grinned. "I like that, too... but we don't have enough food on board."

"True. And... faster we do this, faster we're home. Or so it will feel."

"Right."

They headed down the hall to the cryonics area. This ship had twenty pods in total, split ten per side of a hallway with a tiny infirmary at the end.

Kerys paused by the first room on the left. "Well, this is it."

Gina, one foot in the room across the hall from her, also stopped. "Yeah."

They faced each other.

"Thanks," whispered Gina.

"You don't have to—"

Gina smiled. "I do. You saved my ass twice when I gave up on myself."

"Maybe once. Second time I just chickened out. Couldn't shoot someone I cared about."

"You care about me?" Gina raised both eyebrows.

Kerys stared at her for a long minute. "Yeah. I do. Still working out the details."

"Details?"

"Yeah. Super close best friend, sister, combat survivor buddy, or... something more."

Gina's cheeks darkened. "Kiss?"

Kerys fidgeted, not expecting her joy at hearing the word. "I was kinda hoping you'd say that."

Gina leaned closer.

After a second's hesitation, their lips met. She found it far different from being with Will, much *much* gentler and more loving—not possessive. Butterflies danced across her stomach. Kissing a woman felt simultaneously strange and exciting.

Eventually, Gina pulled back. They stared into each other's eyes, barely an inch between their noses.

"Well? What do you think?" whispered Gina.

"So nice… I don't know what to think anymore…" Kerys bit her lip. "Let me sleep on it?"

"Heh." Gina chuckled. "See you in three years?"

"Something like that. Yeah." Kerys hugged her tight.

Gina squeezed back.

For a while, it seemed she'd never be able to make herself let go. They'd both survived something unbelievable. No matter what happened going forward, Gina would forever be part of her life.

"Are we going to stand here the whole time?" asked Gina. "My legs are about to give up."

"Still sore?"

"Yeah. Not as bad as yesterday, though. I think I'm gonna be okay." Gina let go and took a step back. "Pod time."

"Okay."

Kerys backed into the stasis room behind her and approached the console by the stasis pod. Kissing Gina was strange on so many levels— but not unpleasant. She needed time to sort out if she had true feelings for another woman or if it came from her elation at surviving and joy at managing to at least save *one* person from Will's idiocy.

If I really wasn't into women I would never think like this. Oh, Averie… maybe I did have a crush on you.

For the first time since things got weird with Will, the future no longer seemed scary, but exciting. Lights came on overhead as well as in the pod when she tapped the black screen. A strip along the top displayed a countdown to the shift out from translight. The system would know when the ship disengaged from the faster-than-light system, and automatically wake anyone in pods.

Aside from the countdown, a single green 'go' button filled the square screen.

Tap.

‹Press A to self-enter cryonic suspension or swipe your medical identification to assist another.›

"Oh, that's nice." She pushed 'A.'

The stasis pod opened.

"Please enter stasis pod for pre-cryonic scan."

She remembered that part from the flight out. The system needed to measure her body mass and vitals to calibrate itself. Kerys sat on the edge of the cushion, staring at her toes, not knowing how to feel about what happened… or Will in particular. *So many dead. The only reason I'm here is because he couldn't let go of me. Hmm. How about that? I guess he really did love me… in a psycho possessive sort of way.*

With a sniffle, she set the dog tags in the drawer of the small table next to the pod, swung her legs up, and reclined on soft, white cushions.

The lid closed part way, and a blue grid of laser-light appeared over her.

"Scanning," said an electronic female voice. "Please remain still."

She stared at the pure-white ceiling beyond the transparent lid. "Guess you're right, sarge. It is kinda comforting to hope there's something out there when the bullets are flying over your head, even if no one's really listening."

I'll try to get along with Mom if I make it home alive. I swear I'll even go there for Christmas dinner from now on.

The system chirped. "Calibration complete. Self-entry to cryonic stasis ready. Biometric data matches employee record for Loring, Kerys. Please provide verbal activation code 'Commit A-A-eight-one' to initiate."

"Might as well do this. Damn, I hope I don't dream this time." She took a breath, let it out slow, and said, "Commit. A, a, eight, one."

A soft, mechanical whirr emanated from below as the pod closed around her, sealing with a soft *thump*. In a moment, the air took on a crisp, clean coolness. A little metal prod extended upward and delivered an injection to her right arm. Her limbs grew leaden. The strong overhead lights dimmed.

"All right, kiddo." Kerys closed her eyes and pictured her little brother's smile as she surrendered to the oncoming drowsiness. "I'm coming home."

---

fin

ACKNOWLEDGMENTS

Thank you for reading Wayfarer: AV494!

This is the third edition of this book, edited slightly for a somewhat less depressing story. Skip this next sentence if you picked the book up and went straight to the end matter. When I first wrote this story, I somehow ended up clinging to the idea of writing a 'final girl' trope story where only the main character survived. It never quite sat right with me, and ever since the book originally released, I'd been second-guessing that decision to blindly follow the trope. So, the edit you have hopefully just read happened. Still a high body count, but the one character I most regretted killing off no longer dies—and Kerys isn't quite stuck seeming so clueless purely because the 'final girl' thing required everyone else to die.

I'd also like to thank Dean Samed for the amazing cover, and Lee Sheridan for editing. Additional thanks to Tony Healey for the idea of writing a 'space thriller.'

ABOUT THE AUTHOR

Originally from South Amboy NJ, Matthew has been creating science fiction and fantasy worlds for most of his reasoning life. Since 1996, he has developed the "Divergent Fates" world, in which *Division Zero, Virtual Immortality, The Awakened Series, The Harmony Paradox, and the Daughter of Mars series* take place. Along with being an editor at Curiosity Quills press, he has worked in IT and technical support.

Matthew is an avid gamer, a recovered WoW addict, Gamemaster for two custom RPG systems, and a fan of anime, British humour, and intellectual science fiction that questions the nature of reality, life, and what happens after it.

He is also fond of cats.

Visit me online at:
    Facebook: https://www.facebook.com/MatthewSCoxAuthor
    Pinterest: https://www.pinterest.com/matthewcox10420/
    Goodreads: https://www.goodreads.com/author/show/7712730.Matthew_S_Cox
    Email: mcox2112@gmail.com

OTHER BOOKS BY MATTHEW S. COX

Divergent Fates Universe Novels
Division Zero series

- Division Zero
- Lex De Mortuis
- Thrall
- Guardian
- Harbinger
- The Shadow Fixer

The Awakened series

- Prophet of the Badlands
- Archon's Queen
- Grey Ronin
- Daughter of Ash
- Zero Rogue
- Angel Descended

Daughter of Mars series

- The Hand of Raziel
- Araphel
- Ghost Black

Virtual Immortality series

- Virtual Immortality
- The Harmony Paradox

Prophet of the Badlands Series

- Prophet's Journey
- Prophet's Mercy

Divergent Fates Anthology

(Fiction Novels - Adult)

The Roadhouse Chronicles Series

- One More Run
- The Redeemed
- Dead Man's Number

Faded Skies series

- Heir Ascendant
- Ascendant Unrest
- Ascendant Revolution

Temporal Armistice Series

- Nascent Shadow
- The Shadow Collector
- The Gate to Oblivion
- The Queen of Discord
- The Burning Alchemist

Vampire Innocent series

- A Nighttime of Forever
- A Beginner's Guide to Fangs
- The Artist of Ruin
- The Last Family Road Trip
- The Phantom Oracle
- How Not to Summon Demons
- Ordinary Problems of a College Vampire
- A Vampire's Guide to Surviving Holidays
- An Introduction to Paranormal Diplomacy
- A Vampire's Guide to Adulting
- How to Stop a Vampire War in Six Easy Steps
- Ancient Vampire Death Cults and Other Annoyances
- Hunting Vampires for Fun and Profit

Standalones

- Wayfarer: AV494
- Axillon99
- Chiaroscuro: The Mouse and the Candle

- The Spirits of Six Minstrel Run
- Sophie's Light
- The Far Side of Promise anthology
- Operation: Chimera (with Tony Healey)
- The Dysfunctional Conspiracy (with Christopher Veltmann)
- Of Myth and Shadow
- The Girl Who Found the Sun

Winter Solstice series (with J.R. Rain)

- Convergence
- Containment
- Catalyst
- Catacombs

Alexis Silver series (with J.R. Rain)

- Silver Light
- Deep Silver
- Silver Quarrel
- Silver Crucible

Samantha Moon Origins series (with J.R. Rain)

- New Moon Rising
- Moon Mourning
- Haunted Moon

Vampire For Hire series (with J.R. Rain)

- Moon Master
- Dead Moon
- Lost Moon
- Vampire Destiny
- Infinite Moon
- Vampire Empress
- Moon Elder

Maddy Wimsey series (with J.R. Rain)

- The Devil's Eye
- The Drifting Gloom
- Dark Mercy

- Primal Wrath

<u>Samantha Moon Case Files series</u> (with J.R. Rain)

- Blood Moon

Immortal Operative (with J.R. Rain)

- Broken Ice
- Broken Wing

Four Elements series (with J.R. Rain)

- The Elementalist
- The Black Rose
- The Wakefield Curse

Witches series (with J.R. Rain)

- The Witch and the Hangman

Young Adult Novels

The Eldritch Heart Series

- The Eldritch Heart
- The Cursed Crown
- The Sapphire Soul

Evergreen Series

- Evergreen
- The World That Remains
- The Lucky Ones
- Nuclear Summer
- The Nuclear Frontier
- The World We Make

Progenitor Series

- Out of Sight

- Out of Mind

Diary of a Teenage Fey

(Short story series)

- Elder Horror
- The Hag of Barrow Falls
- Babysitter's Nightmare
- Lharakki
- Bauble for a Soul
- Simulacrum
- Amorphous
- Manticore

Standalones

- Caller 107
- The Summer the World Ended
- Nine Candles of Deepest Black
- The Forest Beyond the Earth

Middle Grade Novels

The Adventures of Ubergirl series

- My Dad is a Mad Scientist
- Aliens Ate My Homework
- The End of all Halloweens
- Dr. Infinity and the Soul Smasher

Tales of Widowswood series

- Emma and the Banderwigh
- Emma and the Silk Thieves
- Emma and the Silverbell Faeries
- Emma and the Elixir of Madness
- Emma and the Weeping Spirit

Standalones

- Citadel: The Concordant Sequence

- The Cursed Codex
- The Menagerie of Jenkins Bailey

www.ingramcontent.com/pod-product-compliance
Lightning Source LLC
Chambersburg PA
CBHW020300200626
46814CB00006BA/2009